PRAISE FOR CAROLYN BROWN

Small Town Rumors

"Carolyn Brown is a master at writing warm, complex characters who find their way into your heart."

—*Harlequin Junkie*

"Carolyn Brown's *Small Town Rumors* takes that hotbed and with it spins a delightful tale of starting over, coming into your own, and living your life, out loud and unafraid."

—*Words We Love By*

"*Small Town Rumors* by Carolyn Brown is a contemporary romance perfect for a summer read in the shade of a big old tree with a glass of lemonade or sweet tea. It is a sweet romance with wonderful characters and a small-town settin͗"

—*Aᵤₒnna Loves Genres*

"Carolyn Brown continues her strea͟ ͟   heartfelt novels with *The Sometimes Sisters*, a story of estranged sisters and frustrated romance."

—*All About Romance*

"This is an amazing feel-good story that will make you wish you were a part of this amazing family."

—*Harlequin Junkie* (top pick)

"*The Sometimes Sisters* is [a] delightful and touching story that explores the bonds of family. I loved the characters, the story lines, and the focus on the importance of familial bonds, whether they be blood relations or those you choose with your heart."

—*Rainy Day Ramblings*

The Strawberry Hearts Diner

"[A] sweet and satisfying romance from the queen of Texas romance."

—*Fresh Fiction*

"A heartwarming cast of characters brings laughter and tears to the mix, and readers will find themselves rooting for more than one romance on the menu. From the first page to the last, Brown perfectly captures the mood, as well as the atmosphere, and creates a charming story that appeals to a wide range of readers."

—*RT Book Reviews*

"A sweet romance surrounded by wonderful, caring characters."

—*TBQ's Book Palace*

"[A] deeply satisfying contemporary small-town western story . . ."

—*Delighted Reader*

The Barefoot Summer

"Prolific romance author Brown shows she can also write women's fiction in this charming story, which uses humor and vivid characters to show the value of building an unconventional chosen family."

—*Publishers Weekly*

"This story takes you and carries you along for a wonderful ride full of laughter, tears, and three amazing HEAs. I feel like these characters are not just people in a book, but they are truly family, and I feel so invested in their journey. Another amazing HIT for Carolyn Brown."

—*Harlequin Junkie* (top pick)

The Lullaby Sky

"I really loved and enjoyed this story. Definitely a good comfort read when you're in a reading funk or just don't know what to read. The secondary characters bring much love and laughter into this book—your cheeks will definitely hurt from smiling so hard while reading. Carolyn is one of my most favorite authors. I know without a doubt that no matter what book of hers I read, I can just get lost in it and know it will be a good story. Better than the last. Can't wait to read more from her."

—*The Bookworm's Obsession*

The Lilac Bouquet

"Brown pulls readers along for an enjoyable ride. It's impossible not to be touched by Brown's protagonists, particularly Seth, and a cast of strong supporting characters underpins the charming tale."

—*Publishers Weekly*

"If a reader is looking for a book more geared toward family and long-held secrets, this would be a good fit."

—*RT Book Reviews*

"Carolyn Brown absolutely blew me away with this epically beautiful story. I cried, I giggled, I sobbed, and I guffawed; this book had it all. I've come to expect great things from this author, and she more than lived up to anything I could have hoped for. Emmy Jo Massey and her great-granny Tandy are absolute masterpieces, not because they are perfect but because they are perfectly painted. They are so alive, so full of flaws and spunk and determination. I cannot recommend this book highly enough."

—*Night Owl Reviews* (5 stars and top pick)

The Wedding Pearls

"*The Wedding Pearls* by Carolyn Brown is an amazing story about family, life, love, and finding out who you are and where you came from. This book is a lot like *The Golden Girls* meet *Thelma and Louise*."

—*Harlequin Junkie*

"*The Wedding Pearls* is an absolute must-read. I cannot recommend this one enough. Grab a copy for yourself and one for a best friend or even your mother or both. This is a book that you need to read. It will make you laugh and cry. It is so sweet and wonderful and packed full of humor. I hope that when I grow up, I can be just like Ivy and Frankie."

—*Rainy Day Ramblings*

The Yellow Rose Beauty Shop

"*The Yellow Rose Beauty Shop* was hilarious and so much fun to read. But sweet romances, strong female friendships, and family bonds make this more than just a humorous read."

—*The Reader's Den*

"If you like books about small towns and how the people's lives intertwine, you will love this book. I think it's probably my favorite book this year. The relationships of the three main characters, girls who have grown up together, will make you feel like you just pulled up a chair in their beauty shop with a bunch of old friends. As you meet the other people in the town, you'll wish you could move there. There are some genuine laugh-out-loud moments and then more that will just make you smile. These are real people, not the oh-so-thin-and-so-very-rich that are often the main characters in novels. This book will warm your heart, and you'll remember it after you finish the last page. That's the highest praise I can give a book."

—Reader quote

Long, Hot Texas Summer

"This is one of those lighthearted, feel-good, make-me-happy kinds of stories. But, at the same time, the essence of this story is family and love with a big ole dose of laughter and country living thrown in the mix. This is the first installment in what promises to be another fascinating series from Brown. Find a comfortable chair, sit back, and relax, because once you start reading *Long, Hot Texas Summer*, you won't be able to put it down. This is a super fun and sassy romance."

—*Thoughts in Progress*

Daisies in the Canyon

"I just loved the symbolism in *Daisies in the Canyon*. As I mentioned before, Carolyn Brown has a way with character development with few, if any, contemporaries. I am sure there are more stories to tell in this series. Brown just touched the surface first with *Long, Hot Texas Summer* and now continuing on with *Daisies in the Canyon*."

—*Fresh Fiction*

the
Empty
Nesters

ALSO BY CAROLYN BROWN

CONTEMPORARY ROMANCES

The Perfect Dress
The Magnolia Inn
Small Town Rumors
The Sometimes Sisters
The Strawberry Hearts Diner
The Lilac Bouquet
The Barefoot Summer
The Lullaby Sky
The Wedding Pearls
The Yellow Rose Beauty Shop
The Ladies' Room
Hidden Secrets
Long, Hot Texas Summer
Daisies in the Canyon
Trouble in Paradise

CONTEMPORARY SERIES

THE BROKEN ROAD SERIES

To Trust
To Commit
To Believe
To Dream
To Hope

THREE MAGIC WORDS TRILOGY

A Forever Thing
In Shining Whatever
Life After Wife

HISTORICAL ROMANCE

THE BLACK SWAN TRILOGY

Pushin' Up Daisies
From Thin Air
Come High Water

THE DRIFTERS & DREAMERS TRILOGY

Morning Glory
Sweet Tilly
Evening Star

THE LOVE'S VALLEY SERIES

Choices
Absolution
Chances
Redemption
Promises

the
Empty
Nesters

CAROLYN BROWN

Published by Montlake Romance, Seattle

www.apub.com

Amazon, the Amazon logo, and Montlake Romance are trademarks of Amazon.com, Inc., or its affiliates.

ISBN-13: 9781542043007
ISBN-10: 154204300X

Cover design by Laura Klynstra

Printed in the United States of America

*This book is for Georgia Hennard and Carolyn Young,
with appreciation for all your amazing support!*

Prologue

*I*n their years in Sugar Run, Texas, Tootsie and Smokey Colbert had had so many neighbors that they'd lost count. One by one, families in the four other houses on their block had moved in and moved away. Now, all were sitting empty.

At least they were until the first day of July, the hottest day on record in San Antonio and all the little surrounding towns. Tootsie kept a watch out the window as three big strong men—military, from the way they were dressed—unloaded the U-Haul trailers. They laughed and every so often stopped to sit on the curb and drink a beer. Smokey would like this bunch for sure since he was a retired veteran. But what interested Tootsie more than the hunky guys were those three young women and the three little girls running from one house to the other. It had been years since they'd had children on the block.

"Smokey, hurry up with those cookies," she yelled.

"I can't make the oven cook any faster." He came up behind her and wrapped his arms around her. "I like their music and that they're wearing army fatigues. We're going to get along with these folks just fine, darlin'."

Country music blared from the radio in the middle house on that hot July day in Sugar Run. One of the men—a tall, dark, and handsome type—grabbed a woman around the waist and two-stepped with her out there on the lawn. A little girl with dark hair tugged on his arm, and he scooped her up and made it a three-way dance.

"I can't wait to invite them to a cookout in the backyard tonight. I'm sure after moving all day, they'll appreciate having a grilled burger or hot dog, and that way they'll feel welcomed to our block," she said.

"There's the timer. The cookies are ready. Why don't you get those on over to them?" He moved away from her and hurried to the kitchen.

She and Smokey had been married for more than fifty years. The good Lord hadn't seen fit to bless them with children, but He had given them lasting love and friendship. She looked out at the new families, and her heart yearned for grandchildren. "In a minute," she muttered. "I'm looking at them."

~

Even standing in the living room of her new home with boxes all around her, Carmen could hardly believe that she was actually living off base for the first time since she and Eli had married. And as an added bonus, it was a few miles farther away from her mother-in-law, who'd thrown a fit when Eli married her and hadn't gotten over it even yet.

Eli picked her up and twirled her around until they were both dizzy and laughing, and then he fell back on the sofa with her on top of him. "I love you, Carmen Walker. We're going to be so happy here."

"Let's fill up this house with memories and have our fiftieth anniversary right here." She moistened her lips with the tip of her tongue as she went in for a long, passionate kiss.

Eli was panting when the kiss ended. "Now that, darlin', sounds like a good plan."

"Mommy. Daddy. Where are y'all at?" their five-year-old daughter, Natalie, called out from the front door. "We got cookies!"

Carmen stood and tidied up her dark-brown hair. She'd never heard of the army sending a welcoming committee to folks who moved off base, but then this was the first time she had a house that the military didn't own.

"Natalie said I could come in." An older lady, even shorter than Carmen, carried a platter of cookies into the living room. "I'm Tootsie Colbert, and this is my husband, Smokey. We just want to welcome all y'all to our block." She handed the platter to Carmen.

"And invite you to a backyard barbecue tonight. I make a mean hamburger and some pretty fine grilled bologna. We thought we could get to know each other—y'all are going to be hungry after all this work," Smokey said.

Eli set the cookies on a box and extended a hand. "That sounds great. I'm Eli Walker. This is my wife, Carmen, and I see you've already met Natalie. Right pleased to meet y'all."

Smokey shook hands with him. "Same here, and we're glad to have y'all moving in. Whole block has been too quiet this past three months."

"Well, that's about to come to an abrupt end," Carmen giggled. She was what her grandmother used to call *slap silly* that day. Part of it was because she was so tired, but Carmen never in her life dreamed that she'd own a home. Granted, the bank officially owned it for the next twenty years, but it was *her* house. She could decorate it however she wanted and paint the walls whatever color she wanted, and the military had no say-so.

She'd come from the wrong side of the tracks down south of San Antonio and had been working as a bartender when she met Eli. It had been love at first sight for her, but she'd always felt like maybe he'd married down. It hadn't taken long for her to realize that his mother felt the same way.

∼

That evening, Tootsie had a table set up with beer and whiskey for the adults and a different one with chocolate milk, soda pop, and three kinds of juice for the children. They had country music playing from a CD player over in the corner, and the whole backyard smelled like charbroiled burgers. She liked the ladies she'd met that day—that they were army wives put an instant connection between all of them. She'd walked a mile, or maybe she should say thirty years, in their shoes.

"Happy?" Smokey stopped what he was doing and kissed her on the forehead.

"Very, very happy. I'm going to have good friends. I can feel it in my heart." She rolled up on her toes and wrapped her arms around his neck. "And the little girls are precious. I hope that these families stay here for years and years."

"Maybe they will," Smokey said and then went back to his grilling.

Diana and her husband, Gerald, were the first to arrive that evening. Their daughter, Rebecca, the tallest of the three little girls, ran through the backyard gate ahead of them and went straight for the bean-toss game Smokey had set up in the yard.

Dark-haired Gerald was one of those men who made women turn around for a second look. Well over six feet tall, he had a confident swagger to his walk. Diana wasn't short by any means. Tootsie guessed her to be five feet, eight or nine inches tall. She had red hair that flowed down her back and gorgeous mossy-green eyes, and from the way she carried herself, Tootsie wondered if she had modeling experience.

Diana handed Tootsie a box of doughnuts. "I'd have baked something, but my kitchen still looks like a thrift store. So I found a cute little bakery a couple of blocks away and got these."

"You didn't have to bring a thing, but thank you." Tootsie put them on the dessert table with the chocolate sheet cake Smokey had made that afternoon. "First thing you'll learn about me is that I don't cook. Well, maybe I should revise that statement. When Smokey was off to God knows where, doing what only God and the government knew about, I didn't starve to death. I can survive, but Smokey loves to cook."

"You may be the luckiest woman among us all," Diana whispered.

4

"Hey, is this where the party is?" Carmen called out as she came through the gate with a box from the same pastry shop in her hands. She laughed when she saw one just like it on the table. "Maybe we should've had a committee meeting so we didn't all bring the same thing."

"What don't get eaten tonight will be good for breakfast," Tootsie said as she took the box from Carmen.

Eli went straight to the grill. He and Smokey were about the same height, which would put him just under six feet. He didn't quite have the swagger or the good looks that Gerald had. His light-brown hair was cut military-style, and his green eyes set in a round face gave him a boyish, almost shy look. The way he looked over his shoulder at his daughter, Natalie, endeared him to Tootsie.

Before Tootsie could carry the box to the table, the gate opened, and Brett, Joanie, and their daughter, Zoe, brought in a third box from the pastry shop.

"I hope that those don't have a lemon pie in them," Joanie said as she handed the box off to Tootsie. "Looks like we've all been to the same place."

"Which is fine by me," Tootsie said. "It's my favorite shop, and within walking distance. Maybe we can all four go for coffee and a girls' morning out once y'all get settled."

"Sounds good," Joanie said.

She wasn't as tall as Diana but certainly not as short as Carmen. They all kind of reminded her of a singing group she'd seen somewhere in her travels. Diana was the tall redhead. Carmen was the short brunette. And Joanie was the blonde that stood between them if they were lined up by height. She had brown eyes and was a little on the curvy side. Brett was between Gerald and Eli in height and had dark hair and the clearest blue eyes she'd ever seen on a man.

A good mixed group, Tootsie thought as she watched the little girls playing with the bean-toss game. Even the kids. Rebecca was all skinny

5

legs at this age and constantly humming while she played. Natalie was a little shorter and heavier. Zoe was the prissy one. Tootsie predicted that Rebecca would be musical when she was a little older. Natalie was a tomboy type, so she'd play basketball. And Zoe, no doubt about it, she'd be a cheerleader.

But it didn't matter what they did or didn't do; Tootsie was glad to have them all living on her block.

∼

Later that night, Joanie read Zoe a book about living in a new house, tucked her into bed, and stayed with her until she fell asleep. Then she went into her new bedroom to sleep with Brett for the first time in their new home, and the last time for at least three months. He was team leader of a Special Forces group of five people that included Gerald and Eli. They had a mission, and right after that, they were scheduled to teach a class in desert survival.

She curled up beside him and laid her head on his chest. She'd known what she was getting into when she married Brett, and for the most part she'd accepted their lifestyle. But what she'd give right then for at least a week with him in this new place—well, that couldn't be measured in dollars and cents.

"I like Tootsie and Smokey." She bit back tears. A good army wife didn't cry and throw fits. She held down the fort while her husband was gone.

"Me, too, and I feel better knowing you girls have a good neighbor." Brett pulled her even closer to his side. "But I don't want to talk about neighbors tonight. I want to hold you and make memories to last me for the next three months."

∼

Diana awoke the next morning, and it took several seconds before she remembered that they'd moved the day before. She eased out of bed and went straight to the kitchen, where she stirred up pancakes. When the guys were leaving on a mission, she always sent Gerald away with his favorite breakfast.

Rebecca came wandering into the room and crawled up on a barstool. "Pancakes? No, Mama, not Daddy's pancakes." Her little chin began to quiver. "I don't want him to go. He's supposed to stay with us now that we gots a house."

"He's got to go away for a little while and make some money to pay for this house," Diana explained.

Rebecca crossed her arms over her chest and blew her dark hair away from her face. "Then give it back. I don't want him to leave."

Gerald appeared at that moment, swept her off the barstool, and spun her around. "It's only for a little while, and you've got all of your friends right here on the same block. Y'all can play all day, every day, and not just have playdates."

"I'd rather have you," she said. "Don't go, Daddy. Stay home with us."

"I wish I could. I promise, after a few more years, I'll be here so much that you'll want me to leave." He chuckled.

Rebecca did pretty well during breakfast, but when the knock came at the door and she knew that it was time for her daddy to leave, she burst into tears. "I hate goodbyes," she said as she ran to her room.

Diana opened the door to find both Eli and Brett standing there. Their expressions said that they hadn't had any easier a time at their houses. "He's giving Rebecca one more hug."

The sound of Gerald's footsteps on the hardwood floor preceded him to the door. "I did the best I could, darlin'."

"She'll be fine. Call me when you can, and come home in one piece." She raised her head for that final kiss.

"Do my best," Gerald said, and then they were gone.

She slid down the back of the door in a house that wasn't familiar yet, that had days of unpacking to do, and waited. In less than a minute, someone knocked again. She got up and opened the door for Carmen and Joanie. Natalie and Zoe went straight back to Rebecca's room.

Carmen carried a box of tissues. Joanie had a bottle of orange juice. The usual fare for the mornings when their husbands left for an extended time. They made it to the kitchen before the tears started. Diana pulled a bottle of champagne from the cabinet and mixed mimosas. Carmen passed out tissues, and Joanie got out three glasses.

"Champagne shouldn't be used for days like this. It's a celebration thing." Diana wiped away tears.

"We *are* celebrating." Carmen tossed a fistful of tissues into an empty paper bag. "We're rejoicing in the fact that one more time we've held it together like good little army wives. We didn't scream and bawl like our daughters, even though we wanted to. We were strong."

"And now we can fall apart." Diana filled three glasses and touched hers with the other two, then reached for another tissue.

Chapter One

Over the past thirteen years, the ladies who lived on the same block in Sugar Run had been through wars, rumors of wars, death, divorce, fears, and joys, but nothing had prepared Carmen, Diana, and Joanie for the day they walked away from the army recruiter's office in downtown San Antonio. Each of their daughters had enlisted and would leave in less than an hour, heading to Fort Sill, Oklahoma, for basic training. Backs straight, the three mothers managed to keep smiles on their faces until they were all inside Diana's van, and then the waterworks started.

"I need a drink." Diana wiped at the never-ending tears with a tissue, then passed the box around.

"This is ten times—no, a hundred times—worse than when Eli deploys. But, good God, Diana, it's eight o'clock in the morning. If we start drinking now, we'll be passed out by noon," Carmen sobbed as she blew her nose and tossed another fistful of tissues into the plastic trash bag Diana kept in the van.

Diana pushed a strand of red hair away from her wet cheeks. "Passed completely out sounds good to me, and if you'll remember, we always have mimosas when the guys leave on missions."

Joanie took a compact from her purse and checked her reflection, then broke down into more weeping. "Zoe doesn't look a thing like me.

She's got Brett's dark hair and blues, and since she's got nurse's training, they'll probably send her to some god-awful country. She took ballet, for God's sake, and she was a cheerleader. She doesn't belong in a foreign country seeing soldiers with their legs blown off."

"In the words of Jimmy Buffett, 'It's five o'clock somewhere,' so let's go to Diana's." Blotches spotted Carmen's translucent skin from crying so hard. Several strands of dark-brown hair had escaped her ponytail and hung limp like a frayed flag of victory on a rainy day. "At least Zoe will be able to tell you where she's going. Natalie passed that language test with flying colors. She'll be put somewhere to translate, and you know what that means. Everything will be classified, and she won't be able to talk about it."

Diana started the van and then laid her head on the steering wheel. "This is worse than kindergarten, isn't it?"

"Yes," the women agreed.

"We were able to pick them up at the end of the day back then," Joanie sighed.

Carmen stared at the front of the recruitment center. "I wanted one more glimpse of her, but I guess they went out a back door. I prayed every day from the time that Natalie was born that she'd do anything rather than join the service. I didn't care if she flipped burgers at the local McDonald's for the rest of her life, but oh, no, she made her daddy proud. He's over there in God knows where, doing God knows what, and I'm the one left at home with the empty nest," Carmen declared. "And yes, I need a good stiff drink. Maybe two or three."

"That would be great. I'm not ready for an empty house." Diana sniffled as she put the van in gear and headed north toward Sugar Run, population 3,412, according to the city-limit signs on either end of town.

Diana had known when she married Gerald that she'd spend months alone when and if he was deployed. She'd accepted that, and when he divorced her for another woman, she'd lived through that, too, with the help of her friends. She'd raised Rebecca on her own for the most part, and even though the teenage years were unbearable at times, she'd gotten past them. But seeing her only child leave for the service—that was more than a mother should have to bear after all she'd already endured.

She parked her van in the driveway of her small three-bedroom house—the place where she'd raised her daughter for most of the child's life, and the house that she called home. When she got out of the vehicle, she could hear the high school band practicing its fight song. The fact that the house was close to the school had been a plus when she and Gerald had looked at it the first time. The music brought back the memory of Rebecca when she was in the fifth grade and learning to play the flute. At the time, Diana had kept earplugs in the kitchen drawer to be used for that hour every afternoon; now she wished she could go back in time to those days.

With Carmen and Joanie following her—the daughters had teased them all about starting a singing group like Pistol Annies—Diana crossed the yard and unlocked the door, leaving it open for them to come on in. She tossed her purse and sweater onto the sofa and kept going right through the small dining room into the kitchen, where she opened the cabinet door to the liquor supply.

"I'm having a double shot of Jack Daniel's to start with. Y'all can mix your own." Diana poured up her drink and carried it to the living room. She kicked off her shoes, sat down on the end of the sofa, and drew her feet up. "Rebecca's going to have a tough time. Her room looks like a dumping ground. Bed's unmade. Clothes are scattered on the floor, and there's a quarter inch of dusting powder covering the top of her dresser. She may get kicked out and sent home the first week. Of course, as much as I already miss her, I don't want her to fail."

Carmen moved Diana's sweater and purse to a rocking chair and sat down on the other end of the sofa. "My Natalie will be fine on that part of it, but I worry about her temper. If something doesn't make sense to her—like algebra—she fights against it. But she'll be okay with keeping things straight. She could go into her room at midnight with no lights on at all and put her hands on anything she wanted. She got her looks and her OCD from her father. I guess that'll do her well in whatever part of the intelligence field they train her for. Don't they have to be super organized?"

"Yes." Joanie sank into a spot between the two women and sipped a glass of coconut rum. "And Rebecca will be all right, too." She patted Diana's knee. "Basic training for her will be like she told us once about history tests. You memorize it. Pass the test. Then you forget it and go on. She's strong, and she's independent. She may end up being one of the elite few that get sniper training."

Diana threw a hand over her eyes. "Dear God, I don't want to hear that."

"We have to be strong for them." Joanie's chin quivered. "But I've watched too many television shows about medical stuff. Zoe's had technical-school training to be a nurse, but she's never seen a field hospital with bloody towels on the floor, and she's never lost a patient. I worry about her the first time one of her patients doesn't make it."

"Zoe's tough. They all are." Diana tried to convince herself as well as her friends. "When we start to miss them, we need to remember that they've driven us batshit crazy the past year with their senioritis and their too-big-for-their-britches attitudes. God, this house is going to be like a tomb without her." Diana finished off her whiskey. "Besides, y'all do realize we're worrying for nothing. They've got to get through basic training and then Advanced Individual Training before they go into their actual fieldwork. We'll have to take it one day at a time for the next couple of months. Right now, I'll just be glad when the first part of basic is over and they can call us."

"That'll be at Halloween," Carmen groaned. "For the first time ever, Natalie and I won't decorate the house for Halloween together." She got up and went for another drink and returned with half a wineglass of coconut rum. "Nine months of carrying them, then we basically raised them on our own while our husbands were deployed or got sent someplace to train other officers. And now they're gone, and we won't see them for Halloween or Thanksgiving. And who even knows about Christmas? It's not fair."

"We'll see them right before Christmas at the graduation at Fort Sill," Joanie reminded her. "And if we're lucky, they might not be sent to their AIT until after the holidays, so we could possibly get one of those rent-by-the-week places in Lawton and spend Christmas Day with them."

~

Carmen glanced around at the house that was basically the same floor plan as the one she lived in on the other end of the block—living room, small dining area, kitchen, hallway to three bedrooms and a bath and a half. Now all three homes were going to be downright lonely. "And have Christmas dinner all together like we've always done," she sighed. "I might be able to survive the next few weeks with that goal in mind. After this drink, I'm going home. You've got work to do, Diana McTavish, and besides, you are not a nice drunk. If you have another double shot, we'll have to put you in restraints to keep you from driving up to Oklahoma and bringing Rebecca back home with you. Remember how you were on her first day of kindergarten?" She patted her friend on the shoulder.

"I was afraid someone would make fun of her because she was so tall and skinny. I just wanted to be there in case they made her cry." Diana set her empty glass on the coffee table. "And besides, y'all were just as bad as I was."

"I made an excuse to go to the school at noon." Joanie finally smiled.

"And I sat in my car and watched Natalie when it was time for recess," Carmen admitted as she got up to leave.

"Y'all will come back this evening, right?" Diana asked.

"Sure we will," Carmen said.

"Don't we always?" Joanie finished off her rum and took the glass to the sink. "But work is what we all need now. Not having hangovers tomorrow morning."

"Speak for yourself," Diana said.

"We're only half a block and a phone call away. If any of us feel the world dropping out from under our feet, we can get back together in less than five minutes." Carmen carried her empty glass to the kitchen, rinsed it, and put it into the dishwasher. "I'll see y'all later. I'll bring a pan of lasagna for supper."

"I'll try to be sober," Diana called out.

"I'll make fresh yeast rolls, and, Diana, you'd better be able to make dessert," Joanie scolded.

"Does Jack Daniel's count as dessert?" Diana joked.

"It does *not*." Carmen put a lot of emphasis on the last word. "Our girls aren't the only females who have to be tough. We've got to hold down the fort."

"Is she going to be all right?" Joanie whispered as she and Carmen walked out to the end of the driveway. "We've at least got husbands who've got our backs. She's only got us."

"We've been through worse than this," Carmen said. "And she's lived through a cheatin' husband and a messy divorce."

"Thank God we're here for each other." Joanie headed out to the right.

"Amen." Carmen went in the opposite direction. They had met when their daughters were all just babies and their husbands had been assigned to the same team. And then they'd all moved to Sugar Run the same summer just before their girls started kindergarten. With their husbands gone so much of the time, they wanted to be close to each

other. Other army wives had come and gone through the years, some living in Sugar Run for a few months, others a couple of years, but none of them had maintained the long-term friendship that Diana, Joanie, and Carmen had.

Carmen unlocked the door to her house, tossed her purse on the foyer table, and went straight for Natalie's bedroom. She threw herself onto the bed and inhaled the vanilla scent of her daughter's perfume still lingering on a throw pillow. After a while she got up and made sure all the wrinkles were gone from the bed and the pillow was put back at just the right angle. Then she heard the mail carrier opening the squeaky lid to the mailbox and hurried out to see if maybe she'd gotten a note from Eli.

The lady still had an envelope in her hand and looked shocked when the door flew open. "I was just about to ring the doorbell. You need to sign for this one, Miz Walker."

Carmen scribbled her name beside the X and took the manila envelope. "Thank you," she said, hoping that it was from Natalie. It would be just like her to send something cute because she knew her mother would be sad.

She rushed into the living room, sat down on the sofa, and carefully opened the end of the envelope. From the heft of it, she could tell there were several pages hiding inside. She slipped the stapled pages out, expecting to see a silly drawing, only to read in fairly large letters, DECREE OF DIVORCE.

"That's not funny, Natalie," she chuckled. "Just because you're leaving home doesn't mean we're getting a divorce. I might have thought about it when you were so rebellious this past year, but we . . ." She stopped at the sight of her name and Eli's at the top of the page.

She sat in stunned silence, paralyzed from her eyes to her toes. She wasn't dying, but her life flashed before her at warp speed—weepy goodbyes, joyous homecomings, happy times, bad moments, scary events.

Finally, she found her voice and started to scream, a guttural noise that sounded like a dying animal.

~

"Okay, Smokey, you've got to help me out here." Tootsie Colbert stared at the picture of her husband in his dress uniform. "Should I go on the trip by myself in memory of you, or do I sell the motor home and forget all about it?"

She listened intently for a minute, cocking her head from one side to the other. "Of course I can drive the sumbitch. I drove it home from the dealership, didn't I? That's not the issue. I'm not sure I can go to the old house without you. It's where we spent our honeymoon, and you won't be there."

She rolled her eyes toward the ceiling. "You could at least give me a sign. If folks can see Jesus on their toast, surely you can throw something out here. Maybe a cloud in the shape of a big-ass RV?"

Smokey had been gone just shy of a month, and this trip had been weighing on her for the past week. She and her husband of more than sixty years had gone to their vacation place near Scrap, Texas, for a month in the fall to celebrate their anniversary. At the beginning of their marriage, it hadn't been possible every year, not with Smokey in the military, but they hadn't missed going for the past two decades.

"Come on, just a little something," she begged. "Peace in my heart one way or the other will do just fine." She got up from her comfortable rocking chair and went to the back door to stare at the enormous motor home sitting in her backyard. What had she been thinking? Using a chunk of their savings for that monstrous thing was pretty silly at their age.

While she was standing there, she heard the most god-awful sounds—something like a coyote with its foot caught in a trap. She hadn't heard that kind of noise since she lived in northeast Texas—up there in the rural area around Scrap. Coyotes were a problem in most parts of the state, but she'd never even heard one howling in Sugar Run.

She threw open the door and realized it was coming from Carmen's house next door. Without even stopping to put on her shoes, she raced across the lawn, threw open the yard gate, and hurried to Carmen's back door.

Having never been blessed with children, she and Smokey had adopted the three army wives who lived on their block. The women had each had a precious little girl when they moved to Sugar Run thirteen years ago, and the kids plus their parents had breathed life back into a tired old neighborhood.

Without even knocking, Tootsie tried the back door only to find it locked, but that awful sound swelled. Tootsie's heart pumped so hard that she had to stop a second for breath when she made it to the front porch. Someone had to be attacking poor Carmen, the smallest of her kind-of-adopted daughters. Should she go back home and get her pistol or just use whatever was handy, like a lamp, to take care of the villain? Another scream convinced her that she'd better just take her chances with whatever she could find to fight with. But first she had to catch her breath again.

She put her hands on her knees and inhaled deeply before she slung open the door and hurried to Carmen's side. The poor girl was curled up in the fetal position on the end of the sofa. The painfully raw sobs coming from her throat had traveled all the way to Tootsie's house.

Tootsie sat down beside her and gathered her into her arms like a mother with a hurt child. "Is it Natalie? Please stop this, Carmen. You are breaking my heart."

"Not Natalie," she said before the sobs overtook her body again.

"Eli?" Tootsie asked.

Carmen pointed at the papers lying on the floor. "Divorce."

"That son of a bitch." Tootsie grimaced. "What in the hell is he thinking, serving you with that today of all days?"

"What am I going to do?" Carmen's teeth began to chatter. "This can't be happening. Eli is not divorcing me."

"We'll get through this. I'm going to get you a good strong shot of brandy to calm your nerves." Tootsie cussed all the way to the kitchen. "I asked for a little sign, Smokey, not a bomb."

Coming back into the living room, she put a glass in Carmen's hand and said, "Drink this. All down in one big gulp. You've got to stop shaking."

Carmen straightened her legs and took the glass, but her hands shook so badly that she couldn't get it to her mouth.

Tootsie took it from her and held it to her lips. "All of it in one swallow. You're in shock. The first thing we have to do is get that under control. I'll get a blanket and call Diana and Joanie, and then we'll all talk."

With a nod that looked more like a spasm, Carmen obeyed. "Call them now, please."

While Tootsie was making the call, Carmen's phone rang. She sat up and answered without even looking at the caller ID. "Hello," she whispered.

"Carmen, is that you?"

Eli's voice brought on more sobs. "Why did you do this?"

"I've been unhappy for months," he said, "but I held off until Natalie graduated."

"But today of all days." She cried even harder.

Tootsie handed her a fistful of tissues. "I'll talk to him."

"Who's there?" Eli asked.

"Tootsie is right beside me. Want me to put it on speaker?"

"No! I do not. I just want you to sign the papers and get this thing settled. I don't want to be married to you anymore. And I'm not sure that it wasn't a mistake in the beginning. It just took me all these years to figure it out."

He'd used that bitterly cold tone with her once before.

When she'd told him she wanted to take online courses to get a degree, he'd disagreed with her, but she'd done it anyway, and he'd been so angry that she thought that frost would fly out of his ears when he talked to her.

"I'm not signing shit until I talk to a lawyer," she told him.

"I don't love you anymore," he said.

She felt as if someone had reached inside her chest, yanked out her heart, thrown it on the floor, poured gasoline on it, and set fire to it. "But I still love you." Her breathing was labored. "I'm not throwing out our marriage like a sack of garbage." She stopped and blew her nose. "We can go to counseling and work this out. We can spend more time together now that Natalie is out of school." Begging seemed so clingy, but this was her marriage, and she'd do anything to save it.

"It's too late for that," he snapped.

"Not for me it's not, and now I'm hanging up so I can process this crap."

∼

Joanie slumped down on the sofa in her living room, and the memories of the last nineteen years washed over her like a hard-driving rain. She and Brett had been high school sweethearts from the time she was in the ninth grade and he was a sophomore. She'd lost her virginity to him just before he went to the army right out of high school. Then they'd married the next year when he finished his AIT training and she'd graduated.

Her phone rang, and she fished it out of her purse. Thinking it was probably Diana, she answered it without even looking at the caller ID. "Are you all right?"

"Good morning to you, too, darlin'. I knew today would be rough on you, so I had to hear your voice this morning before I left." Brett's deep southern drawl always helped her on a bad day.

"I'm sorry. I thought it was Diana calling. She's having a rougher day than any of us," Joanie explained. "I wish you were here, Brett. Leaving Zoe at that recruiter's office was the hardest thing I've ever done. I've cried all morning."

"It's not fair that you had to do this alone," Brett said. "I should've been there to support you. We just got our orders changed this morning. We had thought we'd be home by Thanksgiving, but we've got to stay a little longer. The new idea is that we'll get to be there for Christmas. I'm hoping to arrive in time for Zoe's basic-training graduation. Maybe we can go away for a week or two, just the two of us, after that. I can put in for leave, and we could spend a week on that little beach in Florida that we like."

"Promise?" she asked.

"As much as I'm able to," Brett said.

"Brett, I feel so guilty that I've still got you. Diana has no one now but us and Tootsie." Her voice quivered as much as her chin.

"I heard a catch in your voice. Please tell me you aren't crying. I wish I was there to hold you or that we could talk awhile longer, but I've got to go. I wanted to give you a heads-up so you'll be there when the mail carrier comes. Eli's lawyer sent out divorce papers to Carmen. They're coming in the mail today."

"Sweet Lord!" Joanie stood up so fast that it made her dizzy. "Why would he do that? Is it another woman?"

"It's been a long time coming. He didn't want to file until Natalie was through school, but it's been a tough year on him having to wait this long. I'm glad that he finally got things going for the divorce," Brett said.

"I *asked you* if it's another woman." Joanie fell backward onto the sofa.

"Just go be with her, Joanie. What goes on between Eli and Carmen is their business. He's calling her before we leave to be sure the papers got there. I really do have to go. I'll call you as soon as I can, and we'll be together as a family right before Christmas. Love you," Brett said.

"Love you," she said, and ended the call.

Joanie tossed the phone on the other end of the sofa and began to pace the floor. Five years ago Gerald had divorced Diana for a younger woman. Now Eli was divorcing Carmen. In five more years would *her* marriage be on the rocks?

Her stomach clenched into knots, but she didn't know if she was hungry or nauseated because of what was happening. This was simply too much drama, too fast, for her to take in. She went back to Zoe's room, lay down on the bed, and let the aura of her daughter's presence from that morning soak in for half an hour.

"Okay, enough," she said out loud as she got up. "The mail will be here anytime, and we need to be there for Carmen when she gets that damned letter. I can't procrastinate another minute." She muttered to herself as she headed out the door, only to see that her mailbox was already stuffed. "Dammit!" She jerked her phone from her hip pocket and hit the speed dial for Diana.

"You finished crying?" Diana answered.

"No, but now it's for a different reason. Meet me on the sidewalk. Carmen needs us," she said. "And bring the rest of that bottle of wine she was drinking and the rum, too."

"Good Lord, did Eli die?" Diana sounded out of breath.

"No, but it might have been better if he had."

Diana met her halfway between their two houses with a bottle in each hand. "What's happened?"

"Eli sent divorce papers, and I think they've already been delivered. Brett called and gave me a heads-up. The mail doesn't usually come until after lunch, but it came early today. We should've already been there with Carmen." Joanie charged on to the other end of the block.

"I should've brought more than two bottles," Diana said, keeping pace.

Joanie rapped on the door but went on in before Carmen could answer. "Where are you?"

"In the living room," Tootsie yelled. "I was just about to call y'all."

They found Carmen curled up on the sofa under a fluffy throw with unicorns on it. Papers were strewn about on the floor, and her phone was ringing. Tootsie had pulled up a rocking chair and was holding her hand.

Joanie pushed the coffee table back a few feet so that she and Diana could sit down in front of the sofa and laid a hand on Carmen's shoulder.

"We're here," Diana said.

Joanie held Carmen's hand. "Brett called. We know."

Diana took her other hand. "The sorry bastard picked the worst day in the world to have those damned papers delivered. Have you even talked to him about it yet?"

Carmen nodded. "He called a few minutes ago. I told him we need to give us another chance. We can't throw out twenty years of marriage like it's the garbage. We can go to counseling, and now that Natalie is out of school, we can spend more time together."

"Son of a bitch is blamin' her," Tootsie said through clenched teeth.

"How could it be your fault?" Joanie asked.

"I was too wrapped up in Natalie and didn't give him enough attention." Carmen pushed back the covers and sat up. "Did I really do that?"

"Hell, no! When the husbands are home, they're showered with attention," Joanie answered. "Sorry bastard should have at least had the decency to tell the lawyers to wait until you'd had time to get used to the empty nest."

"I'm making us all a stiff drink. I don't care if we just had one at my house. We need another." Diana headed for the kitchen and returned with four glasses, each with two fingers of whiskey, on a tray.

Carmen held the glass in her hand for a full minute, then set it down on the end table. "I've had enough liquor. It doesn't make the pain go away, anyhow. I'm not going to sign the papers or get a divorce. I'll work harder. I don't want to lose Eli."

"Well, I need it." Diana patted her on the knee. "You are in denial. That's the first stage of divorce grief, and we're here to keep reminding you that this is all on Eli. I've been where you are, remember? Without a good counselor, and all y'all, I'd have never gotten through it. And, honey, it takes two to want to make a marriage work. One can't do it alone."

"His family never thought I was good enough for him. I barely made it through high school, and I came from the wrong side of the tracks." Carmen grabbed a fistful of tissues and blew her nose. "Evidently they were right. But I can be better. I'm just a year away from having my teaching degree. And we can get through this; I know we can."

Carmen pushed the throw to the side, stood up, and folded it neatly, then began to straighten up the living room. "He'll see. I can do better. I can keep a better house, make better meals, and give him all the attention he wants."

"You raised his daughter, and you've always supported him in everything. The only time you even went against him was when you told him you were going to get your teaching degree even if it took you ten years," Diana said.

"God, I wish I could just disappear and get my head wrapped around all this. If he would only come home, so we could sit down and talk, we could tear those papers up." Carmen picked up the glass, threw back the whole drink like a cowboy in an old western movie, and picked up a dustcloth.

"But he can't come home for another two months at least," Diana reminded her.

"But . . ." Carmen started to cry again.

"We'll figure out later what needs to be done. Right now, we've got to get through this hellacious day. Stop what you're doing and sit down.

You're an excellent housekeeper and cook. This is not your fault." Joanie stood up and took the dustcloth from Carmen's hands.

"I'll let you have my job, and then I'll get a soup can and stand on the corner collecting dimes if it comes down to it, or you can move in with me if you lose this house. I've got a spare room now," Diana offered.

"I'm not getting a divorce," Carmen declared. "My grandpa used to say that anything worth having is worth fighting for, and I love Eli with my whole heart. I'm going to fight him on this."

"But, darlin', from what you're tellin' me, he's not willing to fight, and it takes two to make it work," Diana said again.

"You need to get away for a little while and get some perspective," Tootsie said.

"Let's pool our money and blow it all on a trip to Paris. We can shop and have lattes in little bistros," Diana suggested.

Joanie sighed. "That's a pipe dream. We probably don't have enough money to even get to Paris, Texas, between the three of us."

Tootsie leaned down and kissed Carmen on the forehead. "I'm going home now. I've got something I have to see about, but I'll be back either later or tomorrow morning."

"Thank you, Tootsie, for everything." Carmen's chin quivered.

"No thanks necessary, and no more tears. Any man who'd do this to his wife ain't worth cryin' over. Y'all girls are my family—I ain't got blood kin left with Smokey's passin'." Tootsie pulled a tissue free and dabbed her eyes, and then she put the whole box in Carmen's hands.

"Joanie, a word," Tootsie said as she started toward the door.

Joanie followed her outside and said, "Don't worry, Tootsie, we'll stay with her the rest of the day and tonight. You can come back anytime."

"That's just what I wanted to hear. I'll have things worked out one way or the other by morning." Tootsie headed next door to her house without another word.

Chapter Two

"Yoo-hoo, where are y'all at?" Tootsie's soft southern voice floated through the house.

"In the living room," Diana called out.

Carmen had finally fallen asleep on the sofa at midnight. What little sleep Diana and Joanie had gotten was in recliners, and that was in fifteen- or thirty-minute spurts. Diana had gone to pieces when she got the divorce papers five years ago, but she'd known they were coming. Gerald had told her weeks in advance about his affair, and she'd had a little time to get prepared. Poor Carmen had been hit with it out of the clear blue sky. Diana remembered thinking that she'd felt like she'd been shot in the gut with a 12-gauge shotgun when the papers arrived in the mail. Carmen probably felt like she'd swallowed a hand grenade.

Diana had gotten over her ex-husband, but it had taken lots of counseling, both the professional and the friendship variety. It had taken her a couple of weeks to go from denial to the next step, and each one of those levels had been an ordeal that she couldn't have made it through without Carmen, Joanie, and Tootsie as her support system.

The aroma of bacon and salsa wafted across the room as Tootsie set the platter on the coffee table. "As you all know, I'm a terrible cook, but I can make a good breakfast burrito, and I know y'all didn't eat much yesterday."

Then from a tote bag she pulled a bowl of cantaloupe chunks and a sack of doughnuts from their favorite shop just down the street. "Now let's eat up and talk. Things always look a little brighter after we've slept on them." She put a burrito in Carmen's hands. "One bite at a time. One minute at a time. One hour at a time. That's the way we're all going to get through these horrible emotional events we're having to deal with right now."

Diana swallowed the lump in her throat and took the first bite. She had to eat since Tootsie had been so sweet to bring them food, but it tasted like sawdust mixed with onions.

Carmen nibbled on the burrito. "Things look better than they did yesterday, and there's always hope. When Eli gets back from this mission, I'm going to make him talk about reconciliation. We've just grown apart, and we can fix that."

Tootsie gave her a quick hug before she sat down beside her. "Have you talked to Eli today?"

"No, but he loves me. I know he does, even though he has doubts, and I'll always love him. With some counseling, we can get through this."

"You've got to get through the denial before you can move on. That's a fact, and we're not going to argue about it. I've reached the guilt stage of grief since Smokey died. I keep asking myself why in the hell we didn't go on all the trips we'd planned instead of waiting so long to get the RV. There's motels everywhere. We should have packed our bags and gone." She picked up a burrito. "I thought nothing could be worse than seeing our pretty girls go to the service yesterday morning. I wanted to go with y'all, but I'd have been a big old bawlin' baby. They didn't need that, and neither did any of you. But I want y'all to know that Smokey was so damned proud of them when they decided to serve their country. The way he went on and on to anyone who'd stand still and listen, why, you'd swear they were his granddaughters by blood."

"I'm not in denial," Carmen protested. "I really think Eli and I can work this out."

"So did I, even though Gerald had cheated on me," Diana said. "Just know that we are here to support you, no matter what happens."

Tootsie laid a hand on her heart. "Yes, we are, and with that said, I've been makin' plans since yesterday and finalized them this morning. The only thing y'all have to do is agree with them."

"What kind of plans?" Diana asked.

Tootsie lowered her voice. "Y'all got to promise not to think I'm crazy."

"We'd never think that about you," Diana declared.

"Okay, then, even though it was a month yesterday since Smokey passed away, I still talk to him," Tootsie said between bites. "I was visitin' with him yesterday morning about our anniversary trip that we take every fall. I needed a sign to know whether to go or not. It'll be sad to go without him but even sadder to stay home and wish I'd gone."

"I'm so sorry," Carmen apologized. "With all this going on, I forgot. We should be comforting you, not getting taken care of."

"It's being needed that keeps me going. I know he can't really answer me, but, by damn, he can send me signs, and he sure sent one in a big way yesterday," Tootsie explained.

"How's that?" Diana asked.

"With the divorce papers."

"What?" Carmen frowned.

The wrinkles around Tootsie's eyes deepened when she smiled. "Smokey and I vowed to each other that we'd live to be ninety, and then we wouldn't fight the good Lord if He wanted to come and get us. When Smokey's heart stopped when he was only eighty-two, I knew that God had other plans."

"I'd forgotten that this is the time of year you and Smokey usually went away for a few weeks, but what has the divorce got to do with that?" Joanie asked.

"Oh, I'm going," Tootsie said. "I'm going to make the trip, just like we planned, and stay at the old house up in Scrap, Texas. Only now I'm making different plans for the trip back. I think it'd be nice to take the motor home to Lawton and see the girls graduate from basic training, don't y'all?"

"Oh, Tootsie, that is so, so sweet," Carmen said with more enthusiasm than Diana had heard from her since the day before. "But we'll worry about you out there on the road in that big vehicle all by yourself."

"Y'all are going with me, so pack your bags. Smokey's favorite nephew, Luke, is going to drive me. Y'all haven't met him. Since he's grown-up and not a little boy anymore, I only get to see him at the Colbert family reunion up in Paris in November each year and when he can get off to come to Scrap for Thanksgiving. He did come to the funeral, but things were so stressful, I hardly even realized he was here. He sold his company—some kind of software thing—this past month down in Houston, so he's got some free time," Tootsie said.

Diana sucked in a lungful of air. "Tootsie, we can't do that. We can't leave for a month."

"Two months, maybe more," Tootsie argued. "And why not? We'll be in Lawton in time for the graduation."

"But what if . . . ," Joanie started.

"When's Brett coming home?" Tootsie asked.

"He's hoping to meet up with me in Lawton for the graduation," Joanie answered.

"Carmen said yesterday that she wants to run away. Diana can do her insurance coding work from anywhere. So what's the next excuse?" Tootsie asked.

"What if I need to be here for the divorce?" Carmen asked.

"Are you going to sign the papers? Is he being fair about everything?" Tootsie asked.

"I have no idea," Carmen answered. "I can't make heads or tails out of that stuff. I just know that it says *Decree of Divorce* across the top."

"I thought so. I took the liberty of calling my lawyer to represent you. Don't worry about the money. He was Smokey's best friend, and he's doing it as a favor to me. If you'll let me take the papers with me, I'll pass them on to him. Then y'all can keep in touch by phone about the whole rest of it," Tootsie said. "Any more excuses other than that you just don't want to be stuck in a camper or an old house back in the woods with an old woman?"

"Tootsie, how can you say that?" Carmen asked. "We love you. You've been a surrogate mother to us and a grandmother to our girls ever since we all moved in."

Tootsie's chin started to quiver. "Well, that's the only reason I can think of that you'd make me take this trip alone."

Carmen raised her hand. "I'm in."

Diana took a deep breath and held it while she thought about the whole crazy idea. Tootsie was right. She could do her work anywhere. Being able to stay at home for Rebecca is what made her agree to do the work in the first place. All she needed was her laptop and the internet. But being cooped up with three other women in an RV, even if it was huge—and a strange man—she wasn't so sure about that. Still, she couldn't stand to stay at home with no friends around her at all for the next two months. Finally, she let the air out in a whoosh. "When are we leaving Sugar Run?"

Tootsie cocked her head to one side. "Friday morning. You with us, Joanie?"

"Well, I'm not stayin' home alone. So I have until tomorrow morning to get things packed up and ready?"

Tootsie clapped her hands. "This is going to be so much fun. I can just hear Smokey laughing with happiness. And yes, Friday is the day, and we're leaving here at seven thirty in the morning. That would've been Smokey's eighty-third birthday. We're staying in Texas City the first night and going to the Old Smokey Cook-Off on Saturday, then leaving that area on Sunday."

"Old Smokey?" Joanie asked.

"We planned this trip all summer. He thought the cook-off would be a hoot since it has his name," Tootsie said.

"Was he going to drive that big-ass RV?" Diana asked.

"Nope, I was," Tootsie answered. "But Luke volunteered, and I didn't want to hurt his feelings. You've got the rest of today to get ready, girls. Pack light. If you forget something, there's Walmart stores everywhere. I'll be taking these papers with me." She swept out with the sheaf of papers.

"Did we really just agree to do this?" Carmen whispered.

"I think we did," Diana answered. "But we could back out. We could think about it overnight and break the news to her tomorrow."

"Not me," Carmen disagreed. "I said I wanted to run away, and then she comes in with that invitation. It's an omen. I'm going. I'm trying to remember what she and Smokey talked about when they got home right before Christmas. What did they do up there in the woods for a whole month? And how big is this house? Are we going to be sleeping in lofts on mattresses?"

"It's terrible, but I can't remember," Diana said. "I'm still in shock that we're even considering running away, but yet it's kind of exciting, isn't it?"

"Oh!" Joanie gasped. "We didn't even ask what kind of money we need. We can't let her pay for the fuel for that gas hog or food—we have to eat."

"We have to do that no matter whether we're at home or out on a trip," Diana said. "But let's get it straightened out now about the gas." She pulled her phone from her hip pocket, called Tootsie, and put it on speaker.

"I'm so glad you called," Tootsie started without even staying hello first. "Y'all know that I'm a horrible cook, so here's the deal. Y'all take turns making food for us every day we're on the trip, and I'll pay for the gas and the supplies."

"Tootsie, the gas for this trip will be really expensive," Diana said. "The only way we'll consider it is if we can buy the food, too. We'll gladly do the cooking."

"Smokey left me well fixed, and I have no one except y'all and Luke, and he's not blood kin. I'm payin' for the trip whether y'all go or not, so I'll hear no more about the fuel bill. It'll cost me less to buy groceries and have home-cooked meals than for me and Luke to go out every night. So that's that. Tell Carmen the lawyer is running by my place to get the divorce papers on his way to the golf course this morning. I may not be able to cook, but I did hold down a job as a secretary in the courthouse until I was sixty-five and retired."

"Yes, ma'am," Diana said as she ended the call.

"Well?" Carmen asked.

"I'd forgotten that she worked at the courthouse," Joanie said.

"So to answer your question about what they did up there in the woods, I guess Smokey cooked and they just relaxed." Diana picked up a chunk of cantaloupe with her fingers.

"We've all been tied in knots so long—I can't imagine relaxing," Carmen said.

"Me, either, but it sounds pretty good," Joanie said. "Do y'all feel like you are flat-out drained?"

"Above and beyond." As Carmen nodded, her phone rang. She took one look at it and paled. "It's Eli."

"We're not going anywhere." Joanie propped her feet up on the coffee table.

~

With shaking hands and a knot in her stomach the size of a watermelon, Carmen answered the phone. "Hello, Eli."

"Put it on speaker," Diana whispered.

Carmen hit the right button and laid the phone on the coffee table.

"Good morning, Carmen. Did you sign the papers?" he asked.

"No, and I'm not going to until my lawyer looks over them and I'm absolutely sure that this is the right thing to do. I think we should see a counselor and put this on hold for six months," she said.

"Things haven't been right between us for a long time. Counseling isn't going to help. We need to do this as soon as possible, kind of like ripping off a Band-Aid." His voice still had that cold edge to it, like the day before.

"Of course things haven't been good between us. I've been busy raising our daughter and trying to get a degree to help out with the finances. You're gone all the time. We just need some time together to rekindle our love," she said.

For several seconds there was silence on the other end of the phone. "I fought it for a long time, I really did."

"Wait. Fought what? You sure weren't fighting me. I'm not giving up on us, Eli. I love you and always will." Her heart thumped in her chest, and her pulse was racing as fast as it did after she jogged in the evenings.

"I'm not going to counseling. It's over. Accept it and sign the papers," he said.

"You'll be home for Natalie's basic-training graduation. Brett told Joanie that the team is coming home then, and I'm not signing anything until we talk face-to-face," Carmen said.

"Don't be like this, Carmen," he said.

"How do you expect me to be? I've stayed home and tried my damnedest to be a model army wife. I never cheated on you one time. I raised our daughter, most of the time alone, and now you don't even have the decency to tell me you're considering a divorce until after you've filed? Come on, Eli, how would you feel if the roles were reversed?"

"I'm being fair. Until the divorce is final, you'll still get the same amount of money each month," he said.

"Fair is trying to make this work, not just being sure I can pay the mortgage and electric bill," she said. "Give us six months. If at the end of that time, you still feel the same, I'll sign the papers. I'm not speaking to you about this again until my lawyer tells me what all this legal shit means. Goodbye, Eli."

"Wait a minute," he yelled. "I've only got another few minutes before I have to hang up. Can't you be reasonable? You don't need to pay a lawyer. I've already done that. Read the papers. You'll see that I'm not being unfair."

Carmen looked around at her home, the little brick house that she was so proud of. Did the papers say it would be sold and what equity was in it would be split? Or did they say she could keep the house if she took over the payments? Natalie barely remembered a time when they didn't live here. This was her home, and what if Carmen couldn't keep up the mortgage on what she'd make at minimum wage before she got her degree? It would be her fault that Natalie's home was gone.

"What's the big hurry? Didn't you just say that my money for keeping a home for our daughter will keep coming in until the divorce is settled? I'm not rushing anything. I may delay the signing for a year so I can finish my classes and get a job as a teacher."

Joanie patted her on the back.

Diana gave her the thumbs-up sign.

"Nothing—not a therapist, not even God—is going to change my mind. It's over. Accept it and move on," Eli said.

She ended the call, jumped up and ran to the bathroom, leaned over the toilet, and brought up everything she'd drunk and eaten in the last hour. Diana held her hair back while Joanie wet a washcloth with cool water for her face afterward. The taste in her mouth was horrible, so she grabbed a bottle of mouthwash and rinsed it, then gagged at the taste and dry heaved until her sides and throat hurt.

"I'm sorry," she whispered. "Why is he so determined to get the papers signed?"

"No need for apologies," Diana told her. "I think you held my hair a few years back when I was in the same frame of mind you are right now. Only difference is, I was begging in person, and you're doing it on the phone. And if I remember right, Joanie threatened to shoot him if he didn't get out of the house. It's just payback time. I'm going to make you a club soda with a little lemon twist. It'll help."

"And, honey, evidently he's given this a lot of thought to want things to go quickly." Joanie took her by the hand and led her to the sofa, made her stretch out on it, covered her with a throw, and sat down on the floor beside her.

Diana brought her the drink. "Here, sip on this. You did good on the phone. If you'd let him bully you into signing those papers right now, you'd have always felt like a doormat."

"Why can't he just give it some time? What's the rush? Can't he see I need a while to even adjust to the idea?" Carmen gasped and ran back to the bathroom. This time she put the toilet lid down and sat on it, bending forward until her head was between her knees. "I feel like I'm going to faint."

Joanie got another cold washcloth ready and handed it off to Diana, who flipped Carmen's dark ponytail to the side and laid it on her neck.

"How am I going to tell Natalie?" Carmen groaned.

"You're not. That's Eli's job." Diana handed the cloth back to Joanie, who ran it under the cold water again and then wrung it out. "When she can make and receive calls, he can explain it all to her, and she can make up her own mind about how to handle it. Thank God she'll be through basic training before he comes home and she has to face him. She may be small, but she's got a temper, and she's liable to light into him."

"But we share everything. How can I even talk to her in two or three weeks without telling her?" Carmen asked.

"By then, you'll be over this first initial shock, but don't you dare tell her. Eli's the one who messed up, not you," Joanie said. "Think you can make it back to the sofa?"

"I don't know what I'd do without y'all." Carmen's chin started to quiver again.

"That's what friends are for," Diana told her.

Chapter Three

Diana eased open the door to her daughter's room. Where had the years gone? It was only yesterday that she would've gone in and shaken Rebecca awake so she'd have time to eat breakfast before early-morning band practice. She sat down on the edge of the bed and looked around at the mess. Clothing on the floor, shoes flowing out from the closet door, one drawer hanging open on the chest of drawers, and at least a hundred pictures stuck around the mirror on her dresser.

"But if I touched a single thing, you'd know it the minute you walked into the room," Diana muttered.

Even though her suitcase was packed, her laptop was in its case, and she'd even remembered a jacket and an umbrella, she couldn't force herself to get up off her daughter's bed and go over to Tootsie's house. And yet, she wouldn't let herself call and back out of the trip.

"I'm not deserting you," she said out loud. "It's not like I couldn't wait for you to grow up and leave home so I could take a vacation alone. This is the hardest thing I've done since the day I signed divorce papers."

Get out of my room. Rebecca's voice came through loud and clear. *I'll clean it when I get home on leave.*

The message was definitely a strange one, but it gave Diana the courage to leave. She checked the thermostat, made sure that the lamp in the living room was set to come on at six every evening and go off at seven in the morning, and locked the door behind her.

～

Joanie had a second cup of coffee that morning and fretted about the trip. Zoe should have been in the kitchen with her at that time of day. She would have just come in from the two-mile run she'd started doing the first of the summer. She'd said she was getting in shape so that basic training didn't whoop her ass. Joanie had seen her daughter in cheerleader action for four years—there was no way that anything they could throw at Zoe would get the best of her. She touched the senior picture of Zoe sitting in the kitchen window.

What if Zoe faded now that she'd left the house? Would Joanie be able to close her eyes and remember all those times? What if she couldn't even remember what Zoe looked like without pulling up one of the hundreds of pictures she had on her phone?

Joanie's front door opened, and Diana yelled, "You ready?"

"Not really." Joanie rinsed her coffee cup, dried it, and put it away.

"Second thoughts?" Diana peeked around the kitchen door.

"Oh, yeah, lots of them," Joanie answered.

"Me, too, but I imagined Rebecca demanding that I get out of her room. I took that as a sign that we should go," Diana said.

"I haven't gotten up the nerve to even look in Zoe's room. I'm afraid if I go in there, I'll back out of this trip. This will be the first time ever I've gone anywhere without her," Joanie sighed.

"Me, too." Diana gave Joanie a sideways hug. "This empty-nest stuff stinks."

"Yes, it does," Joanie answered as she turned off the kitchen light and rolled her suitcase outside.

It was only a matter of crossing her and Carmen's yards to get to Carmen's porch.

"Carmen," Diana shouted from the front door, "are you ready?"

"I'm not going," her voice echoed from the back of the house.

Joanie gave Diana a long look, and the two of them headed down the hallway. They found her stretched out on Natalie's bed, arms crossed over her chest and eyes staring at the ceiling.

Diana got her by the elbow and pulled her up to a sitting position. "You are not dead. You've got some fight left in you, so get up."

Joanie's heart hurt for Carmen. She'd probably wither up and die if Brett sent divorce papers, especially at that time. "We're not leaving without you, and if you say the word, we can have a six-foot hole dug when he gets home. Right in the front yard. Think about how disappointed Tootsie will be if you don't go. She's done so much for us these past thirteen years. Remember how she came over here and sat with Natalie when she had her tonsils out? And how many times did she and Smokey take the girls for ice cream and a movie just to give us an evening alone?"

"Y'all can go. I'll be fine. Tootsie will understand," Carmen argued.

"Are you packed?" Diana asked.

Carmen nodded. "But I can unpack. I can't leave my daughter. What if Natalie gets kicked out of basic and she comes home and I'm not here?"

"If she gets booted out, then she'll have to call you to come get her." Diana drew her up to a stand. "And we're just as close to Lawton in the northern part of Texas as we are right here in Sugar Run."

Carmen balked when Diana pulled her toward the door. "I can't."

"Yes, you can." Joanie got behind her and gave her a gentle push. "If you can't even do this, then how are you ever going to fight Eli about this divorce? If you stay here all alone with no support, you'll be by yourself when he comes home. If that happens, he'll steamroll right over you. But if that's what you want, then when we come home, we'll help Natalie pick out a real good mental home for you," Joanie said with a shiver. If she were in Carmen's shoes, she might really end up in a facility for folks with broken minds. "Think about how hard it would be on Natalie to see you in a place like that."

Carmen flipped her off and stormed out of the room, got her suitcase by the handle, and said, "I'll never put Natalie through that shit. Let's go."

~

Luke Colbert was actually looking forward to being semi-unplugged for a few weeks. He'd have his device to use if he just had to have internet, but for the most part, he'd be on vacation. Fall weather was perfect for sleeping out under the stars and getting a brand-new perspective on what he wanted to do next with his life. Spending the days on the road definitely had an appeal. Had he not been so involved with technology, he might have been a truck driver.

"Holy crap!" he exclaimed when he saw the size of his uncle's motor home. "I'd forgotten how big that thing is."

"You're here!" Tootsie ran out the back door, threw her arms around him in a fierce hug, and then scooted up on tiptoe to kiss him on the cheek. "Let me look at you. I swear to God, you look more and more like Smokey did at your age every year. Same light-brown hair and that little cleft in the chin. Only thing is that he had brown eyes, and yours are blue. Go on and put your things in the storage space. I left a spot empty under the motor home for you to stow your gear. The girls should be here soon, and there's room inside for their stuff."

"Why did you buy such a huge motor home when there was only the two of you? That thing must sleep six people," he said.

"Eight if we use the overhead bed," she said.

Then all of what she'd said dawned on him. "Did you say some other people are going? I thought it was just us."

"I hear the front door opening now—you'll meet them. I can't tell you how excited I am this morning to have all y'all goin' with us. Smokey is every bit as happy as I am."

"Who? What?" He raised an eyebrow.

Before Tootsie could answer, three women came through the back door, each rolling a suitcase along behind her, with a laptop case slung over one shoulder and a purse over the other.

"Who are these people?" he whispered. Aunt Tootsie had done wacky things in the past, but she should have told him before now about this. At least given him a chance to back out of the drive. Hell's bells, he didn't even know these women.

He squinted a little and recognized the tall redhead from Uncle Smokey's funeral last month. Aunt Tootsie had said she was more than a neighbor when he asked who she was, but then she got called away to the kitchen. He hadn't seen her again until right that moment.

"These are like my daughters. Remember Smokey talked about them last year when we were in Scrap?" Tootsie said out of the side of her mouth. "They need to get away for a while. I need their support since Smokey can't be here to go with me."

Luke might not have liked having so much sprung on him, but he loved his aunt Tootsie. Uncle Smokey had been like a grandfather to him. No way would he hurt her feelings by saying a negative word.

"Hello, ladies. I'm Luke."

The tall redhead stuck out a hand. "I'm Diana McTavish. Thanks for driving us. I don't think any one of us could handle that thing. Anyone ever tell you that you look a lot like the pictures of Smokey when he was young?"

"Yes, ma'am, all the time." He shook hands with her and turned to find a short brunette with blue eyes at his elbow.

"I'm Carmen. Tootsie told us that Smokey's favorite nephew would be our driver."

"How d'y'do." He tipped his cap toward her. "The feeling went both ways. Uncle Smokey was my hero."

"And I'm Joanie," the blonde said.

"Well, it looks like we're all here now, and we've been introduced," Tootsie said.

Luke nodded and asked, "Could I help y'all with that luggage?"

"We've got it. We got the tour of the motor home last night. Tootsie has shown us exactly how much room we have and where we'll be sleeping," Joanie answered as she headed toward the RV.

"But thank you." Carmen forced a smile that didn't erase the sadness in her eyes.

"Looks like you've got baggage of your own." Diana hung back. "You looked surprised to see us. Didn't Tootsie tell you that she'd invited the neighborhood?"

"Not until about thirty seconds before you arrived." He picked up his suitcase and the zippered bag holding his two-man tent. "But I'm fine with it if she is, and I assure you, I'm a safe driver. So are all y'all's husbands military?" He opened the hatch and shoved his things inside.

"Was, is, were," Diana answered. "I'm five years divorced, but my ex is still military. He and Joanie's and Carmen's husbands are part of a black-ops team that we can't even ask questions about. Carmen got divorce papers two days ago. She's in denial. Joanie's still married, and her husband will be home for our daughters' graduation from basic training in December."

One divorced. One getting a divorce. One happily married.

He'd been looking forward to a few weeks of quiet introspection, not female drama. If his aunt could really drive this monster of an RV herself, he'd seriously consider hightailing it back to Houston.

But she'd only driven it home from the dealership less than two miles—taking it on a long trip was a whole different ball game. He'd feel horrible if anything happened to her because he was too stubborn to drive this circus.

~

For the past five years, Diana had been too busy with her job and taking care of her daughter to even consider another man in her life. Add that to the fact that Gerald's new wife was jealous of any time that he spent with Rebecca, and Diana refused to even go out one time for fear that she might fall in love. What if the new guy in her life became more important than Rebecca? Or heaven forbid, if he wanted children. Diana loved her daughter, but just the thought of starting to raise another child gave her the hives.

Still, it had been nice when Luke sized her up and down like maybe he liked what he saw. Could that have possibly been a slight spark between them when he shook her hand? He looked to be about her age, which would put him up near forty, but men aged differently than women, so he might be a little older or maybe a year or two younger.

"Listen up," Tootsie said when they were all in the RV. "See that sign hanging beside the door?"

Diana pulled her reading glasses from her purse and read aloud:

MAY GOD GRANT YOU ALWAYS
A SUNBEAM TO WARM YOU
A MOONBEAM TO CHARM YOU
A SHELTERING ANGEL SO NOTHING CAN HARM YOU
LAUGHTER TO CHEER YOU
FAITHFUL FRIENDS NEAR YOU
AND WHENEVER YOU PRAY
HEAVEN TO HEAR YOU.

"Amen," Joanie and Carmen said in unison.

"Smokey gave me that sign for our first wedding anniversary. It hung above our bed through countless military moves. I'm grateful for y'all to help me get through losing Smokey. Now start up the engine, Luke, and let's get this wagon train on the trail just like Smokey wants me to do." Tootsie wiped a tear from her cheek. "Dammit! I promised Smokey I wouldn't cry."

"He understands," Carmen said.

"I know, but this trip is to honor him, not to become a dramafest." Tootsie sat down at the U-shaped dinette and took a candy bar from the full dish on the table. She peeled back the wrapper and said, "This is for you, Smokey. I know how much you loved Snickers."

Luke started the key in the ignition, and Diana could almost hear the engine sucking up expensive gasoline. But if this is what would help Tootsie find closure for Smokey's death, and maybe even help Carmen get through the denial stage, then she was all for it.

Luke surprised her when he drove the huge motor home out of the backyard and managed to make the turn onto the street without bumping a single curb. But what impressed her even more was how the crystal candy dish didn't even slide across the table.

"Next stop, Texas City," Luke called out over his shoulder.

"Actually it's Oakridge Smokehouse Restaurant in Schulenberg. Smokey and I always stop there for lunch on the first day. They make great barbecue, and their pickles are amazing. Smokey was partial to their German sausage and sauerkraut. I can't wait for y'all to see the inside of the place. It's just like walking into an old barn," Tootsie said.

"Sounds great," Joanie said. "I love sauerkraut."

"Not me." Diana shook her head. "But barbecue sounds really good. Did you already make reservations at a campground for tonight?"

"The trip is all planned out. That's what I was doing all afternoon on Wednesday. When we get over around Beaumont, I'll be spending the evening with an old friend, Delores. We were a lot like y'all—close friends who stood by each other when our husbands left us at home for weeks on end. I'd invite you to go with me, but I'm selfish enough to want to have some time with her all by myself," Tootsie told them. "And my friend Midge—I've known her since we were toddlers—lives up near Scrap. I'll be seeing her while we're there. Don't mean to be desertin' y'all, but she's been pretty sick, and she's my last living childhood friend. Enjoy the ride."

~

Enjoy the ride. Carmen almost groaned. She'd much rather be at home trying to get this crap with Eli sorted out. But she'd never let Tootsie down, and this trip meant so much to her. She pulled her phone from her hip pocket and checked for texts. Tootsie said the lawyer would call her when he'd had time to look over the papers. A part of her wanted to know right now. The other part hoped the attorney played golf every day and didn't read over the papers until Christmas so that she and Eli could talk face-to-face and get this thing worked out without a divorce.

There were no texts or messages from Eli, but then, realistically, she didn't expect anything. It had been only two days, and she hadn't done what he wanted—like always. Looking back, she'd never denied him anything, except when he threw a fit about her getting her teaching degree. But he'd gotten over it, and he'd get over this, too.

Diana set her laptop on the table and started working on whatever it was that she did for the insurance company. Joanie took out a Kindle and started reading a book, and Tootsie moved up to the passenger seat beside Luke. None of them, not even Diana, who'd been through a divorce, realized that she was willing to lay it all on the line for her marriage.

She pulled up the hundreds of pictures she'd taken of Natalie during her senior year and flipped through them, one at a time, remembering all the events as if they'd just happened yesterday. When the phone rang and Eli's picture popped up on the screen, she fumbled it and almost dropped the thing on the floor. She answered it on the third ring. "Hello."

"I haven't got long. Have you made a decision?" he asked.

"Is it Christmas?" she asked coldly, then softened her tone. "I'm not rushing into anything. I haven't read the papers or heard from the lawyer."

"It's pretty simple. We'll sell the house, split the equity down the middle. You can keep your car if you take over the payments. You can have the furniture. I want my clothes, my guns, and my—"

She raised her voice. "Stop!"

"Problem back there?" Luke asked.

"I'm sorry," Carmen said. "I wasn't talking to you."

"Who are you talking to? Was that a man's voice I heard? What's going on, Carmen?" Eli slammed the questions at her in rapid-fire succession.

"I was talking to Luke. He's Tootsie's nephew, and he's our driver." She went on to tell him where they were going.

"You've left Sugar Run on a whim? Are you crazy? What if Natalie bombs out and needs you? God, you never were smart, but this takes the cake." Eli's voice got louder with every word.

"What if Natalie bombs out and needs *you*? Have you told her that you're divorcing me? I'm going on the trip because I need some space. Are you really going to take the house?" Carmen shot back at him. "Did you wait this long so you don't have to pay child support?"

"No, I didn't, and I'll tell Natalie when the time is right. I'm waiting until the divorce is signed and final," Eli said.

"Then you won't have to tell her, because—"

"There are no buts, maybes, or becauses, Carmen. Either sign it or I'll get a court date set up right after I get home. We'll let the judge take care of it," Eli said. "Goodbye."

His picture disappeared. Seemed fitting to her right then. She looked up to see Diana peering over the top of her laptop, and Joanie had laid her book to the side.

"Dear Lord, what am I going to do? He's determined. If I don't sign the papers, he's going to take this all to court. Has he found another woman?" Her voice sounded hollow in her ears. "He's going to sell the house, and we'll split the equity. That's not much because it's got a second mortgage on it. I'm scared out of my mind. What if he's been cheating on me? What if he really isn't going to give us a chance? I won't have a home. I don't have my degree finished. My heart is being ripped out of my chest—I shouldn't love him, but I do." Carmen laid her head on the arm of the sofa and shut her eyes tightly. "Please tell me this is all a nightmare."

"I can't," Diana answered.

"It's like death," Carmen whispered and then clamped a hand over her mouth. "I'm so sorry, Tootsie. I shouldn't have said that."

"Why not?" Tootsie turned her chair around to face them. "It's the truth. We're going through the same grieving process. I lost Smokey, and you are losing your marriage. It's painful and scary as hell. I've never lived by myself, either. I married Smokey right out of high school, like you did Eli, and the thought of being alone the rest of my life terrifies me. If he makes you sell the house, you can move in with me, or you can live in the motor home until you figure things out."

"Thank you," Carmen said, but it did little to ease the tightness in her chest. Diana's invitation hadn't, either.

"You are forgetting something important," Diana said. "You have three-fourths of a degree. Just one more year, and you'll be able to teach elementary school anywhere in Texas. You could use what you've already learned to get a job and finish up your degree at night. Stop selling yourself short, girl. We've all proved for years that we can live on our own."

~

Guilt dropped over Joanie like a thick fog. She could live on her own, but Brett was coming home in a couple of months. There'd be those first few days when they couldn't keep their hands off each other. Then it would settle into a normal routine of him going to work, her going to the hospital and the nursing home to volunteer, and in a few weeks or months, she'd get a call. He'd be gone again—classified. He'd call when he could—he loved her.

She hated those calls, but at least she would have Brett for a little while. Poor Carmen would never know that elation of homecoming again, and Diana hadn't had it for years. She picked up her Kindle again and went back to reading.

Tootsie got up out of her chair, went to the back of the motor home, and came back with a book, which she put in Carmen's hands. "I've found that a good book will make you forget your troubles."

"I'm really not in the mood to read." Carmen tried to hand back the book.

Tootsie shook her head. "It's not a request. It's an order."

"She made me read after Gerald left. I thought she was crazy." Diana smiled. "But after I'd read five books in a week, I figured out that she was one smart cookie. When I was reading, I didn't think about him at all."

"How come no one ever recommended that one to me?" Joanie asked.

Carmen read the first paragraph and smiled. "You can read it when I finish."

Carmen was a slow reader, so it would be Christmas before she finished the book. Joanie settled back in her seat and continued reading the book she'd pulled up on her Kindle.

At noon, Luke steered the motor home into the parking lot of a barbecue joint. Joanie hated to put her Kindle aside long enough for lunch, but she was hungry. The aroma of barbecue blended with all kinds of other delicious flavors floated across the parking lot as they got out of the motor home.

"It's my day to cook, so lunch is on me," she said.

Tootsie waggled a finger under her nose. "This is my trip, and you're doing me a favor by keeping me company on it, so I pay for gas and food. If you want a souvenir or a bag of candy when we make our stops, then that's on you. But don't argue with me about food or fuel."

"Yes, ma'am," Luke said. "But it doesn't rest easy on me to let a lady pay for things."

"Then we'll compromise," Tootsie said. "Here's my credit card. You keep it, fuel up the motor home when it's needed, and pay the café and grocery store bills with it. And if I catch you switching cards to use one of yours, I will fire your ass and send you home. I can drive this rig if I need to. Understood?"

"Yes, ma'am." He smiled.

Joanie bit her lip to keep from giggling. A big handsome man like Luke backing down from tiny Tootsie was truly something funny, but the expression on Tootsie's face said that she was as serious as a heart attack.

"Now that we got that settled, let's go get some dinner, or lunch, if y'all want to call it that. I didn't eat breakfast because I knew this was where we were stopping." Tootsie led the way across the parking lot.

"Bossy, ain't she?" Luke chuckled.

Tootsie whipped around with a wide grin on her face. "Yes, I am, and don't none of y'all forget it."

Joanie's phone rang as they were entering the restaurant, so she stepped back to take the call.

"Hello, darlin'. Is breakfast ready?"

"It's noon here in Texas, Brett." Her hands shook as she sat down on a bench right outside the door. Just hearing his voice always made her happy, but there was that feeling, just for a second, that he would be calling with bad news.

"Where are you? I hear traffic."

"You're never going to believe where I am right now." She told him the same thing that Carmen had relayed to Eli earlier. "I figured Eli would've filled you in."

"He did, but we decided Carmen was just shootin' him a line of shit because she's mad at him over this divorce," Brett said. "I can't believe you're making this kind of move without discussing it with me."

"There is a *me* outside of us, and I've had to rely on *me* a lot more than *us* our whole marriage, so it never occurred to me to ask your permission." She was on the defensive and knew it, but there didn't seem to be a damned thing she could do about it.

"Hey, don't go getting radical on me," Brett said. "I called to tell you I love you, not fight with you."

"Okay, then, truce," she said. "I love you, too."

"How's Carmen holdin' up?" Brett asked.

"Not good, but then she got slammed with this thing. I imagine she feels a lot like she got a shotgun blast in the gut. Why'd Eli do this? Is it another woman?"

"I'm not sayin' anything, but he's determined, so Carmen might as well sign the papers and get it over with." Brett's brevity spoke volumes.

"Is it?" she pressured.

"I've got to go now. I'll be glad when I can talk to Zoe again. I miss her so much," he said.

Changing the subject to avoid the inevitable—that's what Brett always did. And she always, always found out the truth eventually.

"Well, darlin', if it is another woman, this is where I draw the line," Joanie said. "I stood by when Gerald divorced Diana and even went to some family events when he brought his new woman. I felt guilty every time, but I won't do this again, Brett. I'm not taking another woman into our home and treating her like a friend."

"Eli and Gerald have been my teammates for almost twenty years," Brett said. "I didn't turn my back on Gerald, and I won't on Eli."

"Well, I'm damn sure not turning my back on Carmen," Joanie said.

"I don't expect you to," Brett groaned.

"Stay safe and come home to me," she whispered.

It *was* another woman. There was no doubt in her mind.

Joanie shoved the phone into her purse, plastered a smile on her face, and went into the café. She spotted her group at a table near the back, pointed toward the restroom sign, and headed that way. She sat on the toilet and leaned her face against the cool metal wall of the stall. Why did life have to be so damned complicated, and what had driven Eli into another woman's arms?

"You okay in there?" Carmen's voice sounded concerned. "Is everything all right with the team?"

"Everything is fine. He was calling to tell me that he loves me," Joanie said.

Idiot! She doesn't need to hear that. Eli calls to tell her that he's determined to get a divorce, and you say something like that, the pesky voice in Joanie's head fussed at her.

"Okay, then," Carmen said. "I just came in to check on you and wash my hands. Got lemon juice on them when I squeezed it into my sweet tea. Hey, do you think Luke is kind of cute?"

"You already looking for a rebound feller?" Joanie asked.

"Nope, but Diana might be," Carmen said.

50

"No way." Joanie pushed out of the stall and went straight for the sink. "After Gerald, she swore off men."

"I understand that completely, but she didn't swear 'on' to ladies, either," Carmen said. "I've decided that I'm not feeling sorry for myself anymore. I can do this. I could do it better if a rich old aunt would leave me her rundown house like in the story Tootsie gave me, but since I don't have a single wealthy person in my family, I'll have to make it on my own. I'm beginning to think I can."

"Yes, you can." *And I hope that I'm wrong about another woman because that'll knock you back into the Ice Age.*

Chapter Four

They stopped at a lovely RV park that evening that had a gorgeous, albeit narrow, walking trail around the edge of the bay. Several people were out and about, many of them moving at a much faster speed than Diana, who felt like she was holding them back by stopping to smell the brisk air or pick up a pretty leaf every few feet. So she sat down on a bench and let the majority of them go on by. She was engrossed with watching the sunset—no artist in the world could ever capture the essence of all those swirling oranges, yellows, and pinks radiating out from the orange ball as it slowly dipped down over the far horizon.

"Beautiful, isn't it?" Luke said.

She jumped and jerked her head around. "You startled me."

"Sorry about that. It wasn't intentional," he said.

"But yes, it is beautiful with all the colors reflecting in the water. What brought you out tonight? Tired of all the drama?"

"Not so much. Tootsie is in her bedroom with the door shut. I think she talks to Smokey, but if that's the way she copes, I'm not saying a word. Carmen and Joanie are both reading, so I didn't want to listen to music and disturb them. But mainly, I just wanted to stretch my legs. Driving all day puts all kinds of kinks in my neck and body," he said. "And you? Why did you disappear right after supper?"

"I try to take a walk every day," she answered. "Like you said, riding all day or sitting in front of a computer makes me need to stretch my legs, too."

"What kind of work do you do?" he asked. "I noticed that you kept pretty busy, and then when we stopped for gas, you took your computer inside to use the Wi-Fi. I've got Wi-Fi installed in the motor home if you need to use it, so we're covered."

"Thank you so much—I hadn't even thought to turn my wireless on. That simplifies things a lot. I do insurance work. They send me files. I work on them and send them back. Boring once I learned all the codes, but it's kept the bills paid the past five years." She slid a sideways glance at him—just the right amount of scruff to be sexy, but not enough to fill in that cute little chin cleft.

"Five years?" He raised an eyebrow. "I'm sorry. I don't mean to pry. That's my biggest fault. I'm a computer geek who hasn't learned social manners." The streetlamp beside the bench lit up his blue eyes.

"It's okay," she told him. "I was already working at this job when I got divorced. My daughter, Rebecca, graduated high school last May, and she, along with Natalie and Zoe, all left for basic training last week. That's pretty much the story of my whole life. Now that I've shown you mine, you can show me yours." She turned to face him, crossing her legs and sitting on the bench.

"Computer geek pretty much says it all. I graduated high school at sixteen and joined the National Guard at eighteen to help finance the last two years of college. I got my degree at twenty and went to work for a prestigious firm in Houston. Didn't like having a boss, so I started my own software company. Sold it and made a bundle. Now I'm trying to figure out what I want to do. I'm too young and hyper to do nothing, so I'm thinking of starting up another company after the first of the year," Luke said.

"How young?" She'd guessed him to be somewhere close to her age. He'd been at Smokey's funeral, but she'd seen him only in passing.

Someone had said that he was Smokey's nephew, but like Carmen and Joanie, she'd been busy consoling her daughter.

"I'm thirty-one," he answered. "And you?"

Diana cocked her head to one side. He hadn't been lying about being socially awkward. "It's not polite to ask a woman her age."

"Sorry." He shrugged.

"I'll be thirty-nine next month." And that was entirely too much age difference for her to have felt a little spark when they'd shaken hands earlier that day.

"What day?" Luke asked.

"The fifteenth."

"I'll be thirty-two on the twenty-eighth. We should have a celebration." He stood up. "We'll probably still be at the cabin, so we can make ice cream, and I'll bake us a cake. Aunt Tootsie doesn't do too hot in the kitchen."

"You cook?" Diana asked.

"If I hadn't been so into computers, I would've probably been a chef. You need to rest some more, or can we walk together? It won't be long until dark," he said.

"I'm not that old." She popped up on her feet and headed on down the path.

"Hey, I'm not calling you old." Luke fell in beside her on the narrow trail. "Kind of amazed me that y'all all have daughters old enough to enlist in the army. The way Aunt Tootsie and Uncle Smokey talked about y'all, I figured you'd be at least fifty."

"Well, thank you for that," Diana said.

"You must've all married pretty young," Luke commented.

"I was nineteen and had a year of medical billing training. Joanie and Carmen were right out of high school," Diana said. "What about you? Ever been married?"

He shook his head. "Not many women out there who'd love me for who I am rather than what's in my bank account."

"That's sad." Diana drew in a long breath and let it out slowly so he wouldn't realize that keeping up with his fast pace was making her pant.

"Here we are." He pointed at the tent he'd set up when they first arrived. "I'd invite you in for a nightcap, but my space is limited, and I don't have any liquor."

"Thank you, but I'd better get on inside. You could come in with me. We have lots of space and liquor, and I bet we could get a rousing game of gin rummy going." She put a hand on the outside of the motor home to brace herself.

Luke opened the door for her. "Well, thank you. That sounds better than reading a book by flashlight."

"Hey, we made a little pitcher of margaritas, and we're getting out the cards. I thought y'all might be showing up soon," Tootsie said.

"And I made a pan of brownies." Joanie pointed to the top of the stove. "I'm surprised at how well stocked the pantry is in this thing."

"Smokey took care of doing that before he passed on," Tootsie sighed. "He did love to cook."

"And we all loved to eat his cookin'," Carmen said. "I'll pour up the drinks, and then we'll play cards. Canasta or gin rummy?"

"Canasta gets my vote, in honor of Smokey. He loved that game almost as much as he loved dominoes. And before you ask, his favorite set is in the dresser drawer. We never went anywhere without cards, dominoes, and a couple of those thousand-piece puzzles," Tootsie said.

"Canasta it is," Joanie said.

"I remember working those puzzles with Uncle Smokey the fall I spent with y'all up at the old house," Luke said. "One of my favorite memories. To me, it was like fitting the pieces of computer code together to make a video game."

"You always did have a big brain in your head." Tootsie helped Carmen serve the drinks. "Smokey was proud of you."

Luke blushed slightly. "He'll always be missed. Now about this card game? Shall I deal?" He shuffled the cards with the dexterity of a blackjack dealer in a casino. He was smart, he could cook, and he liked puzzles and card games. Plus, he was downright cute with that chin dimple and those blue eyes.

If only he were ten years older, Diana thought as she sipped her margarita.

~

Fall was the time of year that Joanie would start shopping and sometimes even wrapping gifts. The Christmas tree always went up the day after Thanksgiving, and she liked to have presents ready to go under it. Even if it was only for a day or two, Brett was usually home, and she could pretend that they were a normal family instead of a military one.

Even though the aroma of barbecue filling the air at the Smokey Cook-Off that Saturday morning was far different from the ham, bread, and sugar cookies Joanie always baked, she was still reminded of the happy days of the past. A gust of wind spun a little tornado of fallen leaves right in front of her. Zoe would have already had her phone out and been taking pictures to send to Brett. She stopped in the middle of the gravel pathway and dug in her purse for a tissue.

Diana whipped one from her purse and handed it over to her. "It's tough doing these kinds of things without our girls, isn't it?"

"So you were thinking the same thing," Joanie said.

"If it was about taking our girls to the carnival or the State Fair of Texas, you know I was." Diana pointed toward the next vendor. "That looks good. Want to get one?"

Luke waved at them from a few feet away with an enormous ear of corn. He motioned toward the empty places at the picnic table where he was sitting, and Diana nodded.

"Zoe loves this kind of place. Corn on the cob is her favorite." Joanie pointed to a vendor as she and Diana got in line behind a young couple wearing "Just Married" T-shirts.

"Congratulations," Joanie said.

"Thank you." The young woman smiled. "We just got married yesterday."

The guy pulled his bride close and kissed her on the forehead. "And we've got a whole week of honeymooning before I go back to base."

"Don't that bring back memories?" Diana whispered.

The lady snuggled up close to her new husband. "Are y'all military wives?"

"Were." Diana nodded.

"And am still," Joanie answered. "Here's wishing y'all many years of happiness."

"Thank you," the guy said as he handed the vendor a bill and he and his bride walked away with an ear of corn.

"Remember when we shared things with our husbands?" Diana chuckled.

Joanie stepped up to the window and ordered two cobs with extra butter. "Oh, yeah, but then the honeymoon ended. Remember when that day came in your marriage?"

"The first time Gerald went on a six-month deployment." Diana took the stick holding the corn from Joanie when she offered it.

"You got it. We'd had this meet and greet so the wives could get to know each other. That was the evening the two of us and Carmen became best friends," Joanie said. "I found out I was pregnant after Brett left. By the time he got home, I was six months and had gained forty pounds. It must've been a shock to him."

"I was pregnant when Gerald left, and he barely made it home in time for Rebecca's birth." Diana started toward the picnic bench where Luke waited. "At least we had our babies' fathers in the delivery room with us."

Joanie followed behind her. "Do you think that maybe that's been a problem all along? Eli didn't bond with Natalie—she was two months old when he held her for the first time."

"No, I think there's another woman. He's acting the same way Gerald did, refusing to go to counseling and try to work things out. The main difference is that I had the money saved to buy Gerald's equity in the house since I'd worked the whole time we were married. And he had to pay child support, which helped with all of Rebecca's school activities. Poor Carmen would be out in the cold if it wasn't for us."

"I'm with you, but I'm basing my suspicions on the fact that Brett won't tell me that it's not another woman. Code of brotherhood and all that shit," Joanie said out of the side of her mouth.

"Why are you whispering?" Diana asked.

"I see Carmen and Tootsie headed this way. Tootsie's bright-orange pantsuit stands out really well," Joanie told her.

"Hey, y'all!" Carmen called out from no more than six feet behind them. "Tootsie and I have been lookin' for you. I was just thinking about taking home a side of ribs for supper tonight."

To see Carmen in a good mood lifted Joanie's spirits. Bless Tootsie's heart for what she was doing to help them get through all this turmoil.

"Remember now. I won't be having supper with y'all," Tootsie said as they made their way to where Luke waited. "I told you about Delores, my friend—she lost her husband a while back, and now that Smokey is gone . . ." Tootsie hesitated and wiped a tear from her eye.

"Did she have kids?" Diana asked.

"Yes, she did, and none of them live close to her. I'm lucky to have y'all on the same block. Smokey and I didn't always go this route, but when we did, we stopped to see her. Anyway, she's going to pick me up tonight, and we're going out for supper, so y'all are on your own," Tootsie answered.

"Y'all want some corn anyway? Luke is saving us places at that table over there." Joanie pointed. "And, Tootsie, I know how much you love ribs, so we'll save one for you."

"Thanks, darlin'. Carmen and I already had our ear of corn. We'll just sit with y'all and Luke while you eat yours," Tootsie said.

Tootsie, Joanie, and Carmen sat down across the table from Luke, and Diana took a seat next to him. Other than when she was going through the divorce, Joanie had never seen Diana fidget with nerves. She was the rock in the friendship, always taking the bull by the horns. She'd been sad when the girls had left last week, and angry at Eli, but to show vulnerability—that wasn't Diana's style.

Now all Joanie could see was a bundle of nerves, and it had to do with Luke. The guy was kind of cute, but nothing like hunky Gerald with his jet-black hair and dark-brown eyes. Add that to the fact that Diana hadn't been interested in dating since her divorce, not even when she'd had several chances. *Every one* of those fellows had been sexier than Luke. It didn't make a bit of sense to Joanie.

"How much longer y'all want to stay?" Luke asked.

"I've seen all I need to and eaten more than I needed to." Tootsie covered a yawn with her hand. "It's only a two-hour trip over to Beaumont, so there's no rush."

Carmen stretched and then checked her watch. "It's almost one o'clock already, and I could use a long nap."

Diana shot a knowing look across the table toward Joanie. Carmen never slept during the day. She was the hyper one of their group—the one who was always up and doing something. If she wasn't studying for her degree, then she was making some craft to take to the church arts-and-crafts show to support mission trips.

"Then I'll stop by a rib wagon and buy supper and meet y'all at the motor home." Luke waved over his shoulder as he disappeared into the crowd.

The buzz of conversations, children's laughter, and tired babies fretting all blended together and slowly faded away as the four women made their way back to the motor home. They'd removed their jackets and were settling in for the ride to Beaumont when Luke walked through the door carrying a paper sack. He put it in the cold oven and went straight for the driver's seat. "Next stop, Beaumont, where Aunt Tootsie will run away to her friend's house for the evening and supper."

"That was fun, but I ate far too much. I'll have to jog six miles tonight for the corn alone. I bet each ear had a whole stick of butter on it, and I ate two of them in addition to a barbecue sandwich at lunchtime," Diana said.

"Smokey would have loved it." Joanie settled into her place behind the table.

Joanie could hardly wait to get Diana alone that afternoon, but they were more than an hour down the road before Carmen and Tootsie both declared that they couldn't keep their eyes open another minute. Carmen crawled up on the top bunk, and Tootsie left her seat and went to her bedroom on the other end of the motor home.

Before Joanie could say a word, Diana opened her laptop.

"Hey, you don't work on Saturday, and you already mentioned that you were caught up until Tuesday morning, so what're you doing?" Joanie asked.

Diana shut it and smiled. "Old habits die hard. I keep thinking maybe I'll hear something from Rebecca or that she'll post on Facebook. What's on your mind?"

Joanie peeked around the wall to be sure that Luke had his earbuds in place. His head was bobbing to whatever music he was listening to, so the coast was clear. "What was that at the festival? You got all antsy when you sat down beside Luke, and y'all came in at the same time last night after you'd gone out for a walk."

Diana shrugged. "It's time for me to start dating. I feel something stirring inside my heart, but it's not Luke." She lowered her voice to a whisper. "Guess how old he is?"

Joanie drew her brows down and pursed her lips together. "Since Smokey was past eighty and he's a nephew with the Colbert name, he has to belong to a brother." She drew numbers in the air with her forefinger. "He's forty or forty-five, and that's saying he belongs to a younger brother."

Diana shook her head. "He has to be the son of the youngest of Smokey's brothers. He'll be thirty-two next month. He's seven years younger than I am. Do you realize that he wasn't even shaving yet when Rebecca was born? That's kind of weird. Nature might be telling me that it's my time to have a relationship now, but she's also yelling at me to do it with a man my age."

"I've been telling you that for the past four years. A year of mourning is enough, especially when it's the death of a marriage. There's life to live." Joanie lowered her voice. "Now what about Carmen? Is she going into depression? She never takes naps."

"I remember after a few days, I decompressed. Slept every afternoon for a week," Diana whispered. "Then one day I woke up and the anger had set in. This is pretty normal."

Joanie nodded. "I know depression is one of the steps to healing, but I can never remember the order."

"It's right before acceptance. I think that's where Tootsie is. Talking to her friend tonight will be good for her. Want a glass of tea? I'm going to make one for myself." Diana got up from the table and in a couple of strides was at the refrigerator.

"I'd take one," Luke called out from the driver's seat.

Diana instantly blushed. "Coming right up." Then she turned back to Joanie and mouthed, "How much did he hear?"

Joanie raised a shoulder in a shrug. Diana was so much in control that she never blushed, so what was really going on between her and Luke?

Diana poured a disposable cup of tea, put a lid on it, and carried it to him. "There you go."

"So you think Aunt Tootsie is depressed?" Luke asked.

"It's all part of the process," she said.

He motioned toward the passenger chair. "Sit with me. I got tired of music about the time y'all started talking about depression. I'm bored. I need someone to talk to me so I don't fall asleep at the wheel."

Yeah, right, Joanie thought as she opened her Kindle to read. *There is nothing between them. Seven years' age difference might be a problem at thirteen and twenty, but they're both over thirty now, so the issue isn't there anymore.*

~

"Well, we can't have our driver falling asleep, can we? Would you rather have some strong coffee?" Diana asked as she went back to the kitchen area to pour glasses of tea for herself and Joanie.

"No, this has enough caffeine to keep me awake for another hour," he said.

She set her glass in the cup holder, then sat down, adjusted the seat so that her long legs had more room, and buckled herself into the passenger seat. "You ever wonder why you can get a ticket if both parties sitting in these chairs aren't strapped in, and yet, all four of us can wander around back there without a seat belt?"

"There are definitely strange laws on the books," Luke answered.

"I've noticed that you've been listening to country music most of the time. Why did you turn it off?"

"They were starting to play more alternative rather than classic country. I like Strait, Jones, and Travis Tritt. Guess Uncle Smokey kind of marked me in that area, too. I like to cook, like his kind of music, and love spending time outside when I get the chance." Luke put on the blinker to get off at the next exit, then turned it off.

"Why'd you do that?" Diana asked.

"What?"

"Almost get off the highway on that last exit?"

"Aunt Tootsie," Luke answered. "She needs to rest. I was camped out right below her window last night, and she spent most of it talking to Uncle Smokey. If I stop, she'll wake up."

Cold chills chased down Diana's spine. "Is she all right? You don't think she needs to see a psychiatrist, do you?"

"She's fine," Luke answered. "I talk to him, too, sometimes, just not out loud. It's all part of her healing process. Go back to music for a moment—what kind do you like?"

"Hard metal rock," she said.

"For real?" Luke's blue eyes widened out as big as saucers.

"No, I'm joking," Diana laughed. "I like country music, mostly the old stuff like you mentioned, but I do like some new artists like Midland, Blake Shelton, and Luke Bryan."

"Blake isn't exactly new. He's been around for years now. Remember when he had a mullet?"

"Oh, yeah, he's always been a pretty boy," Diana answered.

"You go for the pretty boys, do you?" Luke slowed down and checked the GPS on the dash. "It's only a few more miles before we turn off to go to the campground."

"How far off the road is it?" Diana suddenly realized that she'd put her entire life in Tootsie's and Luke's hands. Now that was trust she didn't even realize she had after her divorce.

"Another five miles, but it's got an indoor heated pool if y'all want to do a few laps. Believe me, when we get to the old house, there won't be any swimming this time of year."

"Just how big is Scrap, Texas?" Diana asked.

Luke chuckled and then laughed out loud. "There is no more Scrap, Texas. It's not even on the map and doesn't have a city-limits sign anymore. It's not even in the ghost-towns-of-Texas listings. There's just an old map hanging in the living room that dates back to the early part of the last century. It used to hug the Red River."

Diana frowned. "Not even a convenience store?"

"Nope," Luke replied. "We'll have to drive to Paris or Clarksville to even get gas for the motor home or groceries."

"But . . ." Diana had so many questions, she didn't know where to start.

"Aunt Tootsie's grandma and mama grew up there. When her grandma moved to Clarksville, she left the house to Tootsie's mama, and then it was passed on to Aunt Tootsie. There's no town. I don't think there's even a zip code—just miles and miles of farmland and five acres of timber with an old two-story house set back in the trees."

"Why has she kept it?" Diana asked.

"She and Uncle Smokey honeymooned there, so it's a special place. Here's our exit." Luke tapped the brakes. "Ten minutes and we'll be parked and set up for the night. Want to take another walk after supper?"

"Love to," she answered.

She always walked at least a mile in the evenings—in the summer heat or the bitter cold winter. It cleared her head of all the clutter and got her ready for another day. Nothing said that she couldn't be friends with Luke, and it would be rude to tell him no when he was driving them.

Nothing says that you can't be more than friends, too. Smokey's gruff voice popped into her head.

He's too much younger than I am, she argued. *Good Lord! Now I'm talking to Smokey, too.*

Chapter Five

Tootsie was surprised to see Delores behind the wheel of the same old big boat of a car that she'd been driving the last time Tootsie and Smokey stopped by her place. She leaned into the driver's-side window and gave her friend a quick hug. "You want to come inside and meet the kids?"

"Another time, darlin'. It's a chore for me to get in and out, and going up those little steps into your motor home—well, let's just say I'm still clumsy, and I don't want to break a hip. Get in. Supper will be ready when I get you back to the house," Delores told her.

"How are you holdin' up?" Delores asked as she backed her bright-red car away from the RV park and headed into town.

"Pretty good, I guess. I still talk to Smokey a lot, and I mean I talk out loud to him. I prop up his picture and pretend he's right there with me," Tootsie admitted.

"Honey, it's been ten years since Jimmy died, and I still talk to him all the time. Those old soldiers were our life. We can't just turn it off like a water faucet." Delores stopped at a traffic light and then made a right-hand turn. "Talking to them keeps them alive to us, and that's all right."

"So you still live in the same house? You talked about downsizing last year when we stopped by."

Delores pulled into the circular driveway of a two-story redbrick place. "Yep, this is where Jimmy's spirit is. I looked at a couple of smaller houses and even at a retirement home at the kids' insistence, but I couldn't do it." She got out of the car, picked up her cane from the back seat, and slowly made her way to the porch. "Come on in."

Tootsie followed her inside and closed the door behind them. She removed her jacket and laid it on a chair in the foyer. "I hope you didn't go to any trouble. I was really just expecting you to send a car, and we'd visit in a restaurant."

"Where's the fun in that? I can still drive. I still make a mean bologna sandwich, and it *is* Saturday night." Delores hung her cane on a hook beside the kitchen door.

"You remembered!" Tootsie rushed across the floor and hugged her. "Saturday-night supper at your place was my favorite time of the week, especially when Jimmy and Smokey were off to God only knows where."

Delores had to stoop a little to wrap her arms around Tootsie. "I thought we'd keep our tradition. Sandwiches with all the fixin's, potato chips, Kool-Aid, and chocolate ice cream for dessert. Then we can have a glass of cheap wine and pretend the kids are all in bed asleep."

"You are the best. What can I do to help?" Tootsie asked.

"You can make your own sandwich and fix your own plate. We'll take it out to the screened-in porch. We can use those trays over there." She pointed to the other side of the cabinet. "We'll put them on our laps like we did when we started the tradition. It's a lovely evening. You can almost smell the salt air coming off the bay tonight." Delores set out a platter with meat, cheese, sliced tomatoes, lettuce, pickles, and onions. "This is just like when we were neighbors in base housing."

"Your four kids sat around the little kitchen table, and we put our plates on our laps in the living room." Tootsie set about making her sandwich. "How are the kids?"

"Strung from here to hell," Delores answered. "One in England, where he retired after getting out of the service. One in upstate New

York. Third one is in Florida. She moved down there to be near my folks when they got older. My baby boy is finishing up his last year in the army. He says he and his wife are retiring in Arizona."

"Do they ever get home at the same time?" Tootsie asked.

"Not since Jimmy's funeral. I miss those days when they were little and I had to depend on you to help me raise them," Delores said. "But enough of that. Let's eat and talk about what's going in your life since Smokey passed on. I missed getting a letter from you this month, but I'm not fussin'. I know you've been busy."

Tootsie put her sandwich, her drink, and a fistful of chips on a tray and carried it out to the porch. "We should be trying to change our thinking and learn to take advantage of this new modern-technology world, where we can pick up the phone and call someone without paying long-distance fees."

Delores followed her. "My hands go to sleep after I've written three sentences, but I just wait a little while and go back at it."

"Gettin' old ain't for the weak," Tootsie said. "But we could start calling every month instead of writing."

"Yes!" Delores said. "First Saturday of the month good for you?"

"Sounds great. You've got my number." Tootsie made a mental note not to forget.

Delores nodded in agreement. "Now tell me about things in your world. Are you driving that big-ass RV? You still got the same neighbors?"

Tootsie caught her up on everything, in between bites of the best bologna sandwich she'd had in years, ending with, "And now I'm on the road with those girls and Luke. I think there's a spark, or 'vibes,' as the younger generation calls it, between him and Diana, but there's also an age difference. She's about six or seven years older than he is."

"Pffft!" Delores threw up a hand. "What's age when it comes to love? I was two years older than Jimmy."

Tootsie leaned forward. "Maybe it's lust instead of love."

"Well, we lived through the free-love era, so we've done seen it all," Delores giggled.

"Amen to that. I couldn't wait to burn my bra." Tootsie laughed with her.

"I would've been ahead of you, but I was busy settin' out the logs." Delores slapped her knee and laughed even harder.

~

Luke had looked forward to a walk in the nice brisk breeze all day, but now he wished he could go back to the campsite, crawl into his tent, and read until he fell asleep. Being around Diana brought out his awkward and shy side, and he didn't like it—not one bit. He'd been more comfortable around her than he'd been with any woman he'd ever met, and then she found out his age. Now he was back to being that computer geek with a bashful streak.

The pungent aroma in the air was rotting leaves, and the cool night wind would turn downright cold before long, but he loved fall. He tried to find something to talk about, but nothing came to mind until he flashed on an image of Aunt Tootsie and Uncle Smokey's marriage license hanging above the sofa in the old house.

"You'd never guess where they got their nicknames," he said.

"Who?" Diana asked.

"Tootsie and Smokey." A hard wind blew so many leaves from a pecan tree that it reminded him of snow.

"I never thought to ask. The names just kind of fit them. Surely that's not what's on their birth certificates," she said.

"Tootsie's is." Luke kicked a rock out of the pathway with the toe of his boot. "Tootsie Arlene Green, now Colbert. Smokey's real name is Samuel Luke Colbert. I was named after him."

"Why would anyone name a child Tootsie?" Diana asked.

"She says her mama named her after her two best friends. One was Arlene, and the other's name was Othalene. She just couldn't see naming a little baby girl Othalene Arlene, so she used Othalene's nickname, which was Tootsie."

"Tootsie fits her better than Othalene, for sure," Diana said.

"Uncle Smokey got his nickname in the army. When the city boys asked him where he was from, he'd tell them that he lived so far back in the sticks that they had to use smoke signals to communicate with folks in the next town," Luke told her.

"I thought it might be from that old movie *Smokey and the Bandit*, but that's way funnier." Diana smiled.

The uncomfortable silence returned. What had he done wrong? He'd never been really good with small talk or women—that was the curse of being a computer geek. Diana didn't ask anything else or start another conversation—maybe that night she wanted to be alone with her own thoughts.

But Luke liked the sound of her voice too much to let it go, so he finally asked, "Do you like to read? I've noticed that Carmen and Joanie read a lot. You just work all the time. I was a lot like that, too, until I sold my company. I buried myself in my work and forgot to live."

"Did you like what you did?" She sat down on a park bench beside the path. "Is that a golf course right there?"

"The brochure I got when I checked us in said there was a six-hole course on the grounds, so I guess it is. Do you play?"

"Nope," she answered. "You?"

"Not me," he answered. "Like I said, I've always been a workaholic." He sat down on the other end of the bench. "It gave purpose to my life at the time. But about a year ago it became boring, so it was time to sell out and move on. I'm thinking about starting a new company where I'll produce computer software that can design lighter-weight and better prostheses for our war veterans. There's lots of that kind of thing out there, but I've got some ideas to improve on what's available now."

"That sounds amazing." The wind whipped her shoulder-length red hair into her face.

Luke stopped himself from reaching out to tuck it behind her ear. "It's just a way to give back to all the veterans. For Uncle Smokey."

Diana pulled a rubber band from her pocket and twisted her hair up into a ponytail, then zipped up her lightweight jacket. "I hope Tootsie starts to feel better when we get to the house. Do you think it'll be colder up in northern Texas? I didn't bring a heavier coat."

"It can get pretty chilly. I went up there a couple of times for Thanksgiving so Uncle Smokey and Aunt Tootsie would have some company. A couple of times we got an inch of snow. Want my sweater?" Luke asked. He started to unbutton the cardigan.

She shook her head. "I'm fine for now—just wondering if I'd packed the right stuff."

"There are stores all along the way, and it's only a half-hour drive to Paris. We usually make weekly trips down there to get supplies," he said.

"In the RV?"

"Nope, not in the RV. We'll do that in Uncle Smokey's old truck. It's about thirty years old, but it still runs like it's brand new."

"Why would they keep a truck and only use it a couple of months out of the year? Until this year, they'd drive up there in their car, right?"

"That many trips into town on those roads would shake the hell out of their Caddy. And believe me, Aunt Tootsie treats that car like family." Luke chuckled. "Age, on a truck or on a person, makes no difference. It's how well they're maintained that matters."

Why, oh, why, couldn't he have smooth pickup lines like other men? Luke asked himself. What he'd just said could be taken as an insult. She might think that he thought she looked like an old pickup truck at her age, when in reality she was downright gorgeous. He wouldn't be a bit surprised if she still got carded at bars when she ordered a drink.

"I didn't mean that you're old," he stammered.

"I didn't take it that way." Diana smiled. "I took it as a compliment. Thank you for saying it, because I've sure been feeling old this past week."

"I wouldn't know why. You're a beautiful woman, Diana." He stopped and stared at the sunset over the golf course.

She turned to face him. "I'm tall and gangly. I have red hair and freckles. I'm old enough to have a daughter in the army . . ."

He laid a hand on her shoulder. "Beauty is in the eye of the beholder, not in a bathroom mirror. I think you are gorgeous."

"Well, thank you again. It's been a long time since anyone said something that nice about me." Diana blushed.

He removed his hand, and they continued on, but the silence wasn't nearly as awkward as it had been before.

Chapter Six

*C*hocolate-chip pancakes with bacon on the side had been the traditional Sunday-morning breakfast since Natalie was a toddler. Carmen awoke with that on her mind and had already slung her legs off the top bunk before she remembered where she was. All the events since Wednesday flashed through her mind like she'd pushed the fast-forward button on the remote control.

She pulled her legs back up and covered her head with the blanket. She wanted to just stay in bed all day. Everyone had been so good to support her that she couldn't be the drama queen and ruin the trip for everyone. Why didn't Eli just come home? If she could talk to him in person for only a week, maybe they could get all this sorted out. He'd taken emergency leave when his mother had her appendix removed, and that was just day surgery.

She threw the covers back and glared at the ceiling. Her imagination took control. The only reason why Eli wouldn't want to face her was if he'd been cheating on her. What did the woman look like? Was she smarter than Carmen? Was she younger? Did his mother like her?

Sitting up and taking a deep breath, she tried to put the negative thoughts out of her mind. She crawled down the ladder at the side of the bed and peeked around the kitchen area to see Luke at the stove. She was fully covered in her pajamas, but it just didn't seem right to parade around in front of another man in her night clothing. She grabbed up the clothes she'd laid out on the foot of her bed the night before and dashed into the bathroom, where she dressed in jeans and a T-shirt, brushed her teeth, and pulled her dark hair back into a ponytail at the nape of her neck. She dropped her folded pajamas on the bed, and in half a dozen steps she was in the kitchen area.

"Good mornin', Carmen. Coffee is made. Biscuits are about done, and sausage gravy is ready. I'll have this bacon fried in a few minutes. How do you like your eggs?" Luke asked.

"Scrambled," she answered.

"Me, too, so I'll go ahead and make enough for everyone. They'll all be up pretty soon." He cracked a dozen eggs in a bowl and whisked them until they were frothy. "Maybe we'll just take our breakfast out to the picnic table. It's a beautiful morning, but it's a little nippy. You might need a jacket."

"I'll get my sweater." She moved back to the lower bunk bed and pulled a cardigan from her suitcase.

When she returned, he handed her a plate. "You can go ahead and get your food ready. I'll bring out the coffee and juice."

Carmen tore open a couple of biscuits and covered them with gravy, added four pieces of bacon on the side, and then dipped into the eggs to finish filling up her plate. She carried it out to the wooden picnic bench that was provided at each campsite, took one look at the full plate, and wondered what she was thinking. She never ate this much breakfast, not even when she'd skipped supper the night before.

Luke brought out a tray with coffee mugs, small glasses, and carafes of coffee and orange juice. Then he went back inside and returned with his plate piled even higher than Carmen's. "I hardly ever make a big breakfast just for me, but this morning I was thinking about Uncle Smokey and the way he always made this kind of food up at the old house."

Carmen took a deep breath. "Being out here is nice."

Luke poured coffee and juice for both of them. "I love being out-doors, especially in the morning."

"Natalie would love this. We had a Sunday tradition of pancakes and bacon before we went to church, and sometimes we'd eat on the patio."

"Did all y'all go to services together? Did Aunt Tootsie go with you?" Luke asked.

"No, she and Smokey went to a different church, but all of us army wives went together. The girls were all pretty involved with the youth group. This is our first Sunday without them." She started with the gravy first.

"Can I ask you something kind of personal?" Luke's brows drew down in a serious frown.

"Sure." She nodded.

He'd made breakfast, so she owed him at least one question. She just hoped that it didn't have anything to do with the divorce. For the first time since Wednesday, she was really hungry.

"Is Diana seeing someone? She said she'd been divorced five years, so I was just wondering if she's in a relationship."

"She hasn't had time for a boyfriend, or so she says," Carmen answered. "We've tried to set her up with guys, but she's refused us every time. She's devoted herself to Rebecca, pretty much like Joanie and I did with our girls. Except both of us have a husband some of the time, and she didn't."

"Thank you." Luke's smile turned brighter than the sun rising over the horizon.

Carmen bit off the end of a crisp piece of bacon. She realized why he was asking and wanted to slap herself on the forehead. Eli said that she'd had pregnancy brain when she was expecting Natalie. Maybe now she had divorce-brain syndrome—DBS—that would excuse a lot in the next few weeks.

"If I can ever get up the courage, I'm going to ask her out to dinner while we're at the old house," he answered. "But can this stay between us? I don't want things to get weird while we're all cramped up in the motor home."

"Won't we be just as crowded in the house?" Carmen asked.

"No, because y'all are staying in the house, and Aunt Tootsie says I'll take over the motor home when we get to Scrap," Luke explained.

"I can keep your secret," Carmen agreed. She wasn't jealous—well, maybe a little bit. Her marriage was falling apart at the seams, and Diana could have a fresh start if she was willing.

"Thank you," he said.

"But you do realize that she'll be thirty-nine next month." She couldn't ask if Luke was just looking for a good time, but she couldn't bear to see Diana in pain again.

"And I'll be thirty-two. I'm attracted to her like I've never been drawn to another woman—not that there's been that many in my life. I've been too busy for even friendships. Maybe it's a wake-up call that it's time to get serious about settling down. Maybe it's Uncle Smokey trying to see that I have a loving partner, like he did. Whatever it is, I want to explore it further," he said.

There was no way in God's great green earth that Diana would ever go out with Luke, Carmen thought. He was so totally different from Gerald, who'd been the love of her life. Gerald was six feet, four inches of pure muscle, dark haired and dark eyed—"sex on a stick" is what Diana had called him. The girls all privately agreed. But Carmen would keep Luke's secret, even if he didn't have a snowball's chance in hell.

"Good morning." Tootsie came out of the motor home with a full plate in her hands. This morning she was wearing a red sweat suit, and her blonde hair looked like she'd just stepped out of a beauty salon.

Carmen patted her own brunette ponytail. "How do you do that, Tootsie?"

"What?"

"Wake up looking all put together," Carmen said.

"Honey, I learned years ago to do my own hair. Smokey liked big hair, so I've always kept it blonde and piled up high on my head. I'd take it down, and he'd brush it for me every night before bed, and in the morning I'd get it all fixed while he made breakfast," Tootsie said.

"That is so sweet," Joanie said as she joined them. She was wearing gray sweatpants and a matching top. She poured a cup of coffee and took a seat beside Tootsie. "And to whomsoever made this food, thank you."

"That would be Luke." Carmen nodded toward him.

Diana appeared in jeans and a zipped-up hoodie with a biscuit stuffed with bacon and eggs in her hands. "Coffee out here?"

Luke poured a cup and scooted down on the bench to make room for her. "Is that all you're eating?"

"I have to have coffee before I eat anything. This little biscuit is just the appetizer. I plan on eating more after this." Diana picked up the cup and took her first sip. "Good and strong. So where are we headed to this morning, Tootsie?"

"Jefferson, Texas. We should be there not long after lunch. I figure we'll park the motor home, and this afternoon we'll catch the little shuttle bus they run downtown to the antique stores. They open at one o'clock on Sunday, and if y'all want to, you can probably take a tour of the Gone with the Wind Museum. It's by appointment on Sunday, but I think I can make a call and get you in today," Tootsie said.

"Have you been there?" Luke asked.

"Several times. Smokey knew that was my all-time favorite book, so we have the movie and the book, plus the new books about Rhett Butler and Scarlett. I'll have to show you my party dress sometime," Tootsie said between bites. "I wore it to the first big military party that Smokey and I had to attend. Smokey had his dress uniform, but I was a little country girl who didn't have a damn thing to wear to a formal dinner. So I pulled a Scarlett O'Hara."

"And that is?" Luke asked.

"You didn't!" Diana gasped.

"I really did. I took a panel of the green velvet curtains down off the living room windows, thanked Smokey's aunt Gertrude for giving them to us as a wedding gift even though I hated them at the time, and made myself a beautiful dress for the party," she said. "Just like Scarlett O'Hara did in the novel."

"I'd love to have seen that." Carmen had been to several fancy parties with Eli. But she'd always felt like a wallflower and had kept to the shadows or visited with Joanie and Diana, back when she was still going to the events. Looking back, Eli hadn't paid a lot of attention to her at those affairs. She'd always chalked it up to him needing to mingle, but now she wondered.

"And I bet you were the belle of the ball," Diana said.

"Smokey thought so, and his opinion was the only one that mattered to me," Tootsie said. "I'll make arrangements for whoever wants to go see it if anyone is interested. I'm planning on hitting the antique stores myself. I always pick up a little something to take to the house. Last year I got a lovely pink Depression-glass bowl. I'd love to find another piece like it."

What Tootsie said about Smokey stuck in Carmen's head—when was the last time Eli had paid her a compliment? She drew her eyebrows down and tried to remember. It was more than a year ago. They'd gone to the traditional July Fourth cookout at Tootsie and Smokey's. He'd kissed her and said that she looked nice. But when they got to the party that evening, Smokey had said that Tootsie was more beautiful than the fireworks show would be. It kind of put a damper on what Eli had said, but then he'd never been one to gush.

To get her mind off that, Carmen kept sneaking looks across the table to see if there were sparks between Diana and Luke. He might not be a hunky black-ops soldier like Gerald—with his dark hair, square-cut chin, and broad shoulders—but Luke really was a handsome guy with that cleft in his chin and those clear blue eyes. His sandy hair and the scruff on his face reminded her of someone, but she couldn't remember who—maybe someone she'd seen on one of the television series she liked to watch or the cover of a book.

She almost clapped her hands when she remembered where it was. Natalie had gotten into a reading binge after graduation, and there was a duke on the cover of one of the books in her room that looked enough like Luke to be his brother.

"What?" Diana finally caught her staring. "Do I have egg on my face?"

"I was just looking at your hair with the sun shining on it," Carmen lied. "It looks like copper."

"Exactly what I was thinking." Luke smiled and nodded.

~

Diana had never been attracted to blond men, but after what Carmen said about her hair, she was fascinated by the gold streaks that the morning sunrays created in Luke's. The little vibe between them when his shoulder touched hers was further proof that she really needed to get back into the dating world. Maybe when she got back home, she'd go out with that doctor from the hospital where Joanie volunteered, if he was still single. It had been at least six months since Joanie had tried to fix her up with him, and the past week had sure proven that a lot could happen in only a few hours.

"Okay, now I'm ready for a real breakfast." Diana got up and swung her legs over the seat.

"And we're all finished, so you can eat on the road," Tootsie said.

"Fair enough," Diana agreed. "And I'll even volunteer to do the kitchen cleanup since I slept in a little longer than y'all did this morning."

Carmen raised a hand. "If that's the case, then I'll have to help you, because I'm planning on eating another biscuit with strawberry jam in it. And I would love to go to that museum. Natalie and I have watched *Gone with the Wind* a dozen times."

"I'll wash and you can dry," Diana suggested.

"I'll take care of the paper plates out here and get things ready to roll." Luke offered Diana his hand. When she took it, he pulled her up to a standing position. "You going to the museum?"

She shook her head. "No, I'd rather go with Tootsie to the antique stores."

"Me, too." He cleared the table and shoved the paper plates into the trash barrel.

"I'll go with Carmen." Joanie picked up the tray with the dirty coffee cups and carafes on it. "I love *Gone with the Wind*. That Scarlett is my kind of sass."

Tootsie held the door for her. "Yep, she's always been my idol, too."

Carmen took the handle from Tootsie and followed her inside. "After the inspiration she gave you for your party dress, I'd love to see it sometime."

"I'll do you one better than just showing it to you," Tootsie said. "You're about the same size I am. When you get past all this divorce shit, I'll let you borrow it to wear on your first formal whatever with a handsome hunk of a guy."

"It'll be rotten by then," Carmen assured her. "Maybe you'll wear it when you date again."

Tootsie drained what was left of the coffee into her cup and turned off the pot. "Honey, it really would be rotted away to nothing if it's waiting on me to wear it again. Smokey Colbert was my first and only love, and I'm too damned old to even look at another man. I've got you girls and your daughters to keep me busy. I don't have time for anything or anyone else."

"Hey, now. What about me? Don't you have to look after me, too?" Luke asked as he entered the motor home.

"If you'll move out of Houston to a place closer to me, I'll include you in that." Tootsie shook her finger under his nose.

"It could be arranged," Luke said.

Diana wondered what it would be like if he lived closer. What if he asked her out? Would she accept?

Joanie poked her in the arm. "Your eyebrows are drawn down like you're arguing with yourself."

"You're right. I was," Diana answered.

"About what?" Tootsie asked.

"A crazy notion that would never work. You said you've got another book for Carmen when she finishes the one she's reading. Can I read it? I promise I'll get it done before she needs it." Diana quickly changed the subject.

"Sure thing." Tootsie headed to the back of the motor home.

They were on the road when Diana and Carmen finished cleaning up the breakfast dishes. Carmen headed to her bunk to read more of the book that Tootsie had given her. Diana went to her bed with the one that Tootsie lent her. She hoped that by reading she would forget about the way her heart had tossed in that extra beat when Luke's shoulder had touched hers earlier while they were having breakfast.

~

Tootsie was glad for a door that closed, offering her a little privacy in the tiny bedroom in the motor home. She picked up Smokey's picture and sat down on the bed. "Well, darlin', I made it through the first two things without you. We went to the Old Smokey Cook-Off yesterday, and I stayed strong. The barbecue was good, but not as good as what you make. And it was real nice to have the girls and Luke with me. I'd have been lost out there in the crowd all by myself. And last night I saw Delores. We talked about the past, and I felt old and alone, probably like she has since Jimmy died. The difference is her kids are all scattered across the world, and ours are right here with me. I know they aren't blood kin, but if we'd adopted like we talked about all those years ago, they *could* be, so that's my story, and I'm stickin' to it." The corners of her mouth turned up.

Her phone rang, and she answered it with a sigh. "Hello, Midge."

"How you holdin' up?" Midge had been Tootsie's friend since long before either of them could walk. Her voice sounded even weaker than it had when Tootsie had talked to her a couple of weeks ago.

"Pretty good," Tootsie answered. "How are you feelin' these days?"

"I've got hospice now, but I'm glad you're coming to Scrap so I can see you one more time. Sissy was going to call, but I wanted to hear your voice. I'm supposed to tell you that the house is ready, the truck has been taken to town for servicing, and the leaves are raked. But you know that's a never-ending job this time of year." Midge was panting for breath by the time she finished the last words.

"Hello, Tootsie. Sissy here." Midge's younger sister sounded tired. "We have it on speakerphone. Midge can't talk very long at a time, but like she said, she wanted to hear your voice. And I wanted to tell you that there's a pot roast in the fridge for your first day, and I bought a few groceries—just the staples, milk and bread and such. The thermostat is set, so the house should be warm, and the beds are all fresh. Anything else I need to have done before y'all get here?"

"No, I believe you've covered everything. You shouldn't have done so much, Sissy, but thank you." Tears welled up in Tootsie's eyes. Midge was the last of the little group of girls that she'd started school with three-quarters of a century ago. Gloria, Midge, and Tootsie had been inseparable, best friends from the time they were toddlers in the church nursery and then through all twelve years of school. "I'll be down there to see y'all day after tomorrow. We'll get settled, and then I'll come spend the day."

"Thanks. We'll have a long visit," Midge said.

"See you then. Will you be here for dinner?" Sissy asked.

"Before that. First thing in the morning," Tootsie told her.

"We'll have the red carpet laid out," Midge said, and then there was a pause.

"I took the phone off speaker and brought it to the kitchen. The hospice nurse says maybe a week but probably only a couple of more days, and that might be stretching it. I'm so glad you're coming. It will mean the world to her to see you," Sissy said.

"This breaks my heart." Tootsie's voice cracked.

"Mine, too, but I've seen her suffer so much these past three months that I've told God to take her when He's ready. I just hope He don't come before you get here. Be safe," Sissy said. "It's time for her pain medicine, so I have to go now."

Tootsie stared at the blank screen for a long time before she laid the phone to the side and turned her focus back to Smokey's picture. "Midge will be gone within a week. I talked to her and Sissy today. I'm going to see her on Tuesday. I'd go tomorrow, but I've got to get the girls all settled in first. Sissy says the house is taken care of. I expect she had one of her grandkids do it this year. Losing you and seeing Delores with a cane, and now losing Midge and knowing that Gloria's been gone for years—it's almost too much to endure."

~

Luke's mind went around in circles as he drove north that morning. The last time he'd made this trip with Tootsie and Smokey, he'd been a little boy, so he didn't remember much about Jefferson. When he traveled to see them by himself, he seldom had time to stay more than one night. So he'd fly in to Texarkana and rent a car to drive on up to Scrap. Now he wished he'd sold his company a year before so he could have visited them more.

"Want some company?" Diana asked as she slid into the passenger seat.

"Love some," he said. "I was just feeling guilty that I didn't spend more time with Aunt Tootsie and Uncle Smokey before he died. They've always been so active and full of life; I guess I just thought they'd be that couple forever."

"Life doesn't come with guarantees. All of us felt the same way when Smokey dropped with his heart attack. One evening he was grilling steaks for us; the next morning he was gone. Guess it's a lesson to all of us not to take a single moment for granted," she said.

"Amen," Luke agreed.

Tootsie came out of her room, got a root beer from the refrigerator, and took it to the table. "I had two best friends the whole time I was in school. Gloria died ten years ago, and Midge is at the end of her life. I'll be going to see her on Tuesday and probably spending the whole day."

"I'll be glad to go with you," Diana said.

"We can all go." Joanie scooted around on the bench and draped an arm around Tootsie's shoulders.

"There's only room for two in the pickup truck, and there's things I need to say to Midge, so I'm going alone." Tootsie laid her head on Joanie's shoulder.

"So y'all've been friends for more than seventy years?" Carmen got down off the bunk and slid into the booth on the other side of Tootsie.

"Probably longer than that. Her mother was Tootsie, and Gloria's was Arlene. They were my mother's best friends, and those are the folks I'm named after. Gloria was named for my mother, and Midge for my grandmother. We were in the church nursery together and started and finished school at the same time. Now it's just me and Midge, and I need to spend some time with her," Tootsie said.

"Is she in a nursing home?" Diana asked.

"No, her sister, Sissy, is taking care of her. Sissy was one of those change-of-life babies and was born when we were all sixteen. Midge's kids have all passed away, so when she got too sick to live alone, Sissy took her into her house. She's got hospice." Tootsie's voice cracked.

"I'm going with you whether you like it or not," Luke declared. "I'll drive and stay in the truck, or else I could go on down to Clarksville and pick up any supplies we might need for the week. But you shouldn't be driving alone under these circumstances."

"I'll agree if you'll just drop me off and then come back and wait until I'm ready," Tootsie said. "That'll give you girls a day to get settled in and get the lay of the land."

"Fair enough," Luke agreed. "If Midge is really bad, we could forgo the Jefferson stop and drive on to Scrap this afternoon. That way you could go see her tomorrow instead of waiting another day. We could be there by suppertime."

"I promised Joanie and Carmen a tour of the Gone with the Wind Museum," Tootsie answered.

"And we can do that another time. Maybe we'll make a day trip down there in the motor home between now and Thanksgiving." Carmen patted her on the arm. "Midge is more important right now."

"If you're sure, that would be great." Tootsie dabbed at her eyes with a napkin.

Luke raised his voice. "Next stop, Scrap, Texas."

"You want your seat up here in the front?" Diana asked.

"No, darlin', I'm going back to my bedroom to watch *Designing Women*. I've got all the seasons on discs, and it'll help pass the time from here to there," Tootsie said. "Anyone who wants to join me is welcome."

"I'll make a bag of popcorn," Joanie said.

"I'll bring root beers." Carmen slid out of the booth and headed toward the refrigerator.

Luke glanced over at Diana, expecting to see her unfastening her seat belt.

"I'll join y'all after a bit. I'm going to stay up here for a little while longer," Diana said.

Luke's job meant that he spent hours and hours alone, so he didn't mind driving with no one to talk to. But he did like being able to catch a sideways glimpse of Diana whenever he wanted.

Chapter Seven

ootsie had always gotten antsy when she and Smokey got close to Scrap, but that afternoon it was even worse than usual. She picked up Smokey's picture and held it close to her heart.

"It's going to be tough to go in the house without you, darlin'. In all our travels, this was the home base, even after retirement. I was a fool to think it would be the same without you. If I didn't need to see Midge tomorrow, I'd tell Luke to turn this rig around and take us back to San Antonio," she said.

Stop it! I left you with three beautiful girls and a nephew. They all need help in one way or another, and you're the one they'll be leaning on, so buck up, sweetheart. I'm always with you in spirit, if not in the flesh. Smokey's voice was so real that the short hairs on her neck stood straight up.

"You rascal, you could have been talking to me all the time." She shook her finger at the picture. "I might feel your spirit, but what I want to feel is your arms around me when I walk into the house."

She waited and even looked up at the ceiling, but Smokey didn't have anything else to say.

The motor home almost came to a stop, and then Luke slowly turned to the left. Tootsie went to the window, drew back the curtain, and looked at the trees lining the short lane. The sugar maples had already lost half their leaves, but what remained were deep red, orange, and yellow all mingled together. She opened the window slightly and breathed in the brisk fall air. Most folks called this football weather, but not Tootsie. This was going home to Scrap, Texas, weather, and suddenly she couldn't wait to get into the house.

Luke brought the motor home to a stop. Tootsie hurried to the door and swung it open. "Home!" she squealed. "We're here, and it hasn't changed a bit."

I'm waiting for you, darlin'. Let's go in and let the memories begin, Smokey whispered in her ear.

Tears flooded her eyes as she planted her feet on familiar ground, the fall leaves crunching under her as she made her way from the motor home to the front porch. She hesitated a moment before she used the key to unlock the door. Smokey wouldn't really be there when she went inside. He'd never be with her in the flesh again. She finally took a deep breath and thought about the last time they'd been there. He'd kissed her at the door, like always, and said, "Let's go in and let the memories begin."

"If that's all I've got, then I'll be grateful for every one of them," she muttered as she opened the door and took the first step inside the old house. Nothing had changed. The forty-year-old sofa was still sitting against the far wall of the living room, and the matted and framed marriage license was still hanging above it. Stairs off to the right led up to three bedrooms and a bathroom. She headed straight ahead through a small kitchen and peeked into the utility room and bathroom before she went through the archway from the kitchen into the dining room.

After she'd made her way around the table and past the buffet, she stared at the door a full minute to build up her courage. Finally, she reached out and put her hand on the knob and turned it. She closed her eyes tightly as she stepped into the bedroom she and Smokey had shared for twenty of the sixty years they'd been coming here.

"You're right, darlin'," she whispered as she opened her eyes wide. "Your spirit is here. Don't go away. I've got to get the girls settled in, and then I'll be right back."

She stopped at the door and looked back, imagining Smokey propped up on pillows at the head of the bed. He had a book in his hands, and he looked up and smiled at her. "I love you, Smokey. Thanks for giving me that memory."

She rushed back through the house to find Luke holding the door for them as they brought their suitcases inside. "Luke, you can take that luggage up to the landing. Y'all girls can choose your rooms in a few minutes, but first let me show you through the rest of the house. It's not very big, but after the motor home, it seems like a huge place. This side of the downstairs is fairly open. Living room, kitchen, utility, and small bathroom—mine while we're here." She gestured toward each as she spoke. Then she ushered them into the dining room. "That room right there"—she pointed to the open door—"used to be a formal living room. When Smokey had a knee replaced about twenty years ago and couldn't maneuver the steps so well, we turned it into our bedroom. Smartest thing we ever did. We dang sure didn't need a formal living room, and we were both getting too old to climb stairs."

"I thought we were coming to a little cabin in the woods, not a big house like this," Joanie said. "Who takes care of this when you aren't here?"

"My friend Midge did before she took sick. Now she and Sissy hire a handyman to take care of it for us." Tootsie remembered that there was no *us* anymore, just a *me*. She wiped a tear away before anyone else could see it. "I'll get my suitcase and bring it in while y'all get settled."

"I'll take care of that for you." Luke followed her outside and handed her a clean white handkerchief. "How are you holding up?"

She wiped at the tears that had begun a steady flow down her cheeks. "Not so good. I can feel Smokey in the house, but . . ." She stepped up into the motor home and sat down in the passenger seat. "Feeling him here, even imagining him here, isn't the same."

Luke knelt in the space between the two seats and wrapped her up in his arms. "I knew it would be tough. I've got this hollow space in my chest that's putting a lump in my throat. I can't imagine what you're going through."

She patted him on the shoulder. "I was so wrapped up in my own feelings, I didn't think that you'd be grieving, too."

"We've got each other to lean on," he said as he slid into the driver's seat.

"Yes, we do." She handed the handkerchief back to him. "But for now I've got to get myself together and be strong for the girls. They're empty nesters, you know, and that's every bit as big a grieving process as what we're going through, plus poor Carmen is dealing with the divorce. Being needed is a big help."

Luke nodded. "Yes, it is, and we all pretty much need each other in one way or the other, don't we?"

"That's what family is all about. And family don't always mean blood kin." Tootsie's mouth turned up in a slight grin. "Don't ever think that I don't need every one of y'all to get me through this hard time. Without you four kids, I'd probably go batshit crazy."

"Aunt Tootsie, there isn't a single one of us who can lay claim to bein' a kid," he chuckled.

"To me, you'll always be a bunch of kids," she said. "And I'm grateful for every one of you. Now let's get my things together and take them inside before the girls come out here in force to see if something's wrong. Are you going to be okay in this motor home all alone?"

"Hey, I'll be just fine. Don't worry about me, Aunt Tootsie. I've got the biggest place of all of us, but I do plan on coming in and out the back door and using that bathroom so we don't have to take this monster thing to a dump site every few days," he said.

"Good idea. We never lock the doors when we're out here, so that won't be a problem." She twirled her seat around and started toward the back bedroom. "I changed the sheets this morning, so this room is yours until we leave."

"I can use a twin bed." He followed her down the narrow hallway.

"Nonsense." She picked up Smokey's picture and a small jewelry box from the dresser. "You'll use this room. You can carry the suitcases into the house for me, and thank you, Luke, for coming out here with me."

"My broad shoulders are available anytime you need anything," he told her as he picked up the baggage and started outside.

~

Carmen was busy hanging her clothing in the antique armoire in the room to the left of the hallway when her phone rang. She saw Eli's face appear on the screen and left the door hanging open to rush to answer it.

"Hello." She crossed her fingers like she did when she was a little girl and wanted something badly.

"Have you thought about signing the papers?" His tone left her feeling like she was talking to a complete stranger.

"No, I haven't, and I'm not going to until we get some couple's counseling." She backed up until her legs hit the bed, then sat down.

"It's too late for that. I didn't want to tell you this, but it seems to be the only way that you're going to understand that our marriage is over. I never meant to hurt you. It wasn't my intention, and Kate and I tried to walk away from the attraction," Eli said.

"So it *is* another woman causing all this? Is she aware she's breaking up a family?" Carmen's world fractured in front of her. Permanently. Separate households.

The silence was so heavy that it seemed to suck the oxygen right out of the air.

"Are you still there?" Eli asked.

"I'm here," she answered.

"Kate knows about you and that we have a daughter. We tried to fight it, but about six months ago, we gave up and followed our hearts," he said.

"You were sleeping with her when you came home the last time!" Carmen yelled at the top of her lungs.

Joanie and Diana hurried into the room and sat on either side of her. Carmen hit the button to put it on speaker.

"It wasn't easy on me, either. Lying there with you and wanting to be with her," Eli said.

"For the love of God!" Carmen's voice got even louder. "Why didn't you just tell me then? This is downright cruel! I can't believe you're telling me this."

"You need to understand that it's over and just sign the papers," Eli said. "And I didn't tell you then because I wanted to wait until Natalie had graduated."

"She's been out of school four months," Carmen reminded him.

"Yes, but then she was going into the service, and it was easier just to let things go until she left," he said.

"And you wouldn't owe a bit of child support, right?" Carmen asked.

"I'm not that person," Eli protested.

"No, you're just the bastard who sleeps with his wife and wishes he was with his girlfriend," Carmen said.

"Call me what you want," Eli said, "but just sign the damn papers."

"So tell me about Kate. Is she younger than me? Prettier than me? Better in bed or maybe smarter?" Carmen's voice broke.

"I'm not going there with you," Eli said.

"Why not? You made love to me and wished it was her, so why not tell me more about the woman that you brought to our marriage bed?" Her voice sounded downright cold even to her own ears.

"I didn't bring Kate—" Eli started.

"If you wished you were with her when you were with me, then it's the same thing. How many more women have you slept with and then fantasized about when you were in bed with me?" Her voice raised another octave or two.

A dead silence told her that her fears about those nights he went to the gym just might be true. "Answer me! When did you start cheating on me?"

"When you were pregnant with Natalie," he said.

"How many have there been?" she whispered.

"Come on, Carmen. I'm not going there."

"Did Gerald and Brett know?" Her voice quaked.

"Some of the time," Eli said. "They've known about Kate from the beginning. *Now* will you get the papers signed?"

"You got her with cheating; then you can lose her the same way. What makes you think this will work anyway?" she asked through clenched teeth.

"I'm retiring. Kate's enlistment is up, and my twenty is in. I'm doing things different this time. I love her like I've never loved anyone, and we're both ready to settle down."

Carmen hung up on him, threw the phone on the floor, and fell backward onto the bed. "Did you know about this, Joanie?"

"I didn't," Joanie gasped. "I swear to God, I didn't. Brett didn't tell me. Lord, I hope I'm not next in line. I'm sorry. This isn't about me. What are you going to do now?"

"I don't know. I can't imagine telling Natalie that her dad wants to divorce me. Now all this? I'm glad she can't have mail or phone calls right now." Carmen sat up and then stood. "Right now I hate him. I mean, I really, really hate him. If I had those papers in front of me, I'd sign them just to get him out of my life." She began to pace the floor. "He slept with me and felt like he was cheating on her. That's basically what he said, isn't it?"

Diana nodded. "That's exactly what he said. Even Gerald wasn't that harsh when he told me he'd been seeing another woman. I always liked Eli, but I'd better never lay eyes on him again, or I just might do something that will land me in jail."

"Where is the mad-as-hell step in that grieving process y'all've been talking about?" Carmen asked. "I think I found it, but I'd like to know how many more of these steps I have to endure until I get to the end."

"Two, but if you're really determined, you can bypass the depression one." Diana stood with her and gave her a hug.

"Right now I'd like to bypass however many miles it is to where Eli and Kate are shackin' up and beat the shit out of him with an iron skillet," Carmen said.

Tootsie huffed and puffed as she entered the room. "I heard a man's voice. What's going on?"

Diana filled her in while Carmen continued to pace from one end of the bedroom to the other.

"Sorry sumbitch," Tootsie growled, "telling her all that on the phone."

"*Coward* is the word you're lookin' for," Diana whispered.

Tootsie sat down on the edge of the bed to catch her breath. "He should have told her when he was home last. You've got fifteen minutes, Carmen, to throw your hissy. Go out in the yard and shake your fist at the heavens. Damn him to hell on a rusty poker. Whatever it takes, but when the time is up, you have to move on."

"Why? I want to be mad for a long time," Carmen said.

"Because he's got power over you when you let anger eat away at your heart, and he shouldn't be given that kind of control," Tootsie said. "It's not easy, but that's what you have to do."

"Did you go through this when Smokey died?" Carmen's mouth was so tight the words could barely get out.

"Yes," Tootsie admitted. "And one night I went outside, stomped and cussed like a sailor, beat the hell out of a metal trash can with a baseball bat, and was about to start in on the motor home when I realized what I was doing. You want a bat?"

"I live right next door to you, and I didn't hear any of that," Carmen said.

"I waited until y'all were all gone. It's two miles to the nearest neighbor out here, so if you want that bat, it's in the garage. Just don't use it on Smokey's pickup truck. The trees, the horse apples—all fair game. There's also an ax out there and a bunch of logs out back that could use chopping into firewood. Don't reckon you know how to do that, do you?"

"I was raised out in the country, and all we had was a woodstove to heat the house in the winter. I'll be back in time for supper." Carmen stormed down the stairs and slammed the kitchen door behind her.

~

"You think one of us should go with her?" Joanie asked.

"No," Tootsie answered. "This is something she needs to work out for herself. We can support her, but she needs to get that anger out."

"Did you really work over a trash can?" Diana asked.

"Oh, yeah, and I felt better when I got done. What did you do?" Tootsie threw the question back.

"I broke every plate in the cabinet throwing them at Gerald's picture hanging on the wall. Then I cleaned up the mess and went out and bought a whole new set that he had never eaten off of. The next day, I threw my mattress on top of my van, took it out in the country to a landfill, and set fire to it. No man has slept in my bed since then," she said.

Joanie sucked in air so fast that it made a whistling sound. "You mean you've been celibate for five years?"

"I didn't say that," Diana said. "I said no man has slept in my bed. There have only been a couple men since then, and one night in a motel was all I needed to see that I didn't want to see either of them again."

"But I swear right now, and you can get out a Bible for me to lay my hand on if you want to, that I'm finished with the army family parties." Joanie hit her fist against her palm. "Brett can go without me if they have a barbecue or a picnic. It was tough enough to go when Gerald brought in his new woman, but you asked me to do it to be there for Rebecca. This time the girls are grown, and I don't have to endure seeing those two with their new women."

Tootsie stood up and headed for the door. "Y'all get unpacked while Carmen is out there choppin' wood or beatin' up a trash can. Sissy put a pot roast she cooked for us in the refrigerator for supper tonight, so we don't have to cook. Luke says he'll make some biscuits and a salad, and I can make a pretty decent pitcher of sweet tea, so we're all set for when Carmen comes back inside."

"Yes, ma'am." Diana headed back toward her room. "And, Tootsie, don't come runnin' up those stairs like that again. You scared the bejesus out of me the way you were all out of breath."

"I thought someone was attacking Carmen. The bad thing is that I forgot to grab my pistol," Tootsie threw over her shoulder as she started downstairs—a lot slower than when she'd come up them.

"Did you really do that with the dishes and the mattress?" Joanie asked as she followed Diana into her room and sat down on the bed.

"Yes, I did, and I gave all his clothes to Goodwill. He was so mad when he came for them that it made it worth the time and energy it took." Diana smiled at the memory of the fit.

"Did it really help you get past all the pain?" Joanie asked.

"A little bit, but then that damned week of depression hit. Remember that?" Diana hung up her things in the armoire and filled the empty dresser drawer with her underwear and nightshirts.

"God, I hope I never have to go through this kind of thing, but I'm terrified now that it could happen to me." Joanie barely got the words out of her mouth when her phone rang. She darted across the hallway and grabbed it from the nightstand.

"Brett, I'm so glad you called. Tell me you love me," Joanie whispered.

"I love you, darlin'," he said. "I just talked to Eli. How's Carmen holdin' up?"

"She's outside working out her anger on a pile of firewood. She's got an ax in her hands, so maybe it's a good thing that Eli is a million miles away," Joanie said. "Now tell me you're never putting me through this kind of hellish nightmare."

"You know me better than that." She could hear him smile. "I love you, Joanie."

"Gerald loved Diana at one time, and Eli loved Carmen. Things change," she said.

"Since Carmen is out chopping wood, I take it y'all are in Scrap, wherever the hell that is, now?" Brett changed the subject.

"We're here," Joanie answered. "We're just getting unpacked and settling in. Diana, Carmen, and I have bedrooms on the second floor, but we have to share a bathroom. It has one of those old claw-foot tubs in it that I can't wait to get in with some bubbles and bath salts."

"Is Tootsie staying in the motor home?" His voice sounded kind of distant, as if he didn't really want to talk to her. Was it possible that he'd seen women in the past or maybe was stringing one along now? Was she in the bathroom taking a shower while Brett called her?

"No, she has a bedroom on the ground floor. Luke has the motor home now." She eased the bedroom door shut. "I think Diana may be attracted to him."

"It's about time she moved on with her life," Brett said.

Did his comment mean that he was moving on with his—without her? Her chest tightened at the idea. He'd never given her reason to believe he was cheating, but then Carmen hadn't a clue, either, until the divorce papers were dumped in her lap.

"He's seven years younger than she is," Joanie whispered.

"That's nothing. Kate is fifteen years younger than Eli," Brett said.

Sweet Jesus in heaven! Was Brett defending Eli because he was seeing someone?

"Holy crap on a cracker! That means she was just a little girl when Natalie was born. That ought to go over like a dead mouse in the church punch bowl with his daughter," Joanie said.

A long silence on the end of the line made Joanie hold the phone out from her ear to make sure she hadn't lost the connection. "Are you still there?" she asked.

"Eli didn't tell Carmen that Kate is only twenty-five, did he?" Brett asked.

"No, just that he's leaving the service when his enlistment is up. Retiring so he can be at home with Kate and do things different this time," Joanie said.

"It'll be easier on Carmen than it's been for Diana . . ." Brett let the sentence hang in the air. "Kate is from Kentucky, so they'll be living out there."

"Well, that's a bit of good news at least. Then I won't be the bitch who refuses to go to picnics with her," Joanie said.

"My time is up. Got to go on a fake mission with a bunch of green recruits. I'll call when I can," Brett said.

"Love you," Joanie whispered, but he was already gone, and he hadn't told her that he loved her. A cold chill ran down her back, and her hands went all clammy. Diana opened the door and peeked inside. "Are you all right? You're as pale as a ghost."

"You're not going to believe how old Kate is," Joanie whispered.

"After this past week, you could tell me that aliens were parachuting out of the sky and I'd believe you," Diana said.

Chapter Eight

Carmen set an eighteen-inch log up on an old tree stump, drew the ax back, and brought it down with a vengeance. The log split perfectly down the middle, leaving two sides to fall on either side of the stump.

Just like my marriage, she thought as she picked up another piece of wood. This time she swung and hit a knot. The shock jarred her slim body so badly she dropped the ax. She bent forward, hands on her knees, and got hold of herself, then picked up the ax, repositioned the wood, and went at it again.

Just like me, wanting to hold on to what is already split. I'm just throwing knots in the inevitable. She swung at the log and split it this time.

Two hours later, her muscles were screaming in pain, but there was at least one rack of firewood split and ready to be stacked. She ignored her aching shoulder and arm muscles and carried an armload to the end of the house where she could see a little of last year's wood still racked up. When that job was finished, she picked up the ax to split more wood, but the aroma of food wafting from an open kitchen window said that supper was almost ready.

She sat down on the cold ground and leaned back against the stump. Life went on. It didn't seem to matter that her heart was broken, that she'd put her trust in a man who'd betrayed her from the beginning of their marriage. Life didn't care about all that. It just wanted oxygen, food, and water to keep going.

"But how does it go on with a broken heart?" she muttered.

No answers fell from the cloudy skies above her. Nor did the north wind whip a few into her head. So she stood to her feet.

I can do this. I am strong. I can get over this and go on with life. My broken heart will mend. My dignity will be restored, she thought with each step toward the house.

Her dark hair stuck to her sweaty face, and she cried until she was sure her eyes were red and swollen, but once she stepped inside, she realized Tootsie had been right. She felt a hell of a lot better.

"Perfect timing," Tootsie said when she entered the house through the back door. "Supper should be on the table in ten minutes."

"I'm going to take a quick shower. I'll be down by the time it's ready." Carmen took the stairs two at a time. She removed her dirty, sweaty shirt and jeans, peeled her underwear down her thighs, and left them all on the bathroom floor. She wished she had time for a long hot bath in the deep tub, but that wasn't possible in such a short time. She adjusted the water temperature, drew the curtain, and stepped under the spray.

If only she could wash Eli out of her heart like the dirt and sweat from her body, but that wasn't going to happen with one simple shower—or phone call, for that matter. She shampooed her hair, rinsed it, and turned off the water. Drying her body in a hurry and then wrapping her hair in a towel, she was amazed that she felt better than she had since the divorce papers had arrived. Maybe there was something to be said about that old adage—when you're mad or sad, work it off. If that was the case, she might be chopping wood forever.

"Something sure smells good," she said as she approached the dining room.

"Sissy left a pot roast in the refrigerator," Diana told her. "Luke made biscuits and a salad. Tootsie put together the sweet tea, and we set the table. Do you have something to show for your anger, or did you opt to tear up a trash can?"

"There's enough firewood to finish filling up the woodshed. We should have enough for a month if we want a full blaze, or longer if we just want to have a small blaze in the fireplace to roast marshmallows," Carmen answered.

"Fireplace?" Diana asked.

"Check out the living room, behind that tall folding screen thing," Joanie said.

"We're back in the boonies, here," Tootsie reminded them. "Luke, you can have Smokey's place at the head of the table. I'll sit by Carmen right here, and Joanie and Diana can have the other side."

"You sure about that? I can sit at the other end," Luke said.

"I don't like seeing an empty place where he sat," Tootsie said. "It makes me sad, so please."

"Yes, ma'am." Luke pulled out Tootsie's chair for her.

"Thank you. Smokey always did that, and I like it," Tootsie said. "And he always said grace, so you can do that, too."

Luke took his place, bowed his head, and gathered them in a simple prayer.

~

Diana sat to Luke's right, and every time their hands brushed as food was passed around the table, a little spark shot through her. Yes, sir, it was time to get serious about moving on.

"What time are you and Luke going to see your friend tomorrow?" she asked Tootsie, mainly to get away from her thoughts about how she'd like to wrap her arms around Luke and kiss him.

"Right after breakfast. Y'all need to take stock of what's here and make a list for what you need from the grocery store. Luke can go take care of that while I'm spending time with Midge. We'll plan on going to the store once a week on Monday." Tootsie took two biscuits when they came her way.

"So then, Tuesday, it's my turn to do kitchen duty. Wednesday, it's Diana's, and Thursday, it's Joanie's?" Carmen asked.

"Why in that order?" Luke asked as he put a serving of roast, potatoes, and carrots on his plate and sent the dish on to Diana.

"Alphabetical," Carmen said.

"Then I'll come in after Joanie, so Friday's my turn." He took a bite of the carrots. "I hate raw carrots but love them cooked in a roast."

"You're taking a turn?" Diana asked.

"Sure, I am. Just like Uncle Smokey, I love to cook," Luke said.

"Okay, then, I have two days this week. And I agree with Luke. Cooked carrots are great—raw ones not so much." Carmen popped a bite of biscuit in her mouth. "I'll have my list ready before bedtime. Is anyone allergic to anything?"

"Not an allergy, but I hate bell peppers in anything," Tootsie said. "Love jalapeños, chili peppers, or even banana peppers, though."

"Anyone else?" she asked.

"Butterscotch," Luke snarled.

"And I planned on making butterscotch pies for dessert and butterscotch chocolate-chip pancakes for breakfast on my days," Diana teased.

Carmen giggled. "Yeah, right. You don't do butterscotch, either, not since your divorce."

Luke raised an eyebrow.

"Her ex-husband loved butterscotch pies and those yucky pancakes she just mentioned," Joanie explained.

Diana ignored them and set about eating her supper. So Luke didn't like butterscotch—that was sure enough a big plus in his favor.

"Oh, and I'll make a stop at the liquor store, so put down what you'd like from there as well," Luke said. "Uncle Smokey always put a case of beer on his list, but I really never acquired a taste for the stuff. I like a little nightcap of Jameson if I'm going to drink anything at all."

There's another plus, Diana thought. *Gerald hated whiskey and had to have a beer or two every night. I'd like Luke better and better if only he were my age.*

~

Tootsie was reminded of Smokey's breakfasts that morning. Carmen had rustled up enough ingredients to make biscuits and sausage gravy for breakfast. She'd also made oatmeal-raisin muffins that were right tasty with a little butter and honey. Evidently the ladies had compared notes, because from the list Tootsie had seen that morning, they weren't having the same thing twice all week.

She and Smokey had had a long talk the night before. Well, actually, she'd done most of the talking. He hadn't really said a single word, but he'd told her he'd always be right there with her. She'd laid his pillow longways and snuggled up to it. That didn't help much until she got up and put a few drops of his shaving lotion on the pillowcase. Then she slept like a baby.

Getting into the old pickup truck the next morning was another battle. Vehicles had changed a lot in the last twenty or thirty years. Very few had bench seats these days. She smiled at the memories of taking trips with Smokey in this vehicle—of sliding across the bench seat to snuggle up to Smokey's side, and curling up on the seat with her head in his lap to sleep the last hundred miles to wherever he stopped when his eyes got too heavy to drive anymore.

She was still thinking about that when Luke pulled into the driveway at Sissy's house. "Did I get it right?" he asked. "You said the first left after the traffic light and the third house at the end of the cul-de-sac."

"You remembered very well. Give me a call when you're finished with the shopping, and we'll see how things are going," Tootsie said. "If she wants me to stay all day, you might just want to go home and come back to get me later this evening."

"Whatever you want or need, Aunt Tootsie." He left the engine running but got out and jogged around the front of the vehicle to open the door for her. Tucking her arm in his, he led her past a flower bed brimming with multicolored mums and onto the porch of a white brick house that looked pretty much like all the others on the circle.

"Thank you." Tootsie reached out and rang the bell.

Sissy opened the door and motioned her inside. "Come in. She's awake this morning and ready to see you. I haven't seen you in years, Luke, but I'd recognize those eyes anywhere. They're just like Smokey's. Come on inside."

"Thank you, but I've got some errands to run. I'll be back in a little while," Luke said as he took a few steps back.

"We'll look for you later, then." Sissy ushered Tootsie on inside and closed the door. "She drifts in and out a lot, so be ready for that."

"Has hospice been here today?" Tootsie asked.

"Earlier this morning," Sissy answered.

"Do I need to know anything else before I go in there?" Tootsie whispered as they neared the open bedroom door.

"Nothing I can think of," Sissy said. "Midge, darlin', she's here."

Midge raised her hand and said, "I'm so glad"—she panted a moment before going on—"to see you. Sissy, bring the box."

"It can wait until later, can't it?" Sissy asked. "Y'all have some catching up to do."

"No, I don't want to die without giving them to her myself," Midge said.

"You're not dying today." Tootsie bent down and kissed her on the forehead.

"Yes, I am, and I'm glad you're here with me when I take that first step into eternity." Midge patted the side of the bed. "I'm not afraid, but it'll be good to have you with me. You'll be here"—she stopped and inhaled deeply several times—"to see me off, and Gloria will be on the other side to welcome me into the next life." With shaking hands, she brought out a remote and pushed a button to raise the head of the bed. "Sissy got me this new fancy bed."

"We've got one like it at home." Tootsie sat down beside her. "Helped with Smokey's snoring to raise his head up a little."

"Helps with my breathing." Midge's eyes shut, and her breath came in shallow bursts.

Sissy came in and set a box on the foot of the bed. "When she wakes up, tell her that it's right here."

"She says she's dying today," Tootsie whispered.

"She's hung on to see you, but when she goes is up to God, not her." Sissy gently closed the door behind her.

"I got a deal with God that I didn't"—Midge had to stop for air—"tell her about. That box is for you."

Tootsie scooted to the end of the bed and removed the lid of the cardboard box that had once held copy paper. Separated and tied by ribbons by the year that they were written were all the letters Tootsie had ever sent her. More than sixty years' worth, the older ones sporting faded ribbons, the newer ones still bright and shiny. One a month for all those years.

"Want you to have them back. Lots of history there," Midge said.

Tootsie grabbed a tissue from the nightstand and dabbed at the tears running down her cheeks. "I can't believe you kept all these."

"Went back and read them over and over." That took all of Midge's air, so she had to wait a minute to continue. "You need to buy water-proof mascara."

Tootsie giggled even though the tears, stained black, kept coming. "You need to turn up your oxygen."

Midge's giggle was barely audible, but her weary eyes glittered. "We had good times. Take a little nap with me." Her eyes closed again, and Tootsie kicked off her shoes and crawled up into the bed beside her.

Midge reached for Tootsie's hand and held it tightly. "Twinkle, twinkle," she said.

"Little star," Tootsie sang the next two words of the lullaby. When they had been little girls and were allowed to have a sleepover, they had sung that song just before they went to sleep at night. Gloria never could carry a tune and sounded like a toad-frog, but Tootsie and Midge never said a word. Tootsie wondered if God had given Gloria a beautiful singing voice in the next life. She closed her eyes and said a silent prayer that God would let Midge breathe easy and run and play when she got beyond the pearly gates.

Memories played through Tootsie's mind in living Technicolor as she lay there beside her oldest friend, holding her hand as she tried to breathe. The three of them had been inseparable from her earliest memories. When Gloria died, she and Smokey had been stationed in Germany, and there was no way she could come home for the funeral.

Midge's eyes popped open. "Gloria is here!"

"Honey, Gloria has been gone for years. Remember she had that brain aneurysm?" Tootsie said.

"I know that," Midge whispered. "But she's right there at the end of the bed."

A cold shiver made its way slowly down Tootsie's spine. Suddenly, she realized how lucky she was that Smokey had simply sat down in his chair after Sunday dinner and was gone when she went to wake him up to watch the ball game with her. He hadn't had to suffer like this. One minute he was there; the next he was gone. The shock had been almost more than she could bear, but she wouldn't have wished him back if he had to endure what Midge was going through.

Sissy came in with two pills. "Time for the pain medicine."

"Don't want it. Gloria has come for me." Midge's voice was barely a whisper now.

"Don't be silly. You know what the hospice nurse said. If you let the pain get away from you, then it's twice as hard to get it under control." Sissy held them out to her.

Midge shook her head. "No. I want a clear head when I go with Gloria."

"Okay, but tonight you're going to hurt," Sissy fussed.

"Tonight I'll be in paradise." Midge squeezed Tootsie's hand.

Who did Smokey see just before he went to sleep that Sunday afternoon? Tootsie wondered. *Was it one of his old army teammates, or maybe Luke's father, who was his youngest brother?* She hoped that when it was her turn to go, it would be Smokey who was in the room with her.

I'll be there for you, darlin'. His voice was so clear in her head that she turned to see if he was with her now.

Midge drifted off again, and Tootsie let her mind wander back to the girls. Was Carmen out chopping more wood again? What would happen if she swung wrong and got a cut? They didn't even have a vehicle to get them into town unless they drove the motor home. She wasn't sure if Luke had even left the keys so the girls could use it in case of an emergency. She was so busy worrying about Carmen that she didn't realize Midge had taken her hand away until she caught movement in her peripheral vision.

She jerked her head around to see Midge stretching out her fingers and then closing them, as if she were holding someone's hand. Then with a slight shudder, she took her last breath. Midge's hand fell back to the bed, and Tootsie covered it with hers.

"I guess you and God really did have an agreement," she whispered as she slung her legs off the side of the bed. She found Sissy sitting in the kitchen washing a few dishes.

"She's gone," Tootsie said.

Sissy sucked in a lungful of air and let it out slowly. "Is it wrong of me to be relieved?"

Tootsie wrapped her arms around the younger woman and said, "No, darlin'. She's at peace now, and I really believe that Gloria came to usher her out of this world. She was holding my hand until the last minute, then she reached out toward someone and took her last breath."

Sissy began to sob. "But that don't make giving her up any easier, does it?"

"Whether it's sudden or a long, painful journey, it's never easy to let them go." Tootsie cried with her. "Let's go sit with her a few minutes before we call the funeral home."

Sissy clasped Tootsie's hand in hers, and together they went into the room and sat in a couple of folding chairs beside the bed.

"She looks so peaceful," Sissy whispered. "Like she's just sleeping."

"She didn't fight going," Tootsie told her. "Have you made arrangements?"

"She did all that two months ago. No funeral, just a graveside service. That's to be tomorrow morning. She hated the idea of embalming, and she wanted a plain wooden box. I'm to line it with the quilt our mama gave her for her wedding present and put her in her wedding dress. It's just a little blue dress with white pearl buttons, and I'm to make sure that the pillow under her head has a case on it with embroidery that I did," Sissy answered.

"Then that's exactly what you should do. Flowers?"

"She wanted pink carnations like the corsage that Ralph bought for her on their wedding day," Sissy said.

"Can I please buy those for her casket piece?" Tootsie had to swallow hard to get the words around the lump in her throat.

"She'd like that." Sissy started to weep again.

Tootsie pulled a tissue from the container and handed it to her.

"I'll be lost without her," Sissy said. "She's all that was left except me, and yet I'm glad that she's not suffering anymore. I feel guilty for that."

"You've heard of the seven steps of grief, right?" Tootsie asked.

"The hospice nurse gave us all the points when she started with us," Sissy said.

"I'm only a few miles away, Sissy. I can be here in twenty minutes if you need me or if you want to come up to the house and spend some time away, either one." Tootsie grabbed a tissue and blew her nose.

"Gloria couldn't sing, and you sound like a three-hundred-pound trucker when you blow your nose or sneeze," Sissy giggled. "Midge said that just yesterday when you called and said you were coming today instead of tomorrow."

"She's right about Gloria and me, but *she* was clumsy." Tootsie laughed with her.

"Are we crazy?" Sissy asked. "Sitting here beside my dead sister and laughing?"

"She's probably giggling with us, and I like to think that she's doing it from the bottom of her chest and not wheezing for every breath anymore," Tootsie said.

Sissy squeezed her hand. "Me, too."

The laughter stopped, and more tears began. Tootsie pulled her hand free and said, "I'll stay with you until the funeral home comes for her, and I can stay tonight if you want me to."

"Two of the ladies from our Sunday-school class will be here as soon as I call them to help with the food that will be coming in. We'll have a dinner here tomorrow after the services. They'll spend the night and be here to take care of things in the morning while we're at the cemetery. She'll be buried in the Manchester Cemetery with Ralph and her children. The family will be together again." Sissy patted Midge's hand. "Her hands always get so cold. I have to remember to tell the funeral director that I don't want her hands crossed over her chest. She needs to have them under the quilt."

"We should write things like that down so we don't forget anything. We should do everything just like she said." Tootsie gestured for a pen.

Sissy opened the drawer of a bedside table and brought out a small notebook and a pen. "She liked to keep this handy to make notes."

Tootsie flipped it open. "There's nothing here now."

"We tore out the last page she wrote on this morning before you arrived. It had a note to give you the box of letters. I guess that was her final message," Sissy sighed.

Tootsie thought of Smokey's final message. After Sunday dinner, he'd given her a hug, kissed her on the forehead, and said, "I love you, darlin'."

Sissy removed her phone from the pocket of her shirt and called someone named Henrietta. Within five minutes, two ladies were at the house, and only a few minutes after that the funeral-home director was there to take Midge away. Tootsie walked beside the gurney all the way to the hearse, kissed her friend on the forehead, and told her goodbye.

She watched the vehicle pass her old red truck at the end of the driveway. One was taking away her last living childhood friend; the other was on the way to take her home. Luke bailed out of the truck and jogged across the yard. He opened his arms, and she walked into them.

"She's gone." Tootsie laid her head on his shoulder. "I'm the only one left of the three little girls who grew up together. I'm so glad that I came today instead of waiting until tomorrow."

"What can I do to help?" he asked.

"You can wait right here. I need to go tell Sissy that I'm leaving. She's got everything under control. Tomorrow morning at ten o'clock we need to be at the Manchester Cemetery for the service," Tootsie said.

"Why so quick? Can all her family make it that fast?" Luke frowned.

"It's what she wanted, and she hated the idea of embalming. Plus, the only family she has is Sissy, and whatever friends are left probably live within a fifteen-mile radius. News travels fast amongst folks in this area. I'll be right back. Wait for me in the truck." Tootsie broke free from his embrace and crossed the yard to the porch.

～

The first thing Diana found out that Monday morning was that there was no internet service in Scrap, Texas. She sat down on the top step of the porch and fretted about whether to call her supervisor and explain the situation. Maybe she should just take a couple of weeks' vacation time and then fly back to San Antonio. When she heard the rumble of a vehicle turning into the driveway, she shaded her eyes with her hand and watched the truck as it came closer and closer.

Tootsie looked like she'd been through a wringer backward when Luke helped her out of the truck. She forgot all about her job situation as she jogged over. "Are you all right? You're pale as a sheet."

"I just lost my last childhood friend. I'm so glad that I went today." Tootsie wiped tears from her eyes.

"I'm so sorry." Diana threw an arm around her shoulders and fell in beside her. "What can I do?"

"Y'all being here with me is the best thing you can do for me right now. Letting me be part of your lives and be needed," Tootsie sighed. "Now, you need to go help Luke get the groceries and supplies in the house."

"Yes, ma'am," Diana said and then yelled as she opened the door, "Carmen. Joanie. Tootsie needs you."

Luke already had two bags in each hand when she got back to the truck. "This is going to be tough on her. She just lost Smokey a month ago and now Midge. And her army wives friend, Delores, is failing."

"Got any ideas about what we can do to help?" Diana picked up a couple of bags and followed him to the house.

"Keep her busy so she doesn't have time to worry and think. She's probably already seeing her own end in sight," Luke suggested. "And by the way, you look nice today. That sweater is the exact color of your eyes."

"Thank you."

It might have seemed strange to someone else, but with all the recent events, his comment was a life preserver in the midst of an ocean—a simple compliment to hang on to when the stormy waters of life were sweeping over her.

"I hope she lives to be a hundred," Luke said. "She and Uncle Smokey have been like grandparents to me. I don't want to think about life without her."

Diana had faced death with her own parents and then more recently with Smokey. But just the thought of losing Tootsie brought tears to her eyes. She blinked them back, but that little niggling voice in the back of her mind said that Tootsie was the same age as Midge.

Carmen swung the door open for them. "Tootsie says that she's going to help put things away. I told her that we could do it all, but . . ."

"She needs to stay busy," Diana whispered. "Let her do whatever she wants."

After a brief nod, Carmen went out to the truck and hauled in more bags. "Who'd have thought that five people would eat up this much food in only a week?"

"I hope there's some extra in those bags, because we need to show up at the dinner after the funeral tomorrow with a casserole or a dessert in our hands," Tootsie said.

"I'll make hot rolls," Joanie offered. "Folks often forget to bring the bread."

"I could do a chocolate sheet cake." Diana unloaded the bags. "It only takes thirty minutes from start to finish. I'll make it in the morning so it will be fresh."

She pushed away the thoughts of what people would bring to the house when Tootsie died. Lord have mercy! She had to stop thinking about such things. She made a silent vow to spend more time with Tootsie when they got back to Sugar Run.

"Thank y'all. Smokey did that kind of thing when we had to go to funerals before. Thank God y'all came with me, or I'd be takin' in store-bought cheesecake or a vegetable tray," Tootsie said. "When we get this stuff put away, I've got something to say while we have dinner. Thank you for cooking while I was gone, Carmen."

"Tootsie, I'm so, so sorry." Carmen's eyes floated in tears as she hugged Tootsie. "What can I do?"

"You're here with me, and you've got a nice little dinner made. Let's eat. My mama always said that food and friends were a great comfort," Tootsie said.

Luke sniffed the air. "I smell something spicy."

"It don't take much to make a gingerbread with warm lemon sauce for dessert," Carmen told him. "It's in the oven with the casserole."

"Good Lord, I'm going to gain fifty pounds while we're here." Tootsie's smile didn't quite reach her eyes.

"And you'd still be tiny even if you did," Diana told her.

When they finished reloading the pantry, refrigerator, and freezer, they gathered around the dining room table, sitting in the same places that Tootsie had assigned the day before. Luke said grace, and then Tootsie raised her glass of tea.

"What are we toasting?" Diana asked.

"To Midge and to lifelong friendship," Tootsie said.

"To Midge," they chanted as they raised their glasses and took a drink.

"I've got something to say now while we pass this food around the table. I don't want to be mollycoddled. Midge was ready to go, and although I'll miss her, I'm glad she's gone. Seeing her like that broke my heart and helped me see what a huge blessing it was that Smokey had good health up to the last minute of his life." She stopped and took another sip of her tea. "I'm already in the grieving process, and I don't intend to go back and start all over with denial. I'm going to let Midge go with dignity, in her own way and her own time."

"That's good, Aunt Tootsie," Luke said.

"And now for the rest of the story . . ." Tootsie glanced around the table. "I'm very grateful that y'all are on this journey with me."

Diana's breath caught in her chest. Had Tootsie insisted that they go with her because she was sick and knew this would be her last trip?

"We're the ones who are grateful that you brought us along. We need this time with you to get through our own problems," Carmen said.

"When we get old, the biggest blessing in the world is simply to be needed," Tootsie said. "Now enough of that. Tomorrow we'll go to Midge's service, have dinner with Sissy and the people who loved Midge, then come home to live, love, and make an attempt at happiness. That's what Smokey would tell me, and that's what we're goin' to do. I hope I live to be a hundred, but if my time is up tomorrow, I hope I die like Smokey did." She snapped her fingers. "One minute on this side of eternity and then, in a single breath, on the other side."

"Yes, ma'am," Carmen said.

Life, love, and happiness. Life, one doesn't have a choice about. Love is negotiable. Happiness—that's the tough one, Diana thought.

Chapter Nine

iana hated funerals, but there was no way she wouldn't go with Tootsie to support her the day of Midge's service. But by midafternoon, she felt like the walls were closing in on her. Tootsie was surrounded by people she knew, so Diana thought it was all right to slip out the back door. She rounded the corner of the house and walked through the yard and into the pecan orchard out beyond that. She'd gone quite a way into the wooded area when she found a log with all the bark peeled off that made a perfect bench.

During the past month, too much sadness had surrounded her, and she needed a break, something to take away the heaviness that felt like a cold, wet blanket on her shoulders. Too much change, too quickly, was taking its toll on her. First, Smokey dying, then the girls leaving, Carmen's divorce, and now Tootsie's best friend was gone. She heaved a sigh of relief just knowing that Tootsie hadn't wanted the whole bunch of them to join her because she was sick, too.

Thank goodness she, Joanie, and Carmen had all packed a Sunday outfit just in case Tootsie wanted them to go to church with her. But the flowing muted-green skirt and matching emerald cardigan Diana had brought with her sure weren't what she'd call right for a funeral. A north wind rained leaves down around her and went right through her thin sweater. She gathered the front of it in a fist to pull it closer to her and watched a squirrel dash up one of the trees, harvest a pecan still in the green hull, and scamper down to the ground to dig a hole and bury it.

"I wish I could bury a lot of things like that," she muttered.

Tootsie sat down beside her. "Amen. I had to get away from all those people. It brought back too many memories of the dinner we had after Smokey's funeral. I'm feeling like I'm next in line."

"Don't get in a hurry." Diana laid a hand over Tootsie's. "Drag your feet a little. Heaven is timeless, so Smokey won't realize how many years it takes you to get there."

"I never thought of it like that," Tootsie said.

"A sweet little elderly lady at church told me that when my folks died while I was in college. I went into a depression, and she brought brownies over to my apartment. I told her how I felt, and she really gave me a lecture that ended with that idea. That my parents were in a place where there were no clocks or calendars, and they'd want me to live a full life so that when I joined them, neither they nor I would have regrets. But sometimes these days I feel a lot overwhelmed, so I know you do, too." Diana picked a few yellow leaves from Tootsie's hair.

"I guess I'd better get back in there before I'm missed, but thanks for the encouragement. Maybe I *will* drag my feet since I'd really like to stick around long enough to see all of y'all become grandmothers." Tootsie stood up and headed back toward the house.

That grandmother business is a long, long time in the future. Rebecca is only eighteen. Diana frowned.

You were only twenty when she was born, Diana's mother's voice reminded her.

"What are you thinking about that's so serious?" Luke sat down where Tootsie had been.

He startled Diana so badly that she jumped and would have fallen if he hadn't caught her. She quickly righted herself, and he released her.

"Being a grandmother," Diana admitted.

"How do you feel about that?" Luke asked.

"I have no idea," she said.

"You're still young enough to have more children, so maybe you'd rather start all over and refill your empty nest." He brushed the falling leaves from his dark pants.

"Not me. Been there. Done that. Have several T-shirts to prove it, and I'll get used to the empty nest," she answered with an inward shiver. She missed Rebecca so much that her heart ached, but the idea of starting over again at her age almost made her break out in hives.

"That sounds pretty definite." He sat down beside her again.

"It's the truth. What's so funny about it?" She pulled her cardigan tighter around her body.

He removed his leather jacket and draped it around her shoulders. "It's not really funny—but it is. I've never been a father and never will be. Mama didn't believe in vaccinations, so I had the mumps and a high fever to go with them before I ever started school. That's one of the reasons I've never been in a really serious relationship. Most women want a family . . . I didn't see a reason to start something that I couldn't finish."

She inhaled, and the aroma of his jacket—something woodsy and masculine—put a few extra numbers on her pulse rate. "Are you sure that you can't have kids?"

"Yep." He nodded. "Had the test run, and they said I'd have about a one-in-a-million chance of ever getting a woman pregnant."

"Why'd you even have it done?" she asked.

"Mama always felt guilty about not letting the doctor give me the vaccinations." He shrugged. "When she was on her deathbed, I told her the doctor said there was a chance I could have a family. That seemed to help her, and it wasn't the worst lie. You ever told one like that?"

"Oh, yeah." She smiled. "When did you lose your mama?"

"When I was in college. Yours still living?" he asked.

"Lost them, her and Dad both, when I was in college, too," she answered.

"So there you go." He moved closer to her and took her hand in his. "We've got a lot in common. No parents. You don't want more children. I can't produce babies. Evidently, that's why we've escaped out here to a pecan orchard free of sadness. I'd tell a joke just so we could laugh, if I could think of one. They say laughter is good for the soul."

She glanced over to find him staring at her. She felt as if he were seeing right into her soul. He let go of her hand and draped his arm around her shoulders. Then, ever so slowly, he leaned toward her. His eyelashes closed and rested on his cheekbones. The tip of her tongue darted out to moisten her lips. She wanted him to kiss her, wanted to see what the attraction was all about, but just before their lips met, that pesky squirrel dropped a pecan from a low branch and hit her right on top of her head. Even though it was only about half the size of her thumb, it felt like a boulder.

She jerked back and grabbed her head. "Ouch!"

"What?" Luke's eyes flew open.

"Blame it on that squirrel sitting up there." She pointed up. "He doesn't appreciate PDAs during a funeral dinner. He's throwing pecans."

Luke's chuckle turned into a laugh.

His laughter was so infectious that she giggled. "I guess Madam Fate is telling us that even though there's an attraction here, we should think long and hard about this age difference."

"You're attracted to me?" He sounded shocked.

"Yes, I am." She nodded. "But you've got to remember I've been divorced for five years, and I can count on the fingers of one hand how many dates I've been on. So it could be that I'm just ready to—"

Before she could say another word, he tipped up her chin and kissed her. It started out sweet but then deepened into something longer and more passionate. No one had ever sent shivers down her spine with a first kiss, not even Gerald, but she shouldn't compare the two. With Gerald, it had been the first time for both of them, and they hadn't been quite sure how to position their noses.

"Hello!" Carmen's voice floated through the air. "Tootsie says that it's time for us to leave."

"We'll talk later," Luke said as he stood up.

Diana handed him his coat, and together they took a few steps toward the house.

"There you are. It's a little chilly out here, isn't it?" Carmen shivered.

Depending on whether you're making out like sophomores in high school, Diana thought, *or just sitting like a bump on a log, watching a squirrel bury pecans.*

"Little bit," she said, "but I had to get away from that heavy feeling in the house."

Luke lengthened his stride and went on ahead of them. "I'll see y'all in the house."

"I hid on the front porch swing," Carmen admitted. "Sissy has a quilt out there, so I wrapped up in it. I wish I could say that I found all the answers to this divorce thing, but I didn't. It was peaceful, though."

"Let's hope this is the end of cold weather and that all we have is sunny days for the next few weeks."

"You need to get out of the forest so you can see the sky," Carmen said. "The reason we're leaving is because there's a storm brewing off to the southwest. Tootsie's afraid if it starts to rain, we'll get that big motor home stuck in the mud on the way back to Scrap."

"What's the weatherman saying?" Diana slowed down so that Carmen didn't have to run on the way back to Sissy's house.

"That we've got a solid week of rain and possible thunderstorms. Sissy said she's so glad that God gave us a sunny day for the graveside services. Even though it's nippy and there's a wind, at least we didn't have to shiver under umbrellas today."

"Amen to that." Diana caught her first glimpse of the storm clouds rolling in from somewhere down around Paris. A bolt of lightning flashed, and thunder followed it in a few seconds.

Tootsie leaned out the door of the motor home and motioned them to hurry. "We've got to get home," she yelled when they were close. "That thing's coming on fast. Sissy just heard that there's a tornado on the ground in Paris, and we're right in line for it. I don't want to be in this tin can or stuck on the road, either, when it gets here."

Diana and Carmen jogged the rest of the way and had just gotten inside when the first big drops of rain hit the windshield. The twenty-minute drive to the house took twice that long, but the rain had slackened off slightly when they arrived. The four ladies dashed inside, leaving Luke to get things leveled and the extension cord plugged in to the electrical outlet on the side of the house.

Was this an omen? Diana wondered as she climbed the stairs to change clothes. Did it mean that the kiss she'd shared with Luke would only bring on a storm in their lives if she let it go any further?

There you go, overthinking everything. Her mother's voice was back in her head. *Why don't you just move forward?*

Diana hurried up to her room and stripped off her wet clothing, hung it over the back of a ladder-back chair to dry, and pulled on a pair of gray sweatpants and an oversize T-shirt with Minnie Mouse on the front. *Mama, he's rich, and I barely make it from one paycheck to the next.*

What's that got to do with anything? her mother continued to argue.

"Hey, you decent?" Joanie asked, knocking on the bedroom door.

"Come on in." Diana was glad for the interruption so she could get her mother out of her head. "Sounds like the storm is over."

"Look out your window," Joanie said.

Diana crossed the floor and drew back the floral curtains. "Good grief! That is one eerie look out there."

"Tootsie says it's the color of a tornado, and everything has gone all still and weird. She sent me up to bring you downstairs so we can get into the cellar until it's passed through," Joanie told her.

"Where is this cellar?" Diana asked.

"Cellar is right out the back door. The noise that sounds like a freight train off in the distance is the storm coming at us. We've seen our share of tornadoes in Sugar Run, so you should remember the sound," Joanie said as she darted out of the room.

"I wasn't thinking of a tornado at this time of year." Diana ran down the stairs to find Luke waiting for her in the kitchen.

"Come on." He grabbed Diana's hand and held it tightly when the wind tried to force them back into the house as they rushed to the cellar. He sent her down before him and then closed the door behind in a hurry.

"I hope either the house or the motor home is still standing when this is over," Tootsie yelled above the turmoil. "If they're both gone, I guess we'll hitch us a ride to town and catch a bus back to Sugar Run."

"That is a lot of noise out there," Diana hollered. "Wouldn't you be sad if you lost everything?"

"Sure I would, but I've got you four kids, so I haven't lost everything even if the storm takes the house and motor home with it," Tootsie replied.

Diana's hand still tingled from Luke's touch. Maybe her mother was right about analyzing everything to death. But when Gerald announced that he'd been seeing another woman and wanted a divorce, it had shocked the hell out of her. She'd vowed nothing would ever sneak up on her like that again. So far she'd managed to avoid any more heart-breaking surprises.

Old wooden benches lined two sides of the cellar. Shelves, probably built when Tootsie's mama or grandmother canned vegetables and fruit in the summer, covered the third wall. Tootsie, Carmen, and Joanie sat across from Diana and Luke. The noise got louder and louder, and then suddenly everything became so quiet that it was creepy.

Rain and hail began to pelt the metal can over the vent on top of the cellar. Luke took a deep breath and climbed the steps. "Uncle

Smokey always said that when it starts to rain, the bad part is over, so we can go back to the house now."

"If we've got a house," Tootsie said.

"I'm going to think positive." Luke put his back against the door and pushed. "Y'all get ready to run from here to the house, soon as I open the door. It sounds like that hail is pretty good sized."

Bigger than a pecan thrown from a tree limb, Diana thought as she hung back to let Tootsie go first. If any of her friends slipped and fell or got knocked out by a hailstone, she could at least pick them up and carry them to safety. That was one of the benefits of being almost six feet tall.

"What are you waiting for?" Luke asked her as hailstones the size of Ping-Pong balls bounced off the cellar door.

"Are they all inside?" she asked.

He nodded.

She took the steps two at a time, made it halfway across the short distance, slipped on a pile of hail, and fell flat on her back. Hail and rain beat down on her for a full ten seconds before Luke scooped her up in his arms, slung her over his shoulder like a bag of chicken feed, and carried her into the kitchen.

~

"What happened?" Carmen blinked several times before she could believe what she was really seeing. "Why are you carrying Diana like that?"

Luke bent slightly forward and set Diana on her feet, then put his hands on her shoulders. "Are you okay? Is anything broken?"

"Only my pride." She rubbed her hip.

"You've got red dots on your face," Joanie said.

"Hail coming down at about fifty miles an hour will do that to you." Diana put her hands over Luke's. "Thanks for the lift into the house. It was like I flew."

His grin brightened the whole room. "Picking you up was nothing after working out with weights in the gym."

"I thought you were a computer geek." Carmen cocked her head to one side. There was something between them—vibes, sparks, whatever it was called these days—and she hoped that Diana thought long and hard before she got involved with another man. A heart couldn't stand two hurts like what Gerald had dealt her, or like Eli was pushing off on her, herself, these days.

"I am exactly that." Luke removed his hands and took the towel that Tootsie offered him. "But I found out that I'm also very fond of food. Sitting at a desk meant I had to give up doughnuts, potato chips, and cookies, or else I had to hit the gym four days a week. Since I have no willpower over food, I chose the gym." He dried his hair and handed the towel to Diana.

Were the extra ten pounds she'd gained since she and Eli married what made him go looking for another woman? No, that couldn't be the excuse, not when he admitted that he'd been cheating since she was pregnant, and that was only a year after they were married. It had to be something to do with her weight, though. Maybe if she'd paid more attention to her looks and the scales, he wouldn't be leaving her.

"Stop it," Diana whispered.

"What?" Carmen asked.

"I can tell by the expression on your face you're thinking of Eli and blaming yourself," Diana said.

"You know me all too well," Carmen sighed. "I was thinking that I might start going to the Y when we get back home. Want to join me?"

Luke had said he had no willpower over food, so he exercised. She had no willpower when it came to Eli, but the gym surely couldn't fix that. However, it could help her take those extra ten pounds off, and she might feel better about herself.

"If Diana doesn't want to go exercise with you, I will," Luke said. "Only let's go to a real gym instead. Anyone else want to go with us?"

"I might want to go, too," Diana said. "I've been thinking about it for a while."

"Not me," Tootsie said. "I'll just eat what I want and get fat and lazy. Speaking of that, let's make hot chocolate and watch a movie. We don't get cable up here, but we've got a whole stack of movies in the cabinet over there." Tootsie shivered as she started toward her bedroom. "And let's light a blaze in the fireplace to get this chill out of the house."

"I'll do the chocolate," Carmen offered, "and make a bag of popcorn to go with it."

Luke picked up a box of matches and crossed the room. "Uncle Smokey always left it ready in case it was cold when they arrived. It takes the electricity a while to heat everything up."

"Well, I'm going to my bedroom and putting on some more comfortable clothing, and then I'm going to tell Smokey all about that tornado that passed over us. We are one bunch of lucky folks to have a house still standing," Tootsie declared.

"I'll go through the movies," Joanie offered, and gasped when she opened the cabinet doors below the television. "Oh. My. Goodness. Look at this selection, and they're alphabetically arranged. Everything from *Steel Magnolias* to seasons of *NCIS* and *MacGyver*."

"I love *MacGyver*," Carmen said as she used a whisk to stir the hot-chocolate mixture in a saucepan. Before she and Eli could afford cable, they'd watched reruns of the original *MacGyver* for entertainment. She'd make popcorn. He'd have a beer, and she'd have a diet soda pop, and they'd cuddle under blankets on the sofa. That was before she got pregnant—before he had the first of what must have been several flings.

"Then we'll binge out on that one this rainy afternoon," Joanie said. "We've got the first and second season, so that might even keep us busy through tomorrow if it's still raining."

"Oh, it will be." Luke got the kindling going under the logs. "The weather report says it's going to do this all week, and there's flash-flood warnings. Now I'm going to dash out to the motor home, put some dry things in a plastic bag, and bring them in here to change. These wet things are giving me chills, but at least I don't have to try to dodge the hail. I think it's stopped." He opened the door and sucked air through his teeth. "The hail brought a blue norther with it. I bet it's dropped twenty degrees out there."

As soon as he was gone, Carmen turned to Diana, who was watching the popcorn in the microwave. "What's going on with you and Luke?"

"Nothing," Diana answered, but she didn't look at Carmen.

"Did you hit your head when you fell?" Joanie laid the two *MacGyver* DVDs on the coffee table in front of a well-worn, buttery-soft leather sofa. "I call shotgun on one of the recliners." She pointed toward a matching brown leather chair.

"Did you?" Carmen hip-butted Diana.

"What?"

"Hit your head? That's the only way you'd be addled so badly you'd lie to us about nothing between y'all. It's plain as the flat little snout on a pig's face," Carmen said.

"I kissed him. It felt good. It won't happen again. Not only is he younger than me, but he's rich as Midas. He's too good a man to have his friends teasing him about a cougar who married him to get at his money," Diana admitted in a monotone.

Carmen whipped around, her eyes bulging. "Holy crap!"

"What shocks you? That I kissed him or that I said I was a cougar?"

"The latter," Carmen whispered. "Looking at you two, no one would ever know that you're older than him."

"Now, as Ma used to say on *The Golden Girls*, picture it: The Steakhouse in San Antonio in five years. Rebecca is married and has a new baby. Someone comes up and thinks she's his wife and the baby is his. Imagine how embarrassed he'd be."

"Honey, in five years, he'll be five years older, and no one is going to think that. You're just borrowing trouble," Joanie said as she sat down in front of the fireplace and flipped her wet blonde hair over her shoulder so the heat would dry it. "And besides, one kiss doesn't mean he's going to drop down on one knee and propose next week. It just means that y'all might like to spend some real time together after we get back home and things settle down from all this drama."

Carmen backed away from the stove and pulled her dark-brown hair up into a ponytail. In five years, would she be ready to kiss another man? She didn't think so. Not even in ten years. She'd given her heart to Eli. He'd shattered it into a million pieces, and like poor old Humpty Dumpty, all her friends and all the miracles in the world couldn't put it back together again.

~

The rain fell in sheets, cold wind blowing behind it. Hoping it would let up in a few minutes, Luke tarried at the motor home. His waterproof tote bag was packed with a change of clothing and his laptop in case he got bored with *MacGyver* episodes. He seldom watched television, but if the women all liked that show, there was no doubt it was some kind of chick flick.

When he gave up on the rain ever slackening off, he took a deep breath, picked up his bag, shut the door behind him, and took off for the house in a hard run. He was as wet as if he'd fallen fully dressed into a swimming pool by the time he reached the porch. Cold rainwater ran down and dripped off his chin, droplets of it sticking to his eyebrows and lashes. He hated to go inside and track mud across the hardwood floor, but it was that or stay out on the porch and freeze to death.

"Hindsight," he muttered. "What I should have done was get into some warm pajama pants and stay in the motor home." He opened the door and ran in the longest strides he could take from there to the downstairs bathroom.

"What's the hurry?" Diana asked.

"Don't want to ruin the flooring," he shouted as he passed by her in a flash. He was shivering from the inside out by the time he dropped his wet clothing on the floor. A good hot shower would warm him up before he got into dry clothing, but he didn't want to take the time when the ladies already had popcorn and hot chocolate ready. He grabbed a towel, dried his body and hair, got dressed in a pair of flannel pajama pants and a T-shirt, and threw a flannel shirt over that. Once he'd pulled on a pair of thick socks, he hung his wet things and the towel over the shower stall.

He went straight to the fireplace to warm his hands after he left the bathroom. "Unless you have to go out for something, stay inside. That rain is colder than ice water. If the temperature drops any more, we may be in for an ice storm."

"It feels like night, and it's only three thirty," Tootsie said as she snuggled down with a fluffy throw in her favorite recliner. "I'm sure glad y'all are here. This would be a dreary day without company."

Joanie handed her a cup of hot chocolate and a bowl of popcorn. "Drink this. It will warm you from the inside."

"Thank you, darlin'!" Tootsie held the mug in her hands to toast them before she took a sip. "I heard y'all talking about *MacGyver*, so let's get him on the television. I like him really good, but the actor I really like is that handsome George Eads that plays Jack Dalton. Now there's a man after my heart. He kind of reminds me of Smokey."

Luke set his laptop on the end table, took a throw from a rack sitting behind the sofa, and settled down to see what this television show was all about. He'd seen George Eads in a few episodes of *CSI*, so maybe it wasn't totally a chick flick.

"Before we get started, thank you to whoever cleaned all the water off the floor," he said.

Diana raised a hand. "That would be me. It wasn't a big job. You were almost flying."

"I tried." He liked the idea that Diana had cleaned up after him. That was almost personal, even if it was just water from the floor. "I should've stayed out in the motor home."

Tootsie sipped her hot chocolate and then set it on the table between her and Joanie. "That's nonsense. Water can be mopped up off floors, and we'd have missed you."

Diana settled in between him and Carmen, her hip touching his. Joanie picked up the remote and started episode one. He was immediately drawn into the show, but he enjoyed watching Diana's expressions as much or more than anything else. Joanie hit the pause button after they'd watched two episodes, and they all made sandwiches to eat in the living room while they watched MacGyver use paper clips and plastic straws to get out of tight places.

At ten o'clock, Tootsie yawned and said, "You kids can watch this until dawn if you want, but I'm going to bed."

"Me, too," Carmen said.

Luke looked at the hard rain still pounding against the window. "Guess I'll get a cold shower on the way to the motor home."

"Nonsense!" Tootsie spit out one of her favorite words. "You can sleep on the sofa until it lets up."

"I'm getting partial to that big king-sized bed. I've got plenty of dry clothes, so I'll just run between the raindrops." He got to his feet and rolled the kinks out of his neck. "Anyone want to walk me out to the motor home?"

"Honey, I love you, but I wouldn't get out in that weather for Jesus," Tootsie said.

"Then I guess I'll go by myself. If I don't make it in for breakfast, y'all can figure I slipped and fell, bumped my head on something, and drowned in the pouring rain," he teased.

"Poor baby," Carmen shot back as she gathered up the empty cups and bowls.

"Enough about bumping heads and dying," Tootsie said. "I don't want to go to another funeral for at least ten years. And now I'll have the hymn they sang at the service today stuck in my head while I'm trying to sleep."

"Which one?" Carmen asked.

"'I'll Fly Away,'" Tootsie answered.

"I'm sorry, Aunt Tootsie. That was insensitive of me to bring up such a thing after this morning," Luke apologized.

"Accepted. Now good night to all y'all."

"Good night," all four of them sing-songed as she left the room.

Luke stood up to leave next and said, "If it's still raining tomorrow, maybe we can watch some more of that show. I liked it."

He darted outside before anyone could say anything, and sure enough, he was soaking wet all over again by the time he reached the motor home. He went straight to the tiny bathroom, hung his dripping clothing on the hook on the back of the door, and took a quick hot shower. When he got out, he dressed in sweat bottoms and a shirt and crawled in between the sheets on the bed. It took a few minutes to warm up a spot, but once he did, he fell right to sleep. He dreamed about Diana for the second night in a row. This time they were both older and sitting on a porch swing watching a couple of little children play in the yard. He knew they were Rebecca's kids, but they were calling him Grandpa.

He awoke, shivering in total darkness. Rain was still coming down like it meant business, but the electricity was out. Using a flashlight, he located the closet and was packing a bag again when he found an old yellow slicker hanging at the very back. He put it on, picked up the bag he'd packed, and ran from the motor home to the house. He built up a blaze in the fireplace, and using the quilt from the back of the sofa like a sleeping bag, he stretched out on the floor. He was warm and dry, and the fire threw off enough light to keep it from being so damned dark. Hopefully by daylight the power would be back on, but if it wasn't, they could survive. He shut his eyes, and hoping that he'd pick right up on the dream he'd left behind, he went to sleep.

Chapter Ten

*D*iana awoke from a nightmare, her whole body clammy and her hands shaking. She sat up in bed and opened her eyes, but there were no shadows, nothing but total darkness. She held up her hand and brought it close to her face but couldn't see it until her eyes readjusted to what little light there was.

"No electricity," she muttered. She threw the covers back and crawled out of bed and was amazed that the bedroom was still reasonably warm. She remembered seeing the breaker box in the utility room off the kitchen, so she headed that way. "Hopefully it's just a matter of throwing a switch."

In the complete darkness, she hit her knee on the nightstand, bent to rub it, and smacked her forehead on the old iron bedstead. She seemed to be the only one awake, and the house would cool down rapidly if the switch that had flipped controlled the heating unit.

It was no different from when she was at home in Sugar Run. She'd make her way to the back bedroom closet where the breaker box was located and take care of things. But at home she knew her way around her bedroom in the dark; here, not so much. Holding her hands out in front of her, she found the chest of drawers. The chair where she always dropped her purse was just to the left of that. She felt her way carefully but still bumped her shin on the chair before her fingers located it.

"If this is what it's like to be blind, I never want to lose my eyesight," she muttered as she searched her purse by feel for the flashlight. She found it and pushed the bottom, and nothing happened.

"Dammit!" she swore under her breath. "The battery is dead." Then she realized that what she was holding didn't have a key chain on the end.

"Lipstick," she giggled as she fumbled around again, finally bringing up the flashlight. She held her breath as she pushed the button and bit back a shout when a small ray of light appeared.

The tiny thing was to help you find a keyhole, so it didn't offer a lot. She focused it on the floor and took one step at a time. She'd made it halfway down the stairs when something hit her on the cheek. She'd forgotten about the chain that turned on the light at the top of the stairs. It wasn't all that big, but the crystal ball at the end hit her square in the eye.

"Ouch!" she groaned. She threw the tiny ray of light upward and sat down on a step until the ball stopped swinging. Then she got up and made her way to the bottom. Once there, she held up the flashlight so that she wouldn't stumble over an end table or a kitchen chair.

A really nice blaze was going in the fireplace, throwing not only warmth throughout the room but a golden light. She frowned, remembering that Luke had banked it so that nothing but embers were glowing before he'd left the evening before. Had Tootsie gotten up in the night, found the electricity was out, and put more wood on the fire? If so, that meant that they hadn't popped a breaker but that the power was out in the whole area. She held up the flashlight to light the way to the kitchen and didn't even see the big lump on the floor.

One minute she was taking a step, the next she stubbed her toe on what she'd figured was an ottoman and was falling forward. The flashlight flew out of her hand and landed on the floor, and suddenly she was lying on top of Luke. His eyes opened, and his expression registered total shock. She tried to roll to the side but couldn't because his arms were wrapped around her, her breasts pressed against his hard chest.

His hands, splayed out on her back, jacked her pulse up at least ten notches more. Suddenly she was too hot, and his lips were too close. Even though his face looked eerie with the light shining on it from the side, she wanted to lean forward and kiss him.

She couldn't breathe—not only from having the wind knocked out of her but because of a desire to throw back the quilt and crawl inside the cocoon with him.

~

Tootsie pulled up the covers around her neck and still couldn't get warm. She turned toward Smokey to snuggle up against his warm back, only to realize that she was holding on to a cold pillow.

"I miss you so much," she sighed. "You were always there to keep me warm on these cold nights."

Rain beat on the window like BB pellets, and all was darkness when she finally sat up in the bed. "Dammit! The electricity is out," she moaned. "I've got four kids here and no power. What am I going to do, Smokey?"

First you check the breaker box, remember? His voice was clear enough that she made sure he wasn't lying beside her. She grabbed the flashlight from the nightstand drawer and started across the cold floor. A burst of warm air hit her when she opened the door. She heard a noise like something falling, then heavy breathing.

Starting back to get her pistol, she caught sight of a bit of light in her peripheral vision and followed it to the living room, where she found Diana stretched out on top of Luke.

"Well, well!" she said. "Am I interrupting something here?"

Luke sat straight up, rolling Diana off to the side. "No, ma'am. I was out cold, and suddenly Diana fell on me."

Diana sat up beside him. "I didn't know he was—"

Tootsie laughed out loud. "I was teasing y'all. I can see you're both dressed and that Luke is wrapped up like a cocoon in that quilt. Why don't we look at the breaker box? 'Course I'm thinking the electricity is blown for the whole area. That's not unusual up here when it storms. Might be out for a few hours or days if this weather don't let up."

"I'll go check it. Y'all might want to grab a blanket and claim either a recliner or the sofa to stay warm." Luke got free of the quilt, stood to his feet, and started that way only to bump his leg on a chair. "Mind if I use one of those flashlights?"

Tootsie handed him the one she had and then sat down in the recliner. "I can leave the door to my bedroom open, and heat rises, so y'all should be fine upstairs until the power comes back on. But it's not going to be as warm as usual. Hope y'all brought plenty of clothing, because the washer and dryer won't be working."

"We'll be fine." Diana moved from the floor to the sofa. "We caught up the laundry yesterday, so we've got plenty to hold us for a few days. That's a minor thing compared to cooking."

Tootsie pointed to a clock hanging on the wall. "Smokey bought that ugly thing years ago after we spent a day without electricity. I hated the damn thing, but the next time the power went out, I learned to appreciate it. At least we knew what time it was. He changed the battery when we got here every fall and then when we left and kept extras in the kitchen drawer. Lord, I miss that man. He was so organized."

"It's not the breaker." Luke slumped down in the recliner. "Three thirty. We've still got hours before it's time to get up." He yawned. "I'm going to curl up in my makeshift sleeping bag again. Y'all going to sleep right here or going back to your rooms?"

Tootsie eased up out of the recliner. "I'm going back to bed, but I'll leave the door open to get some of the heat from the fireplace."

"I'll just pile on another blanket and go back to bed." Diana picked up her flashlight and headed toward the stairs. "See y'all when daylight comes. Maybe the power will be back on when we all wake up again. Good night."

"Good night," Tootsie and Luke said at the same time.

Tootsie turned her eyes back toward Luke. "We'll make you a softer bed for tomorrow night if we're still without power. Smokey bought one of those air mattresses when his old army buddies came to visit one fall, but we didn't need it, so it's still in the box somewhere. And we'll have to get out the generator and hook it up. It's only big enough to run the refrigerator and freezer, not the heating unit, but at least we won't lose all our food."

"I'll be fine, Aunt Tootsie, and I'll keep the fires burning to keep the chill off. Last weather report I saw on my phone said the rain was supposed to continue through Friday, but the temperatures are well above freezing." He yawned again. "If I had a fireplace in the motor home, I'd stay out there."

"And miss all the fun of having a tall redhead fall for you," Tootsie teased.

"Not for me, on me." He grinned.

"Potato. Pa-taw-toe. Ain't much difference," she threw over her shoulder as she started back to her room.

She snuggled down into the covers, laid her hand on the extra pillow, and whispered, "You're never going to believe what happened, Smokey." She went on to tell him all about Diana's fall. "And they were both embarrassed, so it proves that there's something going on there. What would you tell me to do about that? Ignore it and hope it goes away? Or encourage it?"

Smokey didn't have any words of wisdom for her.

"No electricity. Cold house and cold rain. You could at least whisper something in my ear." She waited and then sighed. "Okay, then, good night, darlin'."

~

135

The sound of rain falling all night gave Carmen the first good night's sleep she'd had since the divorce papers had been served. She checked the time on her cell phone and found that it was seven o'clock, so she pulled the chain on the antique lamp on her bedside table, and nothing happened.

"Bulb must be burned out," she muttered as she slung her feet over the side of the bed and pulled a sweatshirt over her head. With clouds still covering the sky, very little light came through the window. It seemed like a sign to her as she struggled to find two matching socks. Her marriage had grown dimmer by the day, but the storm wasn't really over yet.

Diana met her in the hallway. "Electricity is off."

"How are we going to make breakfast?" Carmen asked as she followed her downstairs.

Diana shrugged and dodged the crystal ball just in time. "The fireplace?"

"Good mornin'," Joanie said cheerfully from the kitchen. "I guess we're going to pretend that we're camping out today."

In the living room, Luke was bending over a big cast-iron skillet set up on an apparatus above the blaze in the fireplace, and the smell of bacon filled the whole room. "Soon as this is cooked, I'll make us a skillet of camp breakfast."

"And that is?" Diana asked.

"Potatoes, peppers, and onions cooked together, and then when that's done, I scramble eggs in with it," he answered.

"I lit lamps so we can see," Tootsie said.

Carmen looked around the living room at several oil lamps burning brightly. "I thought those were for decoration."

"Honey, when this house was first built, it had no electricity or water. Lamps were necessary, and they come in real handy when we lose power. My parents had the place wired and plumbed when they moved in. The only thing Smokey and I wished they'd have done different was put in a propane cookstove for times like this. We talked about having a gas stove in the motor home, but Smokey liked electric ones better. I may change it out to propane when I get home, just in case we ever get in a bind like this again," Tootsie explained.

"Wish I'd known that all I had to do was light one of them last night," Diana grumbled.

"And miss all the fun of falling on top of me?" Luke joked.

Carmen whipped around. "What happened?"

"I only had a little flashlight, and it didn't throw nearly enough light. I thought he was one of the ottomans." Diana blushed.

"I might have been sleeping on the floor, but I don't like to think that I look like a footstool." Luke grinned.

"I stumbled over him and fell. It was an accident," Diana stammered.

"And I found them all tangled up together like a bunch of baby kittens," Tootsie giggled.

"Now we want the real story," Joanie teased.

"That's their story, and they're stickin' to it," Tootsie chuckled.

"It's the truth, and the bacon is ready," Luke said. "Joanie, do you have the potatoes all cut up?"

"All ready when you are," Joanie said. "And thanks so much for taking my day. I've never cooked over a fire like that."

"I'll take care of the fire and food as long as we're without power," Luke said.

Diana groaned.

"What? You don't like that idea?" Luke asked.

"No, it's my job that I'm worried about. I need to send things to the company on Wednesdays and Fridays at the latest. Then they send me work on Mondays and Wednesdays. No internet or—"

"I can help there, too. I have a device on my laptop that lets me access internet anywhere, anytime. But we'll be running on battery and not electricity, so you'll have to be careful how much power you use," he warned. "I keep extra batteries for my business, so if you use up all yours, you can use my computer to send your work."

"Thank you. That's a load off my mind," Diana said.

"Now that we've got everything figured out about how we're going to survive in the wilderness, let's get the table set." Carmen tugged on Diana's arm and motioned for her to follow her to the pantry.

"Paper plates and plastic cutlery," Tootsie reminded them. "There's no hot water to do the dishes."

"What's going on?" Diana whispered.

"I think this storm and power outage is a sign. Eli has been cheating on me for years. Couples therapy probably wouldn't fix that. He's betrayed all the trust I put in him," Carmen said.

Diana gave her a side hug. "Without trust, there is no marriage. That's what my counselor told me when I was trying to hang on to what was already gone. The only thing left is for you to get what is legally yours and to learn to survive."

"That's sure enough not easy." Carmen drew in a long breath and let it out in a whoosh.

"No, honey, it's not, but you will live through it, just like I did," Diana said. "We've had each other's backs for the past eighteen years. Remember when the girls all got mono at the same time?"

"And when I had that miscarriage two years after Natalie was born? I thought for sure I'd lose my mind from worrying about if I caused it, because Eli didn't want more children and I wouldn't tell him I was pregnant," Carmen said.

"Are we remembering times when we had to lean on each other?" Joanie joined them at the middle of what Carmen said. "If so, how about when I fell off a ladder and broke my arm? The guys were gone, like they always were in any major problem, so y'all had to help for six weeks. You gave Zoe her baths every night and fixed her hair for school every morning, Carmen. And you did the cooking and cleanup for me, Diana."

"What would we do without each other?" Carmen tiptoed and hugged Diana. Joanie took a few steps forward and made it a three-way hug.

"We're sisters, not by blood but by the heart," Diana said. "You won't ever be without us."

Chapter Eleven

The whole idea of cooking over an open fire, eating by candlelight, and listening to rain hit the roof wasn't so bad the first day. But after breakfast on the second day, Joanie was ready to make a meal on a real stove, ready for the sun to shine through the window, and ready to use the lamps for decoration again. She'd gone to her bedroom and pulled a quilt up over her as she tried to read by the dim light coming through the window.

Carmen rapped on the doorjamb and stuck her head inside Joanie's room. "Are you as tired of this as I am?"

Joanie motioned her inside. "Worried as much as I'm tired of it. I don't want to be without a phone if Brett calls or if Zoe gets kicked out of basic."

"Don't worry about that." Carmen sat down in an old wooden rocking chair and set it in motion with her foot. "Luke's got a charger for his computer, and he's got spare batteries. He can keep our phones powered up. I love this place. It's like going back in time—from the iron bedsteads to the rocking chairs—and it's peaceful. I don't even mind eating soups cooked over the open flame. But I hate not having hot water. My hair feels like a grease pit. I'm tempted to take a cold shower and wash it."

"I will if you will." Joanie laid the book she'd been reading on the coffee table. "But something else is on your mind other than electricity and boredom. I can see it in your face."

"I'm going to let Eli have the divorce, but I'm not giving up everything. I'm going to fight him for the house. I'll find a job and take over the rest of the payments. The lady at the base where we take our clothing donations has been after me to come work for her for years. She takes care of a couple of dozen children at a time—those who've been separated from their parents or who have no legal parents. I may call her when I get home and see if there's still an opening," Carmen said. "But my home is Natalie's place to come to when she has time off, and I refuse to sell it."

"Okaaay." Joanie dragged out the word.

"That doesn't mean I'm not still angry," Carmen said.

"Understandable." Joanie tried to imagine how she would feel if she were walking in Carmen's shoes. One of those icy shivers chased down her spine when she thought of how distant and hasty Brett had been when he called the last few times.

Carmen swallowed a couple of times. "My marriage is like a dirty paper plate. It's time to throw it away. Even with counseling, things wouldn't ever be the same."

A loud clap of thunder rattled the windows at the same time Diana joined them.

"Well, that startled me," she said.

"As much as falling flat out on top of Luke last night?" Joanie teased.

Diana sat down on the edge of the bed. "No way. It'd take more than thunder to give me that kind of shock. I think I came in on Carmen saying her marriage is like paper plates."

"She's right about things not being the same," Joanie said and then turned her attention to Carmen. "You might be able to start all over and rebuild what you had, but it would take even more than the twenty years you've already put into the marriage."

"Why?" Carmen leaned forward, and the chair stopped rocking.

"Because you started out with a foundation of trust," Joanie answered. "Eli threw a hand grenade on that, and it's all shattered. Now you'd have to start with distrust, with wondering if he'd ever cheat on you again."

Diana nodded with every word. "That's what my therapist told me. It's not like starting from ground zero. It's more like digging a six-foot hole and trying to climb out of it after a hard rain."

Carmen kept rocking. "It doesn't mean I'm instantly over his cheating, but let's move on. What about this little spark between you and Luke?"

"It hasn't disappeared, but neither have the reasons for not encouraging it." Diana stood up. "Break time is over. Back to work. Have to get another several hours in before I can borrow Luke's gadget and send the files to the office."

"In other words, you're not going to talk about the vibes," Joanie teased.

"You got it." Diana waved as she went across the hallway to her bedroom.

Joanie remembered those first few flirtatious days with Brett. They both thought they were the first ones to ever discover love. Maybe that all-powerful emotion was what men craved when they were looking middle age in the eye. It definitely would make them feel young again. Was Brett looking over his shoulder at the past, like Eli, and wondering if he could re-create his youth? Was that why he was so rushed lately when he called? Previous deployments had allowed for time on the phone.

"Hey," Tootsie yelled from the bottom of the staircase, "anyone up for a game of dominoes?"

"Be right down," Carmen shouted and then turned to Joanie. "You comin'?"

Before she could answer, her phone rang, and she nodded. "It's Brett. He lately only has a few minutes, so don't start without me."

"Hello, darlin'," she answered the phone.

"Hello, I've got maybe five minutes at the most," Brett said. "So how's living in the backwoods?"

"It really is great except when there's no electricity. We're without power here for the second day now. I'm just glad it's not winter," she answered. "What's goin' on in whatever neck of the woods you're in?"

"Classified, for the most part. It seems like I've been keeping secrets forever," he said.

Joanie held her breath, fear gripping her heart. He was about to tell her that he wanted a divorce, too.

"Are you still there?" Brett asked.

"Yes, I'm here," she whispered. "Go on."

"I'll have my twenty years in about the same time as Zoe gets out of basic training. I'm thinking about retiring," he said. "I didn't want to mention it until I'd thought it over."

Tears welled up in her eyes. He and Eli were both leaving the military, and his next words would be that he had a new woman, too.

Stop it! That niggling voice in the back of her head screamed at her. *He's never given you any reason to doubt his fidelity.*

"Joanie, I know this is a lot to spring on you, but I had to think it through first. The team is splitting up since Eli and Kate are both leaving anyway," he said.

"Okay . . . ," she stammered.

"You sound like you're about to cry. Are you disappointed?" he asked. "It's just that I've been offered a civilian job. It's a nine-to-five teaching job at a private security firm, and it pays very well. Our plan was to stay until I had thirty years in, but . . ." He paused.

Joanie was speechless. She opened her mouth to talk, but words wouldn't come out. She'd dreamed about the day that Brett would retire from the service, but she'd never let herself think about that day coming sooner than another decade. There was no other woman. He'd been distant because he was trying to figure things out.

"If you don't like the idea, I can turn down the offer, but it's a good one and seems like a sign coming right now," Brett said.

"I love it," she spit out in a hurry. "I'm teary eyed, and, God, I wish you were here so I could show you how much I want you to do this. Where's the civilian job located?"

"That's the kicker, darlin'. We'd have to move away from Texas. I'd be working out of Washington, DC. I've been looking at apartments in Arlington, Virginia. That's only about three miles from one place to the other. You'd have to leave Carmen and Diana," he said.

"You are serious about this?" She pinched her leg to make sure she wasn't dreaming. "Have you told Gerald and Eli?"

"Yes, I'm very serious, and no, I haven't told them. Don't intend to until I get your thoughts on it. I was approached last year, but I had another year to put in before retirement. A couple of days ago, I got called again, and . . ." He paused and then went on. "And something you said about family affairs with Gerald and Eli and their new women stuck in my mind. I asked myself which was more important to me—my family or my friends? You came out at the top of the list."

"When do we put our house up for sale, and when do I start packing?" she asked.

His laughter was like honey to her soul. "I won't start the job until March first, but I have to give them an answer in the next two weeks."

"Do you need to think about it?" Joanie felt as if she were floating on air.

"Not since I've talked to you, but to be on the safe side, let's both do some serious thinking about it for one week anyway," he suggested.

"And now, after laying that bomb in your lap, I really have to go. I'll call when I can, and I hope the power comes back on real soon."

"Love you so much, Brett." She wanted to kick herself for doubting his faithfulness, even for a minute.

"Love you," he said.

She held the phone to her chest for a long time. Just the idea of Brett being home every evening would be the best Christmas present ever. Then suddenly the feeling disappeared. How in the world was she ever going to tell her two best friends that she was moving more than a thousand miles away from them?

~

Old habits die hard. On Friday afternoon, Diana flipped on the light as she started into the bathroom, then quickly switched it off, fussing at herself the whole time because she knew that there was no electricity. But she could have sworn the light fixture above the sink had come on.

"Figment of my imagination," she muttered. It had to be that the flickering candle she had carried carefully into the room had flared up because of a draft. She tried the switch again, and there was light. She tried it three more times, flipping it on and off, on, off, on, off, before she blew out the candle and washed her hands.

She went back out to the dining room, where the rest of the folks were deeply engrossed in a game of Monopoly by lamplight, and turned on the light fixture above the table. "Look what I discovered. I wonder how long it's been on and we didn't know it?"

Luke pushed back his chair. "I'll go take care of the generator. And I betcha we'll all be looking for places to recharge our laptops and phones."

"Praise the Lord!" Tootsie raised a hand toward the ceiling. "And I mean that in a very serious way. I've been wondering if I was going to have to show up at the Colbert family reunion on Sunday with store-bought food. This will be the first reunion I'll attend without Smokey, so everyone will be looking to see what I brought."

"Aunt Tootsie, we all know your talents are not in the kitchen," Luke said on his way out the door.

"Well, I'm still glad that I don't have to go with a can of corn and a loaf of bread," she said. "Now, you three girls tell me what we're taking."

"Chicken and dressing. I'm going to put the chicken in a slow cooker right now and let it cook all night so the broth will be rich," Carmen said.

"Cranberry-orange salad and a chocolate cake," Joanie offered.

Tootsie rubbed her hands together. "You should make a sample cake tonight just so we can be sure the oven is baking just right."

"I'll be glad to." Joanie pushed back her chair.

Tootsie looked up at Diana. "And what are you making for us to take?"

"Marinated vegetables and taco casserole." Diana smiled. "I'll do the vegetables tomorrow morning and the casserole Sunday morning so it'll be fresh."

Tootsie clapped her hands. "We're going to have so much fun. I can't wait to introduce y'all to all Smokey's relatives. He's been talkin' about y'all for years."

"I didn't know we were invited," Diana said. "We can just cook and send it with you and Luke."

"Oh, no." Luke came in from the garage. "Y'all have to go with us, and one of you has to pretend to be my girlfriend so Aunt Mary Lou will stop trying to fix me up."

"I'm married." Joanie held up her left hand to show off her rings.

Carmen shook her head. "I'm not even divorced yet."

Luke looked over at Diana and wiggled his eyebrows. "I guess it's you. Wear that pretty outfit you wore to the funeral."

"Oh, no!" Diana threw up both palms.

"Why not? It'll only be for a few hours, and he's right. Mary Lou has been drivin' him crazy for years." Tootsie said.

"You owe me. I've been letting you use my device to send in your work. I can always refuse to let you have it anymore," Luke teased.

"No PDAs." Diana held up a finger.

"Done," Luke agreed.

"No telling my age." Another finger shot up.

"Wouldn't dream of it. Why, Aunt Mary Lou might pass clean out at the thought," he teased.

She laughed in spite of herself. "And no telling anyone about me falling on top of you." The third finger joined the other two.

"You got it, but I really hate giving up that last one. It would have my uncles all in stitches." Luke winked.

"Okay, we've got that settled, and the power is back on, so I can really see y'all's faces." Joanie motioned for everyone to sit down. "I've got news."

"Is it about Eli?" Carmen melted into a chair.

"Are you pregnant? You've been acting strange the past few days," Diana said.

"No, it's not about Eli, and I'm definitely not pregnant, thank God," Joanie answered. "I have to admit that I've been worried. Brett has been so abrupt when he calls that I was afraid that—"

"That he was following in Eli's footprints," Carmen finished for her.

"It's understandable that you'd have doubts," Diana said.

Joanie rolled the dice and moved ahead five spaces. She landed on the Go to Jail space. "I feel so guilty about not trusting Brett that I deserve to be in jail. Okay—here's the deal. Brett has an offer from a civilian firm to teach survival skills to private security recruits, and he thinks he's going to put in his twenty-year retirement papers."

"Oh, my gosh!" Diana squealed. "That's amazing news."

"When? Where?" Carmen jumped up to hug her and almost knocked the Monopoly board on the floor.

"He'll be home for good after Zoe gets out of basic, and . . ." She dreaded saying any more, but these were her friends. "And we'll be moving to a suburb of Arlington."

"That's not so very far away," Tootsie said. "It's only a couple of hours from Sugar Run over to Dallas, and Arlington is right there. You can come back to see us every week."

"Arlington, Virginia. He'll be working out of Washington, DC, but we won't move until spring," Joanie said all at once and watched their faces turn from happy to sad in an instant. "Please be happy for me. I can't stand it if you're not."

Tears rolled down Carmen's face. "I'm happy for you, but I'm sad at the same time. We've been through so much together, but I'd have gladly moved with Eli if it would have saved my marriage."

Tootsie's chin quivered. "I moved many times with Smokey. I'd never hold you back, but at the same time, I'll miss you so much."

Diana's world took another downward spin. She couldn't say that she didn't want Joanie to go, because that might be the very thing that kept her marriage intact. And yet she couldn't bear to think of not seeing her again. Finally, she leaned down, hugged Joanie, and said, "All I got to say is that you'd better rent or buy a house with a couple of extra bedrooms and make sure your phone is charged at all times. I refuse to ever say goodbye, but when the time comes, I will say 'See you later' and mean it with my whole heart. We will make a way to visit at least every other month."

"That's good," Tootsie said. "Delores and I have decided that we need to stay in touch more often than we have in the past. You girls hold to that every-other-month idea, and make it work."

Diana patted Tootsie on the shoulder. "Not only us. You're part of this family, so you have to make time for visits, too."

"Thank you." Tootsie's voice broke. "We are family, aren't we?"

Diana hugged her. "Of course we are. We're all here right now living under the same roof."

"And it takes more than blood and DNA to make a family," Carmen said from across the table.

"Well, then, we'll take the motor home anytime y'all want to. Maybe we'll meet in the middle, like somewhere around Nashville part of the time. That way none of us have to go as far." In her usual manner, Tootsie was already making plans for them, and Diana loved her for it. "And Luke can drive us so we can all be together a few times a year."

"I'm sure willing," Luke said.

"If we move in March, then we could plan a Nashville trip in May," Joanie said.

"And we can do coffee together every morning like always, only on FaceTime." Carmen still didn't look happy, but she was trying. Bless her heart, she'd been through so much the past couple of weeks.

"We're so lucky to have been able to raise our girls on the same block all these years," Diana said. "Most army wives would have moved half a dozen times in thirteen years. We're just lucky that the team got to stay at Camp Bullis all this time."

"And that the government wanted to keep it together." Joanie paid her phony money to get out of jail. "I wonder what will happen to the team now that Eli and Brett are both retiring. Will they just start a new one, or will they get replacements and maybe let Gerald be team leader?"

"Who knows? It's the government. But on driving y'all, I'm glad to do that anytime you want," Luke offered.

Diana had forgotten that Luke was in the room. She whipped around to find him standing so close to her that she could see the small crow's-feet around his eyes. The scruff on his face was a little longer than usual, but then he couldn't really keep it well groomed without his electric razor.

"That's so sweet of you, and we may take you up on that more often than you realize," Tootsie said.

"Thank you." Diana held her hands behind her back to keep from reaching up and touching his face to see if the light-brown hair was as soft as it looked. "Now that we have power, I'm going to go upstairs and get to work. See y'all at suppertime. Whose turn is it to cook? We've gotten off schedule with the funeral and no electricity."

Luke raised his hand. "I'll take care of it tonight, and we can start all over tomorrow with Carmen, then Joanie on Monday, since we have the reunion on Sunday, and you on Tuesday, Diana. How's that?"

"Great," Diana muttered as she escaped to her bedroom and picked up an old magazine to fan her face. Lord have mercy! She had to get over this infatuation with Luke.

A rap on her door startled her so badly that she threw the magazine halfway across the floor. "Come in," she said, expecting it to be Carmen.

Luke slung open the door and held his Wi-Fi device. "Thought you might need this."

"Thank you," she muttered as she took it from him. Warmth spread from her fingertips through her body when her fingers brushed across his palm. She took a step backward and laid the device on the bedside table. She figured she'd see his back as he left the room when she looked up, but he'd taken a couple of steps closer.

He traced the edge of her face with his forefinger, sending heat waves all the way to her toes. "You were named right, Diana. She was the goddess of the hunt, the moon, and nature in Roman mythology. She even had the power to talk to animals."

It was downright geeky and nerdy but yet still the most romantic thing anyone had ever said to her. Before she could say a word, his lips closed over hers in a searing-hot kiss that weakened her knees. Age, time, place—the universe stood still, and the only people occupying the whole world were Luke and Diana. She felt like a goddess when his arms went around her and drew her even closer.

One kiss led to another and still another. They were both panting when they heard someone coming up the stairs, and they stepped back from each other. "How long are we going to deny this thing between us? Something stirred in my heart when we shook hands the first time." Luke locked eyes with her.

Diana heard Carmen's door open across the hallway, so she took another step back. Then Carmen rapped on the door and stuck her head inside. "Hey, can I come in, or are you busy?"

"Let's talk about it later," Diana whispered to Luke.

Luke nodded. "I'll come back and get the device in a couple of hours. I've got a couple of things to do before I need to see what's going on in the cyber world today."

"You really like him, don't you?" Carmen cocked her head to one side once he was gone.

"No. Yes. Maybe it's just lust, but right now, no matter what it is or isn't, we have too much on our friendship platter to deal with this. You're going through a divorce. Tootsie's still in mourning, and now Joanie is probably moving away from us. That's enough drama for now. I don't need to add romance to it." Diana flipped on the light. "I'll never take being able to do that for granted again."

Carmen sat down on the edge of the bed. "You're changing the subject."

"Yes, I am, and now I'm doing it again. How are you with Joanie moving?"

"Horrible. I can't imagine life without her there every day," Carmen admitted. "But I'm not telling her that, not when it means that she can be with Brett every day and there'll be no more deployments or missions."

"Me, too." Diana sat down beside her.

But her mind wasn't on Joanie—it was on the way her lips still felt hot after that steamy little make-out session and how she had wanted to walk backward to the bed and pull Luke down on it with her.

Chapter Twelve

*L*uke awoke the next morning in the motor home but didn't jump out of bed like usual. He pulled up the covers around his neck and thought about the kisses he and Diana had shared. He'd always heard that in order to really know a person, you should live with them for a little while or at least walk a mile in their shoes. He'd never be able to put his big size 12 foot in Diana's shoes, but he had lived with her for eleven days now, and he liked her a lot. She was strong, independent, and beautiful, and if the little bit of age difference was the only thing between them, he'd convince her that it was nothing by the time he drove them all home to Sugar Run.

He threw off the covers and padded naked to the bathroom. Sleeping in the raw was one of the benefits of living in the motor home alone. The downside was that he missed making breakfast over the open fire and listening to the ladies all brag on him about how good it was.

For years, he'd worked alone, and when he hired a small staff to help with his business, he'd still spent most of his time in his office—alone. He'd thought that was what he liked, where he felt comfortable, but this trip had proved he'd been wrong. He liked being around people and didn't even mind the drama.

He made sure the right guard was on his electric razor and ran it over his face, then brushed his teeth and combed his mop of light-brown hair. Looking at his reflection in the small mirror above the sink, he made the decision that when he started his next company, he was doing it with help from the very beginning. He'd started on a shoestring before and had trouble delegating even when he hired an assistant. It drove them both insane. But this time he was going in fully staffed with an administrative team and a couple of IT specialists to help him. He didn't intend to spend eighteen hours a day at work anymore.

He dressed in jeans and a T-shirt and picked up a jacket but found out he didn't need it when he stepped out of the motor home. The sun shone brightly in a cloudless, beautiful blue sky that morning. He slung the jacket over his shoulder and whistled from the motor home to the house, where he left his muddy shoes on the rug right inside the door.

"Something smells wonderful in here," he called out.

"Bacon, coffee, and waffles with either syrup or canned peaches and whipped cream," Carmen said. "It'll all be on the table in about five minutes."

"Good morning," Diana said from about halfway down the stairs.

His heart threw in an extra beat when he saw her. She really did look like a goddess even though she was wearing a pair of jeans and a faded T-shirt. He nodded and said, "Good morning to you."

She'd said they'd talk later, but there hadn't been an opportunity the day before. Hopefully today they'd find a few minutes alone. He was a patient man, so he didn't mind waiting to actually date her until they were back in Sugar Run. Besides, she had a lot on her mind with the drama of Carmen's divorce and the possibility of Joanie moving away.

"So how do you like your waffles?" he asked when she reached the bottom step. "Syrup? Or fruit and whipped cream?"

"Maple syrup, and lots of it." Diana's smile warmed his heart. "How about you?"

"Same," he said. "See there, we have lots in common. We both like to watch squirrels and like the same kind of waffles. I'd call that a foundation."

"Maybe," she said softly, "but you can't build it on sand. Remember your Sunday-school lessons about that?"

"And that little song they taught us about how the rain came tumbling down?" Luke flashed a bright grin her way.

"Don't even say that word," Tootsie yelled from the kitchen. "I've had enough rain to last me a year. I won't even complain about the heat in Sugar Run next summer after this."

Luke crooked his little finger around Diana's for just a moment; then he let go and headed toward the dining room. "I just hope the sun dries out the yard and road enough today that we don't have trouble getting the motor home out onto it. What can I do to help?"

"Bring the coffeepot in, and fill the cups," Carmen said.

"I'll pour the juice," Diana offered. "Looks like that's all that's left. You're going to be a hard act to follow—but wait, I don't have to follow you because tomorrow we go to the reunion. That means Joanie has Monday, right?"

"You lucked out on that day, but you'll have to cook on . . ." Luke counted days on his fingers. "Next Saturday, and we'll expect gourmet."

"Oh, honey, I make a mean gourmet bologna sandwich with tomatoes, lettuce, mustard, pickles, and even black olives and peppers," Diana teased.

"Sounds like a great Saturday-night supper to me." Tootsie went on to tell them all about the bologna nights she and Delores had shared. "But you've got kitchen duty all day. We can do the fancy sandwiches for supper, but we'll expect to have something great for dinner."

"Like your enchiladas," Carmen suggested. "The chicken ones with white sauce and your special rice and beans to go with them."

"Sounds good to me." Luke finished with the coffee and took his place at the head of the table.

"You'll never want to go to a Mexican restaurant again after you've eaten her food," Joanie said. "Her grandmother came up here from

Mexico when she married Diana's grandfather. Diana learned how to cook from her."

Surely they were kidding. Diana had that milk-and-honey complexion that usually went with the English or Swedish folk. And red hair! They were pulling his leg for sure.

"My grandfather was Scottish and married a Mexican girl. My father married a blonde-haired girl he met while he was in the army and based in England," Diana said. "My daughter, Rebecca, is dark haired and has brown eyes. Her skin is the color of coffee with lots and lots of cream. She's a throwback to my grandmother and is even talented musically, like Grammy. I tell her all the time that as long as she's alive, my grandmother Marie Sanchez McTavish lives on in this world."

Luke found himself wondering what kind of child he and Diana might have. It wasn't even a remote possibility, but the thought wouldn't leave his mind all through breakfast.

~

The kitchen grew crowded and crazy that afternoon. Joanie just stood back and enjoyed the bickering among Diana, Luke, and Carmen for oven time or counter space to roll out pie dough or cut up vegetables. She'd miss days like this so much, and yet when she thought of Brett being home to have supper with her every night—words couldn't describe the joy in her soul.

Tootsie yawned. "There's too damn many cooks in this little kitchen. I'm going to take a nap. If y'all get to fightin', just keep it down, because if you wake me up, I'll be an old bear the rest of the day."

"I'm going to strip down my bed and wash my sheets while we're getting stuff ready for the reunion." Joanie went to her bedroom, sat down on the bed, and sent a text to Brett: I'm all in.

The phone rang immediately. "You sure about this? It hasn't been a week. Did you tell Carmen and Diana?"

"Yes, I did," she said. "And Tootsie says we'll meet halfway every couple of months and spend a couple of days together in her motor home, so it's not like we'll never see each other again, and if you want to go to a yearly reunion thing for the team, that's up to you."

"Things aren't the same here, darlin', since Eli is . . . well, you know . . . and Gerald has encouraged that whole thing from the beginning. It's not the team that it was when we first started, so I doubt that I'll be going to any of the reunions," Brett said. "I'm lookin' forward to a brand-new start in a different place with you."

"Then let's do it. Get the paperwork started, and call the people who offered you the job. When you get home in a few weeks, we'll talk to a real estate agent and make a trip to Virginia to find us a place," she said.

"You are amazing," Brett said. "I'm going to call the company and tell them I'll take the job."

"Time is going to pass so slow between now and Zoe's graduation," Joanie sighed.

"Hey, I went through a few channels and found out that the graduation is December seventh, on a Saturday. I'll be getting in on December fourth. Think you could be in Lawton by then?" he asked. "I'll have a hotel room all ready for us."

"I'll be there with bells on my toes." Everything seemed right now that it was settled.

"I'd rather you be there in that cute little red lace teddy," he whispered.

"Your wish and all that." She made a mental note to get somewhere between now and then to buy some sexy lingerie. That red thing had gotten eaten by the washing machine.

"Love you," he said.

"Love you." The call ended, and she held the phone to her heart. "Please come home to me safe. We're so close to the finish line. Don't get hurt or killed now."

Carmen poked her head into the door. "Are you okay?"

"Just sending up a prayer that Brett comes home in one piece," Joanie answered honestly. "I'll worry until he's here."

"Even more than before?" Carmen asked.

Joanie laid the phone on the vanity. "More than ever, because when he comes home, he'll be here forever. We all live in fear of a black government car driving up to the curb and two uniformed soldiers bringing the news that our husbands were killed in action. But now that the time when he retires is only weeks away, I'm scared out of my mind that something bad will happen."

"If anyone understands, Diana and I do." Carmen slipped an arm around Joanie's shoulders. "Just think, though. You get to tell Zoe good news, and I have to tell Natalie bad news."

"I'm so sorry," Joanie's voice cracked. "But this isn't on you to tell her. It's Eli's job."

"No, it's mine, because she needs to hear it from me. I'm the one who stayed home and raised her. I'm the one who sat up with her at night when she was sick, the one who held her when her first boyfriend broke up with her. Eli has been a good father, but I need to tell her, because she'll need comforting," Carmen said.

"Are you going to tell her before basic is done?"

Carmen shrugged. "I don't think so. It might hinder her, and then that would be my fault. I'll tell her to her face so I can hold her when she cries."

"What if Eli tells her first?"

"I'm going to tell him that the only way I'll sign the papers is if he keeps his mouth shut. If he goes against his word, I'll shoot him."

"If you do, Diana and I'll borrow Tootsie's shovels and bury him so far back in the woods that the coyotes can't even find him." Joanie meant every word. That Gerald's and Eli's actions could cause her to have doubts about Brett made her twice as angry as she might have been.

"Our worlds are sure changing, aren't they?" Carmen started out of the room.

"In a couple of years we're going to look back and see that everything that happened was for the best."

Carmen stopped at the door. "I hope so."

So do I, Joanie thought as she started taking the sheets off her bed.

Chapter Thirteen

Tootsie had always loved the Colbert family reunion, but that morning she awoke dreading it. Even though she'd been a part of the family for sixty years, Smokey wouldn't be by her side when she walked into the church fellowship hall.

But I left you with four kids to take to the reunion, Smokey's voice reminded her.

"Yes, but I miss you. I can get by in the day, even when they're arguing over who gets the oven next or who has rights to the washing machine first, but it's not you, Smokey," she whispered.

My body is gone, but you've still got my heart and my spirit. Take those with you today.

"Oh, I will. Without those I'd refuse to go at all." She threw back the covers when she got a whiff of bacon and coffee. "This reminds me of you so much. You'd sneak out of bed and get breakfast going before I ever woke up."

She waited for a long time, but Smokey didn't have anything else to say. Finally, with a long sigh, she slung her legs over the side of the bed, put on her slippers and a robe, and made her way to the kitchen.

"Good mornin'," Diana said. "You're the first one up today. Coffee is ready."

Tootsie went to the pot and filled a mug, then added two spoons of sugar and enough cream to turn it light brown. "I thought you weren't cookin' until next week sometime."

"I woke up early, so I thought I'd do breakfast this morning. What time do we leave for the reunion?" Diana brought an omelet out of the oven and put in a pan of biscuits.

"Ten o'clock. That'll get us there in time to get our food on the tables and do a little visiting. Grace is said at twelve o'clock sharp. Then we eat and visit all afternoon. We usually gather up our dirty plates and start home around four," Tootsie answered between sips of coffee.

The front door opened, and the sound of Luke's whistling preceded him into the kitchen. "What is that delicious-looking thing on the top of the stove?"

"That would be one of Diana's oven omelets." Tootsie could actually feel the vibes bouncing off the two of them. Why, oh why, hadn't she thought to introduce them a year or even two years ago?

Because Luke always visited us here in Scrap, not in Sugar Run, Smokey reminded her.

He was at your funeral. I could have made them acquainted then, she argued.

Too many people were there, and you weren't really thinking about playing matchmaker. She could imagine Smokey's deep chuckle, and it warmed her heart.

She opened her mouth to fuss at him but then snapped it shut. The kids would think she'd done lost her marbles if they knew how often she talked out loud to Smokey.

"Good mornin', all y'all." Joanie waved as she headed to the coffeepot.

Carmen arrived right behind her. "You take forever to get your coffee dosed up just right. Let me go before you—I drink it black."

"Get up earlier than me if you want to be first in line," Joanie said.

"No bickering on reunion day. Today you'll be good." Tootsie waggled a finger at all of them and giggled. "I always wanted kids so I could say that kind of thing to them."

"Why didn't you have a houseful?" Carmen asked. "You are such a good mama to all of us and a grandmother to our girls."

"God didn't see fit to give us our own children. Smokey and I both had problems, but He did give us y'all in our old age, so we felt blessed," Tootsie said.

"That is so sweet." Diana bent to hug her. "We feel that God blessed us by letting us all move in on your block so you and Smokey could be part of our lives."

Joanie finally finished adding sugar and hazelnut-flavored creamer to her coffee and carried it to the dining room. "Well, somebody got up early. The table is already set and ready."

"Couldn't sleep," Diana admitted.

"Me, either." Luke covered a yawn with his free hand.

What's happened between them that's kept them both awake? Tootsie stole sideways glances at each of them. *Something sure has, because they're fidgety this morning.*

"So you haven't backed out, have you?" Luke nudged Diana.

"Nope, I'm your date from right before noon until four o'clock." The blush that turned her cheeks a faint shade of pink didn't escape Tootsie's all-seeing eyes.

"Why those hours?" Joanie called out from the dining room.

"That's when we get there and when we leave." Diana took the biscuits from the oven and carried them straight to the table.

"Does it involve a good-afternoon kiss?" Carmen teased.

"It does not," Diana declared.

"How about some hand holding or long gazing looks into each other's eyes?" Joanie asked.

"Maybe, since we've got to sell it to Aunt Mary Lou." Luke followed her to the table with the casserole pan in his hands.

Now Tootsie couldn't wait to get to the reunion. Watching Mary Lou's expression when she saw that Luke had brought a tall red-haired beauty to introduce to the family would be a hoot.

~

Diana could put on a fantastic front, but down deep she had a case of nerves going on that morning as they drove the motor home from Scrap to Paris. Acting had never been something she was good at, and now she had to be a pretend girlfriend. She wanted to sell it, as Luke had said. When Luke parked the motor home out on the edge of the church parking lot, she shut her eyes and sent up a silent prayer that she wouldn't blow the whole thing and make a laughingstock out of Luke.

Don't pretend. Just go with your heart, and make it real, the pesky voice in her head said. *You like him. He likes you. For one afternoon, don't fight it.*

She looked up at the ceiling and mouthed, "Thank you."

All five of them carried a dish of some kind through the side door of the kitchen. Once they were inside, several people rushed to give Tootsie hugs and ask how she was holding up. It wasn't Carmen's, Diana's, or Joanie's first rodeo when it came to potluck dinners, and the tables weren't set up any different from when they'd had dinners for army wives who'd lost their husbands on the battlefields. Meat dishes first, vegetables and fruits next, breads beyond that, and desserts last. Iced tea, lemonade, coffee, and water were on a separate table.

A short gray-haired lady with a face like a shrunken potato pushed her walker over to Luke and tapped her wrinkled cheek with a forefinger. He bent down and gave her a quick kiss, then motioned for Diana.

"Aunt Mary Lou, I'd like you to meet my girlfriend, Diana McTavish." Luke draped an arm around Diana's shoulders and pulled her close to his side.

It wasn't difficult to listen to her mind—or was that bit of advice coming from her heart?—and not fight it. It actually felt really good to be close to him and not feel like she should step away.

Aunt Mary Lou's eyes started at Diana's shoes and traveled slowly up past her flowing skirt to the green blouse that was topped with a matching cardigan. She had to raise her head to see Diana's face and red hair.

"A good Irishwoman, I see." Mary Lou nodded. "I'm pleased to meet you."

"My pleasure," Diana said. "But I'm really Scottish, not Irish."

"That's even better." Mary Lou shifted her focus back to Luke. "Hang on to this one. Y'all will make pretty babies."

Diana's cheeks burned so hot that she was sure if she looked in a mirror, they'd be scarlet. "Well, thank you, ma'am. I hope that any babies we might have get his blue eyes." They'd never have children, but saying that had come out so easy that she felt herself falling right into the role of his girlfriend.

"And Diana's gorgeous hair." Luke brushed a sweet kiss on Diana's forehead. "We'll talk more later, Aunt Mary Lou. I want to introduce Diana to Uncle Clarence before he gets to telling his war stories to the other guys."

"You better hurry if you intend to do that." Mary Lou flipped her walker around and headed off toward the group of women surrounding Tootsie.

"You did good. So you want our kids to have my blue eyes?" Luke whispered.

"Of course I do." She smiled up at him.

He brushed a soft kiss across her lips. "That's to make sure they believe that I can really get a woman like you." He removed his arm from her shoulders and laced his fingers in hers.

Clarence met them halfway across the room. A tall, stocky man with bulldog cheeks and deep-set eyes, he reminded Diana of Smokey.

"This is the oldest living Colbert brother since Uncle Smokey passed away," Luke said. "He spent some time in the army during the Vietnam era."

"Yes, I was, and, honey, I can tell you some stories." His deep voice brought Smokey right back to life.

"I bet you can." Diana smiled.

Luke gently squeezed her hand. "We'll have to hear them later. We've got to make the rounds."

"Well, darlin', if you get tired of Luke, I've got an unmarried son still left that I'd love to introduce you to." Clarence winked.

"I don't think I'll ever get tired of him, but if I was to ever throw him over the fence, I just might give you a call," Diana teased.

"And she's got a sense of humor, too," Clarence said. "Smokey talked about you girls so much that I feel like I know you. Is that Carmen and Joanie over there with Tootsie?"

Diana nodded.

"Well, I got to go meet them. Maybe one of them will be interested in my bachelor son." Clarence left them standing there and shuffled over to the other side of the room.

"Do I get an Emmy?" Diana asked.

"Well, darlin', I had a mind to name our red-haired daughter Fiona to keep in line with your Scottish blood, but if you like the name Emmy better, then I won't fight you over it," he joked as he pulled her toward another group of relatives.

"I like Fiona just fine. When's the baby due? Why wasn't I invited to the wedding?" A lady tapped Luke on the shoulder.

"No wedding yet, Linda June," Luke said. "And I would never leave you off the guest list unless we decide to elope to Paris—that's France, not Texas—or have an Elvis wedding in Las Vegas." He turned to bring Diana in closer. "Honey, I want you to meet my cousin Linda June. And this is my girlfriend, Diana McTavish."

Long gray braids hung down the sides of Linda June's body. She wore bell-bottom jeans and a tie-dyed T-shirt. Several strands of multicolored beads hung around her neck, and she sported a peace-sign tattoo on one arm and a butterfly on the other.

"Well, darlin'," Linda June whispered, "if y'all ever want to forget about what society thinks and join my commune, I can make room for you."

The woman had best not make that offer to Carmen. To get away from having to go home to an empty nest, she just might take her up on it. Come to think of it, Diana might throw her laptop in the trash and run away herself.

And leave Tootsie? There was that voice again.

No, she'd never do that, and neither would Carmen. Tootsie had been too good to them to desert her. But it was tempting.

"Thanks for the offer, but we're pretty happy where we are. See you later." Luke pulled Diana in the opposite direction. They went through a door and a hallway and wound up in the church sanctuary.

"Break time. We'll go back for act two in a little bit. That'll involve sitting beside me at the dinner table, but you're doin' good." He let go of her hand and sat down on the back pew.

She melted into the place right beside him. "Linda June is a trip, but I've got to admit, her offer to run away to a commune sounded kind of good."

"Takes all kinds." He brushed a strand of hair from her face. "I hadn't considered a commune." He rubbed a hand across his chin. "But I'll go if you will."

Diana giggled. "I could never do that. Tell me about her. Seems like she kind of got stuck in the hippie days."

"You are so right." He nodded. "She's Aunt Mary Lou's only child. Mary Lou is the oldest child in the Colbert family, and she had Linda June when she was about sixteen or seventeen. So Linda June is probably

166

close to seventy, but she never got past her bell-bottom jeans and all that went with them."

Heat from his touch raised the temperature in the sanctuary at least ten degrees. "Does she have children?" Diana asked.

"About ten or maybe eleven, but only the last five belong to the man she's still with now. From what I understand, they all live in the commune with her. She's the queen bee of the place," he said. "After meeting her and Aunt Mary Lou, you'll break up with me at five after four for sure, and I had my hopes set on this being the foundation of an amazing relationship."

Diana poked him in the ribs. "If I was in love with you, it would take more than a few crazy relatives for me to throw you over the pasture fence. And besides, you haven't met my family. They'd probably put this one to shame."

"Oh!" He raised an eyebrow. "Is that an invitation to meet *your* cousins?"

"No, sir. My cousins would try to seduce you," she teased.

"Does one of them have red hair? I'm a sucker for redheads." His eyes glittered.

"Yes, Molly does, and she has six kids. I think two of them have the same father, but that's only because they're twins. She believes in free will. It would be like dating Linda June, only younger. I'll have to warn you that most of her walls are painted with ketchup or mustard. Or whatever was in the diaper that day. But you go ahead and flirt with her when you come to my family reunion." She patted him on the cheek.

"Let's invite them all to our wedding, darlin'. Molly's kids can smear cake icing on the floor, and Linda June can offer to take them all to her commune." He picked up her hand, brought it to his lips, and whispered, "Aunt Mary Lou has opened the door enough to peek through."

Diana smiled up at him when he kissed her knuckles and then wrapped her arms around his neck, twined her fingers into his hair, and brought his face to hers for a long, lingering kiss. When it ended, she moved over to sit in his lap and whispered in his ear, "Now there's three sets of eyes on us. Man, they really do want to see you settled down, don't they?"

This was turning out to be a hell of a lot more fun than she'd ever imagined. It was like being a sophomore in high school and making out in the back seat of a car, plus the excitement of being just a little devious in tricking folks into believing that she and Luke were a couple.

"I'm the baby of all the grandkids," he told her. "My dad was the youngest child, coming along when my grandmother was past forty. And then he died before any of them, and they think they owe it to the family to see me married. I'm going to kiss you again. Pretend like you like it."

"I'll do my best," she said, just before his hand moved to the back of her head and his lips closed over hers again. She definitely didn't have to pretend that she liked it—not one bit. Chest to chest, their hearts were both beating so fast that they were out of breath when a loud clanging noise ended the kiss. It startled Diana so badly that she jumped up out of his lap in fight-or-flight mode.

"Dinner bell." Luke stood up and took her hand in his. "Everyone gathers round the oldest child in the Colbert family, Aunt Mary Lou, to say grace, and then the feasting begins."

He led her back through the door into the kitchen area, where everyone already had their heads bowed. Mary Lou had pushed her walker to the middle of the circle and waited until Luke and Diana had taken a place beside Tootsie.

"Let us pray," Mary Lou said as she bowed her head. "Father in heaven, thank you for bringing us together one more time for this reunion. Bless our time together, and go with us as we all travel home for another year. Thank you for the hands that prepared this food and for giving our Luke a girlfriend. Amen."

Now she felt horrible for tricking these good folks. It's a wonder God didn't send a lightning bolt right down from heaven to strike her graveyard-dead for what she was doing. But she couldn't say a word, not when it would make Luke look like a fool. She cared too much for him to do that.

When the short prayer ended and everyone raised their heads, all eyes were on her and Luke. He just grinned, raised his and Diana's clasped hands, and said, "Amen!"

Everyone joined in with a hearty "Amen!" and then Mary Lou shuffled to start the buffet line.

"Does it work from the oldest to the youngest for dinner, too?" Diana asked.

"Linda June will help Aunt Mary Lou get her food first, but after that, it's every man for himself. You want to go back to the sanctuary and make out some more, or do you want to eat?"

Diana almost said that she'd rather make out just to wipe that devilish grin off Luke's face. But instead she said, "Oh, darlin', we used up so much energy with those hot kisses that we probably should eat hearty for the next session."

"Smart girl," Uncle Clarence said right behind them.

Diana fought the heat creeping up from her neck to her cheeks. She'd blushed more that morning than she had in her entire lifetime. These poor people were going to be so disappointed next year when Luke showed up again without a girlfriend. Or maybe he would have found a real someone by then.

How does that make you feel? Her mother's voice popped into her head again.

Just a little jealous after those kisses, Diana admitted.

Did you think about the age difference when you were sitting on his lap? Diana shook her head.

Has anyone in this room asked you if you were older than Luke?

No, but I know, Diana argued.

"Are you okay?" Luke asked. "You're a little pale."

"Just hungry." Diana wasn't going to admit that she had voices in her head, not with so many of his relatives hanging on every word and watching every move she and Luke made.

"We can fix that, sweetheart," Uncle Clarence said. "Y'all just come with me." He took Diana by the arm and led her right to the front of the line. "This pretty lady and Luke need to be next," he said loudly. "She's our guest of honor, after all."

Diana was so embarrassed that she wanted to crawl under a table. When she had agreed to be Luke's girlfriend for the reunion, she wasn't thinking it would be such a big deal, and she felt horrible for duping all his relatives. But she was far too invested in the charade now to back out. It would break their hearts and make Luke look like an idiot.

"Thank you, sir," she said.

"That's Uncle Clarence to you, darlin'," he drawled.

She smiled and nodded. "Then thank you, Uncle Clarence."

She focused on all the food to keep from thinking about the pretense and loaded up her plate with little bits of everything until she scurried out of room. Then she carried her plate to a table on the other side of the room from Aunt Mary Lou. Luke sat down beside her with his food, and pretty soon Tootsie, Carmen, and Joanie joined them.

Joanie nudged her with an elbow the moment she sat down. "Where'd you two disappear to?"

"We checked out the church," Diana answered.

"The lady with the walker was peeking in the door, too. What's on the other side?"

Diana said, "Let's talk later."

"Hey, this is the best ham I've ever eaten," Carmen said from across the table.

"Dr Pepper," Tootsie said.

"What?"

"It's Linda June's recipe. All she does is pour a bottle of Dr Pepper on it and bake it slowly," Tootsie answered. "She brings it every year.

170

She and her husband raise their own hogs and chickens and a steer or two every year. She does her own sugar curing and always brings a ham to the reunion, but the secret is the soda pop."

Diana was glad to talk recipes and food instead of what had gone on in the sanctuary. Her mother was right—when she was making out with Luke, she hadn't thought one second about the age difference between them, and she needed some time to sort all that out before she talked about it.

Chapter Fourteen

*D*iana changed into her pajama pants and a tank top and was busy rubbing lotion on her feet when her door opened. Both Carmen and Joanie came in uninvited and crawled up in the middle of her bed.

"It's later now, so talk," Joanie said.

"About?" Diana played dumb.

"We've been patient and didn't say a word about your date, but now we want to hear how you felt about being his girlfriend," Carmen said.

"Don't you dare start without me." Tootsie came into the room huffing and puffing. "I forgot how much energy it takes to get up those stairs."

"Start what?" Diana asked.

"Y'all may be empty nesters because your daughters all left, but I'm one because my husband is gone, so we're in the same boat. That means I get to listen to Diana's side of the story. Mary Lou told me that y'all were in the sanctuary making out like teenagers and that she prayed to God that He'd close his eyes and look the other way. She said losing Smokey was enough for one year, and she didn't have the energy to go to another funeral, so God was to look the other way for a little while." Tootsie kicked off her slippers and got on the bed with the others.

"You've heard it all, then, so there's no reason for me to say anything," Diana said.

"I want to know how it felt to kiss another man," Carmen said. "I can't imagine being even that intimate with anyone other than Eli, and yet, the thought of kissing him right now makes me nauseated."

"Then how could you ever want to stay married to him?" Tootsie asked.

"I hate change so much," Carmen answered. "I've lived with this routine so long that I'm used to him coming and going. But never having that moment when he comes home again, that time when everything is right in my world—it's scary. And thinking about a job is terrifying, too. I can manage money, but what if I screw up at work? I haven't worked at anything other than being a waitress before I married Eli."

"You'll be fine. Have you called the lady at the base?" Diana was so glad that the conversation had turned to Carmen's drama that she fought the urge to wipe imaginary sweat from her forehead.

But then Joanie tapped her on the shoulder and said, "So tell us what it felt like."

"He's not the first man I've kissed or even the first one I've been to bed with since Gerald," Diana answered. "I had a couple of dates, remember?"

"Oh, yeah"—Carmen nodded—"but it's been so long that, by now, I bet you needed to check out videos on YouTube to figure out how to do it."

Diana shoved her backward onto the pillows. "It's like riding a bicycle."

"Have you been wasting Luke's gizmo on YouTube videos?" Joanie teased.

"What's YouTube?" Tootsie asked.

Carmen jerked her phone from the hip pocket of her jeans and pulled up a video of Travis Tritt singing "Here's a Quarter (Call Someone Who Cares)."

"Well, would you look at that," Tootsie said. "Me and Smokey missed out on that thing. Why didn't you girls tell us?"

Again, Diana hoped the spotlight was off her, but Tootsie looked up and asked, "And they have tutorials about kissing on this thing?"

"I have no idea," Diana answered. "But they have them for putting on makeup, knitting, cooking, and all kinds of other things. Rebecca used to watch those makeup ones for hours on end."

"And I can get this on my laptop when I get home?" Tootsie asked.

"Or your television. I can set it up for you," Carmen said. "Now, back to Diana."

"Okay," Diana sighed. "I forgot all about the difference in our ages and just enjoyed the moment. And it was fun being in a relationship for a day. Truth is, I didn't pretend so much. It was kind of like it was real. But now that it's all over, I keep thinking about how tough it will be to tell Rebecca about him."

Tootsie listened to the song all the way to the end and handed the phone back to Carmen. "Rebecca is going to be elated."

"What makes you think that?" Diana extended a hand and pulled Carmen back up to a sitting position.

"Because she came to give me one more goodbye hug the night before she left. She was sad to be leaving you all alone and told me that she wished you'd find someone to make you happy," Tootsie answered.

"Did she really?" Diana was so touched that she got misty-eyed. Her daughter had thrown a pure old hissy fit the first time that Diana went out after the divorce.

"For real," Tootsie answered. "You don't have to make a decision now, but give Luke a chance. Let Rebecca meet him before you throw him out."

Diana fidgeted with the rows of chenille on the bedspread. "This could just be an attraction between us because we're the only two unattached people in this group and we've been spending a lot of time together."

"Maybe so, but it might be something more. Don't close the door to opportunity," Tootsie said. "Just think about it. Now let's talk about Linda June. Lord have mercy. She's past fifty and looks like a hippie. I hope I never get stuck in an era like that!"

Diana glanced at Tootsie's hairstyle and bit back a grin. "Me, either," she said.

~

Carmen's phone rang, and she whispered, "It's Eli."

"Thank you, Lord." Tootsie raised her hand to the ceiling. "At this time of night, I was afraid it might be Natalie." Tootsie slid to the side of the bed.

"Don't leave." Carmen's heart leaped into her throat as she hit two buttons at once, one to answer and one to put it on speaker. Could she really tell him that she was willing to go through with the divorce?

"Hello, Eli. I've got Tootsie, Diana, and Carmen with me."

"I need to speak to you privately," he said.

"Whatever you say, I'll tell them anyway, so this just saves a step in the process. Kind of like you talking to Gerald. Why are you calling so late anyway?" Carmen asked.

"I'm at our house in Sugar Run," he answered. "I came to get my personal belongings and my truck."

"You left the team for that?" *Dammit!* She should string him on for six months to a year. He wouldn't take a week off to tell her to her face what he'd done, but he could do it to get his things. Right now she'd like nothing better than to beat him half to death with a cast-iron skillet.

"I took personal leave time. I had thirty days built up, and the team doesn't need me for what they're doing right now, so . . ." He paused for several seconds. "I'm having the lawyer draw up new papers. All I want is what I'm taking out of the house tonight and my truck. You can have all the equity in it, but you'll have to keep making the payments to keep it. Other than that, I don't think we have anything else to fight about, do we? Will you sign the new revised papers when they come?"

"How dare you go in the house without me there! Is that woman with you? Is she in my house? You better tell me the truth." Carmen felt her throat close up, sending her voice all high and squeaky.

"Hell, no," Eli said. "She's at a hotel in San Antonio. Her son is staying with my mother."

"Oh, I bet your mama just loves that." Sarcasm dripped from her words.

"I didn't call to talk about Mama. I just want to know, now that you're getting everything you want, if you'll sign the papers so this can be finished," Eli said.

"This is damn sure not what I wanted," Carmen said through gritted teeth.

Diana laid a hand on her shoulder. "Eli, this is Diana. You could have waited until she got home to get your things."

"I remember what you did, so I wasn't taking any chances." His tone was cold enough to give them all frostbite. "Gerald was the one who told me this would be a good idea."

"I just bet he did." Diana's tone wasn't a bit warmer than his. "So where are you going? Moving in with the new woman?"

"We're going to Kentucky to live close to her folks," Eli answered. "We've got a U-Haul loaded with her things, and we'll be pulling the truck behind it."

"Are you still coming to Natalie's graduation?" Carmen asked.

"Probably not. She'll need some time to process this whole thing. When she's ready, she'll get in touch with me," Eli said. "Kate and I are getting married as soon as the divorce is done. I'm hoping that Natalie understands and keeps in touch."

"Why so soon?" Joanie asked.

"Because." Every one of them could hear Eli suck in a lungful of air. "Kate and I both are getting out of the service. I put in my twenty-year papers last week. She's already got an offer for an IT position in a firm not far from where we'll be living in Kentucky. I've been offered a job in a security firm."

"So she's been in for twenty years, too?" Carmen asked.

"No, she's only been in for two hitches, but it was time for her to reenlist or give it up, and since she's got a ten-year-old son and . . ." He took another long breath. "Since she's pregnant, we decided to get out now."

Carmen heard the word, but processing it was such a shock that she picked up the phone and hurled it across the room. "You son of a bitch," she screamed.

Diana crossed the room and picked it up. "How can you do this to her over the damned phone? You could've been a man and told her months ago."

"I don't need any of y'all's opinions," he said.

"How could you?" Carmen yelled.

"That's why I want the divorce. We'd like to be married by Christmas. The baby is due in February," Eli said.

"Sweet Jesus." Tootsie moved over to put both her arms around Carmen.

"That means you knew she was pregnant that last night you were home and had sex with me." Carmen's voice was barely audible now, and tears ran down her cheeks. "Does *she* know you did that?"

"No, she does not . . ." He paused.

"When I get home, I'll sign the papers, and good luck to Kate. She can have you, but she'll wonder where you are every single time you walk out the door, because if she got you this way, then someone else can steal you from her the same way," Carmen said.

"That's a mean thing to say. I was hoping we could be civil, for Natalie's sake," Eli said.

"Goodbye, Eli, and good luck with colic, diapers, and selling Girl Scout cookies or whatever. You've never had to do much of that before because you were gone all the time," Carmen said.

"I'm ready to enjoy all that now. Kate is having my son, and I'm adopting hers, so they'll both be mine," he said.

"I don't ever want to see you again, or talk to you, or hear anything about you, so this is the final goodbye." Carmen ended the call.

"I'm so, so sorry," Diana kept saying over and over again.

Carmen hopped off the bed and began to pace. "I wanted more children. I wanted to try to give him a son, but he said one child was enough since he was gone so much of the time. I can't believe this—and he's adopting her kid—and she was pregnant when he was home last time? God, I'm such an idiot. Looking back, I can see that something wasn't right, but I thought *I* was doing something wrong. How do I ever tell Natalie all this? And how's she going to feel when her dad, the man she loved so much that she signed her name on the dotted line for six years of a life like his, isn't even there for her graduation?"

She threw herself on Diana's bed and covered her eyes with a pillow. "I can't think. I can hardly breathe. I need to chop wood or bake cookies or do something. I damn sure can't sleep."

"Okay, then." Tootsie got off the bed and shoved her small feet into her slippers. "Let's go clean house. I try to do a deep cleaning every year, and if none of us can sleep, then we can get on with it. I'll clean out my closet, and you girls can wash windows and woodwork."

"I'll do the ceiling fans since I'm the tallest," Diana offered.

"And I'm volunteering for the woodwork." Carmen tossed the pillow to the side. "But y'all don't have to stay up all night working just because I can't sleep."

"You think we can rest knowing that you're in turmoil?" Joanie asked. "We'll all work until we drop, and then we'll have a living room slumber party."

"I can't"—Carmen's voice broke, and she sobbed—"even begin to thank y'all for standing by me."

"Just payin' you back for doin' the same for me," Diana said.

~

Luke awoke while it was still dark. He laced his hands behind his head and stared at the shifting patterns the clouds made on the ceiling as they moved across the moon. Joanie was putting her house up for sale, and it was on the same block as Diana's. He could locate his new business anywhere, even in the living room of his house, to start out with. And he'd be close to Aunt Tootsie if she needed him.

Would it be awkward if you and Diana had a fling and then it didn't work out? That was clearly Uncle Smokey's voice in his head.

"You're probably right, Uncle Smokey," he said out loud. "I can't imagine living in the same town with Amelia."

It had taken five years to get over that woman—after he'd gotten down on one knee with a three-carat diamond in his hands and visions of circumnavigating the globe with her on a honeymoon, and she'd said, "I'm still in love with my old boyfriend, and we've decided to give it another try."

The sun was rising over the top of the trees off to the east when he stepped out into the yard. He'd gone only a few steps when he heard a noise out in the back. He eased around the side of the house to find Carmen out there with an ax in her hands, chopping wood into fireplace logs.

He dragged an old rusted metal lawn chair over and sat down in it. "You upset about something?"

"I don't want to talk about it," she answered.

He sat there patiently, amazed that someone as small as she was could wield an ax like that and split the wood almost every time.

She tossed the ax on the ground and sat down on the splitting stump. "She's pregnant."

"Who?" His blood ran icy cold. If Diana was pregnant, then she would probably want to be with the baby's father.

"Eli's new woman, Kate. She's going to have his baby, a son, in February. That's why he wanted a divorce so quick," she said.

He didn't realize he was holding his breath until it came out in a whoosh. "And that's why you're out here at the crack of dawn splitting wood?" He got to his feet, picked up an armload of wood, and put it in a wheelbarrow to take to the woodshed.

"We cleaned house until three this morning. I pretended that I was tired enough to sleep so they'd all get some rest, but I've been out here ever since," she said.

Luke didn't claim to know anything about women, but he was a good listener, so he kept piling up the wood until the wheelbarrow was full. Then he took it to the shed and brought it back empty to find that she'd already split several more logs.

"I'm still angry. I wanted a lot of kids, but he only wanted one. Now he gets more, and I'm left with an empty nest."

"Can you have more? I mean, physically, can you?" He began to gather it up as it hit the ground.

"Of course, but I'm thirty-seven years old. And besides all that, after this I'm not sure I'd ever trust anyone again." She laid the ax to the side and wiped beads of sweat from her forehead with the sleeve of her shirt.

"Ever thought of fostering?" He removed his jacket and hung it on the wheelbarrow handle.

"I want my own." She picked up the ax and went back to work. "And now I'm too old, and my attitude toward men stinks. Bad thing is, I didn't cause it. He did."

"Just remember that when you get to feeling guilty over the way you feel right now," Luke told her as he brushed a few chips from the front of his shirt.

"I'm already there," she said. "I shouldn't deny that new baby or that little fatherless boy a daddy. My child is grown and has left home, and Eli would be miserable knowing he had a child that he couldn't be with. It's not the baby's fault. He deserves a father. But why should he have a full-time dad when Natalie didn't? Guilt is about to smother me."

"Kill that pile of wood, and then walk away from it," Luke said.

"Will that fix me?" She shook the ax.

"It will if you do the same with your feelings. Kill them and then walk away. As long as you're in this state of mind, Eli still has power over you. Take it back and be your own person. If you want babies and can't trust anyone, go to a sperm bank and have babies. If you want to finish your degree and teach little children to fill the void, do it, but shake this off and move on." Luke went back to sit in the old rusty chair. He'd learned a long time ago to get past the hurdles life threw at him—looking back at those lean college years and those humiliating months after his botched proposal, sometimes he felt like he should be fifty years old.

Carmen dragged another chair over beside him and sat down. She drew her knees up and wrapped her arms around them. "How do I do that? How do I shake it off when it's all I can think about?"

"You need to get a notebook and write your goals in it, then set about making them happen instead of fretting."

"How'd you get to be so smart?" she asked.

"Experience is what you get when you didn't get what you wanted. I had a T-shirt with that on the front a few years ago. If I've got any intelligence at all, it's because I didn't get what I wanted." He thought again of how awkward he'd felt when he'd been kneeling in front of Amelia and she'd said what she did. He took a deep breath and told Carmen about the only woman he'd ever loved enough to want to give his heart to and share his life with.

"Good Lord! Does Diana know that?" Carmen gasped.

"No, and I'd rather she didn't until the time is right. I don't want her pity, Carmen. I want her to like me for myself, not how much money I have in the bank or any materialistic things I can provide—just for me. So can that be our secret?" Luke asked.

She stuck out her hand. "Yes, it can. Thanks for listening to me rant."

He shook her hand. "Thanks for keeping my secret. Shall we sneak in and cook breakfast? They'll be hungry when they wake up. But I'm starving now, and I bet you are, too. We'll leave their food warming in the oven."

"Sounds great." She stood up, picked up the ax again, and slung it hard enough that half the blade buried into the stump. "Don't want to leave it on the ground. That dulls it."

"Want to go to the store with me later today? Monday is the day I go for supplies," he asked as they walked side by side to the back porch.

"Nope."

"Why? It might help you to get away for a while." He opened the door for her.

"Because you should ask Diana." Carmen switched on the kitchen light.

The smell of cleaning fluid and a scented candle burning on the table filled the air. He was instantly taken back to his house in Houston. He loved the day the cleaning lady came and made everything all shiny, but what he liked most was that aroma when he first entered the house. He always kept either a vanilla or a sugar-cookie jar candle for her to light when she finished cleaning. Today, the scent seemed to be something spicy, like maybe pumpkin pie.

His stomach growled so loudly that Carmen giggled. "Scented candles always trick my stomach into believing that there's food cooking. Let's make pancakes and sausage, and then when the others get up, I'll cook for them. It's not my day to have kitchen duty, but I'll do it anyway."

"I'll start the coffee and get out the skillets," Luke said.

"Diana should fall for you." Carmen grinned.

"Why do you say that?"

"Because you are a good man, and she deserves someone like you. I'll whip up the batter if you'll start the sausage to cooking."

"Nah, I'm really just a computer geek and a nerd. I've never been popular with the women, but I really do like her." He set a cast-iron skillet on the burner and washed his hands while it heated up.

"Leave the water running, and I'll do mine next," Carmen said. "My advice is to not rush her. Let her work all this business about age difference out in her mind. Meet Rebecca and maybe spend some time at Tootsie's so y'all can get to know each other outside of this place."

"I'm kind of thinking about buying Joanie's house," he blurted out, and wondered if maybe he should have kept that to himself.

"That's a great idea. Tootsie will be ecstatic. Joanie will have it sold. And it'll give you and Diana a lot of close time." Carmen tossed a hand towel toward him.

He caught it in midair. "What if things don't work out between us and it gets awkward?"

"Have faith. You'll still be near Tootsie." She put her hands under the water and sucked air. "Dammit! I forgot to put on work gloves, and now I have blisters."

"The blisters will turn to calluses by the time your day rolls around again," he offered.

She shook her head. "Nope. I can work around them for one day. They'll remind me to work on what you said about leaving the firewood and all this anger behind."

"Hey, I thought we were all sleeping until noon." Tootsie yawned as she entered the room and went straight for the coffeepot.

"I'll get some coffee going and bring you a cup." Luke winked at Carmen. "I woke up early, so I thought I'd make myself some pancakes."

"But it's my day to cook, and I couldn't . . . ," Carmen started, then stopped and held out her hands. "Truth is, I couldn't sleep after we got the house cleaned, and I've been chopping wood the past three hours."

Tootsie took Carmen's hands in hers. "You poor baby. I've got some ointment in the bathroom that'll heal these up in a couple of days. Smokey hated wearing gloves, and I've seen him with blisters just like this too many times to count. Come with me. Luke, you get that coffee going. Then you can help her make something simple for breakfast. We don't have to eat gourmet three times a day."

"Hey, what's going on in here?" Diana asked.

"Pancakes and sausage. Coffee will be done in a few minutes. Want to be my girlfriend one more day and start off the day with a kiss?" He couldn't help poking fun.

"You think that's wise?"

She looked so damn cute in her pink-and-black plaid pajama pants and pink tank top that he was afraid if he kissed her once, he'd scoop her up and take her to the motor home for more than a make-out session.

"Probably not." He grinned. "But it would be a helluva nice way to start the day."

Chapter Fifteen

The week went by so fast that Diana could hardly believe it was Friday when she turned in the last of her weekly work that evening. She removed the device that Luke had lent her and laid it to the side, then closed her laptop and stood up to stretch all the kinks from her body. She'd used the vanity for a desk and the bench for a chair. It worked, but it sure left more sore muscles than her desk and office chair back in Sugar Run. Either the kitchen or the dining room table would have been a better choice, but there was entirely too much noise going on in those rooms for her to ever get anything done.

She started down the stairs just as Luke came in the front door. His jeans and jacket were dusty, and a couple of burgundy-colored leaves remained tangled in his hair.

"Well, hello." Luke looked up at her.

"What have you been doing?" He looked so sexy that she wanted to fall into his arms when she got to the bottom of the stairs.

"Couldn't you hear the banging up on the roof? That storm knocked off some shingles and loosened several more. I've been up there all afternoon getting them fixed," he answered.

"I had my earphones in. If another storm came through here, y'all would have had to come and get me, because I couldn't hear a thing." She went down a couple more steps.

"Never fear." The crow's-feet around his eyes deepened when he grinned. "I'll be the knight in shining armor that saves the damsel in distress." He held out his hand.

When she reached the last step, she put her hand in his. "You've got calluses."

"Does that surprise you?" he asked.

"A little bit." Even when they were making out on the church pew, she hadn't noticed that his hands were rough. Working with computers all day should have made them soft.

"This week while you've been in your work cave, I've cut down several trees so Carmen will have something to work out her frustrations on, and I've done a lot of repairs around here. Got to admit, though, this is the first time I've had calluses since I was a teenager and helped Uncle Smokey build the wood shack just off the back porch," he said.

"No wonder you've gone to the motor home right after supper." Comparing Gerald and Luke was like comparing jalapeño peppers to grapes, but she couldn't help it. Gerald had never been one to do much around the house except keep the lawn mowed when he was home. Other than that, he was all for paying someone to take care of it. And here was Luke, whose usual job was sitting in front of a computer all day, and yet he could repair a roof, build a shed, and cut down trees.

He dropped her hand when they'd walked across the living room. "Got to get washed up for supper."

"Me, too," she said. "I'll take the kitchen sink. You can have the bathroom."

With a brief nod, he went ahead of her. As he walked away, a streak of jealousy shot through her. Someday he was going to make someone a wonderful husband, and even though the relationship would be child-less, they'd be so much in love, just like Smokey and Tootsie had been.

"Have you got all your work done for the week?" Carmen pulled off her apron and hung it on a hook beside the stove.

"Yep. Finished the last entry, so I'm free now." Diana soaped up her hands and then rinsed them. "Need some help chopping wood?"

"You ever done that before?" Carmen asked.

"No, but I reckon you could teach me," she said.

"Not tomorrow." Tootsie came in from the dining room. "You're going with Luke to Clarksville in the truck to get some more shingles, and while you're there, y'all can go to the grocery store and fill the weekly list. Luke wants to finish up the roof on Monday since we change the time in another week. He wants to get it done before it starts getting dark earlier."

"And I've filled the woodshed—there's enough there to last through several more years when we come back here for the fall," Carmen said.

"So this is going to be a yearly thing?" Diana asked.

"I'd love it if it were." Tootsie beamed. "Maybe we could get Joanie to come down from Arlington for a few days while we're here, and it could be like our own little family reunion."

"Sounds great to me." Joanie shoved her hands into a couple of oven mitts and took a bowl of macaroni and cheese to the table. "Maybe I can even bring Brett if he can get time off."

"That would be even better," Tootsie said. "These past weeks have been just what I needed to get through some of this grief. Y'all will never know how much all y'all being here has helped."

Carmen raised her hand. "You can double the amount that it's helped you. There wasn't an ax at home or a huge pile of wood that needed to be split. Eli has no idea how lucky he is. I might have used the ax on his head instead of a stick of wood."

"So you're feelin' better?" Luke asked as he entered the room.

"Oh, yeah." She smiled.

Diana reached out and took a leaf from his hair. "You missed one."

"Thanks. Guess the damsel in distress is helping out the knight this evening," he said.

"What's that all about?" Joanie motioned them into the dining room.

"I'm the knight who'll save Diana from tornadoes. She's the damsel in distress," Luke explained.

"Yeah, right. I'm not a little wisp of a girl you can scoop up and put on the back of a white horse." Diana took her seat at the table.

"I beg to disagree," Luke argued. "If I remember right, I saved you from being beaten to death by hailstones when you fell after that last storm. I might not have put you on the back of a white horse, but I got you inside the house."

"Seems like I recollect that." Tootsie winked.

"A damsel can be any size and have any color hair. The knight is always strong enough to save her, and the horse is big enough for both of them to ride. Haven't you seen the animated princess movies?" He seated Tootsie and then took his own place.

"Have you?" Joanie asked.

"I've watched every one of them to see if I could use any of their ideas in the games I created. Let's give thanks for this food before it gets cold." He bowed his head and said a short prayer.

~

Joanie passed the meat loaf around the table, and when she took a bite, a pang of guilt shot right through her heart. She was eating Zoe's very favorite meal that evening, and when she got home, she'd have to pack up everything in her daughter's room. It would be like telling her goodbye all over again, and Joanie dreaded that part of the job awaiting her even more than telling her friends goodbye.

"Is something wrong with the food?" Carmen asked.

"It's delicious," Joanie sighed. "I was dreading the idea of taking down Zoe's bulletin board and packing all her things."

"We'll be there to help," Carmen said. "You aren't going to have to make this move all by yourself. We'll get a bottle of wine and sit on the floor and cry with you when the job is done. I'm glad that Eli has agreed to let me have the house so I don't have to do that for a while, but the time will come when Natalie will want to move all her things to a new place."

"Good Lord!" Diana gasped. "I hadn't even thought of that. It'll take a backhoe to scoop out Rebecca's messy room."

"Amen to that." Carmen nodded. "And thank goodness Natalie got my tendencies toward OCD, and everything has to be in its place. When she moves her things out, each box will be marked and packed like a professional. With a spreadsheet."

Tootsie giggled. "They both got part of me in them."

"OCD is not a good bed partner with messy," Luke said. "And I've never seen your house messy. Not the one in Sugar Run or this one. You're an immaculate housekeeper. Uncle Smokey said he tried for years to get you to hire a cleaning lady, but you'd have no part of it."

"What's on the outside is OCD." Tootsie smiled. "But what's on the inside is Rebecca all over again. Do *not* ever open either the living room closet or the hall closet doors, and only go into my little storage shed in the back if you have your life insurance paid up."

"You're kidding me." Joanie's eyes widened so far that they ached before she remembered to blink. "I figured your closets would look like Natalie's."

"Nope." Tootsie shook her head. "I never was a neat person until I married a career army man. I didn't want to embarrass him at inspection time. But they never opened the closet doors when they did a walk-through, so that was my secret."

Joanie thought of the space under the sink in her bathroom. It was always a jungle, but those were her private things, and nobody ever saw it but her. That would have to be cleaned out, too.

"I just remembered that we'd only lived in the base house a couple of years when we left it for the one in Sugar Run. Moving was downright traumatic—what to take with us, what to sell, what to give away—and every single thing, even as small as a hairpin in the bathroom drawer, had to be handled," Joanie said.

"Yep." Diana nodded. "And you've been in this house six times that long, so just imagine how much junk you've accumulated and will have to go through."

"I'll have to make even more lists," Joanie groaned.

"I've never been in your homes," Luke said. "Are they all pretty much like Aunt Tootsie's place?"

"You know someone in the market for a house in Sugar Run?" Joanie asked.

"I might," he said. "A friend has been looking to relocate close to San Antonio but not in the town itself."

"They're about the same, except that she's got a screened porch and a deck beyond that. She's got two lots, and we've only got one," Joanie answered. "Is this friend someone that would fit in with folks on our block?"

"I think he just might," Luke said. "Tell me more."

"The houses are all what they call spec homes. They've got different-colored brick on the outside, and they sit a little different on the lot, but they're three bedrooms, full bath in the hallway, and a half bath in the master bedroom. About fourteen hundred square feet, which isn't a bad size," Diana told him.

"But they're twenty years old, so they are pretty standard brick homes. You've been in Tootsie's place, right?" Carmen asked.

"Only the day of the funeral, and things were so hectic that I don't even remember meeting any of y'all," Luke answered. "I always visited them in the fall when they came up here to Scrap."

"You were there?" Carmen asked.

"If y'all will remember, we spent a lot of the time on the screened porch with the girls," Joanie said. "They were so upset. Smokey had told them he'd be at their graduation from basic if he had to crawl there on his hands and knees."

Tootsie sniffled. "He'll be there in spirit, just like he's here. Thanks for sharing that. I knew he was proud of them but had no idea he'd said that."

"I didn't mean to make you sad," Joanie apologized.

"It's okay," Tootsie said. "Always, always feel free to talk about my precious Smokey. It keeps him near to me to hear y'all tell stuff that he said and did."

After supper they got out the decks of cards to play canasta but decided that since they had an odd number, they wouldn't play partners. Luke had the biggest hands, so he shuffled the big stack of cards and dealt the first round.

"I remember when Uncle Smokey did this job. Last time I was here, he finally let me do the shuffling. I was prouder than if I'd sold a new game for a million bucks," he said.

"First time we all played this game was at Tootsie's house," Joanie said. "I was Smokey's partner so he could teach me the ropes, and Carmen was Tootsie's partner."

"Where was Diana?" Luke asked.

"She and Gerald took Rebecca to a movie that night. Our husbands had already left on a mission, but Gerald had an extra day," Joanie answered.

"The next morning after he left, we taught her the game to keep her mind off the sadness of telling him goodbye." Carmen arranged her cards in a fan.

Diana's face lit up in a smile. "I remember the first time I beat him. He used it as an excuse to break out a brand-new bottle of Jameson, and we all had a shot to celebrate."

Joanie had to swallow three times to get the lump in her throat to go down. She knew in her heart and soul that she was doing the right thing, but she was going to miss times like this so much.

Make the most of them. Maybe God gave you these weeks so that you could have the memories to take with you to your new place, Smokey's gruff old voice whispered in her ear.

You're so right. Joanie nodded. *It's not the end for any of us but a new beginning for every one of us in some way.*

Chapter Sixteen

*I*t would make more sense for Tootsie or either Carmen or Joanie to go to town with Luke that Saturday since it was Diana's day in the kitchen. When she realized that, she altered her plans after breakfast and put a pork roast in a slow cooker to make pulled pork sandwiches for dinner. If she and Luke weren't home, the rest of the family wouldn't be eating cold cuts, and she'd make chicken Alfredo for supper. All she needed was whipping cream, and she would pick that up at the store.

The truck wasn't as smooth riding as the motor home, but the wide bench seat reminded her of riding with her dad in his last vehicle. She'd wished dozens of times that she hadn't sold it when she was settling the estate, but at that time, she was in college and had a car.

"We haven't had that talk yet," Luke said. "Since we've got some time alone, it might be a good time to do so right now. I'll start. If we met in a church social or in a bar and I asked you out, would you go with me?"

"Maybe," she answered.

"How many dates would we go on before you asked me how old I was?" he asked.

"I have no idea," she answered. "Where are you going with this?"

"Okay, then I've asked you out to dinner and maybe a movie afterward, and I'm even okay with a chick flick," he said.

"Whoa! Who says I like chick flicks? I'd rather have dinner and then go home and cuddle up on the sofa to watch a Bourne DVD. I own all of them, so you can choose the one you like best." She turned on the radio and found a country-music station. She imagined a dimly lit room. She and Luke would be sitting on the sofa. His arm would be around her, and maybe her head would rest on his shoulder.

"That sounds great. So we've been out on one date. I kiss you goodbye at the door and ask you out again. This time I suggest a picnic at a park and then watching the sunset as we talk well into the night," he said.

"That sounds nice." Her thoughts shifted from a romantic evening in the living room, maybe with snow falling outside, to a spring setting. A quilt spread out on the ground, the bubbling sound of a creek close by, the two of them lying side by side and talking about their hopes and dreams.

"Third-date time now, and you still haven't asked me if I'm younger than you are, have you?"

She shook her head. "I'm having too much fun and wondering what you're going to come up with next."

"Then what the hell are we doing dancing around this birth-certificate crap?" he asked. "I'm attracted to you, and you kiss like you feel the same, so if I ask you out when we get back to Sugar Run, will you say yes?"

What he'd said made perfect sense, so she nodded in spite of her doubt. "Dinner and a movie at first, but no commitments. Deal?"

"Are you seeing other guys right now?" He made a turn to get on the highway going south to Clarksville.

"Nope. Are you seeing other women?" Diana held her breath, expecting him to hem and haw like other men she'd dated.

"Haven't been in a real relationship in a decade. I've had a couple of short-term girlfriends, but right now I don't have to break up with anyone, so I won't feel guilty about dating you," he said.

"You might change your mind when you get to know me. I'm Scottish, and I've got a temper. You might not even like me in a dating scenario," she said.

"And I'm honest, so if I do, I'll be up front with you, just like I'd expect the same from you. I just think it's terrible to waste this attraction on something as trivial as age," he said as they passed the WELCOME TO CLARKSVILLE sign.

It didn't take long at the lumberyard to get the shingles and nails that he needed, and then they were off to the grocery store. That took more than an hour, with both of them taking a cart and filling half the list. Diana felt guilty when he whipped out a credit card to pay the bill, but Tootsie would have a hissy fit if they tried to sneak one past her.

They were on the way home and about to make the turn just before the Red River bridge to go back toward Scrap when Luke swerved to miss a cardboard box sitting right in the middle of the road. "Don't like to run over things like that. Never know when a bunch of kids might have put it there with a chunk of concrete in it that will tear up the undercarriage of the truck."

"Or else have filled it up with fresh cow crap so your truck will smell horrible for days. Whoa! Stop!" she squealed as she looked back in the side mirror.

He stomped the brakes and left a long line of black tire tracks as he came to a halt. "What is it?"

"I think there's a baby in that box. I saw what looked like a little hand sticking out one of the holes in the side." Diana opened the door and started running the city block back to the box.

Luke bailed out of his side, leaving the door wide open, and jogged after her, until he saw a car coming from the opposite direction. He stood in the middle of the road, waving both hands until it slowed down. Then he pointed at the box, and the car inched its way forward until the driver rolled down the window a little and came to a stop only a few yards from where Diana was kneeling.

"What's going on? Y'all lose something from the back of the truck?"

"No, but someone left that box in the middle of the road, and there's something alive in it," he answered.

"Be careful. Someone put a skunk in a box, and my boyfriend stopped to see about it and got sprayed." The window went back up, and the lady drove very carefully until she was past.

"Don't open it," Luke yelled.

But he was too late. Diana had already pulled the tape from the top and was throwing back the flaps. When he reached her, both her hands were inside the box.

"Good God, it *is* a baby, isn't it?" he gasped.

"Not a human one, but it's a mama cat that seems to be real tame, and she's got three little babies that don't even have their eyes open. We can't leave them here, and we can't just turn her loose on the side of the road, Luke. They'll all be killed," Diana whispered.

Luke rubbed the calico cat's head, and immediately she began to purr. "Of course we won't leave her. I'll carry her to the truck, but if the flaps aren't closed, she might get spooked and run away."

Diana carefully pulled the tape back up over the flaps and held her hand on the top of the box as Luke took it to the truck. He placed it on the seat between them while she rounded the back end of the vehicle. The moment she was inside and the doors were closed, she opened one flap and started petting the cat.

"It's okay, pretty mama kitty. We'll take care of you and your babies. Why are you turning around, Luke? Is there a shelter in Clarksville?" she asked when she realized that he was doing a three-point turn.

"I have no idea, but I do know we're going to need some litter, a pan to put it in, and some cat food. Maybe the kittens can stay in a dresser drawer with their mama. You rest in the truck with them while I run into the store and get what we need. We can't leave them outside in this kind of weather. Never know from one day to the next if it's going to be cold or if it's going to rain. Aunt Tootsie will let us keep them in the utility room, I'm sure," he said.

"You think we should call and ask to be *sure* sure?"

"Naw." He grinned. "Better to ask forgiveness than permission. Could be that they're just what she and Carmen both need right now, and they'd never know it if Tootsie said no before we even brought them in."

It was only a fifteen-minute drive back to the store. Luke snagged a parking place close to the entrance and was in and out in less than ten minutes. They were easily going to get home in time for Diana to fry a pan of potatoes to go with the barbecue sandwiches.

"Everyone is going to fall in love with you," she crooned to the cat as Luke got behind the wheel and started the engine. "How could anyone do this to such a loving animal?"

"They're just downright mean," Luke answered.

"You ever have a cat?"

"Yes, I did. A big old yellow tomcat that ruled my house until last year. One day I found him on his favorite blanket on the sofa. I thought he was sleeping, but the vet thought he probably died of a heart attack," Luke said. "I love cats and dogs both, but a cat is an easier pet. Dogs have to be walked, and they don't train to a litter pan."

"I'm so sorry." Diana removed her hand from the box and laid it on his shoulder. "What was his name?"

"Bouncer. He'd actually been my father's cat, but when Dad died, I inherited him. He was eighteen years old, so he had a long, happy life and went fast, without much, if any, pain. I like to think that he just went to sleep and never woke up." Luke turned back to the state highway again. "If Aunt Tootsie doesn't want her or the kittens, I'll take them home with me."

And there's another reason you should latch on to him in a hurry. He's good with animals, and I can tell you that little kids flock around him, too. So don't blow your chance at happiness. Diana could hear Smokey's chuckle so clearly that it startled her.

~

Carmen was bored.

All the wood had been split. It wasn't her day to cook, and she'd read the whole book that Tootsie had given her when they had first started on the trip. Yes, it had helped her put things in perspective and made her wish that she'd been home when Eli had arrived. The heroine in the book had put sardines in her ex-husband's car when he came to take it away from her. Carmen would have just loved to have tucked some into Eli's golf-club bag. Let his new pregnant woman, Kate, try to find what was stinking up her house for a week.

She was sitting on the porch, watching the last few leaves fall from the maple tree in the front yard when the old red truck came to a stop not far from her. The back was loaded with bags of groceries, and she'd started out to help when Diana opened the door and hollered at her.

"Come over here and take this in the house first. We found it sitting in the middle of the road."

Carmen wasn't sure she wanted to handle something they'd picked up on the road, but she recognized a cat's paw when it shot out the hole in the side of the box. "Is it a cat? You know how much I love cats and kittens. Eli is allergic to them, so we could never have any of them in our house." She peeked inside the flap and held back a squeal. "Just look at those kittens! Oh, Diana, this is wonderful! Look at their mama."

"You better go show them to Tootsie and get her approval before you start naming them." Diana handed her the box and picked up four bags of groceries.

Carmen held open the door and then followed her inside. "Tootsie, come and see what some evil person did with these poor babies." She dearly loved cats. Her grandmother always had at least a dozen or more backyard cats, as she called them, and Carmen had loved them even better than her doll.

Tootsie hopped up out of her recliner so fast that she dropped the book she'd been reading. "Who did what to a baby?"

"Look, Tootsie." Carmen set the box on the floor, and the mama cat hopped out and rubbed around Tootsie's legs, purring the whole time.

"Oh. My. Goodness. Isn't she pretty?" Tootsie sat down on the floor, and the cat crawled up into her lap. "Did I hear you right? Someone left her in the middle of the road in that box. Were they out of their minds? That's so cruel."

"They should be shot." Carmen moved the box closer to Tootsie. "There's three little kittens, and they don't even have their eyes open."

"Bless their little baby hearts," Tootsie crooned as she reached over with her free hand and touched each of them with a forefinger. "Well, we'll give them a home. I'll keep the mama cat, and y'all can each have a kitten when we get back to Sugar Run."

"Oh, kittens!" Joanie came down the stairs and went right over to pet the cat and then the babies. "I'd love to have one, but with the move I'll have to pass."

"That's okay," Carmen said. "I'll take yours. That way mine won't be lonely."

"And I'll take whatever is left." Luke carried in the last of the food. "But if all y'all want this litter, I'll go to the shelter and adopt one when we get back. I miss having a cat around."

Diana dropped down on her knees. "I'll take one for sure. It'll be company now that Rebecca is gone. I haven't seen you smile like this in weeks, Carmen."

"I'm happy. I mean I'm really happy right now," she said. And for the first time since the divorce papers had arrived, she really was. "I'll sign the papers when I get home, and I'll have a cat." It didn't seem like such a big deal, but for the first time since she'd married Eli, she would have something of her very own without even asking him.

"Good." Tootsie picked up the cat and curled it up in her arms like a baby. "Her name is Dolly because I'm reminded of the song 'Coat of Many Colors' when I look at her. We're going to be great friends."

"And the kittens' names? There's a jet-black one with an orange face, and two yellow ones." Carmen picked all three up and nuzzled them.

"That's for each of y'all to decide, but Dolly is mine." Tootsie eased up on her feet and carried the cat to the recliner. "We're going to get along just fine. Sweetheart, you better enjoy this litter because as soon as we get home and you get them weaned, you're going to the vet for a little operation."

"Diana, you brought them in, so you get to choose the first one; then, if you're serious, Luke, you can choose next, and I'll take the critter that's left," Carmen said.

"I want one of the yellow ones." Luke pointed at the squirming kittens.

"I'll take the other yellow one." Diana held out her hands.

"I'm already in love with this little black one." Carmen handed off the other two to Luke and Diana. "Y'all can fight over how you're going to divide them. One has white feet, and the other has a black tip on its tail."

"Let's fight later." Diana put the kitten back in the box. "Right now, I should be getting some dinner on the table and putting away the groceries."

"I am starving." Luke grinned as he handed his kitten to Joanie. "You babysit, and I'll help Diana. We'll have dinner ready in no time."

Joanie leaned over and whispered to Carmen, "You really do look happy, but so does Diana. What do you think happened, other than finding a box of cats, on that little trip to town?"

"I don't know, but we should make her tell us later tonight, right?"

"Let's all meet in my room after Luke goes out to the motor home," Tootsie said. "I hate climbing up those stairs."

"Deal," Carmen said softly, and then raised her voice. "There were about four mama cats in my granny's barn when I was growing up. They always had a couple of litters a year, and I loved them. I'd spend hours in the barn naming them and playing with them when we went to see her for holidays."

"So this brings back memories?" Tootsie asked.

"Yes, but what it does even more is help bring me closure where Eli is concerned. He's got his new woman and a baby on the way. I've got a cat that I could never have before because of his allergy. Actually, I think he just didn't like cats, and what he said *went* in our house. Now I can do whatever I damn well please. Kate can have the job of upsetting him now," Carmen said.

"Congratulations," Diana called from the kitchen. "You've gone through all the stages if you've got even a little closure."

"If I'm honest," Carmen said, "I'm still harboring some—no, not some—a hell of a lot of anger."

Diana stuck her head around the door. "That, too, will pass with time. Trust me."

Carmen checked to see if she was holding a male or female and then kissed her kitten on the nose. "It's a girl, and her name is Sugar."

"Why'd you name a black cat Sugar?" Joanie asked.

"Because that song from Sugarland called 'Stay' has been on my mind all week. I've been begging Eli to stay with me and work this out, but now, like the song says, I'm telling him to stay where he is and not come back to me. The song has been good for my soul, so her name is Sugar."

Chapter Seventeen

S unday dinner was finished, and everyone had retired to the living room to hug up to the blaze in the fireplace. They had wakened to the first hard freeze and a slow, steady drizzling rain, so Luke had started a fire. Tootsie had in mind for them to go to church over in Manchester that morning, but because the weather was so bad, she'd changed her mind.

Joanie stared into the blaze and thought about Zoe that afternoon. Had her daughter gone to services that morning? Was she able to do any type of volunteer work where she was now, like she'd done at their little church in Sugar Run?

When her phone rang, it took a minute for her to realize that the ringtone meant it was coming from Zoe. She squealed loud enough that she startled Luke, who was sitting on the floor with his back against a hassock.

"It's Zoe! She's calling," Joanie yelped.

"Well, then, answer the thing. She won't have but a minute or two at the most for this first call. There's a pad and pen on the table there," Tootsie said.

"Hello, darlin'. You're on speaker with Tootsie, Carmen, Diana, and Luke. How are you?"

"I'm fine, Mama. It's tough, and I only get a minute to give you my address with this first call. Got a pen ready? Who is Luke?" Zoe asked.

"Luke is Tootsie's nephew who drove us up here to north Texas in Tootsie's motor home. I have a pen now."

Zoe rattled it off, and Joanie read it back to her. "I've got ten more seconds. I miss you, Mama. Next week, we get to talk longer. I want letters, but I'm absolutely not allowed to receive anything to eat, and that's a hard rule. I've got to hear more about you on a trip then. Bye, now. I love you."

"Love you, baby girl." Joanie barely got the words in before the call ended, and she hugged the phone to her chest. "I got to hear her voice. I'm going up to my room to write her a long letter."

"Going to tell her about the move?" Tootsie asked.

"I think I just might. That way when she calls again, we can talk about it," Joanie answered. "Are you missing the army wives' support group back at home, Carmen?"

"Hell, no," Carmen answered with a shiver. "I couldn't stand all that sympathy right now. I'm glad we're gone for a while. Besides, we have each other, and we hardly ever go to those support meetings anyway."

Carmen's phone rang, and like Joanie, she put it on speaker. Natalie's voice broke just slightly when she heard everyone yell her name, but she gave her mother her address, told her that she loved her, and told her no candy, cookies, or anything to eat. Letters were all she could have.

"It's a shame that we don't even need to be told that, isn't it?" Carmen said. "All of us are military, so we've heard the stories of what happens when a mama or granny sends food. I remember when Eli called me the first time in basic training. I wanted to send him a box of his favorite cookies. When he got home, he told me exactly what happened to a kid whose mama sent candy. I'm glad we know those things."

Diana nodded, and her phone rang. It was the same message and the same short phone call, but she was beaming when the call ended.

Just hearing the girls' voices was better than expensive presents on Christmas morning.

Tootsie held out a notepad and pen. "Give me those addresses so I can write them down. I'm going to get a letter ready for all three of them. Did y'all file a temporary address change before we left Sugar Run?"

They all nodded.

"Then if they send a letter home before they get this address, it'll get forwarded." Tootsie eased up out of her recliner and headed to her bedroom. One by one the other three headed upstairs, with Joanie bringing up the rear.

"What about you, Luke?" Joanie stopped halfway up the stairs and looked toward him.

"The sofa is all mine now. I'm having a Sunday-afternoon nap." He yawned as he stretched out on the empty sofa.

"Secrets," Joanie whispered as she followed them to the second floor.

"What's that?" Diana whispered.

"We've all got secrets that we need to tell our daughters, but we'd rather tell them to their faces, not in letters." Joanie stopped at the door of her bedroom.

"I don't have a secret," Diana said.

"Oh, yes, you do. It's a secret if you don't want to tell Rebecca about Luke," Carmen told her. "Hey, I got away without stationery or even a notebook. Either one of y'all got extra?"

"I got you covered. I brought two spiral notebooks," Joanie said. "I figure that the girls won't care if the letters are on fancy paper or not. I'll bring one over to your room. And about that secret of yours, Diana. It goes beyond not telling Rebecca about Luke."

"Oh, yeah?" Diana raised an eyebrow.

"Yep," Carmen said. "I'd be willing to bet that you and Luke discussed something other than cats on your trip yesterday. We were going to have a talk about it in Tootsie's room last night, but we played dominoes so late that she put it off until tonight. Tootsie says that we should have started a weekly meeting among us four as soon as we got here. I guess it's never too late." She shrugged. "Anyway, tonight she says that we're all to be in her room as soon as Luke goes to the motor home."

"Y'all are crazy." Diana smiled. "We talk all the time."

"Maybe so, but we've all still got a secret to tell our girls, and I'm telling Zoe all about mine in a letter, but we're going to discuss everything tonight, and I do mean everything." Joanie went to the armoire in her room, took a notebook from the shelf, and took it back out to Carmen. "You need a pen?"

Carmen grimaced. "I sure wasn't very well prepared, was I?"

Diana whipped one out from the messy bun on top of her hair. "Here you go. It's done its job holding up my hair. Now it can take care of your letter to Natalie."

"I'm tempted to tell her about the divorce right now," Carmen sighed.

Diana gave her a quick hug. "Don't give in to it. She doesn't need to hear that news until she's through basic."

"Diana's right," Joanie said. "And while we're writing, I'm going to send something to Rebecca and Natalie, too. I remember Brett saying that letters from home meant so much."

"Let's all do that. We can tell them about the trip, the kittens, the storm, and all kinds of things." Diana went into her room but left the door open.

"Don't forget the meeting tonight," Joanie called out in a loud whisper.

Sitting cross-legged in the middle of her bed, Joanie realized that other than signing birthday cards or leaving a note stuck to the refrigerator door, she'd never written to her daughter. Should she be silly or serious?

Finally, she decided to go for what was in her heart. She put the pen to the paper and wrote: *My Dearest Zoe, I miss you so, so much.* From there the story fell into place as she told her about the trip and the family reunion. She didn't mention the divorce or the fact that Diana was attracted to Luke. She did tell her that Luke was Smokey's nephew and that from the early pictures in the Scrap house, he looked a lot like Smokey did as a young man. When she wrote *Love, Mama* at the end of the fifteenth page, an hour and a half had passed. When Zoe got the letter, she'd know all about Brett getting out of the service. She wished her two friends could share their stories as easily as she'd done, but that wasn't possible.

~

It was almost eleven o'clock that night when Tootsie brought out a bottle of wine from her secret stash on the top shelf of her closet and piled sugar cookies high on a platter. Meetings weren't held in the South, especially Texas, without food and something to drink, so it was only right that the first official meeting of the empty nesters should at least have something.

In a few minutes the girls were all in her bedroom. "Make a circle in the middle of the bed, and as the oldest member of this club, I'm calling it to order. Old business will be discussed first. Did you all get your letters written?"

"Yes, but we forgot stamps, so we can't mail them until we get to town," Diana answered.

"I always bring a whole roll with me," Tootsie said. "What I don't use to write to y'all and the girls while I'm here, I use up to send out my Christmas cards when I get home. Problem solved. The stamps are in a little box above the fireplace. Help yourselves. Any other old business?"

She waited a few seconds and then said, "Okay, new business. We'll start with Carmen. How are you really feeling?"

"It helps to have a kitten to love, but down deep, I'm still angry, a little bit depressed, and a whole lot antsy," she admitted.

"It'll take time, but one day you'll realize that you hardly ever even think about him anymore," Diana said.

"I believe you, but I sure wish that day would be tomorrow." Carmen finished off her wine and held her glass out for more. "Now, Tootsie, tell us your new business."

"I still talk to Smokey every night and lots of times through the day. Sometimes he talks back to me. Don't tell anyone that I have voices in my head. They'll think I'm crazy, but it brings me comfort to know that his spirit is still with me," Tootsie admitted. "I may never get closure, but I'm strong, and I will survive."

"I'd like to talk to Eli," Carmen said.

"Okay." Joanie set her glass to the side. "I'm Eli. Tell me off."

Carmen narrowed her eyes. "You sorry bastard. I'm most mad at you because you had sex with me and told me you loved me when you walked out the door the next day, and you were planning to leave me for another woman, a *pregnant* woman, the whole time. I always deferred to you on everything because I never felt like I was good enough for you. I gave you my best, and now you're getting out of the army, and you're going to raise her son instead of our daughter. It's not fair." She took a deep breath and went right on. "And besides all that, I couldn't have more children because you didn't want them, and I couldn't have a cat because you said you were allergic. And while we're at it, I hate that living room suite you picked out. I may take it out in the yard and burn the damn thing. I can always use lawn chairs until I can afford to buy another one."

She realized that if she'd been pointing a gun at Eli, she would have unloaded a full clip into him and then shoved in a new one for the next round. She downed the rest of her second glass of wine. "Damn, that felt good."

"Anyone else got anything to say about this new business?" Tootsie asked.

"Just that I did the same thing with a therapist after Gerald left, and you're right, Carmen, it felt damn good to unload on him even though he wasn't Gerald." Diana handed her a second cookie. "You need this to soak up some of that wine."

"Moving on, then, Joanie, you got any new business?" Tootsie asked.

Joanie set her glass on the bedside table. "Hello, my name is Joanie, and I'm carrying around guilt like a security blanket."

"Why?" Tootsie asked.

"I still have a husband that I love very much. My dream of having him home every night for supper is about to happen, and Carmen is going through this divorce, and Diana's already been through one, and it's made her so wary of dating that she's afraid to even give Luke a chance." She stopped for a breath. "Why should I be happy when y'all are in turmoil? Even you, Tootsie—getting your dreams shattered by losing Smokey—and here I am sitting on the top of the world. Why me? What did I do to deserve happiness when y'all don't have it?"

Diana picked up Joanie's glass and handed it back to her. "Give us the guilt blanket. We'll burn the damn thing and scatter the ashes over the Red River. We're so happy for you; not one of the three of us would ever want to throw shade on your sunshine. So let us share in your happiness."

"But I'm the one breaking up the friendship," Joanie groaned.

"No, honey." Tootsie patted her on the knee. "Nothing could ever break up what we have. We're family, and those bonds can't be broken."

"Thank you." She held up her glass. "To family."

They all touched theirs with hers and repeated what she'd said. Then Tootsie turned to Diana. "It's your turn to share."

"Hello, I'm Diana." She grinned at Joanie. "I've been hiding behind a couple of birth certificates to keep from facing an attraction I have for Luke. That makes me an idiot, I know, but I'm afraid to trust anyone even after five years. Please don't make that same mistake, Carmen."

"I'll do my best." Carmen's dark hair fell in front of her face when she nodded. She pushed it back behind her ears and picked up another cookie. "We're getting crumbs on your bed."

"We'll take the bedspread out on the back porch and shake it when we adjourn this meeting. Go on, Diana," Tootsie said.

"So Luke and I had a talk on Saturday." Diana went on to tell them that she realized Luke had made perfect sense. "And so when we get home, Luke is going to ask me out to dinner, and I'm going with him. Then we're coming back to my house, and we're going to watch a Bourne movie."

"And?" Joanie raised an eyebrow.

"And I'm still terrified to tell Rebecca that I'm really dating, as in maybe a serious relationship on down the road a few months or a year from now," Diana added. "And I've never taken a man into the house I shared with Gerald. Sure, I broke the dishes he ate from and gave all his clothes away, but the house itself is where we had good times as well as bad ones. I'm afraid it will be strange having Luke there."

"Yet, it could completely erase any spirit that Gerald left behind. You'll just have to see what happens." Tootsie shared the last of the wine between the four of them.

"What if it doesn't, but then we get really serious—maybe deciding to spend the rest of our lives together?" Diana asked.

"Then you simply move into another house. I told you that Luke sold his company and made millions in the profit. If you get that serious, he can build you whatever kind of house you want. Hell, you can raze the one you're living in and build a new one right there. I'd love having you two close to me," Tootsie said.

"Are you serious?" Diana said.

"Oh, honey, I'm very serious. Luke isn't a rich man like most folks might think. He's just an ordinary bighearted guy who has a shitload of money," Tootsie informed her. "Now do we have any more new business?"

"I can't believe I was so gullible," Carmen said.

"It's all right to be angry. God gave us anger for a reason, and it's fine to use it when we need to. Better to get it out rather than let it sit there in your gut and fester," Diana told her.

"Amen." Tootsie nodded. "I think we pretty well covered it. Now, Diana, you can read the plaque that's over there on my dresser tonight. We'll close with it every time we have a meeting, because we all need to hear it."

"Is that the one that was in the motor home?" Diana asked.

"It is. I wouldn't dream of going anywhere without it. Not even from the motor home to this house," Tootsie said.

Diana read:

MAY GOD GRANT YOU ALWAYS
A SUNBEAM TO WARM YOU
A MOONBEAM TO CHARM YOU
A SHELTERING ANGEL SO NOTHING CAN HARM YOU
LAUGHTER TO CHEER YOU
FAITHFUL FRIENDS NEAR YOU
AND WHENEVER YOU PRAY
HEAVEN TO HEAR YOU.

"I feel better now, don't y'all?" Tootsie said.

"I sure do." Carmen slid off the bed. "When's the next meeting?"

"Every Sunday night from now on, and once Joanie has moved, we'll put her on speakerphone," Tootsie said. "Good, cheap therapy."

"When we get home, I'll bring the wine," Diana offered.

"We'll take turns bringing it." Tootsie grinned. "Now let's all go to bed. I betcha Smokey will have a lot to say to me tonight after he's heard all this."

Chapter Eighteen

iana's sweater and jacket did little to keep the whistling north wind from chilling her to the bone as she carried a bundle of letters to the mailbox. She wasn't used to late October being so cold. In Sugar Run, they'd still be using the air conditioner. She put up the flag to let the rural carrier know there was something to pick up and braced herself for the wind to hit her in the face as she started back. Then she heard the distant rumble of a vehicle and waited to see if it might be the mail truck.

Sure enough, it was, and the carrier put several things in the box, waved at her, and then drove on. She turned around and retraced her footsteps back to the mailbox, kicking leaves out of her way. She gathered a bundle of letters close to her body so the fierce wind wouldn't blow them out of her hands. She did notice that the one on top had Carmen's name on it and Natalie's return address in the upper corner.

"Mail call," she shouted as she entered the house. Joanie came from the kitchen, where she was making dinner, and Carmen ran down the stairs so fast that she almost fell. Tootsie laid her book aside, and Luke took out his earbuds.

"Okay, first one is Carmen's; then there's what looks like a bill for Luke." She handed them out one by one.

"Lucky me. Carmen gets a handwritten letter, and I get a power bill," he grumbled.

"Is it from Natalie?" Joanie asked.

"Yes, it is, and I'm going to take it up to my room and read it five hundred times and cry over every word, even if they're just telling me how many push-ups she's doing and what she's eating." Carmen started for the stairs.

"And another one for Carmen. This one has been forwarded from Sugar Run, so you might want to read it first," Diana suggested.

"Happy Halloween to me," Carmen sing-songed.

"And here's two for Joanie, no, three. This one looks like a card, and it's got Brett's return address." Diana passed them to Joanie.

"And three for Tootsie. Looks like each girl has written to you."

Tootsie held them to her heart. "God love their sweet souls. I love getting mail."

"And the last two plus the mortgage bill are for me," Diana said. "And I'm going to do the same thing that Carmen's doing—go up to my room and read these two letters a dozen times."

"You could stay down here and share them with me since all I got was a bill from the electric company." Luke laid his envelope to the side.

"Do you want to see her cry?" Tootsie asked.

"Good point. I don't do well with weeping women, so go on, and I'll just sit down here and pout over my bill," he teased.

"I've yet to see you pout about anything." Tootsie ripped into her first letter. "But just so you don't start, I'll share my letters with you."

Diana hurried up to her room and laid her mail on the bed. Then she ran her fingers over Rebecca's name in the upper left-hand corner. As if it were a Christmas present, she tore into it, not caring if she ripped up the envelope. She removed the letter, unfolded it, and read through the one page ten times. Rebecca was fine. She'd learned to make a bed with no wrinkles and so tight that she could bounce a quarter on it. The food wasn't what Mama made, but it was good. She'd lost five pounds and was the tallest girl in her group. She missed her mama and couldn't wait until they could have a long conversation. Zoe was struggling a little bit, but don't say anything to Joanie. She'd work it out. Mostly just homesickness. And please, please write letters to her so she wouldn't be so lonely.

Carmen was trying to keep her sobs quiet, but Diana could hear them. She wondered if she should go over to her, but until she could get her own emotions under control, it would simply be a sobbing fest like they'd had that day in the van when the girls all left.

She picked up the second envelope and tore into it, also. Rebecca was glad that she'd gone on the trip with Tootsie. She'd been worried about her being alone, and she'd gotten four letters that day. One from each of the army wives, as she called them, and one from Tootsie. Diana would have to write and tell her that they had a new name now—the empty nesters. Rebecca would get a kick out of that. The second letter covered three pages, and she talked about Natalie and Zoe. Surprisingly, they were having a rougher time with homesickness than she was, but then they'd never been through a tough divorce. She guessed that was what made her tough enough to help them, but it didn't mean that she wasn't a big baby who wished that she could talk to her mama every single night.

Diana laid both letters to the side, blew her nose, and wiped her tears. Hopefully Rebecca was tough enough to accept what she had to tell her about Luke when the time came. In the beginning, after the divorce was final, Rebecca had been in denial. She had declared quite loudly that her father would get tired of his new wife and would come back home where he belonged. By the time a year passed, she'd done a complete turnaround. She didn't want him to come back, but she wasn't ready for her mother to go out with anyone else.

Joanie rapped on her door and then came in without being invited. "Zoe says that she misses us and to tell you and Carmen that she'll answer your letters next time they're given free time to write home. She also says that she got so homesick that she cried for two nights. Natalie and Rebecca sat with her on the bathroom floor until she got things under control."

"Rebecca said the same things. I'm surprised that Zoe told you about the homesickness. She told Rebecca that she didn't want to worry you," Diana said.

"And so did Natalie." Carmen joined them. "It's good just to have words on paper that we can go back and read until the next ones arrive."

"I've got to go back downstairs to put the corn bread in the oven. It's good that I'm cookin' today, or I'd spend hours trying to figure out if there are any hidden messages in Zoe's letters." Joanie tried to smile, but it wasn't very convincing. "Honestly, do y'all think she'll be able to finish basic? And after that she's got AIT. I can't help but worry. She'll feel like such a failure if she gets sent home and Rebecca and Natalie get through it."

"She'll make it," Carmen said. "She's in the same boat I am. Unsure of her decisions and scared of the future, but she's got two friends who'll support her and hold her up, just like I've got. Now let's quit worrying and go make corn bread. I'll help you. If I stay up here, I'll start trying to find messages in Natalie's letters, too."

"Since we can't give out candy tonight, at least we have letters we can send to our kids." Diana managed a weak smile. "God, I miss Halloween at home. Decorating the porch and sitting in the rocking chair giving the little kids candy."

"Me, too." Carmen nodded, and then she and Joanie left the room and headed down to the kitchen.

Diana opened her notebook, intending to start a letter to Rebecca and tell her how much she missed Halloween. But before she wrote a word, she had another idea. She wrote:

Dear Luke,
We'll all get handwritten letters every day or two during the rest of our time here. Doesn't seem fair that
you don't get any at all, so I'm writing to you. This
little trip has meant so much to all of us, and I can't
thank you enough for all you do for us . . .

She went on to fill up a page about how she missed her daughter
but wanted to be strong for Carmen and Joanie, just like Rebecca was
strong for her friends in basic training. Then she folded it, put the
address on it, and tucked it under the dresser scarf to be mailed with
the letters she would write to Rebecca.

~

Luke was messing around on his computer when he found that the
little church only ten miles down the road was having what they called
"Trunk or Treat" that night. He loved giving out candy to the kids in
his neighborhood and immediately decided that he was going to participate in the fun in the church parking lot. He made a phone call to
the number given for information, and when he mentioned that he was
Tootsie Colbert's nephew, the lady invited him to participate.

"I won't be here for supper," he announced at the dinner table and
then went on to tell them what he was going to do. "Anyone want to
join me?"

"Too chilly out there for me," Tootsie answered. "But you go on
and have fun. What are you going to give out?"

"Don't know yet. I'm making a trip to the Walmart store in Paris
to buy stuff."

"Not me," Joanie said. "I'm watching scary movies, like Zoe and I
do every Halloween, though I'll be pretending that she's sitting on the
sofa with me."

"I'm with you," Carmen said.

Tootsie raised a hand. "Count me in, too."

Luke glanced over at Diana. "How about you?"

"I'd love to go," she said. "What time are we leaving?"

"The event starts at five, so maybe three. That would give us time to drive down to Paris, load up on goodies, and get there when it kicks off." Luke was so happy about getting to spend the evening alone with Diana, even if it was just on the drive to the store and home from the festivities, that he could have done a little jig.

"That will give me time to finish up my last little bit of work on the computer." Diana passed around the plate of corn bread. "This is such a good day for vegetable soup."

"And apple crisp for dessert," Tootsie added.

When dinner was finished, Luke went out to the motor home and put in a call to his financial adviser. "I want to put my house on the market," he said. "I'll be out of town until the middle of December, but get it appraised, pick out a good real estate agent, and give them a key."

"Are you sure about that? The market isn't up much right now," the man said.

"I'm very sure. I'm moving up around San Antonio to be near my aunt. My uncle died a few weeks ago, and I want to be a help to her."

"Okay, then, I'll get the ball rolling. Anything else?"

"Not today, but if I think of something, I'll call. And thanks," Luke answered.

"I'm here to serve," he said. "I'll keep you posted on how things go."

At five minutes to three, he crossed the yard to the garage and had good intentions of warming up the truck before he went inside the house for Diana. But she was already in the truck with the engine running and the garage door raised. He slid behind the wheel and put the vehicle in reverse.

"Thank you for getting the chill out of the truck. I had planned to do it myself," he said.

"I got finished with my work a little early, and to tell the truth, I'm excited to get away for the evening. I don't like scary movies," she said.

"But you watch them because everyone else likes them, right?"

A smile spread across her face. "Yep, but I'd much rather be giving out candy this evening to little princesses and astronauts."

That comment shot his pulse up a few notches. He loved kids, always had, and wished that he'd had a brother or a sister, or even two or three of each, his whole life. The biggest disappointment he'd ever had was when he'd learned that he could never be a father—well, maybe not *never*, but who was counting that one chance in a couple of million?

He bought two bushel baskets at the Walmart store, and Diana helped him fill the first one with apples, oranges, and bananas. Then he bought five huge bags of candy and filled the second one. This time Diana noticed that he charged it to his own card and not Tootsie's.

"Now what do I buy?" she asked.

"How about we get one more basket and buy a bunch of those popcorn balls?" he suggested. "When I'm home, that's what I give out. I spend a couple of days making them and wrapping them all up in spooky plastic wrap. The kids in my neighborhood love them. You looked surprised."

"It's just that . . ."

"That what?" he pressed.

"Gerald wouldn't have been caught dead in the kitchen unless it was to make coffee or get a beer from the fridge."

"I'm not your ex," he said. "I'm just plain old Luke Colbert, who enjoys cooking, loves kids and animals, and only served one term in the National Guard, where I was a supply clerk. It's who I am. And you're not my ex, either. That woman wouldn't have ever come to this kind of event with me."

"Ex? You were married?" she asked.

"No, just almost engaged, until that very embarrassing moment when I proposed and she told me that she had decided to get back together with her old boyfriend," he said.

"Oh. My. God! That was downright cruel," she said.

"So was the treatment you got from your ex," he said. "But it's all in the past now. It's only human for us to compare. We can't help it, but hopefully we'll both see that what we have now is better than what we had then."

"And that's why I like you. I can be honest with you."

She liked him!

"As a brother, as a friend . . ." He continued to press a little.

"If I had a brother, I wouldn't make out with him on the back church pew."

"Fair enough." He grinned.

Be satisfied that she likes you, and leave it at that for now, he told himself.

Diana pushed the cart around to where the baskets were located and selected an orange one, and together they filled it with popcorn balls. "Rebecca and I make caramel apples to give out to our special friends. What are we going to do with these baskets when we're done with them?"

"They can be beds for our kittens when we take them home," Luke suggested.

"Home in Scrap or in Sugar Run or, in your case, Houston?" she asked.

"Right now, home in Scrap, but later just home wherever it is. Can you keep a secret?"

"Depends on who I'm keeping it from," she said as she paid out and prepared to push the cart out to the truck.

"From everyone, but especially Joanie, and only for a little while." He opened up the box of big black garbage bags he'd bought and put each basket inside one before tying the tops shut. "That way nothing flies out on the way to the church."

"What's going on with Joanie?" She looked worried.

"Not with Joanie as such, but she's putting her house up for sale, and I'm going to make her a really good offer for it." He held the truck door for her. "I contacted my financial adviser today and put my place in Houston on the market."

"Why would you do that?" she asked as soon as he was in the vehicle.

"Because I want to be near Aunt Tootsie, and truthfully, I want to be closer to you," he said.

"But right on the same block with both of us? Are you nuts? We'll drive you crazy," she protested.

"If you do, I'll sell it and move somewhere else. Right now, it'll do for me to start a new business in, and I won't have to drive so far to date you." He started the engine and drove out of the parking lot.

"I'm flattered, but I hope you don't regret it," she said.

That took a little air out of his balloon but not so much that he wasn't still floating from getting to spend time with her. They arrived at the church parking lot right at five o'clock and had barely gotten parked and pulled their baskets out of the bags when the first kids showed up.

"Trick or treat," a little ballerina said timidly.

"What will it be, darlin'?" Luke asked. "Fruit, candy, or a popcorn ball?"

"An apple." She held out her bag. "And candy, too."

"Misty!" her mother scolded.

"It's all right. One big red apple and a little bit of candy to go with it."

"Thank you." The little girl twirled for them.

After they'd given out candy to several kids, Luke put his hands on Diana's waist, picked her up, and set her on the tailgate of the truck.

"Might as well give it out sitting rather than standing for the next couple of hours."

He put a couple of popcorn balls in the next kids' sacks and turned to Diana. "Having all these children around me, it makes me want to be a father. What do you say we adopt a couple if we make it through the dating stage and into a permanent relationship?"

Diana's look made him feel like he'd grown an extra eyeball right smack in the middle of his forehead. "You are still young enough to be a father, but I'm too old to start all over."

"Forty is the new thirty, and you damn sure don't look or act like you're a day over twenty-five." He wished he could take the comment back. It should have been something to be discussed later on down the road instead of before they'd even gone out on their first date. But that night sitting beside her, he'd realized that he did want children and had spit it out before he'd thought it through.

"If you're serious about wanting to be a dad, maybe we should take a step back here," she said.

"Trick or treat." A little ghost held out his bag. "Can I have a banana, please? I've got lots of candy."

"You sure can, sweetheart." Diana put one in his bag, and he went on down to the next vehicle.

"So you are definite about no children, like in ever, forever and ever, amen?" he said.

"Yes, I definitely am." Her tone left no wiggle room. "I have one and love her, but I would never start over at this point in my life."

In true Luke Colbert fashion, he'd just screwed things up big-time. But in all honesty, he'd just realized that moment that he wanted to be a father. He'd never given it much thought before, but something in the way he felt about Diana had him skipping through the preliminary relationship steps and going straight for the goal line. And he'd spoken up way too soon.

He'd killed it for sure. "So does that mean we don't get to go on date number one?"

"That's up to you, Luke," she answered.

"And that means?"

She shrugged. "I like you a lot. But this is where that age difference comes into play. You're at just the right age to be a father. I'm at just the right age not to want kids anymore. So you know how I feel. That's why it's up to you. We can be friends and neighbors if you buy Joanie's house. Or we can see if we want more. You decide."

"Fair enough." He nodded.

~

Diana had taken her stand, something that she'd never done very well with Gerald. She had a little more backbone than Carmen had had with Eli, but she'd still deferred to Gerald too often. She'd never do that again, not even with Luke, and she really liked him—a lot. Had it been Gerald, the rest of the evening would have been miserable. He'd have gone all cold and distant.

"So tell me, what was your favorite Halloween costume?" Luke's voice still had warmth in it, and his smile was genuine.

"I wanted to be Princess Leia, but Mama said I wasn't wearing a gold bra and harem pants, so I went as Dorothy, and Mama sprayed a pair of my shoes with red glitter," she laughed. "And you?"

"The last year I went trick-or-treating, Mama made me a Superman costume. I slept in it until I outgrew it. Can you imagine me as a super-hero? I'd have done better to have gone as the scarecrow from Dorothy's story." Luke laughed with her.

They were back on familiar ground, but she could still see a heavy black cloud in the shape of a stork right there in the back of her mind.

What if she fell in love with him? What if he regretted not being able to adopt a child?

She tried to shake it off, but it was still there at the end of the evening when they got home. Everyone else was in the living room, watching the tail end of a scary movie. Luke sat down in the empty recliner to finish it with them. She needed to be alone, to analyze things and get them sorted out, to decide whether to nip this attraction she had for Luke in the bud or let it blossom.

"I'm going up to write to Rebecca and tell her all about the kids before I forget. I took pictures with my phone that I'm sending, too. She can share with the other girls. See y'all in the morning," she said.

"Hey, before you go," Tootsie yelled over her shoulder, "we made an executive decision while you were gone. We decided to go to Paris and do some Christmas shopping on Saturday. We might even spend a night or two in the motor home. There's a real nice little park down there, and we can get a driver to take us to town to shop."

"Sounds great." Diana started up the steps.

That was just what she needed. Two nights cramped up in the motor home with Luke underfoot while they shopped. Just looking at toys everywhere would remind her of their huge difference in opinion on the issue of children. Maybe she'd offer to stay home and take care of Dolly and the kittens. That would give her lots of time to really settle it forever and for good that she didn't want another child. She really liked Luke, but if she agreed to adopt a baby, it wouldn't be for the right reasons, and she wasn't sure what those might even be.

She picked up her notebook and started a letter to Rebecca. Three pages later, she'd given her an update on the kittens, who now had their eyes open, and told her how much she'd missed sitting on the porch with her and giving out candy. She'd even related the "Trunk or Treat" tales about the kids and how she and Luke had had such a good time.

But she didn't mention anything about bringing a brother or sister into Rebecca's world, through adoption or otherwise.

When the envelope was addressed and sealed, she went downstairs to get a stamp. Everyone else had disappeared, but Luke was still sitting on the sofa watching *Beauty and the Beast* on his laptop. "This is us," he said.

"You're watching *This Is Us?*" she asked.

He patted the sofa beside him. "No, I said this is us. You're the beauty. I'm the beast."

"No, Luke, you aren't. You are the kindest, sweetest man I've ever met, and I'm very attracted to you. We just have to figure things out."

He shrugged. "Then I didn't mess it up permanently?"

She sat down beside him. "Do you know what I like about you the most? That you are honest and open. Like you said, we can't help but compare. So, that said, I never liked living with a man who couldn't tell me where he was going or how long he'd be gone. I knew what I was getting into when I married him, but I didn't know until a few years had passed that I would hate the secrets so much."

"Thank you." He kissed her on the forehead. "Now about that honest-and-open stuff, I'm not going shopping with y'all. I think a couple of days apart is what we need. The pickup has a bench seat wide enough that the four of you can get in it. Surely one of you can drive a stick shift."

"Why?" she started to argue.

"I'll take care of Dolly and the babies and do a little more maintenance on the yard while y'all are gone. We need a little apart time. I told Aunt Tootsie, and she's made arrangements for y'all to stay two nights in a hotel," he said.

"You're not only open and honest but the smartest man I've ever known." She stood and then bent down to kiss him.

He reached around the laptop and cupped her cheeks in his hands. When the kiss ended, he looked deeply into her eyes and said, "Before I forget. The letter you wrote to me—well, I'll keep it forever. I'll answer it, but I think I'll just slip it under your door or put it in your purse rather than mail it."

"I'll look forward to it." She smiled. "Good night, Luke."

"Good night." He nodded and went back to watching the movie.

She went up to her room and threw herself back on the bed. *Dammit!* Why did life have to be so complicated?

Chapter Nineteen

*I*t was only an hour's drive from Scrap to Paris, and although they were a little crowded with four of them in the truck, Carmen grabbed Tootsie's knee only one time when she was reaching for the gearshift on the floor.

"Where'd you learn to drive this kind of thing?" Diana was amazed at how smoothly Carmen shifted the gears.

"My granddad taught me to drive. He didn't believe in all those gadgets and geegaws, as he called extras on a vehicle, and that's what he considered automatic transmissions. I was surprised that he even bought a vehicle with air-conditioning, but it was West Texas, and it gets hot out there," she answered.

"Well, I never learned to drive this thing, but I can drive that motor home if I need to," Tootsie said. "Smokey said that since I was the one who wanted it, I could drive it. So I proved to him that I could when I drove it home and backed it up in the yard."

"What'd he say then?" Diana asked.

"He said that he was going to sleep the whole way to Scrap this fall," Tootsie answered. "I guess he did in a way, but I'm real glad he woke up every now and then to talk to me."

"He's talked to me a few times, too," Diana admitted.

"And me," Joanie said. "When I was worrying with this move, he came to me in a dream. He was younger and looked a lot like Luke, and he said that all y'all would be fine and for me to think of my marriage."

Carmen took one hand off the wheel and raised it. "I've only heard his voice once, and it was yesterday when he said that we should definitely make this trip."

"I'm glad he's visited with y'all. You are all like daughters to us," Tootsie said. "Now make this next left, and park as soon as you find a place. Our first stop is that little pastry shop on the corner."

Carmen snagged a parking spot close to the door. Diana was the first one out and held out a hand to help Tootsie up the two steps into the shop. "Did you and Smokey come to this place when y'all were in this area?"

"At least once or twice every year." Tootsie went to the counter, laid her credit card out, and said, "We'll have four pumpkin spice lattes, and I'll have two apple fritters. Y'all come on up here and tell the lady what you want. Joanie, you should have chocolate iced doughnuts."

"That sounds wonderful. Can I have two?"

"You ought to order three. They're that good," Tootsie declared.

"Two is enough, especially with a latte." Joanie took a sideways step so that Diana could order.

"One of those bear claws." Diana pointed.

"Make that two," Carmen said right beside her.

"I'll bring them out as soon as I get your lattes made," the lady said.

"What's the plan for shopping?" Diana asked when they were seated around a table near the window.

"We're skipping the stores and going out to the fairgrounds. The first weekend of November, they have vendors that come from all over the United States and set up for two days. There's food of every kind, and there's all kinds of places to buy everything from leather to jewelry. If you can imagine it, we'll be able to find it there," Tootsie answered.

"Kind of like the state fair, only without all the animals?" Joanie asked.

Tootsie nodded as she wrapped up her second apple fritter and put it in her purse. "We'll shop until we drop and then go to the hotel. They serve breakfast in the morning, starting at six thirty. I figure we'll be back at the fairgrounds by seven thirty and start all over again. And I've brought each of you a big tote bag to keep your purchases in."

"Did you and Smokey do this every year?" Diana asked.

"Yep, it's where I always found something unique for y'all and the kids," Tootsie said. "I hadn't thought to go this year, but Diana and Luke need a couple of days apart right now."

"Why would you say that?" Diana asked.

"I'm an old woman even if I don't look a day over fifty." She winked. "But my gut never lies to me. Something isn't right between y'all this week."

"Maybe we're having second thoughts about that dating business." Diana toyed with the napkin dispenser.

"We're not getting into any more of that right now." Tootsie waved her hand around. "These two days are for us girls, with no relationship problems, moving issues, or divorce troubles. We'll have our empty nesters' meeting tomorrow night in my room and discuss all of it then. That way we can have two whole days to clear our minds."

Diana sure wished she could wipe away all thoughts of everything but buying Christmas gifts for the next couple of days, but it would take more than the holiday music playing everywhere to make her believe in miracles.

~

"Okay, now what?" Joanie asked when they reached the fairgrounds and Carmen had parked the truck. "Do we all stick together or go our separate ways?"

"Let's split up and meet back at Smokin' Bob's Barbecue Wagon at noon," Tootsie suggested. "Smokey and I always ate there when we came here."

"See you in a couple of hours, then." Joanie took off in a fast walk. It sure made shopping for the other three easier since they weren't right there. She inhaled deeply when she bypassed a caramel-apple-and-fried-pickle vendor and almost stopped at a cinnamon-roll wagon but forced herself to stay on track. She stopped at a handmade bracelet place and had just bought one for Zoe when her phone pinged. She pulled it out of her purse and read a message from Brett saying that his retirement papers had been filed, and as of December 1, he would be officially retired from the army. The rest of the month would be spent in meetings and helping Gerald choose two new team members. And he'd called a real estate agent so that they could get a jump on selling the house.

She sat down at a picnic table under an awning beside a taco wagon and sent back a heart emoji with a message: Can we talk?

Immediately a sad face appeared. Am with Gerald right now, so no.

She sent a GIF with a bear hugging a heart.

Putting the house in the hands of a real estate agent seemed to finalize the whole thing in her mind. Maybe over the next few days, Zoe would be able to call again, and they could discuss everything rather than waiting for letters to go back and forth.

"I miss hearing her voice," Joanie muttered.

Tootsie sat down beside her. "If you're talking about Zoe, so do I."

"It's a done deal now. December first is the official retirement day for Brett, and he's even called a real estate agent already," she said. "I can't wait to tell Zoe. She's going to be so happy that her dad is retiring and will be home every night."

"Did you already let her know about Brett getting out of the army?"

"In a letter, but—"

"It's not the same as hearing her voice." Tootsie finished the sentence for her. "When Smokey was deployed, we wrote to each other nearly every day, but it wasn't the same as hearing him. For one of his last deployments, I bought us each a tape player, and we made cassettes. Felt really strange at first, but I put his picture in front of me and talked to it, and I listened to those tapes he sent over and over. Sometimes I even put them on continuous play and went to sleep to his voice. I bought all three girls a new leather wallet with lots of compartments. Zoe's looked pretty pitiful last time I saw it."

That was Tootsie—always observant and buying something useful rather than something frivolous. "We've got fifteen minutes before we go to the barbecue wagon for lunch, so I'm going over there to that vendor." She pointed across the gravel pathway. "See that black lace parasol? Abby carries one like it on *NCIS*, and Zoe loves it. I'm getting her that for her second present."

Scratch the idea of always being practical. "She'll squeal when she opens it," Joanie said. "I'm going to check out the scarf vendor right next door to the umbrella one. See you in a few minutes."

Tootsie waved over her shoulder. Thank goodness she always had her cell phone in her pocket and kept it charged. As tiny as she was, she would have been hard to spot in a crowd if they all went looking for her. Joanie found a lovely red-and-green plaid scarf to give to Tootsie at the end of the trip as a small token of her appreciation. Then she bought three more in different colors for the girls. With her luck, Natalie and Rebecca would spend the winter in Florida or California for their training, but like the old adage said, it was the thought that counted.

~

"Hey, it looks like y'all have got some of your shopping done," Carmen said when they reached the barbecue wagon. "Diana got here first and saved us a table. Are we ready to get in line to order?"

"I always get a pulled chicken sandwich with a dill pickle and chips." Tootsie set her bag on the table beside two others. "Smokey liked their brisket, so I can vouch for that, too."

Carmen remembered that Eli loved smoked brisket-and-coleslaw sandwiches. She closed her eyes and made herself think of Natalie, who always thought her father's sandwiches were gross. When she opened her eyes, she was looking up into the aqua-colored eyes of a soldier dressed in camouflage. For a split second, she thought it was Eli, with his close-cut hair and round face.

"Do I know you?" the guy asked.

"I'm sorry. The sun was in my eyes, and I thought you were someone else," she stammered.

"Daddy, Daddy, look what I got!" A little girl with a swinging blonde ponytail danced across the path and tugged on her father's arm. "It's a purple unicorn. Mama got it for me for my birthday."

"Unicorns aren't purple," he teased his daughter.

"Mine are," she protested.

Carmen blinked away the tears that were welling up behind her eyes. There was a purple unicorn on Natalie's bed at home. Eli had brought it to her the last time he was home. So much for forgetting about divorce troubles over the weekend.

"Hey, you all right?" Diana nudged her on the arm. "It's your turn to order."

"I'm fine. Just wool gathering," Carmen said. "I'll have a pulled pork sandwich, a pickle, and corn chips, please, and a tall sweet tea."

She took her food to the table and sat down beside Tootsie, but her eyes kept darting back to the guy and his family, who'd ordered their food and were heading toward a table across the way.

"Looks a lot like Eli from a distance," Tootsie said. "You want to talk about it?"

"Not until tomorrow night—remember the rules? But I do want to talk about this amazing little vendor who had handmade jewelry that she'd made from natural materials." She dug around in her bag, brought out three small velvet pouches, and opened one. "Look at this beautiful blue necklace with brown streaks that I got for Natalie's Christmas."

"She's going to love that. What's that braided rope made of that it's hanging on?" Joanie asked.

"I don't know, but it sure caught my eye. They're all so modern looking, and the girls might like something pretty to wear if they get to go out during their last weeks of training," Carmen said.

~

Diana hadn't gotten a lot of shopping done, other than a small cross-stitched piece for Joanie to hang on her wall in her new house. It simply said "Bless This Home," but the fall colors and tiny leaves that were scattered around the letters would remind her of the time they all shared in Scrap.

Mostly, she'd wandered around or sat on a bench and watched the people, but that little piece of needlework brought to mind the difference in a *house* and a *home*. She'd done her best to keep a home for Rebecca, especially after the divorce. Now she'd have to be careful, or with just her rattling around in their place alone, it could easily turn into nothing more than a house.

Conversation among the four of them had come to a halt while they ate their food. That was fine with Diana because she was trying to analyze the maternal feelings that had washed over her when she'd seen a gangly little girl with dark braids and big brown eyes earlier. In that moment she'd wished that she still had a daughter in the house, one who'd throw her backpack down inside the door instead of taking it to her room and who never got the cap back on the toothpaste.

Rebecca had been gone only two nights when they'd left on their trip—and the first one, Diana had stayed at Carmen's house. The second she'd spent packing and getting ready to leave, but when she got back to Sugar Run, she'd really feel the emptiness. Not that she was ready to change her mind about adopting a child or children. No, sir! But she'd been consumed with her daughter's life since the divorce, and now Rebecca was gone. She thought about the empty house with no one to keep her company—well, that was downright scary.

Joanie pointed at her. "You're awfully quiet."

"It's not polite to talk with your mouth full of food." Diana stood and started putting all the trash in one disposable tray to throw away. They'd run from their empty nests by taking this trip, but they were waiting for them when they got home—Carmen's maybe even more than the others because she had to face hers with no husband or daughter in the house. But then maybe Joanie would have a tough time, too, since she'd be faced with leaving. Diana had heard all her life about how change was good, but that didn't mean it wouldn't be painful.

∼

"I'm plumb worn out," Tootsie said on Sunday evening when they reached the hotel after the second day of shopping. "I barely have enough energy for our meeting, but we all need it, and besides, the wine will give me a fresh burst. Should we get some pizza delivered to go with it?"

"I've eaten too much for two days," Carmen said with a groan. "But I did buy some pecan tassies from a vendor that will go well with the wine."

"And I bought some brown-sugar fudge to take home, but if we want to sample it, there's plenty," Joanie offered.

"I could toss some chocolate-covered pretzels into the mix," Diana suggested.

"Y'all save all that to take home and share with Luke. I tucked a package of Oreos into my suitcase, and since they're dark, I brought red wine." Tootsie got into the elevator. "We'll meet in mine and Carmen's room in half an hour. That'll give us all time to get a shower and into our comfortable pajamas."

"I'm glad we've got rooms right across the hall from each other. My pajamas are pretty ratty," Joanie laughed.

"Sounds like that would be a good present for you." Tootsie was first out into the short hallway when the elevator doors opened. "Which reminds me, Diana and Luke both have a birthday while we're in Scrap. Luke's is on Thanksgiving this year. We'll have a party for Diana on the fifteenth, but we'll combine Luke's with Thanksgiving." She touched her key card to the device on the door. "See y'all in a little bit."

"You want the first shower?" Carmen asked when they were in the room.

"No, you go on ahead. I'll sit down and catch my breath. I'd forgotten how tiring two whole days of shopping can be." Tootsie dropped her loaded bag on the floor and slumped down on the end of the sofa.

She waited until she heard the water running in the shower and then grabbed her phone from her purse. Luke sounded out of breath when he answered on the third ring. "Hello. Y'all havin' fun?"

"We're plumb tuckered out," Tootsie answered. "How's Dolly? Is she missing me?"

"She sits in your recliner and pouts," Luke chuckled. "So what's been going on? Y'all got lots of shopping done?"

"We decided not to talk about our problems for the whole two days," Tootsie said, "and we haven't, but I guess Joanie's move is really happening, because Brett called a real estate agent and got things started. I thought they might back out and he'd decide to get a job in San Antonio, but no."

"Does that make you sad?" Luke asked.

"A little. I'm happy for her, but it's going to be an adjustment for all of us, and right here on the heels of their girls all leaving and Smokey's death. Seems like it's a lot to handle at once." Tootsie kicked off her shoes and propped up her feet on the coffee table.

"How would you feel about me buying Joanie's house?" he asked.

Tootsie almost dropped the phone. "Are you serious? I'd love to have you close by. You don't even need to ask such a thing." She wanted to squeal, but if she did, Carmen would come rushing to see if she was hurt.

"It's just something I've been thinking about this weekend. Don't say anything to Joanie yet, until I make up my mind. But I would like to know who the real estate agent is so I can be first in line to make a bid," he said.

"Oh, Luke!" Tootsie sighed. "That's just the best news I've had in a long time. I'll find out for you. Got to go now. It's my turn for a shower, and then we're all meeting in my room for a glass of wine. See you tomorrow by noon."

"I'll have dinner ready, so don't eat more'n a snack on the way. Good night," he said.

"Good night to you. Kiss Dolly for me," Tootsie said.

"You got it," he said. "And y'all drive safe."

Carmen came out of the bathroom with a towel around her head and wearing a pair of Rudolph the Red-Nosed Reindeer pajama pants with a bright-green tank top. "Your turn."

Tootsie danced a little jig in the bathroom when she kicked off her sweats and underwear. If Joanie had to leave, then the best new neighbor ever would be Luke. She just had to figure out how to get the name of that real estate agent without causing suspicion. When she came out of the bathroom in her royal-blue silk pajamas, the other three were already sitting on Carmen's queen-size bed. They'd already gotten the wine from the refrigerator and four plastic hotel cups. The package of chocolate cookies sat on the nightstand between the two beds.

"I'm calling this meeting to order." Tootsie took her place in the circle. "Old business?"

No one said a word.

"Okay, then, let's get on with the new business. I'll go first this time. These past two days haven't been easy on me. Smokey wasn't there beside me to help me pick out presents, and he won't be in Sugar Run when I get there to fuss about how many Christmas cards I send out. We've all escaped the pain of the empty nest, but in about four weeks, we have to go home and face it. I'm not sure I'll be ready for the first Christmas without him."

Diana poured wine for all of them and held up her glass. "I've been thinking the same thing all day. We needed to escape. That's a fact, but when we get home, the nest is still going to be empty."

"Okay, go on. What's going on with Luke now? Seemed like he was quick to make an excuse not to come with us on this trip," Joanie said.

"I'm glad he didn't come. We both needed to be away from each other for a while." Diana told them about their conversation concerning kids during the Halloween event at the church, but she didn't mention his problems with conception.

"That's a pretty serious discussion before y'all even have a first date." Tootsie broke the cookie apart and ate the icing first.

"We're old enough to know that it's a waste of time and effort to start something that can't be finished." Diana sipped at the wine.

"Well, then it's a good thing that you had these days to think." Tootsie nodded. "Have you changed your mind about starting all over with kids?"

Diana shook her head. "Nope, and I really don't expect that he's changed his."

"You've kind of gotten past the age difference, though, haven't you?" Carmen asked.

"I guess I have." Diana nodded. "Your turn, Carmen."

Carmen took a deep breath and let it out very slowly. "I called Sharlene at the base today. Remember, I told y'all about her offering me a job? Well, I finally got in touch with her. I'll be helping take care of kids who are in the after-school program on the base," Carmen explained. "She says that in the next year or so, she's putting in a day-care center where the base personnel can leave their preschool-age kids. They'll need at least one certified teacher to run it the way she wants to, so it'll work out perfect because I can have my degree by then."

"You think you'd like that?" Tootsie asked.

"It'll pay the mortgage and keep the lights on, and I love kids; plus, I'll be a teacher." Carmen finished off a cookie and reached for another one.

"Joanie, do you want to share?" Tootsie asked.

"I talked to Brett again today. He thinks we should go ahead and send the house key to the real estate agent. The market isn't very good right now, and that would give her a whole month to show it. I keep trying to remember if I left everything in order, because buyers will be opening closet doors. Thank goodness Zoe had just cleaned her room up before she left," Joanie answered.

Diana laughed out loud. "I'm glad I don't have to let a buyer into my place. They'd run for the hills if they saw Rebecca's messy room."

"Is he listing it exclusively or with several Realtors?" Tootsie asked.

"Exclusively with the wife of one of the guys on the base." Joanie divided the rest of the wine between the four of them. "Lindsey's Real Estate out of Sugar Run. They live on the other side of town, and she works out of her garage. He says if we haven't had any bites at all on the place in a month, that we'll go wider when he gets home."

"Sounds like a plan to me. Is that all the new business?" Tootsie yawned.

"Well, I do have one more piece of new business," Carmen said. "I make a motion that we all sleep in tomorrow morning and don't hit the hotel dining room until nine o'clock."

Diana raised a hand. "I second the motion."

"And I third it," Tootsie said. "Now let's join hands, and, Carmen, you can read the sign tonight." She pointed to the little plaque that was now lying on the end table beside Tootsie's bed.

When they'd finished, Diana and Joanie hurried across the hall to their room, and Tootsie sent Luke a text telling him the real estate agent's name. Then she closed her eyes, snuggled down in her bed, and dreamed of Smokey. In the dream, they were sitting on the porch of their house in Sugar Run watching little children run and play on the front lawn. She awoke at midnight with a smile on her face. Maybe the dream meant there would be more children on her block after all.

Chapter Twenty

*E*ight long days passed.

There had been lighthearted banter between Luke and the ladies all week. But underneath, awkward tension still prevailed when Diana was alone in the room with Luke. He was such a good man, and he deserved more out of life than she was willing to give. But with each passing day, she wanted to be with him more and more. To be held and kissed like he'd held and kissed her on the back pew of that church, to know that feeling of closeness, of breathlessness—she wanted it so badly.

They'd just finished breakfast when Diana's phone rang. She squealed when Rebecca's picture appeared on the screen, and answered it on the second ring. "Can you talk longer than a minute this time?"

"Maybe all of five, but don't put it on speaker, Mama. We know about the divorce. Daddy spilled the beans when I talked to him this morning. I called to say happy Veterans Day like we always do on this day, and he told me. Zoe and I decided it was best to tell Natalie," Rebecca said.

"Happy Veterans Day to you," Diana said. "I never would have believed that I'd be saying 'Thank you for your service' to my daughter, but I am. And is Natalie going to call her mama tonight, too? I'm right here with the rest of the folks. Should I put it on speaker?"

"Just tell them all hello for me," Rebecca said.

"So what's going on in your world today?" Diana asked.

"Well, I wanted to talk about this Luke fellow you mentioned. I kind of remember him from Smokey's funeral. Handsome dude. Is he there in the room with y'all, too?"

Diana sneaked a sideways glance over toward Luke. "I want to talk about *you*. It's only about four more weeks until basic is over. Any idea at all where you might be going for training?"

"So Luke is there, too," Rebecca giggled. "Okay, then, we'll talk about me. Natalie and I both tested high in the intelligence field. I'm really hoping and working toward eventually getting into the cyber program, but that's later on down the road, like after officer training school. Still don't know where I'll go for training, but I'm ready to dive into it," Rebecca said.

"And where's the AIT located?" Diana held her breath.

"Goodfellow Base at San Angelo," Rebecca giggled. "I signed up to see the world, and I get sent to a base only a couple of hours from home. But after twenty-four weeks of training, we'll both probably be sent overseas, like maybe Germany."

Six months. At least Diana would have her close by until summer. "How do you feel about that?"

"Well, you could drive down and see me once in a while there, and I enlisted to serve, Mama, so wherever I'm needed is where I'm willing to go, just like Smokey was. And I'll get to see the world."

Scratch any grandchildren for a long time, Diana thought.

~

Carmen's phone rang, and she took it upstairs, answering it on the way up to her room. "I've been sitting in the living room eavesdropping on Diana's call and hoping that you'd call."

"Rebecca's dad told her about the divorce, Mama, and she told me and Zoe. I was mad as hell at first, but I'm over it now. Are you all right?"

"I'm working through it. This trip has helped." Carmen sat down with a thud on the floor beside her bed.

"I saw it coming this summer when he was home. I just didn't say anything because I wanted to be wrong," Natalie said. "He was all the time taking phone calls outside or in the garage, and I heard him whisper 'Love you, too' one time. I convinced myself that he was talking to Grandma."

The lump in Carmen's throat was at least the size of an orange, maybe even a grapefruit. "I agonized over telling you. I didn't want the news to upset you so much that you had trouble in basic."

"I'm just worried about you, Mama. What are you going to do? Can we keep the house? Will you get a job? I can send money home, but it won't be enough to . . ." Natalie paused for a breath.

"Honey, I've already got a job offer, working on the base with children, and we can keep the house. You aren't to send a dime home. You take care of you and enjoy life. Now tell me what's going on with you other than this. Do you know anything about AIT yet?"

"Well, me and Rebecca have been singled out to probably go to . . ." She talked on nonstop about the possibility of training for her job at Goodfellow. "And you can drive down and see me on weekends the six months I'll be there."

"What about Zoe?" Carmen asked.

"She might get a chance at being a combat medic and will be getting part of her training, if not all of it, right there at Bullis. She'll be coming right back to where she started for the training, and her folks are moving to Virginia. Go figure how fate works," Natalie giggled.

"We'll all help take care of her for sure, but that is kind of weird." Carmen laughed with her.

"Give everyone my love, Mama, and tell Tootsie the next time I call we'll put it on speaker so I can talk to her, too. That will probably be next Sunday, if all goes well. It's just great to hear your voice, and please don't worry. We'll be fine. After all, we've spent most of our lives alone. This isn't anything new. Don't get me wrong. I love Daddy, but he's a son of a bitch for the way he's acted," Natalie said. "Love you. See you."

"See you. Love you more," Carmen said.

Since she was a little girl, Natalie had refused to tell Eli or anyone goodbye. She said that was a bad word that made her cry, so she just said, "See you." She'd even whispered those words to Smokey as she walked past his casket at the funeral.

Carmen put her head on her drawn-up knees and took several deep breaths. Natalie knew and wasn't hysterical. That brought her more closure than anything else had until now, including splitting a shed full of wood.

~

Joanie took her call in the dining room and was just hanging up when the rest of the family joined her around the table. "I guess y'all know about everything I do. Can you believe my kid could be coming right back to Bullis, not twenty minutes from our house, and we're selling it and moving to Virginia?"

"I'll take good care of her. Don't you worry one bit," Tootsie said.

"Thank you." Joanie smiled. "One year ago today, we were all having Veterans Day dinner at Tootsie and Smokey's place. I'm wondering what we'll be looking back on one year from today."

"Well, every one of us has been touched by a veteran in some way, and we never know, when we're part of a family like this, what the future holds," Tootsie said.

Joanie cocked her head to one side. "The way you loved Smokey, I'm surprised you didn't enlist full-time, Luke."

"My stint in the National Guard was enough for me. I used the money to pay for my education and start up my business," he said. "I could've gone active duty, but they wanted me to use my techie knowledge for something other than building games."

"And now you're a millionaire and retired at thirty-two," Tootsie said.

"Not until November twenty-eighth." He grinned. "Are we having a party?"

"Of course," Tootsie said. "With turkey and dressing, cranberry sauce, and all that Thanksgiving dinner means. But we're having one in four days that will involve birthday cake and wine for Diana."

"Hmmm." Luke held up four fingers. "Joanie cooked today. I get kitchen duty the next day." Two fingers went down. "That means Carmen is next in line, and Diana is right after that on her birthday. A beautiful woman should not have to work in the kitchen on her birthday, so I'll take her day. It'll be my birthday present to you, Diana."

"And I'll take it with gratitude, so thank you." Diana nodded.

"I'll bring the liquor," Joanie offered. "I stopped at a vendor and bought three quarts of moonshine. I've got apple pie, blackberry, and smoky peach."

Where would Zoe be next year at this time? For that matter, where would Joanie be? She knew she wouldn't be in Sugar Run, but would she and Brett fly or drive to wherever their daughter was for the holiday? Or would Zoe be able to come home for a few days?

"This party is sounding pretty good." Diana smiled.

Carmen pushed back her chair and headed to the kitchen. "Tootsie and I'll do decorations. Anyone want a glass of tea?"

"Not me." Luke stood and waved over his shoulder as he left. "I've got some work to do, so I'm leaving early tonight."

"And I'm going up to my room and getting some of my projects done early so I don't have to work on Friday, since it's my birthday." Diana got up and headed for the stairs.

Joanie reached out and grabbed her hand as she passed. "It's been over a week. Have y'all talked yet? The longer you wait, the tougher it is to get the words out."

"I think the whole attraction is going to die in its sleep," Diana said.

Carmen shook her head slowly from side to side. "From the way he looks at you, I don't believe that it will."

"Talk to him. Do it this week; promise me." Joanie let go of her hand.

"I promise." Diana hurried out of the room.

"You believe her?" Tootsie whispered.

"She's never gone back on her word, so yes, ma'am, I think she'll do it," Joanie said. "I don't like this tension between them. They were teasing and bantering until Halloween. I had high hopes that something would come of it. I haven't seen her like this in years."

"What will be will be," Tootsie said.

"And to finish it like Smokey always did, 'What won't be might be anyway.' Remember him saying that all the time?"

"Yep, I sure do, and he was always right," Tootsie agreed.

Chapter Twenty-One

S aying anything about children had been a stupid thing to do. They had exchanged only a few kisses—hadn't even been out on a date—but Luke had never been good with women. Knowing when to open his mouth, when to keep it closed, and, above all things, how to be romantic had never been his strong suit. He laced his hands behind his head and stared first at the ceiling and then out the window. Dark clouds occasionally obliterated part of the twinkling stars trying to throw a little light on a moonless night.

A howling coyote, a hoot owl, and the steady beating of his heart were the only sounds he heard until there was a light rap on the motorhome door. He glanced at the clock as he jerked on a pair of pajama pants. Seeing that it was one o'clock in the morning, his first thought was that something had happened to Tootsie. He flipped on the porch light and peeked out the narrow door window to see Diana standing there with a worried expression on her face. That put a knot the size of a basketball in his stomach—she was there to tell him that Aunt Tootsie had joined Uncle Smokey in eternity.

He flung open the door and said, "Give me time to get dressed."

"What for?" She shivered as she stepped inside. "You don't have to wear a shirt for us to talk, but it might be a little less distracting if you did."

"Is Aunt Tootsie all right?" He could hardly get the words out.

Diana leaned against the cabinet. "Of course. Oh!" She threw a hand up over her mouth. "I'm so sorry, Luke. I should have led with that. Of course that would be the first thing you'd think about at this hour. She's all right. I'm here to talk about us, and I came at a crazy time because I couldn't sleep for thinking about it."

He flipped on the overhead light, took her by the hand, and pulled her over to the booth. "Shall I make a pot of coffee or pour us some wine?"

"I'd rather have a beer," she said as she sat down.

He went to the fridge, took out two longneck bottles, twisted off the lids, and set them on the table. "I'll be back in a minute."

It took him only a few seconds to pull a shirt over his head, but he took a minute longer to check his reflection in the mirror. "Don't do anything stupid, Luke," he whispered as he ran a comb through his unruly hair.

"Thank you for the beer and for putting on a shirt." Diana smiled up at him when he slid into the booth beside her. "I'll go first since I woke you up and scared you."

"You did give me a start, but I wasn't asleep," he said.

"That makes me feel a little bit better. I like you a lot, Luke, but getting too serious might be putting the cart before the horse." She turned up her beer and took several long gulps.

He scooted around the U-shaped booth until their hips were touching. "This seems a little anticlimactic after the awkwardness that has been between us for the better part of a week."

She laid her hand on his thigh. "Smokey told me when all that went down with Gerald to go to a quiet place where no one would bother me for at least ten minutes. I was to think about living with Gerald without being able to trust him for five minutes—to get the full emotional effect of how that would feel. Then I was to turn it completely around and think about raising Rebecca alone. Whichever one brought me peace, then that was my answer."

"That's a great way to look at things." He reached out to tuck a strand of hair behind her ear. "It's like touching strands of silk."

"That's pretty romantic," she whispered.

"Just statin' facts." He cupped her chin in his hand and leaned in for a kiss. One kiss led to another and another until finally he slid out of the booth and held out his hand.

She put hers in it and pulled him toward the bedroom.

"Are you sure about this, Diana?" he asked. "Seems like this shouldn't happen until a third or fourth date event, and maybe in the penthouse of a fancy hotel, not a motor home in Scrap, Texas."

"As long as we're together, it doesn't matter where it happens. If one time proves we're very wrong about what we're feeling, we might as well find out now," she said.

"That may be the most unromantic thing I've ever heard," he chuckled.

She tugged his shirt up over his head and tossed it on the floor. "Maybe so, but it's the truth. If either or both of us . . ."

He scooped her up in his arms like a bride. "Like the song says, we need a little less talk and a little more action," he said as he kicked the door shut with his bare foot.

~

Diana awoke and for a single second wondered where she was. Then she felt Luke's soft breath warming the tender spot under her ear. She'd thought when she'd impulsively taken him to bed that she'd feel remorse and shame when it was all over, but not in the slightest. She wanted to purr like Dolly when Tootsie rubbed her neck.

"Good mornin'," she said when she realized his eyes were open.

"Mornin' to you." He strung kisses from her neck to her lips. "I don't think it was a flash in the pan."

"Not yet, anyway."

"Are you saying that we'll have to spend more nights together to figure it out?" He propped up on one elbow and looked deeply into her eyes.

"Maybe so." She snuggled down closer to him, liking the way their bodies fit so well together.

"It'll be a trial and a chore, but I'll do my best to endure," he teased.

"Dear God!" she gasped.

"What'd I say? I was only joking," he said.

"It's not you. Look at the clock. We slept longer than I thought. It's almost five, and Tootsie gets up early. I've got to get back over to the house." She threw back the covers and started getting dressed.

"Ashamed of me?"

She flipped on the lamp beside the table so she could see him better. His broad chest with its soft sprinkling of light-brown hair called to her. His grin and twinkling eyes said that he was teasing.

"Darlin', I'm not one bit ashamed of us, but I don't want to answer a gazillion questions when the others wake up. I'd like to bask in the glory of what we have for a little while before we go public with it," she said as she jerked on her pants and socks and then her shirt. "I couldn't find my bra. Can you bring it to me when you come to the house?"

"Or maybe I'll hold it hostage until you come back," he joked.

In one fluid movement, she was sitting on top of him, leaning forward to kiss him one more time. He was right—this was more than a onetime thing. She could flat-out feel it in her heart and soul.

"Why don't we just hang a tie on the door? I think there's one of Uncle Smokey's in the closet." He wrapped his arms around her and rolled with her so that he was holding her close to his body again.

"Sounds tempting, but I don't think so." She unwound herself from his arms and slipped her feet down into her shoes. "See you in an hour or so. I believe it's your day to cook."

He sat up in bed and propped his back against the headboard. "Seems only right that I make you breakfast after that amazing night."

"I'll look forward to it." She blew him a kiss and hurried outside.

She didn't breathe easy until she was in her bedroom. Knowing that she wouldn't be able to go to sleep, she sat down and wrote Rebecca a letter. She didn't mention a word about Luke but told her how much she'd miss their tradition of going out to dinner on her birthday. Then when she heard Carmen and Joanie rattling around in their bedrooms, she gathered up a clean pair of jeans, underwear, and a shirt and went to the bathroom to take a shower. When she finished and was dressed, she peeked out the door, hoping that Carmen and Joanie were both already downstairs. She heard Luke's deep twang and Tootsie's southern drawl coming from the living room. Then Carmen's high-pitched voice piped up, and they all laughed.

"Good mornin'," Joanie said, coming up the stairs. "I forgot my phone. It's got pictures of Dolly and the kittens on it, and Luke said I can use his printer to make a paper copy of them to send to Zoe."

"Hey, I didn't think of that. We can send the girls pictures of this place and some of the festivals we went to, and I've even got a few of Halloween," Diana said, glad that Joanie hadn't taken one look at her and demanded to know why she was glowing.

"They'll be so excited." Joanie retrieved her phone from the bedroom. "And we can write letters to them on the back of the paper where we print the pictures. I figure we can get several on one page."

Diana followed her down the steps, her mind on which pictures would be best to send. "Good morning," she sing-songed as she headed through the kitchen to help Tootsie set the table. "What is that scrumptious smell? Is it pumpkin?"

"That's right." Luke winked. "We've got bacon quiche and then pumpkin tarts for dessert."

"He's showing off," Tootsie teased. "But ain't a one of us going to complain, are we, girls?"

"No, ma'am," they all answered in unison.

"I'm not showing off. It's just that some mornings are better than others, and this is one of them," Luke declared.

"Did y'all talk or something?" Tootsie whispered to Diana.

"We did, and it's all worked out. We will be dating when we get home, but we're taking it very slow," Diana answered.

"Good," Tootsie said. "I was damn tired of the tension around here. I can take you girls bickering, because that's just joking around with each other, and sisters oftentimes argue. But I didn't like that you and Luke were uncomfortable with each other."

"Me, either," Diana said.

Chapter Twenty-Two

$\mathcal{E}$verything settled into a new routine by Friday. Late at night, Diana would sneak out of the house and spend a few hours with Luke, then make it back to her room before daybreak. She'd forgotten it was even her birthday until she came out of her morning shower to the smell of cinnamon floating up the stairs.

"Would you hurry up?" Tootsie yelled from the bottom of the stairs. "Luke is putting the icing on the cinnamon rolls, and they're best when they're right out of the oven."

Diana couldn't have wiped the smile off her face if she'd sucked all the juice from a lemon. She'd mentioned to Luke that she loved cinnamon rolls night before last. "I smell them, and I'm on my way."

"Happy birthday!" All four of the women pointed to the table where Luke was busy lighting a candle that he'd placed right in the middle of a pan of iced cinnamon rolls.

"Blow it out and make a wish," Tootsie said.

Diana whipped her hair to one side, leaned down and closed her eyes, and blew out the candle. "I thought I would be blowing out candles on my cake later on today."

"You will." Luke cut sections, put one on each plate, and passed them out to everyone. "This is just the first of two or three birthday wishes you get to make today."

Carmen forked a bite into her mouth. "Delicious. Now, Diana, we want to know what you wished for."

"Not until she takes a bite, or it won't come true," Tootsie said as she dipped her first bite in her coffee.

Diana cut off a bite, dipped it in coffee, and quickly got it into her mouth before it fell off the fork. "You should forget techie stuff and invest in a café, Luke."

"Your wish?" Joanie asked.

"I wished that someday we could bring our daughters here for a vacation," Diana answered.

Tootsie wiped her mouth with a paper napkin with **HAPPY BIRTHDAY** printed on it. "That can be arranged anytime they all got leave. One or all three can come here with y'all or with all of us. It's open to whoever wants to use it at any time."

"Thank you," Diana said. "Tell us about your honeymoon here. Weren't your folks still living then?"

"Sure they were. Granny and Grandpa had moved into Clarksville to be near her sister, and they gave the place to my folks. I was born right here in this house. Then when me and Smokey got married, Mama and Daddy went on down to Granny's house for a week so we could have our honeymoon alone." Tootsie got a faraway look in her eyes as she talked about it.

"What happened at the end of the week?" Carmen asked.

"They came home in time to see us off to Smokey's first duty station in Georgia. Mama cried when I left. I cried all the way across Louisiana. Smokey didn't know what to do with me. Then we stopped for gas, and I went to the bathroom. The ladies' room had an old cracked mirror above the sink, and I stared at my reflection a long time." Tootsie took the time to eat a few more bites before she continued. "I decided that I loved Smokey more than my folks, my friends, and anything else in the world. So I dried my tears and bought a Coca-Cola in a bottle. That's the only way they came in those days, and I got myself a candy bar to go with it. I promised myself that when I got done with those two things, I was going to make the best of my new life in Georgia. And that if Smokey had to go to Siberia, I'd go with him with a smile on my face."

"And you did, right?" Joanie asked.

"Never had to go to Siberia, but the two winters we spent in the German mountains, I thought I might freeze plumb to death," Tootsie giggled. "But enough about me. Tell me about your best birthday and your worst one ever, Diana."

"Worst was the year that Rebecca was born. She was six weeks old, and Gerald had to leave again two days before my birthday. Looking back, I probably had postpartum depression. Strangely enough, my best birthday was the same one. Carmen and Joanie had both just moved into base housing, one on either side of me. They each had a baby, too, and their husbands were on the newly formed team with Gerald, and our husbands had left on the same mission. They came over that evening with a casserole and their daughters, and we spent half the night talking about everything," Diana said.

~

Carmen reached for a third cinnamon roll. "We've sure been through a lot since that evening. I felt like I was about to drown, and meeting y'all was a lifeboat."

Before she'd taken the first bite, her phone rang. She recognized the number as being the lawyer she'd talked to a couple of times about the divorce. "Hello, this is Carmen Walker."

"Miz Walker, this is Lester Thomas. I've got the revised divorce papers in my hands. Tootsie said it was all right if I called your husband's lawyer and talked to him. This looks much better than that first one, but you are still entitled to alimony if you'd like to pursue that," he said.

"Eli told me about the revision, and I've decided to sign it. If you could mail it to me, that would be great," she said.

"I'll drop it in the post office this afternoon. If you are sure about this, just sign it, and mail it back to me. I'll take care of the rest of it," he said.

"We don't have to go to court or see each other?" she asked.

"Not if you agree on everything. His lawyer and I will meet with the judge in chambers. I'll file it and then send you a final copy. Maybe you should think about it for a while. Once it's signed, you can't go back and ask for alimony. It appears the house you have is the only shared property, and it still has about seven years left on the mortgage. Are you willing to take that on with no job and no alimony? You could at least ask that he make the payments for the first year so you can get your feet under you," Mr. Thomas said.

"I've got a job waiting for me when we get back to Sugar Run, and I want as little to do with him as possible. I'm ready to sign and get it over with. I want to thank you for all your help, though. Please send the bill—"

"Oh, no payment is necessary," he butted in before she could finish. "Smokey was an old golfing buddy, and Tootsie worked for me for years. Smokey talked about you three ladies a lot—like y'all were kinfolks, so let me do this in his memory."

"Then thank you very much." Carmen made a mental note to take the lawyer a basket of homemade cookies and breads when she got home.

Everyone around the breakfast table was staring at her when she ended the call. "You probably heard enough to know that was the law-yer," she explained. "He's mailing the papers here. I will sign them and send them back. I'm hoping it's all done by Thanksgiving so when we take turns around the table sayin' what we're thankful for, I can simply say 'closure.'"

"And start off the new year with a new life," Luke encouraged.

"Amen. And, honey, you don't need anything Eli has in the way of financial help," Tootsie declared. "I've got more money than I'll ever spend, so if you get in a bind, you just let me know."

"Thank you, but I called my friend last night and told her I'd be there for work on December fifteenth. That'll give me a few days to get settled at home before I start. She said the first day will just be paper-work, but after that I'll be working from eight to five every day, and I can have all the overtime I want," Carmen said. "I'd have mentioned it first thing this morning, but this is not about me today. It's Diana's birthday."

"And what better present could I have than knowing that you're actually about to have closure and that you have a job," Diana said. "That's just the best birthday present ever."

"Do y'all realize that in three weeks, we'll all be at our daughters' graduation? And Brett will be home, and the divorce will be done with?" Joanie asked.

"Life sure has taken some strange twists and turns for all of us in the past seven weeks, hasn't it?" Carmen got up and brought the coffeepot to the table to refill all their cups. "It's been good to be here in Scrap, so thank you again, Tootsie."

"Aww, pshaw!" Tootsie waved away the words with a flick of her hand. "It's me that's got the blessing. I was crazy with grief, but coming home has helped me come to terms with Smokey's leaving me so fast."

Luke pointed at the ceiling and frowned. "I think I hear sleet hit-ting the roof. I hope we don't lose power again or, worse yet, have an ice storm closer to the time when we need to leave for the graduation."

Carmen went to the window and pulled back the curtains. "That's exactly what you hear, but we've got lots of firewood cut, and there's still two or three bottles of lamp oil in the pantry, so we should be fine. And if there's ice on the road when we need to leave, we'll get out some skis."

"Or hire us a sled and some mules to pull it," Tootsie laughed.

"I'm going to take mail out to the box and see if we've got letters before the ground gets slick." Luke pushed back from the table and headed to the living room for his coat. "Tornadoes and now an ice storm. Never saw such crazy weather in northeast Texas. Have you, Aunt Tootsie?" He didn't wait for an answer but disappeared out the front door.

"Answer is yes, I have. The winter before me and Smokey got married, it iced over up here, and we didn't get mail for a whole week. Smokey and I wrote to each other every day, and I thought I'd plumb die without his letters," she said. "Weather is like life. It ain't nothing but a cycle. We'll have some cold winters, and then we'll have some that ain't bad at all."

"Know what life really is?" Carmen asked.

"Breathing, eating, sleeping, loving," Joanie offered.

"No," Carmen giggled. "It's a four-letter word."

"Damn straight." Tootsie laughed with her. "And them other four-letter words come in right handy when I'm pissed at the world."

"You got it, Tootsie." Carmen's giggles were so infectious that everyone started in laughing. "And just so y'all know, if Luke brings in some wood that already smells a little scorched, it's because I unloaded a whole wheelbarrow full of four-letter words on those logs when I was splitting them."

Chapter Twenty-Three

They had three days of icy weather, but Carmen insisted on going to the mailbox at the end of the lane every day. The sooner the divorce papers arrived, the sooner she could sign them and be done with it. The first day, she did some fancy footwork to keep from falling either flat on her face or on her butt a couple of times before she made it to the mailbox. The second day, she took a tumble five feet from her destination and had to crawl to the mailbox post to get her feet solid under her again. The third day, she kicked the post. There wasn't even a letter from one of the girls or a damned bill for her efforts.

She heaved a long sigh of relief when she saw the big yellow envelope on the fourth day. "Thank you, God!" she muttered through the scarf wrapped snugly around her face. She gathered up all the mail and stuffed it inside the coat that had belonged to Smokey. It hung to her knees, and the sleeves were rolled up, but it was warmer than the lightweight jacket she'd brought from Sugar Run. Who would have ever thought that the weather could be so different from one part of Texas to another? Bending her head against the bitter cold, she hurried back to the house.

For the next three days, everyone in the house went over the divorce decree, one sentence at a time. Tootsie called the lawyer several times so he could explain the legalese. One week after Diana's birthday and with everyone gathered around her, Carmen signed the papers and dated them November twenty-second. It was just her name on the last page in a seven-sheet stack of paper, but somewhere near the bottom it really should have said THE END.

"Six weeks and two days since Eli got this whole process started. Shouldn't I feel something?" She'd thought there would be relief or perhaps a fresh burst of anger, but there was nothing at all.

"Feelin' a little numb, are you?" Diana asked.

Carmen nodded. "Like I'm hanging in space waiting for . . ." She paused. "I don't know what, but it feels like it'll shock the shit out of me when it arrives."

"It won't," Diana told her. "It's over now, but complete closure takes a while. For me, it was when I realized that I hadn't thought about Gerald in a whole week."

"Then I may never have it, because every day something reminds me of him." Carmen slipped the stack of paper into the envelope and sealed it. "Makes me wonder what he thought when he signed his name."

"Probably that as soon as he got the final decree, he could rush off to the courthouse and marry that girl." Joanie covered her mouth with her hand. "I'm sorry. That was harsh, wasn't it?"

"Life is harsh," Tootsie said. "But he's fixin' to find out the same thing. Being a full-time husband and father isn't easy. I remember when Smokey got out of the service. It took some serious adjustments for us to get used to living together. I used to wish to God he'd get a part-time job and get out of my hair for a little while each day, but we finally settled into a lifestyle that we came to love. Delores said that she had the same problems when her Jimmy retired. Eli is going to have even more adjustments than you will."

"Think I'll ever get used to this new way of life?" Carmen asked.

Diana laid a hand on her shoulder. "Yes, you will. Want me to take that out to the mailbox? It was right nice of the lawyer to send a stamped self-addressed envelope along with the papers."

"I think it'll help if I do it myself," Carmen answered. "Thank goodness Smokey left behind a heavy coat for us to share for the outdoor chores. I'm hoping to have the final papers back by Thanksgiving."

"If they don't make it by then, I'll wrap up a piece of paper for your Christmas present that will have the word *closure* written in glitter on it," Tootsie said.

"That may be the only way I get it." Carmen smiled as she took the heavy coat from the hook inside the kitchen door. She picked up the envelope and almost tripped over her kitten, Sugar, romping around the floor with her two siblings. She laid the envelope and the coat to the side and sat down on the floor to let all three kittens crawl up into her lap.

"Y'all need to name your kittens." She looked up at Luke and Diana, who were sitting on the sofa. "Poor babies should've been named before they opened their eyes, but now that they can see, they're feeling unloved."

"Simba, from *The Lion King.* That's my boy's name," Luke said.

"Nala," Diana said. "That's Simba's friend in the movie."

"Sugar, darlin', I want you to meet Nala and Simba, your siblings. We'll plan playdates for you, so don't be sad when we separate you. Now be nice while I'm gone," she said as she stood and put on the coat.

"I'll go out this afternoon and bring in the mail," Luke offered. "Here's hoping we all get letters today and that they aren't bills."

"I won't argue. It's colder'n a mother-in-law's kiss out there." Carmen started for the door. "And I can testify to that."

But not anymore, Smokey reminded her. *No more trying to please a woman who was never going to think you were good enough for her son, and never again having to sit through a tense meal with her or spend any time with her at all.*

"Well, that's certainly one good thing that's coming out of this," Carmen muttered to herself as she stepped off the porch. Then it hit her that Luke had been going to get the mail pretty often the past couple of weeks. She and Diana and Joanie had been taking turns taking their outgoing letters out in the morning, but Luke was often the one who brought in the mail later in the day. Maybe, she thought, he just likes yelling "Mail call."

Or maybe there's something more going on, Smokey whispered so softly that she jumped to see if he was behind her.

"I think today I'll beat him out here and see who's writing to him. I'll shoot him myself if he's flirting with Diana and getting letters from some other hussy." She put the flag up on the mailbox, slid her envelope inside, and trudged back to the house. The mail person was slow that day, or else they had no letters, because there was nothing for her to take back to the house, but at least the divorce papers were there for him to pick up when he did get there. That brought a good-size measure of closure to her.

Since it was her day for kitchen duty, she forgot about the mail until Luke came inside that afternoon and yelled out the familiar words: "Mail call."

He had letters for everyone, including himself. Carmen watched as he shoved his letter into his hip pocket, and she vowed that she'd not only find out who was writing to him but that he'd pay if he hurt Diana. Her friend had fought a long battle before she would even say that she'd go out with him, so if this wasn't going to be an exclusive relationship, then Diana deserved to know up front.

Chapter Twenty-Four

appy Thanksgiving," Tootsie said when Delores answered the phone that morning.

"How wonderful to hear your voice," Delores said. "Happy Thanksgiving to you, and I'm so glad you called. The kids all came home yesterday and surprised me, but it was for an intervention."

"You been drinking too much?" Tootsie was genuinely concerned.

"No, it's an intervention for me to move to be closer to one of them. They gave me a choice, and I thought about it all night. I don't want to leave the country, so England is out, and I didn't like New York when we were stationed there, or Arizona, either, for that matter. But I do like Florida, so I'm moving there to be near my daughter," Delores said. "You are so lucky that your adopted kids live so close."

Lucky didn't even describe her good fortune when Diana, Carmen, and Joanie had all moved to her block with their little girls that summer more than a decade ago. They'd brought life back into Tootsie and Smokey's world and had truly been a blessing.

"Remember, one of them is moving to Virginia pretty soon after we go home. Closer to you," Tootsie reminded her. "But there's a possibility that Luke will be moving into Sugar Run."

"And you don't have to leave your home or your memories," Delores sighed.

"I hope I get to stay right where I am until they carry me out feetfirst," Tootsie said. "But I've worried about you being all alone in that house; I'm glad you're going to live near your daughter. Still, I know how tough it will be to leave it and all your memories behind."

"The only way I can deal with it is to pack them up and take them with me. Then when I get to my new house, which is actually the guesthouse behind my daughter's place and is right on the beach, I'll unpack them first," Delores said. "I just want you to promise that you'll come visit me."

"I promise," Tootsie said. "And I've got room if you ever want to come to Sugar Run and stay a week or a month or as long as you can."

"You can bet I will," Delores told her. "The kids are here for two weeks, and in that time they plan to get the house on the market. I'll be going home with my daughter."

They talked awhile longer and then ended the call with promises that they would indeed visit each other. "Well, what do you think of that, Smokey? Aren't you glad we bought our house in Sugar Run? I don't have to go to some assisted-living care place when I can no longer take care of myself. The girls and Luke will be right there to help me out."

He didn't answer, so she took that as a sign that he agreed with her.

~

Diana awoke on Thanksgiving morning and was about to get out of bed when Carmen poked her head in the door. "You awake?"

"Just barely." Diana yawned. "Are you bringing coffee?"

Carmen came on in and sat on the bed. "I'm worried, and I don't want to discuss this at the Sunday-night therapy meetings we've been having. I know that you and Luke have reached some sort of agreement, because there's no tension between y'all lately. And I've seen the way he flirts with you with little inside jokes sometimes. But he's getting letters, and I think they're from another woman. I don't want you to go through the pain and hurt again that we've both had to endure."

Diana pushed back the covers and got out of bed. She went to the armoire and got out a pair of jeans and one of her nicer shirts. "Do you remember the first time we got mail from the girls? Remember that Luke got nothing?"

"Of course. I felt sorry for him," Carmen answered.

Diana removed her nightshirt and got dressed. "I wrote to him and snuck it out to the mailbox. After that, he hasn't been left out at mail call. I'm the *other woman* who's been sending letters to him ever since. He's answered every one of them but sneaks them into my purse."

"Well, hell's bells!" Carmen fumed. "That's why you carry your purse downstairs every morning and why he wants to go get the mail every afternoon. What in the devil do y'all write about?"

"Everything." Diana stood in front of the vanity, brushed her hair, and pulled it up into a ponytail. "It's amazing how much more you can learn about a person with letters. I should have told y'all what we were doing at one of our therapy sessions, but it sounds kind of juvenile. Kind of like kids passing notes at school."

"But you're going to tell it this week, right? Because if I've noticed it, you can bet Tootsie has, and we don't want to worry her," Carmen said.

"Of course I will," Diana agreed. *But I'm not telling y'all that I've been spending almost every night in the motor home with him. That's just too damn personal to share, even with my best friends, and besides, I don't want to jinx it before he even meets Rebecca.*

"Well, I sure feel better." Carmen stood and started out of the room. "Now let's go get some breakfast. I hear Tootsie and Luke in the kitchen already."

"Hey, where are you going?" Joanie almost ran smack into Carmen.

"To get dressed," Carmen answered.

"Then wait a minute. I've got something to tell y'all. Brett called first thing this morning to tell me happy Thanksgiving, and guess what, we've got an offer on the house." She clasped her hands together and looked up at the ceiling. "Thank you, Jesus! Things are working out so well that I know I made the right decision for sure now."

"That's great," Diana said.

"I hope we don't get fussy neighbors," Carmen said.

"Well," Joanie went on, "our agent said some guy called and said he wants to buy it sight unseen. We don't even have to negotiate a deal. He bid the asking price. She's getting all the papers ready, and we'll close the deal when we get home. Brett is already looking at apartment websites in Arlington. He figures we'll live in one for six months while we figure out the best place to buy."

"Well, happy, happy Thanksgiving to you. That's amazing news," Carmen said. "Let's tell Luke and Tootsie over breakfast."

She and Joanie went on down to the kitchen to find Tootsie making her breakfast burritos. Luke was sitting on the sofa with a cup of coffee in one hand and Simba in the other. Nala and Sugar were both sleeping on his lap.

"Happy Thanksgiving, and happy birthday." Diana wanted to stop and kiss him, but she just patted him on the shoulder and then sat down on the sofa beside him.

He set his coffee mug on the end table and handed Nala over to her. "They're going to be lonesome when we separate them."

"Yes, they are, but they'll adjust real soon with all the love they'll get." Joanie took Sugar away from him and loved her for a moment, then gave her back and went to the kitchen. "Tootsie, what can I do to help?"

Diana stole a quick kiss while they were out of sight and whispered, "Joanie has news, but we'll talk about it more tonight."

Carmen took Sugar from him once she made it downstairs. "Come here to Mama, you pretty little darlin' girl," she said in a voice usually saved for talking to babies and cuddling kittens and puppies. "You know what I'm thankful for besides the final divorce papers arriving yesterday? I'm grateful that Diana and Luke brought you to me."

Tootsie raised her voice. "Breakfast is ready. It's on the table, so put down the kittens, wash your hands, and get on in here. I don't make my famous breakfast burritos except on special occasions, and it's best to eat them while they're hot."

Tingles danced down Diana's spine when she and Luke reached the kitchen sink at the same time and Luke covered her hands with his and lathered them. "Do you realize that it's only five days until we head for Lawton?" he asked.

She'd known the time was coming, but where had the weeks gone? Nothing would ever be the same again. Carmen was single as of the day before. Joanie was moving. Tootsie seemed to be accepting the fact that Smokey was truly gone. And *she* was in a relationship.

"We've got a lot to do before we leave, but today we're having Thanksgiving and your birthday. Diana is in charge of making a butter rum cake to celebrate both." Tootsie picked up the pitcher of orange juice and carried it to the table.

"Yes, I am, but if you'd rather have some other kind, I can make it instead, or I can make both." Diana rinsed her hands.

Luke handed her the other end of the towel he was using to dry his hands. "Butter rum is my very favorite."

She pulled the towel from his hands. "That's great. It's my specialty. You never mentioned liking it."

"You never said that you made it." He leaned in and whispered softly, "I like all of your specialties."

Diana's blush was so hot that she covered her face with the towel. He tugged it away and handed her a cold cloth. "It's the truth."

"Y'all stop flirtin' out there and come say grace so we can eat," Tootsie called out.

Diana felt another wave of heat moving up her chest to her cheeks. Luke followed her into the dining room and took his place at the head of the table. He bowed his head, gave a short prayer of thanks, and said, "Before we begin, Carmen told Sugar this morning that she was thankful for her. Let's all do our 'what we're thankful for' at breakfast instead of at the dinner. I'll start. I'm thankful that I ever agreed to come on this trip with y'all."

"Why?" Tootsie asked. "And you have to answer in one word."

"Diana," he said as he laid his hand on her knee under the table.

"Luke," Diana said.

"Closure." Carmen nodded.

"Life," Joanie added.

"Kids," Tootsie said. "Now let's eat before my breakfast gets cold."

"No round of questions?" Diana asked.

"Nope, we're all just glad you two done figured out what I saw on the first day," Tootsie answered.

Diana looked around the table at her family—not blood related but heart kin.

Thank goodness you're not blood kin to Luke. Smokey's voice was back in her head with a chuckle.

"Amen," she muttered.

"What was that?" Tootsie asked.

"Just agreeing with all the thanks for today." Diana almost blushed again.

"And now." Joanie took two burritos off the platter and put them on her plate. "For my good news. We've sold the house. The buyer didn't even haggle about the price but bought it sight unseen. I was so happy that step was done that I didn't even think about asking what he was going to do with the place. What if we've said yes and he's going to rent it out to vacationers and y'all get horrible neighbors? I'd just feel terrible if that happened."

"We won't." Tootsie poured a glass of juice and passed the pitcher around the table.

"How do you know?" Joanie sighed.

"I know the buyer," Tootsie said. "He'll be a fine neighbor."

"It's me," Luke announced. "Aunt Tootsie told me the agent's name. I've been in touch with her several times, and I made the offer. You'd all have known it when we go to close the deal, anyway, so now you don't have to worry about me being a bad neighbor."

"Oh. My. Goodness," Joanie gasped. "That means . . ."

"That I'll be living on the same block with Aunt Tootsie so I can help her out when she needs it. And I'll be close to Diana, so we can see each other whenever we want. I'll start my new business in the garage as soon as I get it wired and set up for all my equipment." Luke bit off a hunk of his burrito and gave Tootsie a thumbs-up sign.

"In your garage?" Diana asked out of the side of her mouth. Everyone else was talking at once, so no one heard or even noticed.

"Yep. I reckon it's about the same size as Aunt Tootsie's, and that's plenty big for what I have in mind at the beginning," he whispered. Then he said in a louder voice, "Hey, anyone want a heat-up on their coffee?"

Three hands raised.

"Hey, Diana, would you please go with Luke and bring out the dessert that I worked so hard over?" Tootsie asked.

With a nod, Diana followed him to the kitchen, and he cornered her by the refrigerator. His lips came down on hers in a scorching-hot kiss. "I'm going to love living next door to you."

"I can be stubborn and independent," she said.

"I already know that. Got anything else to throw at me?" He backed away and picked up the coffeepot.

"I'm sure I'll think of something later." She grinned as she picked up the chocolate doughnuts that Tootsie had taken straight from a bag and arranged on a lovely crystal platter.

Chapter Twenty-Five

*D*iana put Nala in the basket with her siblings and Dolly and hurried into Tootsie's bedroom, where everyone else was gathered for their Sunday-night session.

Tootsie had already brought in the customary cookies and wine. "So this is the last meeting we'll be having here. The next one will be back home in Sugar Run." Tootsie passed the plate of Danish wedding cookies and the zinfandel around the group. "We've come a long way from the day y'all decided to come with me on this trip, and I don't just mean in miles. It's been a good journey for all of us. So now I'm calling the meeting to order. Old business?"

"The butter rum cake that we had for Luke's birthday was amazing," Carmen said. "Made me homesick. Diana, you always make those little miniature Bundt cakes at Christmas, and I always look forward to having a slice while Natalie opens her presents. I guess that's old business since we ate it three days ago."

"I finished off the last crumbs that were left just before I came in here," Joanie admitted. "Diana, you've got to promise every Christmas to send me a whole Bundt cake or, better yet, to bring it when we meet for our get-togethers."

"I promise," Diana agreed.

"If that concludes our old business, we'll get on to the new," Tootsie said. "New business, anyone?"

"Yes." Diana raised her hand. "Since my birthday two weeks ago, I've been slipping out at night to be with Luke. And when we get to Lawton, we're going to get y'all all settled—Joanie in the hotel with Brett, and Tootsie, you and Carmen in a trailer park with shuttle service. Then Luke and I are going to have a couple of days to ourselves in a hotel nearby. If you need us—"

Tootsie slapped her on the knee and butted in before she could finish. "Praise the Lord! Now we can talk about it. We knew you were out there with him from the first, but we didn't want to get all up in y'all's business and maybe even jinx it."

"Do you know how hard it was not to say something the last two Sunday evenings?" Joanie laughed. "So tell us about it? Good? Bad?"

"Ugly?" Carmen teased.

"Wonderful. Amazing. And that's all I'm saying. What goes on behind closed doors is our business. Now, does anyone else have any new business before I divide the rest of this wine into our glasses?" Diana asked.

"Whoa! I'm not finished," Tootsie said. "Have you truly gotten over the age difference, and how are you going to tell Rebecca about it?"

"I'm going to introduce her to Luke and let them get to know each other. If and when she asks about his age, I'll tell her then," Diana answered. Hopefully, Rebecca wouldn't even think about their ages, and if she did, she'd be like Joanie and think that Luke was about forty.

"Sounds like a good idea to me," Joanie agreed.

"Now moving on." Diana was eager to get the meeting over with so she could go on out to the motor home and snuggle up in Luke's arms. "I make a motion we stop in Wichita Falls on the way home to do some shopping. I did a little checking, and there's a Victoria's Secret there. Joanie is going to need something other than sweat bottoms and tank tops the first night Brett is home. It's been six months since she's seen him. And we could all finish up our Christmas shopping. When we get home, it's going to be two weeks until Christmas Day, and we'll be busy helping Joanie pack."

"I second that motion," Tootsie said. "We'll go from here to Wichita Falls on Tuesday. Shop on Wednesday, and go on up to Lawton the next morning. What time is Brett getting to the hotel room?"

"He said he'd be there by noon." Joanie picked up a Danish wedding cookie and put the whole thing in her mouth.

"We'll have you there in time for the two of you to spend the afternoon together," Tootsie said. "Looks like it's going to be me and you against the world for a couple of days, Carmen."

"We're strong enough to whip it with one hand tied behind our backs," Carmen told her. "I don't know how I'll feel or act when I get home, but right now I feel like I could fight a forest fire with a cup of water."

"You're going to be just fine, and so am I," Tootsie told her.

"Any more business?" Diana asked as she poured wine for all of them.

"Maybe just a little bit more." Joanie took a drink and said, "Diana, I want to know how you really, really feel about Luke living next door. I'd just feel awful if things don't work and things got all hinky between all y'all."

"I'm going to be just fine with whatever happens," Diana said. "But if that's all the new business, and since y'all already know where I'm spending my nights, I'm going to the motor home."

"Good for you." Joanie gave her blessing.

"And don't try to sneak in before daylight," Tootsie said. "You wake me up every time you put your weight on that third step. It's always squeaked, even when I was a teenager and trying to slip in after my curfew. Now let's hold hands. Joanie, it's your turn to read the words on the plaque."

When that was done, Diana slid off the bed and left the room. She stopped long enough to pet Dolly and the kittens before she went outside and across the lawn to the motor home.

~

Luke flung open the door and opened his arms. She met his embrace and laid her head on his shoulder, their hearts seeming to beat in unison.

"So how did your empty nesters' meeting go?" he asked.

"How'd you know about that?" She took a step back.

"I find out all kinds of things just by keeping my ears open." He kissed her on the tip of her nose. "You taste like wine and sweet cookies."

"You taste like beer and pretzels." She leaned in for a long kiss. "I like it."

"What do y'all talk about at these meetings?" He took her by the hand and led her to the bedroom.

"That's classified, but I can tell you this much: I'm not going to the house in the morning until you go. They know about us, and until we leave, I'm not waiting for them to go to bed before I come out here anymore, or rushing back before they get up in the morning. And I told them that we're sharing our own hotel room in Lawton." She slowly unbuttoned his shirt and ran her hands over his broad chest. "Is that going to be weird for you?"

"Oh, hell no!" He kissed the side of her neck. "We are consenting adults, and we shouldn't have to sneak around like high school kids."

"At least I didn't crawl out the window." She undid his belt buckle.

"If that had been necessary, I would have had a ladder ready for you to climb down into my arms." He slipped her jacket off her shoulders.

"And you said you weren't romantic." She switched off the lights and left the door wide open.

Chapter Twenty-Six

When it came time to leave on Tuesday morning, Carmen lingered a little and was the last one in the motor home. She stopped inside the door and laid a palm on the plaque that read:

MAY GOD GRANT YOU ALWAYS
A SUNBEAM TO WARM YOU
A MOONBEAM TO CHARM YOU
A SHELTERING ANGEL SO NOTHING CAN HARM YOU
LAUGHTER TO CHEER YOU
FAITHFUL FRIENDS NEAR YOU
AND WHENEVER YOU PRAY
HEAVEN TO HEAR YOU.

She'd had those things during the past several weeks. With her big hair and smart-ass attitude, Tootsie hid her wings and halo pretty good, but she was definitely Carmen's sheltering angel. Diana and Joanie had always been faithful friends, and now she could add Luke.

"Read it out loud," Tootsie said.

Carmen's voice shook by the time she reached the last words. "Amen," she said as if she'd just finished a prayer.

Carmen wrapped Tootsie up in her arms. "I'll always, always remember this place. It should be a rehab center for anyone who has a broken heart."

"Or for a heart that's searching for someone," Luke said as he buckled into the driver's seat.

"We may be sad to leave this place, but change is good for the soul, so get the engine going, Luke, and everyone wave goodbye to Scrap, Texas. We'll be back next year if the good Lord is willing."

They all gathered around the back window and waved until the place was completely out of sight.

"Next stop, Wichita Falls," Luke called out.

"And the day after that is Lawton, where our girls are," Diana said.

Joanie took a deep breath and let it out slowly. "And where my husband waits for us to begin our new life."

"Less than two hundred miles and we'll stop in Nocona," Luke called out a mile or so down the road.

"How far is Lawton from there?" Carmen picked up a book and curled up at one end of the booth.

"Less than two hours, so no one needs to get up early," Luke answered.

Diana slid into the booth, opened her laptop, and started to work. "Only four days until we see our girls."

"Thank you so much for leaving early so I can spend a couple of days with Brett before the graduation," Joanie said.

"Hey, girl." Carmen peeked over the top of her book. "We would never, ever cheat you out of that time with Brett."

"That'd be pretty damned selfish." Tootsie took a bag of chips from the cabinet and headed back to her room. "See y'all at noon. I figure we should be close to Nocona about that time. The Dairy Queen there makes amazing burgers, and their nachos are fabulous, plus they've got lots of parking for big-ass motor homes."

Carmen was so lost in her own thoughts about how she would react to a cold, empty house when they got back to Sugar Run that she forgot to turn the pages of her book. *But I'll be busy helping Joanie get packed and ready to move, and then I'll have a job,* she told herself.

Diana touched her on the shoulder. "Are you okay?"

"It's still a little scary. Facing the house and a new job," she admitted. "I just have to remind myself of all I have to be thankful for and not worry about tomorrow."

"Those are words of wisdom," Joanie said. "But it's a tall order."

~

"Oh, yeah, it is," Diana agreed, and went back to putting in codes and numbers, but her mind strayed to the changes that would be made in their comfortable routine back in Sugar Run. Joanie would be gone soon, and Eli and Carmen were divorced, so now there wouldn't be anyone on the block who put up WELCOME HOME banners for their army husbands coming back from wherever the hell they'd been sent.

Once an army wife, always an army wife—she'd heard that for years, but it wasn't necessarily true anymore, not even for Tootsie. Even after Diana's divorce, she'd been happy for her two friends when they made a short-time calendar and crossed off the days to when their husbands would come home.

Change was supposed to be good for the soul, and turmoil created patience, but sometimes accepting either wasn't easy. The serenity prayer that Tootsie insisted they end their meetings with came to mind, and she repeated it silently twice.

Dolly jumped up on her lap, and Diana hugged her close to her chest. "Nala is going to grow up to be a big girl like you real soon."

Joanie laid her book aside and reached over to pet her. "Never seen such a sweet-natured cat in my whole life. If she wasn't a female,

I'd think maybe Smokey had been reincarnated and came back to give Tootsie some company."

"That's Simba's job," Luke called out.

"Maybe Smokey just decided that all of us needed a little extra love." All three kittens tried to follow their mother up on the booth seat, but no matter how high they jumped, they couldn't make it.

Joanie reached down and grabbed each of them by the scruff of the neck, one by one, handing off Sugar to Carmen and keeping the other two in her lap. They were content for a little while, but then they started to squirm, and she put them back on the floor. They bit each other's ears and tails and wrestled until they were tired enough to drop right where they stood. In seconds they were nothing more than a pile of fur, all tangled up together and sleeping.

"They remind me of us." Joanie pointed. "We might argue and bicker, but at heart we're as close as siblings."

"Is bickering kind of like biting each other's ears?" Carmen asked with a smile.

"Got to have a few bad times to balance out the good ones," Luke said.

Kind of like this adoption thing that still hangs between us, Diana thought, but she didn't say the words.

"Okay, I'm changing the subject before y'all get me all weepy again," Carmen said. "How much farther is it to Wichita Falls, Luke?"

"We're on the outskirts of Nocona now, and I can almost smell those burgers Aunt Tootsie was talking about. After we eat, it's about an hour's drive to the mall. And there's a hotel that's accessible from the parking lot," he said. "I checked, and there's places to plug into electricity for a small fee, so I thought we'd just set up camp there. I've made a reservation to stay in the hotel. That way you ladies can have the motor home to yourselves."

"Thank you, Luke," Joanie said. "We've only got two more nights for just us girls, and that means a lot to us."

"You are very welcome," Luke answered.

Dolly hopped off Diana's lap and curled up around her kittens. Luke hadn't mentioned that he was getting a room before now. What if he asked her to join him? She made up her mind that she was staying in the motor home even if Luke did invite her to join him.

Tootsie came out of her bedroom when Luke stopped the motor home in the Dairy Queen parking lot. "Great timing and great nap. Let's go eat burgers and nachos so we'll have the strength to do some serious shopping this afternoon and tomorrow."

"Not me," Luke said. "I'm going to hole up in my hotel room and do some serious work."

"Whoa, boy!" Tootsie pointed at him. "This trip ain't over until we park this sumbitch in my yard. Until then you're on vacation."

"Okay, then I will rephrase." Luke unbuckled his belt and got out of the seat. "I'm going to hole up in my hotel room and pick out what I need to set up shop in my new home. Can I have it all shipped to your address, Aunt Tootsie? And can I please live in the motor home until I get moved into Joanie's house?"

"Of course you can, but I figured you'd be spending most of your nights at Diana's house." Tootsie opened the door and hit the button so the steps would lower.

"Not if Rebecca is home for a few days or weeks before her schooling begins," Luke said. "She'll need time with her mama."

Diana would always remember that moment because it was the very second that she fell hopelessly in love with Luke Colbert.

Chapter Twenty-Seven

They'd shopped. They'd talked until after midnight, drunk far too much wine, and slept in that morning. Had Joanie been home in Sugar Run the two days before Brett arrived, she'd have been baking his favorite pie, cleaning the house, and making a **WELCOME HOME** sign for the front yard. Now it was twenty miles to Lawton, according to the last sign she'd seen, and she felt more like a new bride than a wife of twenty years.

"First time for everything." Diana slid into the booth beside her.

"What?" Joanie kept her eyes on the countryside whipping by at seventy miles an hour.

"I can almost read your mind, even though I've never been in your shoes. Always before when he came home, you and Zoe would meet him at the door, right?"

Joanie turned to smile at Diana. "You have, too, been in my shoes."

Carmen sat down on the other side of the booth. "Nope, she hasn't, and neither have I."

"You've both experienced the antsy feeling when the team came home from a mission or a deployment," Joanie argued.

"Not like this," Diana said. "Tell me if I'm right. When Brett came home, you had a few hours of family time before you had private moments all to yourself with him. Now things have changed. This is more like a honeymoon, even though the two of you've been married for more than two decades."

"It's scary," Joanie answered. "What if we find that civilian life doesn't work for us? We've been military so long that it's who we are."

Diana slung an arm around her shoulders. "You love him. He loves you. That's what will make it work."

"We've all got adjustments to make," Carmen said. "But for the next couple of days, it's okay not to even think of those things."

Joanie sucked in a long breath and let it out slowly. "Thank you both."

"I agree with them," Luke said from the driver's seat.

"So do I," Tootsie said from the passenger seat. "When you walk into that hotel room, all your fears will be gone. And, honey, I'm speaking from experience."

"You've all been a help. You want to come in and see Brett before you go on to the campground?" Joanie asked.

"Nope." Diana shook her head. "We wouldn't interfere in that moment for all the dirt in this great state of Texas."

Joanie looked up in time to see a road sign saying that Lawton was only two miles away. *I don't ever have to cry myself to sleep at night or worry about a couple of soldiers in full dress uniform ringing my doorbell and telling me that he's been killed in action. I get to spend the rest of my life with a husband and not just the memory of a hero.*

"Lawton city limits," Luke called out in a light tone. "Next stop is Joanie's hotel. Please exit through the front doors, and watch your step."

Carmen slid out of the booth so Joanie could get out. "We'll see you at the graduation."

The hotel was at the very next exit, according to the highway billboard. Luke slowed the motor home and made the turn to the right, and she could see the hotel sign.

"And I promise I won't let them get into your Christmas bags." Tootsie unfastened her seat belt and turned around in the seat. "When you're ready for them, they'll be right here in the motor home in my closet."

Joanie stood and rolled her suitcase up to the kitchen area. She could hear her heart beat in her ears, and her hands were shaking. Brett had called that morning to tell her that he'd done all the paperwork and was waiting for her at the hotel.

Luke slowed down, made the turn into the truck parking lot, and got out of his seat. "Let me get the door for you." He pushed the button to bring out the steps and then carried the suitcase out for her.

"It's going to be strange without you right across the hall from me and Carmen," Diana said.

"Don't make me cry. I feel like this is the end of an era already." Joanie hugged every one of them.

"Oh, stop it. We've still got a few weeks in Sugar Run. Get on out of here and have a good time with your husband." Tootsie gave her a little shove toward the door.

"Thanks for everything, Luke," she said as she left the motor home.

He gave her a quick hug. "Thank you for selling your house to me. Now go see your husband—he must be every bit as nervous as you are."

"I hope not. Two of us this antsy wouldn't be good." She smiled up at him and then popped the handle of the suitcase up so she could roll it across the pavement. Luke went back inside, and she heard the engine start up again. When the motor home started to move, she turned and waved until it had made the turn back out onto the street.

As she approached the front doors, they opened automatically, and she headed straight for the elevator to take her to the second floor. She'd taken only a couple of steps when a movement to her right caught her eye, and she glanced that way. Brett stood there in civilian clothes with a big smile on his face. She let go of the suitcase and ran across the room. He wrapped his big, strong arms around her and hugged her for a full minute before he tipped up her chin and kissed her.

"Welcome to the rest of our lives," he said when the kiss ended.

She pushed away from him far enough so that she could look him up and down several times. "I think this life is going to suit us just fine."

"Yes, it is, so let's go get it started." He took her hand in his and grabbed the handle of the suitcase.

The elevator doors opened the instant he pushed the button. Once inside, he took her in his arms again and strung kisses from her neck to her eyelids. She pressed her whole body against his and wished that neither of them was wearing clothes. Finally, his lips settled on her mouth, and the kisses didn't stop until the doors opened again. He got a grip on the suitcase handle again and led her to the room.

When the door opened, she gasped, "Oh. My!"

A bouquet of red roses sat arranged on the coffee table beside a matching ice bucket made of the same sparking crystal as the flower vase. From the sweat on the outside, she could tell that a bottle of champagne had already chilled.

She bent to smell the roses. "Brett, you shouldn't have."

"Yes, darlin', I should have," he whispered as he wrapped his arms around her from behind. "We've got a lot to celebrate."

"Yes, we do." All the anxiety fled. Brett was home for good, and she had him all to herself for two whole days.

~

The sun was shining brightly when Luke maneuvered the motor home into the RV park slot they'd reserved. Carmen noticed that dark clouds were rolling in from the southwest. She hoped that didn't mean storms or, even worse, snow or rain on the girls' graduation exercises.

Luke got everything hooked up and then got his and Diana's suitcases from off one of the bunk beds. "We'll see y'all at the graduation."

"How are we getting there?" Carmen asked.

"Uber," Tootsie told her. "The same way these two are going to the hotel across town, right?"

"You got it." Luke grinned. "If you need anything, just call me. Our car is already here."

"I might need to talk at midnight," Carmen teased.

"Taxis run twenty-four, seven." Diana gave her a brief hug and whispered, "I'm just about as nervous as Joanie."

"You'll be fine," Carmen said, hoping she was right. With bright sunshine on one side of them and black clouds on the other, she hoped that it wasn't an omen that Diana would have a dark moment while she was at the hotel with Luke. Their relationship was fragile right now.

When they were gone, Tootsie looked around the motor home and sighed. "It's kind of like an empty nest right now, isn't it?"

"That's one way of looking at it, but a brighter one is that we've got Dolly, three kittens, and each other," Carmen answered. "I noticed that this park has a lovely little pond. Let's put on our jackets and take a walk around it before those clouds bring down either rain or snow on us."

Tootsie headed toward her room. "Just let me get my coat. And, honey, those are storm clouds. Snow clouds look altogether different. Besides, it's forty degrees out there."

Carmen changed into a sweatshirt and her new coat and the scarf and gloves she'd picked up at the mall the day before. At first she felt guilty about spending the money, but she had a job when she got home. That meant she didn't have to squeeze her pennies until Lincoln squealed. She smiled at the memory of hearing Smokey say that so often.

She'd just sat down to wait on Tootsie when her phone rang. Expecting it to be Diana, she answered it without even looking at the caller ID. "Hello, are you in the hotel?"

"What are you talking about?" Eli's mother's high, squeaky voice was as cold as it had ever been.

"I'm sorry, Barbara, I thought you were someone else." Carmen made herself a vow that she'd never answer the phone again without checking caller ID.

"Evidently," Barbara said. "So are you making money by going to the hotel with men since my son divorced you?"

"No, I'm not. Why are you calling?" Carmen asked through clenched teeth.

"My granddaughter graduates on Saturday. I've sent a card to her father to give or send to her when she has an address. I want her to know that. Since Eli won't be there to tell her, I want you to do so," Barbara said. "I never particularly did like you, but I like this new woman even less. She's mean to me."

"Oh?" Carmen asked. "So you've met Kate?"

"Yes, and that unruly son of hers, too. My son is brilliant until it comes to his choice of women," Barbara snapped.

"And she's mean to you how?" Carmen pushed on even though she didn't really care how the new daughter-in-law treated her own ex-mother-in-law.

"She took my precious Eli off to another state. At least when he was married to you, he was within a day's drive. And when I told them they weren't sharing a bed in my house until they were married, she laughed at me and said they'd just go to a hotel then. They did just that and left that brat of hers here with me," she said. "They thought I should get to know my new grandson. He's no kin of mine, and I don't care if Eli adopts him or not, I'm not ever going to claim him."

Tootsie came in from her bedroom and asked, "Everything all right?"

"Eli's mother," she mouthed.

"Tell her to go to hell," Tootsie said.

"Who's that talking? Are you at the hotel? Is that the man who's going to pay for your favors?"

"I'll tell Natalie that her father needs her new address. Goodbye, Barbara, and good luck with Kate. Maybe he'll let you pick out his third wife and you'll like her."

"You've never been mean before. Why now?" Barbara snapped.

"Guess your son divorcing me for another woman and sleeping with me when she was already pregnant brought out my bad side. Have a great day." Carmen ended the call and put her phone on the table. "I don't want to talk to her if she calls back, so if my phone rings in the next few days, please don't answer it for me. I really need that walk right now. I don't suppose there's any wood to split around here, is there?"

Tootsie chuckled. "Not that I know of. Let's go. We'll just have to walk off the anger."

The air felt like rain when they stepped out of the motor home. Neither of the women even noticed the crunch under their feet as they circled halfway around the pond. Carmen told Tootsie about the phone call. She ended with, "I tried so hard to make that woman like me."

"Well, honey, karma has given her Kate, and it's biting her square in the ass for the way she's treated you. If I'd been you, I'd have divorced Eli years ago just to be rid of her." Tootsie stopped at a bench and sat down. "You walk really fast for a short woman. I need a little rest."

"I'm so sorry." Carmen eased down beside her. "I guess I was trying to outrun my anger."

"Did it work?" Tootsie asked.

"Not really," Carmen answered. "But I noticed that the office for this place has a convenience store. When we get back to it, let's buy a bunch of junk food. We can have chocolate and sour cherry balls and maybe even SweeTARTS while we binge-watch something on television tonight."

"Let's buy enough to last all day tomorrow," Tootsie suggested. "My knees are telling me that the storm coming in is going to bring us a cold front. There's some frozen burritos and corn dogs in the freezer. We'll wear our pajamas and . . ." Tootsie held out her hand. "That's the first raindrop. Maybe we better get on back."

"We should've brought an umbrella," Carmen said when a raindrop hit her on the tip of her nose.

"We ain't sugar or salt either one, darlin'. We won't melt, and we've got dry clothes in the motor home." Tootsie took off so fast that Carmen had to do a slow jog to keep up with her.

They were both drenched by the time they got to the store, but they still took the time to buy a plastic bag full of junk food. The lady asked if they wanted to purchase an umbrella, and Tootsie just laughed. "Honey, it wouldn't do us a lot of good now, but thanks for asking."

When they were back in the motor home, Carmen tossed the bag of food in the kitchen sink and headed straight for the bathroom. Tootsie didn't waste a bit of time getting down the hall and into her bedroom. Carmen dried herself and hung both the towel and her wet clothing on the shower rod. Then she padded out to her bunk bed, opened her suitcase, and brought out the warmest pajamas she had. Old-lady flannel—that's what Natalie had called them last Christmas. Eli had given them to her. She wondered if they had fit his image of her. The thought that he had probably bought Kate a pretty piece of jewelry—or, better yet, something lacy and sexy—made her temper flare again. She threw the pajamas in the trash can and got out her favorite pair of red-and-green plaid pajama pants and her Minnie Mouse T-shirt.

She'd just gotten dressed in them when Tootsie opened her door and said, "You get that candy out of the bag, and I'll stick a bag of popcorn in the microwave."

Tootsie passed by her on the way to the kitchen. "I've got all the seasons of *Chuck* out for us to binge-watch. It's a real cute little show. You'll love it."

"You reckon Joanie and Diana are listening to the rain beating against their hotel windows?" Carmen followed her.

"Honey, I bet they don't even know it's raining," Tootsie laughed. "If we have to have a storm, I'm glad it's today and not Saturday when the girls graduate."

"Amen to that." Carmen thought of a worse storm than Mother Nature could provide—one that involved Eli bringing Kate to the girls' graduation. She had gotten a measure of closure now, but she sure wasn't ready to see him with another woman.

Chapter Twenty-Eight

*D*iana had felt that Rebecca and her friends were still children when they graduated from high school. But a mere six months later, as she watched the impressive military graduation, she could see three young women before her, ready to take on the next responsibility and serve their country. Her heart swelled with pride, and yet tears ran down her cheeks and dripped on her new olive-green jacket.

Luke pulled a snow-white handkerchief from his pocket and handed it to her. She dabbed it against her face and sent it on down the line to Tootsie, Carmen, Joanie, and even Brett, who was sitting at the other end of their little group.

"Thank you," Diana whispered when the hankie made its way back to her hands. She handed it back to Luke, and he stuffed it back in his pocket.

The memory of the day that she and her friends had taken their daughters to the recruiter to enlist surfaced and brought with it a brand-new rush of tears. The girls had been so giggly all the way to San Antonio, and then they'd wanted to go shopping after they'd signed their lives away for six years. The next thing that popped into her head was the day that she, Carmen, and Joanie had left them at that same office. Their daughters had been nervous, but it was more like three teenagers going to their first concert than women who were about to undergo weeks of intensive training.

Now, here before parents, grandparents, and friends were dozens of brand-new soldiers standing so tall and grown-up. The girls all had their hair up and looked so mature that it was impossible to think that they had just been kids a few months ago.

The ending of the ceremony was a little anticlimactic to Diana. After all these young men and women had accomplished, there should have been medals involved or maybe their names called out individually so that each one of them could stand or even come forward and be recognized.

This is not an awards assembly at high school, Smokey's voice scolded.

A smile came through the tears. It was time to recognize Rebecca as an adult. Diana wasn't sure how to go about that, but she was determined to try. Right up until Rebecca found her in the midst of all the chaos, wrapped her arms around her mother, and hugged her tightly.

"I missed you so much, Mama. Some nights I wondered if I'd done the right thing," Rebecca whispered. Then she took a step back and stuck out her hand. "You must be Luke. Mama wrote to me about you."

"Congratulations on surviving basic. That's no small feat." He grinned.

"Hey, I'm Brett. Joanie told me about you." Brett stuck out his hand toward Luke. "Sounds like y'all had a really good time on your trip."

Luke shook his hand. "We sure did. Maybe we can all get together next week for supper at Aunt Tootsie's."

Rebecca moved away from the group to speak to her father, but Diana didn't even notice for several minutes. Then she caught Gerald staring at her over the top of all the folks in their group. He quickly focused his attention back on Rebecca and then the two of them made their way over to her.

"Who'd have thought our baby girl would ever join the army?" He grinned.

"It was wholly her decision," Diana said.

Gerald's wife came from the direction of the restrooms and stepped between them. As usual, she looked like she'd just walked off a fashion-show runway. Every blonde hair was in place, her tight-fitting dress hugged her body, and her matching coat looked as if it had been tailor-made for her. The brooch on her lapel had probably cost more than Diana made in a month, but then, Gerald hadn't chosen his new wife for beauty alone. There was that beautiful bank account that came along with her.

"Diana," the woman muttered.

"Vivian." Diana nodded. "Let me introduce y'all to Luke Colbert. Luke, this is Rebecca's father, Gerald, and his wife, Vivian."

Luke shook hands with Gerald first and then Vivian. "Pleased to make your acquaintance. Y'all should be very proud of your daughter."

"We certainly are," Gerald said. "I understand that you're Tootsie's nephew?"

"That's right," Luke answered, and slipped an arm around Diana's shoulders. "Darlin', we should be gathering up the crew. We've got reservations." Then he smiled at Gerald. "Would y'all like to join us for the celebration dinner? Nothing fancy. The girls only have four hours off base, and they chose Bubba's Burgers and Ice Cream. I can call and add two more if you'd like to join us. Then we're going back to the Baymont lobby to sit around and visit until they have to get back to base."

"No, thank you." Vivian smiled. "We've got to get home to San Antonio. We have friends and family coming to welcome Gerald back from this last deployment, but thank you for the invitation. Come on, honey. Let's go tell Rebecca goodbye and get on the road." She slipped her arm in his and led him away from Diana.

"That went well." Luke grinned.

"If they had joined us, I would have shot you," she whispered.

"But now Gerald can't say that we were selfishly keeping him from spending an important day with his daughter." With his hand on her lower back, he guided her over to where the rest of their group was waiting.

"I'm going straight to Bullis," Zoe was saying. "So y'all can come see me on weekends. If you're still in Sugar Run at Christmas, I can probably have a couple of days off to come home."

"Rebecca and I fly out Monday morning to Georgia. We didn't get to go to Goodfellow after all, but we've been told that we could probably have a few days at Christmas." Natalie had an arm around Carmen. "Want to pick us up in Dallas if we can get a flight?"

"Of course we will," Luke answered.

Rebecca talked with Gerald and Vivian a few minutes, and then she hurried back over to her mother. "I'm so ready to get off base, and I'm starving for a big old greasy burger with french fries and then some ice cream for dessert."

"Well, darlin's," Tootsie said, "we've got the motor home parked not far from here. We can all fit in it comfortably."

"That's wonderful," Zoe said. "We wanted to spend the time together with all y'all as much as we can." She slipped one hand into her father's and the other one into her mother's. "Lead the way, Tootsie."

"Don't expect us to swing you like we did when you were a little girl." Brett's eyes kept shifting from his wife to his daughter. "I'm pretty proud of y'all."

"Y'all?" Zoe asked.

"You for taking this step to serve your country, and your mama for standing beside me for twenty years," Brett said.

"With that in mind." Rebecca stepped between Luke and Diana and, following Zoe's example, slipped a hand in her mother's and the other one in Luke's. "I'd say we've all got a lot of pride right now, but walk faster. I meant it when I said I was starving."

How four hours could pass so quickly was a complete mystery to Diana. It seemed as if they'd only all sat down in the Baymont lobby after dinner when Rebecca pointed at her watch and said, "It's time to go. We can't be late or we'll be in trouble."

"And army trouble is worse than missing curfew at home when we were seniors." Zoe tucked a strand of hair back into the bun at the nape of her neck.

"But not by much," Rebecca giggled. "The only reason I made it through basic was because I had a tough mama."

"Testify, sister." Natalie raised her hand. "The drill sergeant was nothing compared to Mama the night she found out I'd had my first beer. But today I love you for all that strictness." Natalie hugged Carmen for at least the tenth time that afternoon. "This whole day has been amazing, and it's only two and a half weeks until Christmas. Then we can see all y'all again."

~

Luke was on his way out to the motor home to get it warmed up when he heard someone call his name. He turned to find Rebecca jogging toward him. Her long legs and her movements reminded him so much of Diana that he doubted she'd gotten much of Gerald's DNA at all.

"Hey, wait up," she yelled.

When she got to his side, she slowed to a walk. "I wanted to talk to you when Mama wasn't around."

Together they covered the rest of the distance to the motor home. "What's up?" He opened the door for her, and she stepped inside.

"Are you serious about her, or are you just out for a good time? Are you going to break her heart?"

"I hope we're both very serious, and I want a long-term relationship. I care too much about your mother to ever break her heart. Now, let me ask you . . ." He started the engine and turned on the heater. "How do you feel about me? You've only just met me, so that might be an unfair question, but . . ."

"Tootsie has written lots about you in her letters and so have Carmen and Joanie. I hope you're half the man they make you out to be," Rebecca replied. "It's just that Mama has been hurt deeply once, and I want your word that you'll go easy on her. I can see by the way she looks at you that she . . . that she likes you a lot, maybe even loves you."

"I hope so, because I've sure fallen in love with her, but let's keep that between us for a little while. I don't want to overwhelm her. Emotions have been pretty high the past few weeks. I can wait to tell her until she's ready," Luke said. "And I hear them all coming this way now."

"Good talk." She darted off to the bathroom. Her head popped back out of the door for a moment. "Since I've met you in person, I guess I like you." The door closed behind her.

"Where's Rebecca?" Diana was the first one inside. "She said she had an emergency and took off in a run."

"Hey." Rebecca came out of the bathroom before Luke could answer. "The hotel bathroom was in use, and I couldn't wait. Natalie and Zoe and I have an announcement to make right now. Right, girls?"

"No tears when we get to base," Zoe said.

"We want you to be brave like you were when we left," Natalie said. "Just drive up, drop us off, and then leave."

"We all hate goodbyes, and this is the only way we can handle it," Rebecca chimed in.

"You got it," Tootsie said. "We can do that, but we'll make no promises about what happens when you're out of the motor home."

"Fair enough," Rebecca said. "Now let's get this big-ass bus to rolling before we all start crying from just thinking about not seeing all y'all for a while."

"Next stop, Fort Sill army base, Lawton, Oklahoma," Luke called out, and the motor home started forward. "Second stop, Joanie and Brett's hotel. Third stop, Sugar Run, Texas."

"You make a pretty good tour guide, Luke," Brett chuckled.

"I thought we were stopping for a night," Carmen said.

"Change of plans," Tootsie told her. "Luke said he didn't mind driving until midnight, and I'm homesick, so we're taking this *big-ass bus* home tonight."

"Sounds great to me." Carmen yawned. "I may sleep most of the way."

"That's my plan, too," Tootsie replied.

~

They held it together really well when the girls got out of the motor home, but by the time they'd driven away from the base, the waterworks had begun. The women had gone through half a box of tissues by the time Luke drove them to the area where Brett and Joanie had left their car. When they had left the motor home, Luke headed south toward the Oklahoma/Texas border, but the sniffles just got louder. Being the gentleman that he was, he couldn't let Diana cry alone, but he wiped his tears on the handkerchief he kept in his pocket.

Dusk was settling around them when Carmen and Tootsie headed for their beds and a late-night nap. Diana buckled herself into the passenger seat beside him. "We've looked forward to this for months, and now it's over. It's almost surreal."

"Kind of like Christmas," he suggested. "Speaking of that, I told Brett and Joanie that they shouldn't move out until after the holidays so they can have one last Christmas with Zoe in the house. And, Diana, I've already called my financial manager and arranged for flights for Natalie and Rebecca to come home. All they have to do is tell us the dates they can be away from base, and it's a done deal. They can consider it their Christmas present from me. I hate to shop." He grinned.

"And that's why I love you," she said. "Not because you hate to shop but because you are so unselfish and sweet and kind."

He went speechless for several moments following her declaration. When he found his voice again, he asked, "Would you repeat that?"

"I love you," she said. "Plain and simple. And not only do I love you because you are all those things, I'm in love with you because you make me feel special and loved. If that scares you into stopping this vehicle and running . . ."

He slowed to take the next exit and stopped at the bottom of the ramp, made a right, and pulled into a gas station. "We could use a fill-up, but that's not why I'm stopping. I have to hold you when I say this." He got out of his seat and pulled her outside, where he wrapped his arms tightly around her. "I fell in love with you the first time I laid eyes on you, Diana. I want to spend my whole life with you, but the timing—engagement, marriage—can be in your court."

His lips found hers in a long, passionate kiss. By the time it ended, Tootsie and Carmen were looking on from the open door.

"Halle-damn-lujah!" Tootsie squealed. "My prayers have been answered. No rush, Diana, but you do realize that someday I'll be your aunt."

"No, Tootsie." Diana smiled. "You'll always be my mama. That carries more weight than an aunt. But we're in no hurry, and besides, we've got a lot to do before Christmas."

"And we can do it together," Luke whispered.

Diana stared into his blue eyes and saw a bright future with him. She leaned in for a second kiss and didn't care who was watching.

Epilogue

Joanie took a deep breath and inhaled the aroma of the gingerbread that she'd made for breakfast that Christmas morning. Torn wrapping paper was scattered all over the living room floor. Zoe had dashed off to Natalie's house to see what she'd gotten. Brett came from the kitchen with a cup of eggnog in each hand, gave her one, and sat down beside her on the sofa.

"It's lasted through fourteen years." He pointed at the tree in the corner. "Think we should get a new one next year?"

Joanie shook her head. "That one and all the ornaments have too much sentimentality attached to them for me to get rid of them. I still feel like I'm going to wake up and find this is all a dream."

He moved closer and put an arm around her. "I keep thinking that I'll get orders at any minute and have to grab my bag and leave. It'll take a few months of adjustment for each of us."

She leaned her head on his shoulder. "But we'll do it together."

"And we'll enjoy every minute of it." He kissed the top of her head.

~

Carmen stood in the corner of the living room and listened to the excitement in Natalie's and Zoe's voices. Then Rebecca joined them, and

Carmen was reminded of past days when they were little girls. For just a split second, she envisioned Eli sitting on the sofa with a beer in his hand. Then the picture faded, and she thought of all the little kids at her new job who had no family that morning. They'd each have a present under the tree—warm socks, a scarf, or maybe a new shirt—and there'd be a turkey dinner served in the cafeteria. Later, when Natalie, Rebecca, and Zoe all went to the church to help serve a three o'clock dinner and see their friends, she planned to slip away and check on the kids at the base. Maybe she'd even take a big plate of cookies for them to share.

"Mama, we had gingerbread at Zoe's," Natalie said. "Now we need some of your decorated cookies."

"Be careful," she called out. "If you don't do justice to dinner at Tootsie's, her feelings will be hurt."

Natalie draped an arm around Carmen's shoulders. "Tradition says that we have something at all three houses; then we eat dinner with Tootsie and help out at the homeless dinner . . ." She paused for a minute. "We'll miss Smokey so much this year, but we have Luke, and he reminds us of Smokey. We might gain five pounds today, but after basic, we can all three use it."

"Well, far be it from me to get in the way of tradition," Carmen laughed.

"How are you really holding up?" Rebecca asked, coming from the kitchen with a cookie in each hand. "I remember our first Christmas without Daddy. It was kind of sad."

"Yes, it is," Natalie sighed. "But we've all got each other and the best mamas in the world."

"How could I ever be sad with all you sassy girls around me?" Carmen asked. "Don't y'all worry a bit about me. I've got a wonderful job. I'm making new friends, and I've got family right here on my block to support me. Life is good."

And she meant every word.

~

Christmas Day was crazy, with the girls all home and running back and forth between houses like they had when they were kids. Luke had been cooking at Tootsie's for two days. There would be enough food to feed an army rather than just nine people—Diana smiled at that thought this morning. Tootsie had declared that leftovers were just as good as the original meal, so none of them would have to cook for a whole week.

The next few days would be busy, and Diana intended to love every moment of each hour. Rebecca and Natalie would have to leave on the twenty-eighth, and Zoe had to be back at base the next day. Then they'd have three days to get Joanie and Brett all packed and ready for the movers to arrive.

Luke had been there to open presents with them that morning, but then he'd had to rush back to Tootsie's and make sure everything was going according to schedule for the gift opening and the dinner at her house. Diana picked up a long ribbon that had been cast aside when they were opening gifts and dragged it across the floor for Nala. The kitten jumped on it, kicking at it with both hind feet like she was trying to kill a snake. Then Simba came from under the sofa and tried to wrestle it away from her.

Diana eased down on the sofa and watched them play a game of chase through scraps of the wrapping paper that still littered the living room floor. She heard the door open and thought it was probably the girls coming back through her house for another sausage biscuit. But it was Luke, and he saw the kittens, tiptoed around them, and sat down on the sofa beside Diana.

"I'm happier right now than I've ever been in my life." He laced his fingers in hers.

"I was going to wait until later tonight to give you this." She picked up a long, skinny box from the end table and handed it to him. "But since we're alone—merry Christmas, Luke."

"You already gave me a present," he said.

"Yep, but this one is special, maybe even magic or a miracle," she said.

He tore the red paper away to reveal a long black velvet box.

"It didn't come in that pretty box, but I thought it deserved something more than a plain old cardboard one," she said.

He frowned. "A watch? Pens?"

"Look closer," she said as he opened it.

He picked the object out of the box and stared at it for a while before an expression of recognition covered his face. "Are you serious? Is this really . . ."

"A pregnancy test?" she finished for him. "Yes, it is. I guess we won't need to talk about adoption since we found that one chance in a million about six weeks ago. Most likely on that first night I spent with you in the motor home."

He couldn't take his eyes off the stick. "Are you okay with this?"

"Couldn't be better. I won't even be forty yet when the baby gets here." She shifted her position to sit in his lap. "Let's keep it a secret until after the wedding."

"And that's when?" His eyes had misted over.

"Well, the courthouse is open tomorrow, and everyone is here that I'd want at our wedding, so what do you say?" She grabbed a tissue and wiped her own eyes. "I can't ever let anyone cry alone, but, darlin', these are happy tears."

"So are mine." He pulled her closer to him. "I'd say that I only thought this day was the happiest day of my life. You've just given me magic and miracles. I love you so much, Diana." He laid the stick to the side and kissed her.

"Merry Christmas to all of us," she panted when the kisses ended.

Acknowledgments

Dear Readers,

It's not often that I get to write a book in real time—that means I'm writing a winter book in the right season. *The Empty Nesters* was so much fun to work on right here in the winter months. And you'll be reading it during the winter season, so snuggle down under a fluffy throw or Grandma's old soft quilt, get yourself a cup of your favorite tea or coffee or even hot chocolate, and enjoy the reading.

We see ribbons for everything these days, so we really should have one for those of us who have survived the empty-nest syndrome. Spending time with this book triggered many personal emotions from years ago. My son spent several years in the air force, but we still had two daughters at home. Then he came home from the military, and he and both his sisters all got married within fourteen months of each other. The girls got married the same summer, six weeks apart. Talk about a crazy year and then sudden quiet in the house. I hope that *The Empty Nesters* resonates with all you survivors out there—and those of you who will be walking in Diana's, Carmen's, and Joanie's shoes before long. Just remember—the years go by fast, so don't blink.

As always, I have so many people to thank for helping me take this from a rough idea about three mamas whose daughters have enlisted in the army to the finished product you hold in your hands. To Anh Schluep, my Montlake Romance editor, for continuing to believe in me;

to Krista Stroever, my developmental editor who takes a lump of coal and helps me turn it into a diamond; to Erin Niumata, my agent, for sticking with me through all the lean years; to Mr. B, for all he does to make my life easier so I can continue to put out stories; to my family, friends, and fans for the love and support y'all continue to give me— you all deserve a standing ovation with so much whistling, clapping, and stomping that it would raise the roof!

Don't put your reading glasses away. There are more books on the way in 2020!

Until next time, happy reading,
Carolyn Brown

About the Author

Photo © 2015 Charles Brown

Carolyn Brown is a *New York Times*, *USA Today*, *Publishers Weekly*, and *Wall Street Journal* bestselling author and a RITA finalist with more than ninety published books. Her genres include romance, history, cowboys and country music, and contemporary mass-market paperbacks. She and her husband live in the small town of Davis, Oklahoma, where everyone knows everyone else, knows what they are doing and when . . . and reads the local newspaper every Wednesday to see who got caught. They have three grown children and enough grandchildren to keep them young. Visit Carolyn at www.carolynbrownbooks.com.